D0558330

Raymond staggered...

...as another shot whizzed past his head, chunking into the brick and sending shards flying at his back.

They always come at you through other people, they always come at you from the direction you least expect, he thought through the pain. *Can't let it end like this, I can't, I can't.*

The gun spoke again, and it was the loudest sound in the universe.

Other Titles from DarkTales Publications...

The Asylum Volume 1: The Psycho Ward
Tales of Madness by Doug Clegg and others
Edited by Victor Heck

Demonesque
A novel by Steven Lee Climer

In Memoriam: Papa, Blake and HPL
Two Stories by Mort Castle

Scary Rednecks and Other Inbred Horrors
Short stories by Weston Ochse and David Whitman

Secret Life of Colors
A novel by Steve Savile

DeadTimes
A novel by Yvonne Navarro

Clickers
A novel by J.F. Gonzalez and Mark Williams

Eternal Sunset
A novel by Sephera Giron

Moon On The Water
Stories by Mort Castle

Filthy Death, the Leering Clown
A novelette by Joseph Moore & Brett A. Savory

TRIBULATIONS

by

J. MICHAEL STRACZYNSKI

DarkTales Publications

Kansas City, Missouri • Toledo, Ohio • Chicago, Illinois
2000

Published in the United States by:

DarkTales Publications
P.O. Box 675
Grandview, Missouri, 64030

ISBN 1-930997-03-5

PRINTED IN THE UNITED STATES OF AMERICA

For Harlan and Susan
My Friends

The Vermont Corridor

On the one hand, it wasn't the biggest boa constrictor Susan Randall had ever seen. But to be fair, it *was* the first time she'd ever seen one wearing a pink party hat.

Officer David Ryan was laughing so hard he was having a hard time standing. He leaned against the squad car to support himself while his partner, Officer Gerardo Montoya, used a stick to keep the boa from escaping down a sewer drain while they waited for Animal Control to show up.

"Five years on the LAPD and that's the goddamndest thing I've ever seen," Ryan said. Except for the party hat, the boa was a green stain on the darkened lawn, illuminated only by their flashlights and the overhead streetlight as it twisted this way and that. "Hey, Gerry, he's getting away!"

"He's not going anywhere!" Montoya ran in front of the snake, prodding and poking with the stick but never getting too close. He jumped back out of the way as it took a sideways swipe at him, then circled cautiously around the huge snake, looking at Ryan. "You gonna give me a hand here or you gonna just stand there laughing your ass off?"

"Yeah, yeah, hang on."

Because the boa represented a physical danger, however ridiculous, Susan was required by departmental policy to watch from inside the squad car as the two officers herded the boa away from the curb. From what they had been told by the neighbors, the snake belonged to a man who lived in the squat white-washed house behind them. "Guess he figured it was cheaper than an alarm service," Ryan had said. Somehow it had gotten loose and wandered into the yard next door, where the neighbor's two–year–old child concluded that it was a dog and put a party hat on it. Her parents had walked in just as the snake was starting to coil, screamed, grabbed her and ran out the door before calling the police.

Montoya took another poke at the boa. The party hat was now tilted at what Susan considered a rather rakish angle.

"The god–damndest thing," Ryan repeated, laughing. "God–*damn*."

It was the second evening of a three–night ride–along, and so far the experience was less than Susan had hoped for. It was the obvious story, the perennial ever-green story, which was why virtually everyone else at the *Tribune* had done it at one point or another. *Three nights of real life on the mean streets riding with real cops who put their lives on the line day in and day out.* At thirty–two, Susan had been with the *Trib* for five years, working the crime beat for three of them, and had managed to avoid doing the obvious stories for most of that time.

But last week her editor decreed that it was her turn for a ride–along. Hoping to avoid a dull or redundant story, she had checked the duty rosters for Ramparts Division, the busiest and most dangerous division in Los Angeles, and chose the patrol route that had consistently seen the most action. Robberies, muggings, carjackings, high–speed chases and DUI low–speed pur-suits, the Vermont corridor had it all. Everything was on her side: the history of the area, this month's per–capita increase in violent crime, even the weather, which was supposed to be hot all week.

Except that the usually dry Santa Ana winds had cooled, everybody was home watching *The Ten Million Dollar Triangle* (Susan didn't watch TV any-more, how was she supposed to know the show was the hottest thing since chocolate pudding?), and instead of muggers, pimps, rapists and felons, the most dangerous thing they'd come across in two nights was a boa constrictor that at this moment looked more confused than menacing.

But perhaps that was just the pink party hat getting to her.

She looked up in the rear–view mirror as the Animal Control van pulled up behind them. Her reflection was pale, the result of too many nights without sleep, a perception reinforced by her dark hair, which she'd pulled into a tight knot to keep it out of the way of any action they might see but which had not yet materialized. She wore an old pair of blue jeans and a KODO sweatshirt over a T–shirt, clothes she could move in fast if it became necessary, which so far had not been the case.

The side doors of the Animal Control van popped open behind her, as men with nets and ropes and poles stepped out onto the sidewalk.

Susan sighed with relief. Just another few minutes, and they would be back on the street.

She glanced at her watch and wrote down the time in her notebook. *Ten–thirty. Still early.*

With luck, maybe something would happen.

"Any wants or warrants?"

Bending over the squad car's computer console, Officer Montoya punched in the license plate of the Mercedes 2000 they'd been following for the last three blocks. In this part of town, five homeboys dressed down and dirty in a spot-less, brand new Mercedes constituted probable cause for a records check.

"Nothing," Montoya said.

"So it's not stolen?" Susan asked. It was one hour and two moving violations later.

"Not necessarily. It has to be reported stolen before the data shows up here. The owner may not be aware that it's missing yet."

"*If* it's stolen," she added.

The two officers exchanged a glance. She could see from their expressions that all their instincts said the car was hot. But instinct wasn't enough; for a clean bust they needed something they could point to as probable cause.

Suddenly Montoya looked up. "Flash your headlights at him," he said.

"Why?" Susan asked.

He pointed to the car in front of them. "His high beams are on. If you pop a steering wheel to hotwire a car, you can't turn the high beams up or down again."

"Okay, let's see what happens," Ryan said.

He flashed the squad car's headlights. The flash clearly registered in the rear view mirror of the Mercedes.

The high beams stayed on.

"So that means you're going to pull them over?" Susan asked.

Ryan nodded. "Running high beams on a surface street like this is a moving violation." He looked to Montoya. "Let's do it."

Montoya popped the car's bubble-gum lights. A moment later, the Mercedes pulled smoothly over to the curb and stopped under a streetlamp. *Just like they teach in Driver's Ed*, Susan thought, already certain that this would turn out to be nothing more interesting than a *nouveau riche* Hispanic rap group out for a drive.

Flashlights in hand, Ryan and Montoya climbed out of the car and approached the Mercedes on either side. She couldn't hear what they were saying, but so far nobody seemed to be making a move.

Susan squinted. In the glare of the flashlights, she could make out five men in the Mercedes, all dressed in oversized plaid shirts and watch-caps. Typical gang-banger uniforms. The driver was digging in his wallet as Montoya kept an eye on them from just behind the right passenger door.

She was so concentrated on watching what was happening in front of her that she didn't notice the wholly unremarkable white Ford coming slowly up alongside them until she glanced over and saw three other gang-bangers leaning out, hands filling with shotguns and automatic weapons.

Oh my god—

The gang-bangers opened fire. Bright flashes from automatic gun muzzles, thunder roaring from the shotguns, bullets ripping apart the squad car and the Mercedes. *That's why they pulled over so carefully they didn't make any trouble because they were going across rival gang turf to get to their chop shop and they didn't want to attract the wrong kind of attention but somebody noticed somebody noticed—*

Glass shattered and sprayed across the seats. Something sliced across her cheek, and blood ran warm where she touched her face. Then a sharp bang from the car door and something slammed into her leg, upending her in the seat, and she cried out in pain as—

—outside the officers turned, reached for their guns, everything moving slower than it should have been, than it could have been, and the air was torn by more gunfire from the car, the two officers falling, bleeding.

The gunfire went on and on, shredding the Mercedes and those inside.

Then with a squeal of tires, the Ford disappeared into the night.

Susan pulled herself up from the seat. The air was thick with the smell of cordite. Safety glass continued to tumble down around her in a spray. She tried to move, but her left leg was numb, refused to do what she wanted it to do.

On the street in front of her, officer Montoya was shaking, moaning.

Officer Ryan didn't move.

Fighting the pain and hysteria rising in her throat, Susan crawled forward, reaching between the front seats for the police radio, hoping and praying it still worked. She grabbed for it, missed. It seemed farther away than could be possible. She strained to touch it, snared it on the third attempt and dragged it back to her. "Officers down!" she shouted into the mike.

"*Officers down!*"

Susan opened her eyes.

The ceiling raced past her overhead. She was aware of being on a gurney, surrounded by men and women in green hospital scrubs. Something long and hard that tasted of plastic had been shoved down her throat and she was painfully aware of an IV stuck into the back of her hand.

A nurse looked down at her, said something she couldn't make out. It could have been *You're hurt but it's not bad, you'll be okay.* It also could have been *You're burned, but not in bed, your bees are clean.*

She closed her eyes.

She opened her eyes.

She was in a dark room. A monitor beeped beside her bed, in rhythm with her heart. She tried to speak but her mouth was too dry to form words.

A curtain partially surrounded her bed. She was dimly aware of someone else in a bed across the room. In the moonlight, it looked like a young girl, maybe fifteen or sixteen. She was asleep. But even asleep, she looked frightened, her face tormented by nightmares.

Something passed between the moonlight and the window, momentarily blocking the light.

She closed her eyes.

She opened her eyes.

The room was still dark. The girl was still in her bed. But now there was someone else in the room, standing with his back to Susan. He was speaking, but she couldn't make out the words; speaking in the direction of the girl's bed, but somehow not to the girl herself.

Then she felt someone else enter the room, a presence that seemed to loom large in the shadows, filling the room. And with the presence came a sense of anger. Betrayal. Fury. She tried to crane her neck, to see who it was, but was in too much pain to move.

The man who stood with his back to her turned slightly, and spoke to the new arrival. She caught only part of it. *You cannot have her,* he was saying. *She is not yours, she will never be yours. You will go. You will leave her and this place, leave now and forever.*

Susan felt another flash of anger from the latecomer…then the sense of presence diminished. There was now just the three of them in the room. Susan, the girl, and the man, who now turned and looked at her, as though seeing her for the first time.

He looked about twenty years older than Susan, and tall, strikingly so, with a face that was lean and muscular. She couldn't decide if it was a hard face made soft or a kind face made hard. Both qualities were there, punctuated by ice blue eyes that seemed to Susan to hold all the compassion of the world, and all its sorrow. His hair was a salt–and–pepper that had given way to gray at his temples.

He glanced at her chart.

"You've been shot," he said. His voice was surprisingly soft, and had a very faint but pleasant accent, which even in her drugged state she identified as either German or Austrian. Though soft, his voice managed to be firm, as though addressing a student.

She nodded, swallowed. "Yes." The sedatives were pulling at her again, making it hard to form words.

"That's a hard thing to endure," he said. "But for all their pain, the scars do fade with time. At least the ones on the outside. The rest, I'm afraid, are up to you." He studied her for a moment, then added, "You should sleep."

She nodded, and closed her eyes.

When she opened them again, he was gone.

Things Happen

"When I said I wanted a story, I didn't mean an obituary."

Rob Klein, her editor, stood beside the bed where she sat propped up on pillows. She was eating a cold, rubbery *something* that someone had sold to the hospital on the premise that it had once been a chicken. *In life this was* not *a happy bird*, she thought to herself, but kept eating. It was the first solid food they'd let her have since the ambulance brought her in the night before.

He continued. "Leo tells me you deliberately picked the most dangerous corridor for the ride–along instead of letting the dispatcher pick something more appropriate."

"Leo needs to mind his own business." Leo Dexter was over in entertainment features. Always had his nose in everyone else's business. Susan made a mental note to flatten it the next time she saw him.

Rob sighed. It was a resigned, put–upon sound she'd heard enough times to become intimately familiar with it. It was the sigh he always pulled out when he was in paternal mode. Even though he was only ten years her senior, he looked older, a perception reinforced by extra weight and the receding hairline that was already retreating when they first met during Susan's term as a journalism student at LA Valley College.

He had served as distinguished visiting instructor for one semester, at a time when she was beginning to seriously question whether or not she should continue to pursue journalism. She had grown up with the image of journalists reporting in while under fire in Iraq, Kosovo, and elsewhere. She had fallen hard for the romantic image of the journalist as crusader, going back all the way to Edward R. Murrow; there was no greater crusader than a war correspondent. But each of them had to start somewhere, and Susan had made that start as soon as she graduated high school.

But what had started as a passion for truth, justice and the American Way had bogged down in departmental policies and politics, the *coup de gras* administered by instructors who seemed to traffic mainly in horror stories about all the bright–eyed, brash young reporters who had failed in their attempt to fight the system, and ended up driving cabs or flipping burgers the rest of their lives.

Susan had already been repeatedly suspended from the college newspaper for arguing with the editor, refusing to back down on controversial stories, and otherwise infuriating the administration; what chance did she have out in the real world if she couldn't even function in this one? Having barely survived a rebellious childhood long enough to rest on the shores of what she hoped would be her one salvation, her failing optimism put her right back on the express train to self–destruction. She began drinking more than she should, skipping classes, and going to parties instead of doing the necessary but, to her, increasingly irrelevant assignments handed out by her instructors. Her grades were dropping and she found she didn't much care.

Then one semester Rob appeared, speaking to rows of jaded students about things like passion, and drive, and the need for journalists to present truth and fight for what they believed in, with integrity and honesty and as much objectivity as could be mustered. Hearing him speak was like awakening from a troubled sleep and taking a cold, refreshing shower.

She had told him as much, and with his guidance and support somehow managed to get through the rest of her degree before going on to freelance for various newspapers and, eventually, come for an appointment at the *Los Angeles News–Tribune*, where Rob changed her life a second time by hiring her to help cover the crime beat.

In the years since that lecture, he had softened, had gone a little corporate, and looked more often than he probably should at the bottom line. But he still fired her up, and still watched out for her with paternal concern.

There were just some days when it went over better than others.

"You could've gotten yourself killed," he said.

"Rob, for most of the time I was out there, the only thing I could've died from was boredom. Things happen, that's all."

"With you, *things happen* all the time." He sat on the edge of the bed. Susan felt it tilt precariously but somehow managed to avoid tipping over. "Is this okay? Your leg—"

"It's the other one."

"How're you holding up?"

"The doctors say the bullet passed right through the fleshy part of the leg without cutting anything vital. I'll need to use a cane for a few days, but beyond that I should be fine."

"What about…" He pointed to his cheek. Why men felt so nervous about pointing out possible defects in a woman's face was something she never understood.

"It's just a nick, it looked worse than it was. It cut a capillary so it bled like hell but they say it'll heal up great, end up just a fine line in a few months. You won't be able to tell it from the wrinkles."

"That's good," he said, and sighed again.

Susan kept eating.

"Any word on the two officers?"

She nodded. "Montoya took a .45 in the ribcage, broke a couple of bones and nicked his left lung, but the doctors say he'll be okay in a few days."

"What about the other one, Ryan?"

She put down the fork. "They don't know. One of the bullets ricocheted off the car and banged into his skull." She absently touched the bandage where the bullet shard had nicked her cheek, and realized how close she had come to something similar. "He's still unconscious. They say if he wakes up, he'll be fine. If not..." She let the thought trail off.

Rob nodded.

Susan blinked hard, fighting back the memory of Ryan on the ground, not moving. *Stop it*, she thought. *Not in front of Rob, for chrissakes.*

Rob glanced at his watch, frowned. "I should get back to the office before the loonies take over the asylum." He pushed himself up off the bed. "You need anything?"

"No, I'm fine. Thanks."

"So when do you think you can get me the story?"

She smiled. Rob cared about her, in a fatherly sort of way, and he was as good an editor as she'd ever had, but at the end of the day, he was still an editor, through and through. "If I check out okay with the doctors, they'll release me tonight. I'll pull it together and modem it over to you before I go to bed. You'll have it first thing tomorrow morning."

"Good," he said. "I was holding a place for it. Think you can keep it down to twelve column inches?"

"I'll try."

"Then I'll see you tomorrow. Get some rest."

With a wink and a nod, he headed out as an orderly came in. He smiled at her and began to make up the empty bed across the room.

Empty? Susan thought, and memory stirred. *Wait a minute...*

"Excuse me," Susan said. "Wasn't someone in that bed last night?"

The orderly nodded. "She was transferred to a private room early this morning. You were still asleep."

"Oh."

"Strange case," the orderly continued. "Ambulance brought her in yesterday afternoon. Barely conscious, vomiting blood, delirious. She was on her way back from Mexico with her parents when she started to get sick on the plane, then passed out." He shook his head. "Her vitals were all over the place. Tell you the truth, it didn't look good for her. Then, this morning, she seemed perfectly okay."

"What happened to her? I mean, was it poison, or—"

"It's nothing I can talk about, ma'am. I think the family would want it that way." The orderly tucked in the last corner, and started out of the room.

"One more thing," Susan said. "There was a man here last night...I don't know the exact time, but it must've been sometime around two, maybe three in the morning."

"Not possible. No visitors are allowed into ICU after six. Even if an exception was made, there'd be an entry in the log, and there isn't one."

"Look, I know there was someone here. He spoke to me."

"He was here to see you?"

"No," Susan said. "He was talking to the other girl."

The orderly smiled. "Well, then like I said, can't be. Her parents were taking her home to Seattle. She only got off in LA because she fell sick. Aside from her folks, there's nobody local who knows her or even knows she's here."

With that pronouncement, the orderly continued out of the room, shutting the door behind him.

Susan looked down at the remains of the chicken on her plate, and frowned. *There* was *someone here, damn it*. She closed her eyes. She could still see his face.

She opened them again. There was nothing to be gained by debating the issue. The girl was fine, Susan was improving, and as far as could be determined, everybody and everything was all right.

With one exception, but she'd deal with that when she got home.

Home was a two–bedroom Spanish–style stucco apartment in Silverlake, a bedroom community that in recent years had gotten an only partially deserved reputation for being a *gay* bedroom community. Certainly they were its most visible residents, but it was also a place of old family homes and young couples. For the most part it was quiet, friendly, and safe. At least as much as anyplace in Los Angeles could be considered safe.

Balancing carefully with the cane given her at the hospital, she picked up the copy of the morning's *Trib*, which had been yellowing on the driveway since dawn, and gingerly opened the door, closing it again just as the phone rang.

She balanced the phone against her shoulder as she fumbled to put away her keys. "Yeah?"

"Susan? It's me. You okay?"

Susan took a moment before answering. This was the call she'd been expecting—*no*, she caught herself, *specificity of language is our friend*—the call that she had been *waiting for* since last night. The call that had not come, despite all her specificities and her patience.

It deserved a moment of cold silence before she could respond.

"Susan? You there?"

"I'm here, Larry."

"I called the paper this morning, and they said you'd had an accident or—"

"I got *shot*, Larry. Last night."

"Jesus, are you okay?"

"Fine, thanks for asking."

Now the silence was at his end of the line. "I'm sorry, I didn't know—"

"No, you didn't know, because you didn't bother to call, didn't bother to even worry when I didn't call."

"You're out a lot, late at night—"

"Yes, *at the paper*. There's always somebody at the news desk every night, round the clock. They knew what had happened. If you'd called, they would have told you. But you didn't bother."

"Susan, I don't know why you're getting mad at me when I didn't *do* anything. I admit I've been busy. The agency just signed a big deal with Spielberg, and I've been up to my ears trying to get something of my own going. I just called to see if you were okay. You're holding me responsible for something I didn't do, that I didn't even *know* about, and I don't think that's fair. I'm your lover, that doesn't make me a mind reader."

She let the silence return for a beat. On the one hand, she knew he was right...but that did little to change her feeling that he *should* have known, that he *should* have called, that if he cared one–tenth as much as he always said he cared, he would have exerted himself, bestirred himself just an inch to call and check in on her.

And she hated it when he referred to himself as *her lover*. It sounded like something out of a cheap romance novel, and it managed to nicely distance itself from words like *boyfriend* or *fiancé*, both of which implied some kind of emotional obligation, as opposed to *lover*, which implied only the act of sex.

She said none of this, however.

Hating herself for saying it, even knowing she was saying it mainly because she just didn't want to get into an argument right now...she said only, "Maybe you're right. I'm just tired and upset, that's all."

"Of course, hon, I understand. Listen, I know you just got in, so maybe I should let you settle in and get some rest. Long as I know you're okay, that's what matters. I'll check back in on you later, okay?"

"Okay."

She racked the phone and headed for the bedroom, desperate for a shower, a throbbing ache from her leg working its way up to her hip. *Pain killers first, then a shower, then—*

The phone rang again.

She let the answering machine get it and continued into the bathroom, turning on the hot water to let the room heat up.

She stuck her head out long enough to eavesdrop on the answering machine. She recognized Rob's voice in mid sentence.

"—had another homeless guy killed downtown," he was saying. "Looks like we've definitely got a serial killer on our hands."

Just About Right

He had overslept again. He hated it when he overslept. It killed the rest of the day.

The clock read three o'clock. By the time he showered, dressed and ate it would be nearly dark outside. And there was always so much to do.

He sat up, rubbing the sleep out of his eyes with the back of his hand. The palms felt dry and crusty, as they did whenever he worked too hard, the curse of dry skin and hard hands in addition to the blood, but a shower always worked wonders, made his skin feel a hundred percent better.

Three o'clock. He shook his head. How the hell did it get to be three o'clock? Where did the day go? Granted it was a long night, and the work left his muscles with that kind of tight stiffness that only sleep could help, but still, *three o'clock?*

He pulled himself out of bed and staggered into the bathroom, turning on the hot water by feel rather than turn on the lights or open the heavy curtains that helped him sleep. He closed his eyes as steam filled the room, breathing it in and letting it warm him.

His right wrist was still sore from last night's prolonged work. Behind his eyes, he could still see flashes of it, blurred images would continue to soften and dull until they were just an echo, like the afterflash of a camera bulb snapped too close, sharp at first when you close your eyes, then softening, losing shape, until finally you're not even aware of it anymore. Unless you look for it.

And there was no need to look for it. Not now, anyway, there was too much to do and never enough time to do it all. Still, it made him feel better to know it was still there, where he could find it.

Where they both could find it.

He scraped absently at some dried blood under his fingernails, then picked at a piece of lettuce that had worked its way between his teeth as he slept. The air in the bathroom was almost warm enough to satisfy him. He stuck one hand into the shower to check the water, then nodded. Just about right.

He stretched and stepped out of his shorts. The specifics of last night were already going away. In another hour, he wouldn't even think about them. What was done was done, after all, and there was always so much to do. Things to do, people to see. People counted on him.

He was essential, after all.

Not that anyone appreciated it, but as with all things, that would change in time, of that much he was sure.

He stepped into the shower, the events of last night now almost entirely gone, and turned on the shower radio. He soon found himself humming along with Billy Joel's latest, the first really good song he'd done since breaking up with Christy Lee. Yeah, he decided, it was three o'clock, maybe even three thirty by now, but there was still time to get in some television, then go out for a proper dinner.

He pushed the last images away, and focused on his plans for the rest of the day, since there wasn't anything he could do about the rest. For that matter, there was nothing he would choose to do about it.

Why should he?

It really wasn't his problem.

Just sit back, smile, and enjoy the ride, he thought, as the water in the base of the shower turned a coppery brown at his feet.

And Thus Deplete the Surplus Population

Susan stood in the opening to a small back alley off Western Street and shivered. The morning air was cold and damp, and even though the pain in her leg had diminished in the two weeks since she had been shot, allowing her to walk without her cane, the dampness crept into her bones and made her leg ache just as bad as the first morning after.

Ahead of her, yellow POLICE tape had been stretched across the alley to keep out onlookers and curiosity–seekers. Further down, past the police officer standing guard at the scene, a red stain darkened and pooled on the concrete where a fourth body had been found last night, the second since the police had formally decided that there was a serial killer at work.

She checked her notes as she waited for her contact to arrive and, she hoped, usher her past the barricade. It was all she'd gotten from her first call to the precinct. *Victim: male, mid–30s, no name on record yet, found in front of dumpster by old lady chasing her cat. Cat found body, was sniffing at blood. Lady fainted. Woke up to find cat licking her face. Cat had red mouth. Lady fainted again. Finally woke up again and called police. No witnesses to murder, time of death TBD.*

She thought about the old lady and her cat—it was funny, in a grotesque sort of way—and wondered if there was any way she could pry her name and address out of the record for an interview. Then she looked up as Sergeant Mike Devereaux pulled up across the street in a squad car. He was a big man, African–American, and when he crossed the street, heading in her direction, he looked neither left nor right, knowing that no car in its right mind would mess with someone who could tear its front fender off with his teeth. Not long after they'd first met, Susan decided that some people ask for respect, some people demand it, and some people never think about it twice, because it's beyond their comprehension that they wouldn't get it. That was Sergeant Devereaux.

"Got your message," he said, stopping beside her. He looked around and adjusted his belt, which seemed to carry enough in the way of ammunition, handcuffs, pepper spray, bullets, and communications equipment to outfit a small South American rebel army. "Sorry, but I can't let you back there."

"Mike, come on, this is me."

"Oh, I know who you are," he said, and smiled broadly. "You're the woman who gets me in trouble every time I pick up your phone call. Not that I mind, I always figured, live fast, die young, leave a good looking corpse—"

"Well, you're too late for at least one of those," she said. "Would you like to go for two?"

He cocked an eyebrow at her, and laughed. "You sure know how to sweet–talk a guy."

"Figured I had to get your attention. Look, Mike—"

He held up his hands. "If it were up to me, I'd let you go back there. But it's not. We're all getting heat from up top to contain this thing."

"They know something about the killer?"

He started to answer, then looked away.

"What? What is it?"

"I can't tell you," he said. "All I can say is…that *definitely* ain't why they're keeping a lid on this."

"Are you saying they don't know *anything?* They don't have even a clue as to who's doing this, and they don't want people to find out how much they don't know because it'd cause a panic?"

"I didn't say that."

"No, you didn't. But is it true?"

He looked away. Said nothing.

"I notice you're not denying it, Mike."

He shrugged. "I can't get in trouble for what I don't say, right?"

"Right."

"Then I'm not saying anything. Okay?"

She nodded. This morning the Chief of Police had said they were gathering good, solid evidence on the murders, and were *aggressively pursuing several encouraging leads.* Given what she was sensing from Mike, that was a less than truthful statement. *Probably said it to put a scare in the killer, make him back off and go underground for a while. That would buy the police time without another murder while they dig for real clues.*

She looked down the alley, to the dark red stain that pooled on the concrete and splattered the nearby walls. The murder was done out in the open, where anyone walking by could have seen it. She thought about the arrogance and surety of purpose that could enable someone to do that, and weighed that against the chief's statement. *Yeah, I'm sure that'll put a real big dent in his social calendar.*

She checked her notes. "What about the woman who found the body? Any chance I can talk to her?"

Mike snorted. "Get real. Every time she talked to us about it, she'd faint again. Reporters? I think she'd dive off the roof first."

Susan pulled her coat tighter around her. In another hour the morning rush hour would start. "Look, Mike, I came all the way out here, hoping maybe you could give me something. You're a good guy, you've never let me down before, you can't send me away empty–handed."

He hesitated, glancing at the officer standing halfway down the alley. She could sense that he wanted to say something. Truth is, he *was* a good guy, and they'd helped each other before.

"C'mon, Mike…didn't I take a bullet for you guys, and save a couple of LA's finest from bleeding to death in the street?"

"That's not fair."

She shrugged. "It's the only leverage I've got left."

He turned to her, his back to the officer. "Walk with me," he said.

He stepped away from the alley and down the sidewalk, moving out of earshot from the officer guarding the crime scene. She followed until they were halfway down the block. He glanced around to make sure they were alone, no open windows or doors nearby. "You tell anyone you heard this from me and I'll blow up your car," he said.

"It's all deep background, I promise."

"I mean, you can't even *print* it, not now, not until I say it's okay. Deal?"

"Deal."

"Good." He frowned and looked off, trying to find a way to explain whatever it was he wanted to tell her. Finally he glanced back at her. "You know how we figured out all the victims were killed by the same guy?"

"I assumed you found forensic evidence, cloth or fingerprints or hair fibers that were common to the murders but didn't tie into anything in the records that could give you an ID."

He shook his head. "We got none of that. What we got, is a signature."

"He *signed* the bodies?"

"In a way," he said. "See, there's two kinds of serial killers. The first is the killer of opportunity. He looks for his victims out in the open, kills and gets out fast, because he knows that as long as he's in an uncontrolled environment he runs the risk of being caught. The second kind incapacitates the victim and transports him or her somewhere else, to a controlled environment, where he can do whatever he wants, usually involving either sex or torture, for as long as he wants.

"What makes this guy different is that he doesn't fit into either camp. He does his killing right out in the open, but doesn't seem in any rush to get away. He does…what he does…in an uncontrolled environment. He's absolutely unafraid of being seen or captured."

"And what exactly does he do?"

Devereaux let out a low breath. "He's a knife guy. He uses one blade to slit the victim's throat. Forensics says it's a hunting blade of some kind, with serrated edges. After the victim's dead, he uses another blade—we think it's an exacto blade, or some kind of very fine, sharp razor—to slice the inside of the victim's palms. We're talking very delicate work: line after line, cut clean through to the bone, each cut running the length of the palm and maybe a sixteenth of an inch apart. Susan, their palms looked like a piece of beef that had been sliced by a professional meat slicer, the kind you get in a deli. You could run your finger along the ridge, and the cut flesh would riffle, like a deck of cards."

Susan swallowed and looked down, trying hard not to see that image in her mind's eye. "And all the victims had this kind of…mutilation?"

Devereaux nodded. "Some of them had it elsewhere as well…on the face, the throat, the genitals…but all of them had their hands sliced. Anyway, that's all I can tell you, and it's a hell of a lot more than I should have said." He glanced at his watch. "I gotta go."

"Of course."

She walked back with him to where their cars were parked. Without another word, Devereaux crossed the street, climbed into the squad car and drove off. Susan paused by the entrance to the alley and looked down its length, past the yellow tape and the officer standing guard. She tried to imagine the kind of man, the kind of *mind,* that could sit patiently in that alley, as cars drove by and people walked their dogs not twenty feet away, patiently slicing his victim's hands until the flesh could be riffled like a deck of cards. How long would it take? Ten minutes? Twenty?

He would have to have strong, precise hands, the ability to do his work with utter calm, and complete confidence that he would not be discovered.

It was, she decided, an ugly and dangerous combination. And she found she had no longer had any desire whatsoever to go down into that alley.

By the time she returned to the office, the official police report had been emailed over and was waiting in Susan's account alongside the usual flood of spam: junk email from direct sales people and marketers, as well as the usual assortment of ads for sex–oriented websites. They all used the same technique, buying thousands of email addresses, then sending junk mail with subject headings designed to make her think they had been sent by friends. *Hi, it's Julie, look at this!* or *Pursuant to our conversation last week*, or *I knew you'd want to see this.* If she responded, the company would continue to bother her. If she didn't, they simply sold her address to another company and the whole thing started over.

With a few keystrokes, she mass–deleted the spam, sent the police report to her desktop printer, and waited for it to appear.

The *Los Angeles News–Tribune* had been in business less than eight years, turning what had been a twenty–year–plus monopoly by the *Los Angeles Times* into a proper, two–paper town, with all the energy and vitality that such competition produced. The *Trib* was still the new kid on the block, with small, cramped offices in a small cramped building filled with reporters and photographers racing madly out the door to beat the *Times* to a story, then hurrying back hours later to pound the story into the terminals that fed the print–monster across town. Nearly everyone who worked there had a brash, renegade edge that Susan found refreshing, invigorating.

With some exceptions.

"Hey, Susan, how's the downtown renovation–and–gene pool–improvement project going?"

She looked up to see Leo Dexter leaning over the edge of his cubicle, which was kitty–corner to her own. Leo was everything she found offensive in a certain class—or certain lack–of–class—of entertainment and feature writers, foremost being the sure conviction that their opinions were more important than whatever subject they were covering. In his forties, with fine, slicked–back hair that seemed one size too small for his head, Leo was a pudgy man, pale in a meal–worm sort of way, who seemed to perspire all the time, even when the room was air conditioned to within an inch of everyone's life.

As far as Susan was concerned, Leo was a rat and a gossip. You tell Leo something, you may as well tell the world.

She looked up at him, and responded in her usual way. "Shove it, Leo."

He grinned. "Sounds like *somebody* got up on the wrong side of the corpse this morning," he said. "I mean, if you want off the story, all you have to do is tell Rob to put you on something else."

"I don't *want* something else," she said, and turned her attention to the papers dropped on her desk awaiting her return. One of them was a pink phone message. *Larry Dixon's assistant called, 2:10 p.m. Please call back. Dinner?* She put the note aside, with two others that had come in from him the day before. She hadn't decided yet what to do about Larry, and this wasn't the time or the place to think about it.

Wait a minute...

She looked at the note again. *His assistant called. He didn't even have the balls to call himself.*

Well, when you make that much money, I guess you can have your assistant do everything for you, including handle your relationships.

She crumpled up the note and tossed it aside, then pulled the report out of the printer and began to read through it, hoping Leo would take the hint and go back to his cubicle.

He didn't. He never did.

"I don't know how you do it," he said, "keep a story like this interesting, at least to yourself. One more street bum killed in an alley. I mean, what're the odds, right?"

She tuned him out and continued reading the police report. As she'd expected, there was nothing about the mutilation in the two pages the public information office had sent over. *Victim: Rudolph Rypczynsky, age 37, homeless, no known address.*

"I remember the Mayor giving a press conference about a month ago," Leo was saying, "something about cleaning up the downtown area, moving all the derelicts and pushers and pimps somewhere else, and all those protest marches the next day from people who said he was a racist. I'll give you this, whoever's bumping off these people is probably doing more to scare the creeps out of downtown than the mayor's done in the last six years."

Homeless doesn't necessarily mean without relatives, Susan thought. If the murders violated standard serial killer protocol in the way they were committed, maybe it was possible that they violated it in another way. What if the victims weren't chosen at random? What if there was some kind of connection between them?

"What's that line from *A Christmas Carol?*" Leo was saying. "You know the one, it's...right...*and thus deplete the surplus population.*"

She looked back at the name on the fax. *Rypczynsky.*

Come on, she thought, *how many Rypczynsky's can there be in Los Angeles?*

At her touch, the data terminal in front of her flared to life. She accessed the PeopleFinder website the *Trib* had under contract, typed in Rypczynsky, and waited.

Was he *still* talking?

"—and I was thinking that if you want a break from this stuff, I've got two tickets to a revival of *Phantom* at the Pasadena Playhouse."

She focused on him. Was he actually asking her for a date?

"Leo, if you don't crawl back inside your hole and leave me alone, I'm going to take these two Number 2 pencils, shove them in your eyeballs and hang Christmas ornaments off them."

"Fine," he said, his tone dismissive. "I try to extend the hand of friendship and you act like an ass. Suit yourself." With that, he settled back into his chair, disappearing behind the cubicle wall.

Susan turned her attention back to the display. Her inquiry had turned up one address, an apartment in the West Hollywood area. She wrote it down and glanced at her watch. With luck she'd be able to finish what she was doing and get to the address by five. The listing didn't come with a phone number, meaning it was probably unlisted. She hated stopping by someone's home without calling first, but she didn't have much choice.

As she started typing in her notes, she heard from Leo's cubicle, "Is it hot in here? I'm sweating like a pig."

"Touch the thermometer and I'll snap that hand of friendship off at the wrist and feed it to you," she said, and returned to her notes.

It was going to be a long afternoon.

A Moment's Meditation

Raymond Weil had waited for the large black cop and the woman beside him to finish their conversation and drive off before finally popping the car door and stepping out into the street. He'd wanted to see who would show up to examine last night's handiwork, but the turnout was disappointingly small. The police had gotten increasingly better at concealing the exact location of their crime scenes. The single guard posted at the alley was discreetly out of sight, and could have been guarding nothing more interesting than the site of a purse snatching.

He squinted against the brightening sky, checking the windows and rooftops, knowing that just as he was watching and waiting, there were doubtless others doing the same. With a final glance around, he started across the street, joining the flow of foot traffic that was starting to make its way out onto the early morning sidewalks. He buttoned his coat; it was still chilly, and the cold burrowed deep into his bones, which after fifty–one years didn't keep out the chill as well as they once did.

At the entrance to the alley he paused to re–tie his shoelaces, taking the opportunity to glance down the length of the alley, to where the officer stood guard beside a drying pool of blood. More blood spattered the walls and a nearby dumpster.

Just like last time, he thought absently. But was everything the same? That would be the real test.

He hesitated before standing again, feeling unaccountably drawn to the sight at the end of the alley. Something tugged at him from there in the shadows, something familiar. He decided it was probably nothing, but left the feeling on file in case it developed meaning later.

He stood, more slowly than in earlier years, and dusted off his pants where he'd knelt to tie his shoes. Some of the grit remained. He shrugged. He had to get these clothes cleaned soon; who knew what was in them by now?

And he needed a shower. He found he couldn't remember when he'd last had a shower. *Soon*, he thought. *Soon*.

As he walked on past the alley, he wondered absently about the woman he'd seen with the black police sergeant earlier. There was something vaguely familiar about her, but he couldn't quite put his finger on it. He shrugged to himself; he'd come to it in time. He always did.

At the corner, he stopped and looked around, then turned to a woman passing him on the street. "Excuse me," he said, "can you tell me where the nearest church is?"

She was startled by his intrusion into her personal space, but seemed to take assurance when he asked about a church, not a bar or a date. "St. Matthew's, down two blocks that way," she said, pointing east.

He thanked her and started walking in the direction she'd indicated. It was an old neighborhood, and it had been pretty once. Now the six–story concrete apartment buildings were dingy, covered by soot and window grates. Trash lined the streets, and sex shops alternated with stores selling cheap stereos and almost certainly stolen televisions.

He stopped in front of the parish of St. Matthews. The gate leading up to the church was open, a janitor hosing down the sidewalk and the driveway, clearing away debris for any worshippers that might want to come in for a moment's meditation after breakfast.

If it's here, then I'll know I'm right about all this, he thought.

He edged past the janitor, who seemed barely awake in any event, and stepped up the four concrete steps that led up to the church. The front door was locked, but the side entrance that led back to the janitor's office was open. He continued down the hall until he found an open door to the church proper, and pushed through. Incense hung in the air, still pungent, telling him that it had not been aired out or opened since services last night. At least, not by anyone who worked for the church.

He stepped into the center aisle, between the two rows of pews, and studied the interior of the church, knowing that his efforts were hampered by the fact that he didn't know what he was looking for. The last time, the desecration had been both subtle and almost comic. He'd studied every inch of the church and found nothing in the least amiss…until on a hunch he picked up one of the hymnals and found that a nail had been driven through the middle of it, anchoring it to the back of the pew in front of it. Every hymnal in the church had been given the same treatment.

The newspapers didn't even bother to report it, he thought, vaguely annoyed. *Probably figured it was just kids, a prank or something.* He would've been happy to know it was only the work of kids. It was the *or something* part that worried him.

He stifled a yawn. It seemed he was tired all the time, to the point where he was tired of being tired. *Am I really getting that old?* he thought, and wondered, *If anything happens to me, who will take my place?*

He shook his head. It was a rhetorical question. There would always be someone else to continue the work. He should know better than to even ask that question.

Ego, he thought. *Ego and fatigue and it's too early and I haven't eaten and where the hell is it? There's no point doing it if it's so obscure nobody can even see it.*

Why can't I see it? He looked up at the massive crucifix that hung at the front of the church, its eyes downcast toward the altar and the pews. Then it struck him: *Maybe because my seeing it isn't the point. Maybe this was meant for other eyes to see.*

Hoping no one would enter the church and catch him, he stepped past the front railing and up around the altar. He stopped under the crucifix, looked up at it one last time, then turned to look back the way he'd come.

The back of the altar, the backs of the statues of the saints on either side, the back of the stone and marble work, all of it was covered in mud and blood–red paint and what Raymond guessed was probably defecation. None of it could be seen from the back of the church, or the pews. It could only be seen by the priest, and by the figure on the crucifix.

And there was little doubt in Raymond's mind which of those two was really the target, which pair of eyes the Other had most wanted to see this.

He found himself smiling grimly. *You just can't resist temptation, can you? But then, you never could. Isn't that how all the trouble started in the first place?*

Somewhere nearby, a door opened loudly. He hurried past the altar and back down between the pews, hoping to make it out before anyone could find him. He'd gotten what he'd come for: confirmation of his suspicions. The most important thing he could do right now was to avoid being arrested for trespassing, especially since they'd probably try to blame him for the mess. He could not afford to draw the attention of the police.

Once he made it out onto the street, he allowed a sigh of relief, and walked back to his car. He had several more stops to make before he could allow himself to rest.

A message was clearly being sent. But where was the messenger, and even more important…what was the message?

No More Dreams

It was dark by the time Susan arrived at Fountain Street. The address in her hand belonged to a small apartment in a tangle of low–slung bungalows on either side of the tree–lined street, many of them set back one behind the other. Most of the apartments in this area dated back to the forties, pink stucco monuments to a time when gates and fences and window screens weren't necessary, so that the ones added in darker times looked tacked–on and hostile, giving the apartments a feeling that was both paranoid and curiously industrial.

She stepped under a street lamp and checked the address again. *417-B Fountain.* She could find 415 and 421, but so far 417—A or B—was invisible. She backtracked to 412 and found a small path that led through the trees to a courtyard behind the front row of apartments.

Bingo, she thought, and made her way back along the tree lined sidewalk.

Just ahead, she spotted the corner of what was almost certainly 417 just as someone came out of the building. He was turned slightly toward her, just enough to see his profile in the light that spilled out into the courtyard.

She froze. *Can't be,* she thought, and looked again.

It was the same man she'd seen in her hospital room.

"Hey!" she called.

He glanced back but continued walking. He turned a corner, heading around to the other side of the building.

"Excuse me! Mister—" She turned the corner, following after him.

He was gone.

She looked back the way she had come. He couldn't have slipped behind her and gone back that way, and the gate in front of her was locked. Brush and trees lined either side of the walk. *He could've gone through there, maybe hopped the fence into the next apartment complex,* she considered, *but why run in the first place?*

With one last look around, she headed back toward 417-B, wondering if she would find her answers there.

"My Rudy was always good boy," Mrs. Rypczynsky said. She was a heavy–set woman in her seventies, and she spoke with a thick accent, probably Polish, Susan guessed. "He all the time calling, make sure I'm okay. Who would do this to him?"

"That's what the police are trying to find out," Susan said. "I'd like to help also."

"My boy, my boy," she said, crying now and waving a handkerchief at a fire-place mantel covered with photos. Susan noticed that none of the photos showed a Rudolph Rypczynsky older than his middle twenties.

"Do you know what he was doing out there alone the night he was murdered? The police said he was homeless—"

"He not homeless! He had home, right here! He was too proud all the time. I say to him, I say, can you eat pride? Can you sleep on pride? He says you don't understand, mama. I understand plenty. But he don't listen. He was all the time chasing something, some job, never work out. A dreamer. Now, look at him, no more Rudy, no more dreams, no more nothing."

"Do you know if he hung out with any known troublemakers? Anyone who might have wanted to hurt him?"

Mrs. Rypczynsky spit on the floor. "Pah. His friends were creeps. I tell him, you shouldn't talk to such people, they're going to get you in trouble, but again he don't listen. What am I supposed to do? Is this my fault?"

"No, I'm sure it's not your fault," Susan said. "Do you have any names?"

"Names? No, I don't got names, I just see them with my eyes, and I know: trouble."

Susan sighed and looked around the room, which was filled with Eastern European icons, statues of baby Jesus and crucified Jesus, a Jesus with an open heart and a Jesus with spread arms, white Marys and blue Marys and crosses as far as she could see. The sofa beneath her was covered in the same plastic lining that it had probably been delivered with. In the last hour, she'd learned exactly nothing useful about the recently deceased Rudolph Rypczynsky. Protestations to the contrary, it was clear that his mother knew little to nothing of what he had been doing these past twenty years.

Tell the truth, she wanted to say. *You drove him out of the house. Maybe it was money, maybe it was religion, maybe it was him bringing home the wrong woman one night and they spilled something on the sofa and that was the final straw, and he left and you told the neighbors he called all the time because that would prove to somebody, maybe yourself, that it wasn't you who drove him out. You have no idea who he hung out with, who his friends were, where he went or what he was doing out there that night.*

She closed her notebook. "I appreciate you taking time to talk to me, Mrs. Rypczynsky. My condolences on your loss."

The older woman nodded, wringing the handkerchief between her hands.

"Before I go, I'd like to ask you one last question. As I was coming here, I saw a man leave your apartment. A tall man, with gray hair."

"Yes, he came here. He came to talk about my Rudy, same as you."

"Did he say why?"

She shrugged. "I thought he was police."

"Did you ask for ID?"

"No, I just look at him with my eyes, and I see that he is police."

"But did he *say* that?"

"I don't know, I don't remember. But he knew all about my Rudy. He said he wanted to help, same as you. I told him what I knew. That's all."

"I see." Susan tapped on her notebook with her pencil. "Did you by any chance get his name?"

"I don't remember," she said. "I've been very upset, you understand, yes?"

"Of course." Susan stood and dug in her purse for her business card. "Well, if you do happen to remember his name or…anything else that might be useful, I'd appreciate it if you could give me a call."

"Sure, sure," Mrs. Rypczynsky said, accepting the card without standing. "I call."

"Thanks." Susan started for the door and was halfway outside when the older woman called to her.

"His hands were cut," she said.

Susan turned back to her. "Whose hands?"

"My Rudy. The man who was here, he told me that whoever killed my Rudy cut up his hands, like this." She drew quick lines across the palm of her hand. "What kind monster does a thing like that?"

"I don't know," Susan said. "Someone who needs to be put away for a long time."

"Not put away. You hang. Hang the bastard who killed my boy. Pah!" She spit on the floor again. Susan assumed it was a Polish thing.

She continued out the door, letting the screen clatter shut behind her. She still didn't know the name of the man she'd seen, but she had gotten something that was possibly even more important.

He knew about the mutilation even though the police are keeping a tight lid on that. The only ones who know about it are me, the police, maybe a couple more reporters if there have been more breaches of security…but sure as hell it hasn't been on the news and this guy didn't look like any reporter I've seen around town…which doesn't leave a lot of options.

One way or another, this guy knew more than he should. And that was enough to attract Susan's curiosity.

Mrs. Rypczynsky may not have been able to remember his name, but Susan knew one place where she could probably find out.

Tripping Over Brimstone

Convincing her editor to cough up the money for anything out of the ordinary was always a job for Jesus. Plane fare was a particular hot–button for Rob, because he was always sure that somehow or other he was being asked to under-write someone's vacation. *C'mon, Rob,* she'd said, *it's Seattle, what the hell am I going to do in Seattle?*

You'll go see the Mariners.

I'm not a baseball fan.

Then you're going so you can ask Bill Gates if you can have his baby.

Susan crossed her arms and stared at him.

He wrote the check.

Now, twenty–four hours later, she was driving down a tree–lined suburban street in a rented Chevy Blazer, peering through a windshield wet with driz-zle—what Seattle residents called *liquid sunshine*—looking for the address she'd gotten from a contact in the hospital's administration office back in Los Angeles. Once she had the information she needed, she'd called ahead to say she was coming. To her surprise the woman on the other end of the phone agreed to see her, but with the understanding that she wouldn't have much to say.

Which was all right by Susan. All she needed was one name, after all. How hard could that be?

She parked in front of a two–story Cape Cod style house at the ass–end of a cul–de–sac, and killed the engine. As she gathered her bag and her notebook, she glanced up just in time to see a young girl looking out at the street from an upstairs window. Then, realizing she'd been seen, the girl—Susan was confident it was the same one who had shared her hospital room that night—quickly retreated behind the curtains.

Ten bucks says that when I ask to talk to her, they'll say she's sick in bed or at school, Susan thought as she climbed out of the Blazer and started up the walk to the big house.

The Stearns home was a stark contrast to Mrs. Rypczynsky's small apart-ment. It was large, open, and lovingly furnished, with exquisite attention to detail. Dried flowers were propped up just *so* in a small pink vase in the center of the glass coffee table that sat between Susan and Mrs. Stearns. The waiting tea was served in fine–bone china with matching milk and sugar bowls. The sofa, the love seat, the carpets, the throw pillows and the wall hangings were in earth tones carefully arranged so that nothing would clash with anything else.

Not a speck of dust, an old newspaper or a pillow out of place. The house was relentlessly neat. It was, Susan decided, the kind of place that would quickly drive her screaming out into the night.

"I'd be *happy* to let you talk to Cheryl," Mrs. Stearns said, "but I'm afraid her father's taken her out to see her counselor."

Close enough, Susan thought. *Compromise: you owe me five bucks.*

"And what does your husband do, Mrs. Stearns?"

"He works for Microsoft," she said, in a voice that betrayed just a touch of Southern upbringing. Susan guessed Atlanta or thereabouts. "But well, these days, doesn't *everyone?*" She sat back against the sofa and laughed, a quiet and only slightly insincere laugh. "Company humor. And please, call me Gloria."

"I will. Thank you."

Gloria nodded and sipped at her coffee. "So I understand you were in the same hospital room as my little girl."

"That's right. The orderly told me that you were on your way back from Mexico when your daughter became sick."

"Yes. When Cheryl passed out in my arms, I didn't know what to do. I don't think I've ever been that scared before. After all we'd gone through to bring her back, the idea of losing her was…well, it was more than I could bear. Do you have any children, Ms. Randall?"

"Call me Susan. And no, no children yet."

Gloria nodded, as though that answer explained everything about her. "Then you wouldn't understand. When you're holding your own flesh and blood in your hands, and you think she might not make it out alive…" She looked away, biting her lip. "It's a hard thing, Susan. A very hard thing."

"I'm sure it is."

"When we first got to the hospital, the emergency room doctor, Dr. Chang, thought it might have been poison. I told Bill, that's my husband, that those people would stop at nothing to keep her from going back with us, and for a while it looked as if I was right."

"What people?"

She paused, carefully considering her words. "My husband and I discussed this matter at some length after your phone call. We don't want any publicity, we're not looking for anyone's attention. Leaving aside any troubles it might cause for us in the community, it's really for Cheryl's sake. She's been through so much—"

"I understand. I'm not here to invade your privacy. I'm interested in Cheryl's story as background to another story I'm covering. There's no need to dwell on any of it in print. If at any time I need to reference the situation, I'll change all your names and circumstances. I give you my word that there will be nothing in what I write that will point to you or your daughter."

"Well, I guess that's all right, then," she said. "I mean, what's a woman worth if she's not a woman of her word?"

"Nothing at all."

"Exactly." Gloria took another sip of coffee and set the cup back on the table. Susan noticed that her hand was shaking slightly.

"Well, to make a very long and difficult story as painlessly short as possible...about six, seven months ago, my daughter fell in with some bad company. There were these people handing out leaflets near her school for this church, except it was no real church at all, not a proper Baptist or Lutheran church, not even Presbyterian, which as my mother always used to say is about as far as you can get from a real church without tripping over brimstone. I mean, I'd heard about cults before, but I always thought you could tell them by the way they dressed, you know, in those big yellow robes, that sort of thing.

"But these were young people around Cheryl's age, and Cheryl's never really been one to fit in with others. She's very independent, the teachers say, knows her own mind, keeps to herself. But it's lonely sometimes, and there you had these people her own age, offering friendship and something to believe in...well, anyway, I didn't think much about it, I figured it was good for her to get involved with a church here in the area, doing some social work for the less fortunate, and I was very busy at the time, what with several women's organizations I belong to, that sort of thing.

"Well, one day I went upstairs to call her down for breakfast and she was gone. Obviously Bill and I were just frantic with worry. That's when we found out that this so—called church was basically just a cult in disguise. They would arrange to have new members sent down to Mexico, where they would be trained, then sent elsewhere on recruitment missions.

"Now, Cheryl had just turned sixteen, but apparently she'd told the others that she was legal age, which is why they sent her off. When they found out her real age, well, of course they denied sending her anywhere, but we knew she'd gone off with them. We asked the Mexican public affairs office for help, but they didn't do us a lick of good. We had to get her back somehow.

"We got a recommendation from some people Bill met, and they offered to help us find Cheryl. It didn't take a lot of detective work, I mean, cults like this are hard to hide, even in Mexico, especially when you've got kids from all over the world showing up every few days. But we still had to get her out of there.

"For that, we got some...additional help from some people down there. I can't really talk much about that part of it. Except to say that we barely made it out of there ahead of the cult members who wanted to bring Cheryl back at any cost.

"At first she barely recognized us, it was as if...well, almost as if she were somebody else. I'd look in her eyes, and there was such rage there. I don't know if they drugged her, or what, but we had to tussle with her all the way to the airport. Once we got her on the plane, I thought our troubles were over, but then of course she fell sick almost as soon as the plane left the ground.

"If we hadn't had additional help at this end, I think to this day that we would've lost her."

Her voice had fallen steadily as she recounted the events, until the words were barely a whisper. Her eyes were moist, and she rubbed at them with the back of her hand. "I'm sorry, Susan, it still...distresses me to talk about it."

"Of course," Susan said.

"Anyway, that's the end of it, really. I don't know how much else you want to know, but—"

"Just one thing. You said you had additional help at this end of things. What kind of help?"

"That's one of the things Bill and I discussed, and I'm afraid I can't comment on that."

"Would it be okay if I speculated for a moment?"

Gloria smiled. "I suppose."

"During the night when your daughter and I shared a room a the hospital, I woke up and saw a man standing over her." She described him in as much detail as she could remember. "Was he part of that additional help?"

Gloria hesitated, then nodded. "The Bible says we shouldn't lie, and I've lately come to a greater appreciation of that book and its contents."

"Can you tell me what he did?"

"He helped. That's all I can say."

"And you compensated him for this?"

"There were arrangements made."

"Can you tell me his name?"

"No, I'm afraid not. All I can tell you, is that I honestly believe that if he had not been involved, my little girl might not be alive right now."

"Is he a policeman of some kind, an investigator?"

Gloria laughed. "I don't think there *is* a word for what he is, Susan, I truly don't. He comes to people in need, and offers his services. Or they come to him, as we did."

"As I'm sure you know, Gloria, there are plenty of people out there who would try to take advantage of folks like yourself in this kind of situation for personal gain."

"Oh, we know, all right. But that wasn't the case here."

"If you won't tell me his name, can you at least tell me what he did for you?"

"I couldn't say."

"Couldn't as in you don't know, couldn't as in can't, or couldn't as in won't?"

"Let's just say that he was a great comfort to us, and let it go at that. He said he would be with this until the end, and he was." She checked her watch, then stood. "It's late and Bill will be home soon. I should get dinner going."

"Of course," Susan said.

"I'll show you out."

They retraced their steps down the long oak hardwood floor to the foyer, and paused beneath a huge cut–crystal chandelier. "How is Cheryl now?"

"Much better, thank you. She doesn't remember anything that happened once she got to Mexico. The doctor says it's probably trauma, and it's probably better that way. Which is another reason we don't want any publicity about this. We don't want to do anything that might cause her to remember things best left buried."

"Of course. Well, thank you for your help, Gloria."

"My pleasure. Thank you for coming."

Susan started out the door, then paused. "I forgot to ask, what happened to the cult itself, the one down in Mexico?"

"The whole compound burned down," Gloria said. "I hear most of the kids who were there are heading back to their parents now. The leader of the cult was killed. Some say he was shot by his own bodyguards, but we heard that he was killed by some of the folks in a nearby town, who'd seen some of their own children disappear into that place. Either way, he's gone, and though I wouldn't wish hell on anyone, I do think it will probably be deserved this time."

Thanks Loads, Mrs. Rypczynsky

"Mrs. Rypczynsky talked."

"*What?* Talked to who?" Susan stood at a pay phone in the Alaska Airlines boarding area at the Seattle–Tacoma airport, struggling to hear what Rob was saying over the muffled PA voice announcing flights to and from unlikely places made utterly incomprehensible by the surrounding noise level. *Twilight Zone flights*, she called them. "Who did she talk to?"

"*Everybody*. The *Times*, *Reuters*, *AP*, everygoddamnbody. Did you know about this mutilation thing, the sliced hands and stuff?"

Susan rubbed tiredly at her eyes. "Yeah…I knew."

"Why didn't you tell us? We could've had a jump on this thing instead of being caught with our pants down around our ankles."

"It was supposed to be on deep background."

"Well, it sure as hell ain't background now. It's page one on the *Times* and raising hell all over town. It's one thing to find out you've got a serial killer in town without knowing the details, but when stuff like this gets out, well, it tells you just how sick this guy is. Details scare people. A slice–and–dice guy like this is everybody's worst nightmare. So now we've got homeless advocates and social workers and TV actors lined up to protest the fact that nothing's been done to catch this guy, and a quarter million people are afraid to walk the poorer parts of town at night. On top of *that* the DA's office is furious that this stuff got out, because they think it'll compromise their investigation."

"Well, Rob, if it's caused that much trouble, maybe it's a *good* thing we didn't go out with it first." She hoped he would buy the rationalization.

He didn't. "If people are going to go around criticizing the media for leaking this kind of thing, I'd rather it was us than the *Times* because at least it tells you who gets the news *first* around here. Now, if they beat us fair and square, that's one thing. I'd still be pissed about it, but that's the game. But if we had it and didn't go with it…"

He sighed. Even over the phone that sigh carried with it the weight of the world. "Anyway," he said, "it's a mess."

"I'm sorry."

"Yeah, well…it happens, I guess," he said grudgingly. "When's your flight back?"

"We should be boarding any time now."

"You get anything useful up there?" he asked. "Anything we can, I don't know…*print*, maybe? Something to show for the plane fare?"

"I definitely think I've got some good background stuff and some solid leads on the story."

"That was a yes or no question, Susan. I didn't hear a yes or no answer."

The PA system boomed above her. *Althaskar Bearlines announces de-arrival of flight forkey to Mophberg, Debaka.*

"I think they just called my plane," Susan said, not really caring if it was hers or another *Twilight Zone* flight as long as it got her off the phone.

"Susan—"

"I'll call you as soon as I get in, Rob. Bye."

She racked the phone. *Thanks loads, Mrs. Rypczynsky*, she thought. The only good thing to come out of her conversation with Rob—*aside from not being fired*, she reminded herself—was that apparently none of the reports had mentioned the man whose identity she was trying to unravel. Which probably meant that Mrs. Rypczynsky hadn't thought to mention it to anyone, which meant in turn that this far at least, the lead was still hers alone.

Wouldn't hurt to check, though. Once they were in the air, she'd drag out her notebook computer, link it into the news services over the airplane's cell phone system, and do a quick search on the story, find out for sure how much had been reported.

Even if the search turned up negative, as she hoped, that was no guarantee that someone wouldn't stumble upon the information tomorrow, or the next day. She had to jump ahead of the pack somehow.

What was it Gloria had said? She flipped open her notepad and found the quote she was looking for. *"He said he would be with this until the end, and he was."*

If that were true, then it occurred to Susan that there might be at least one coming opportunity to find him.

What she still couldn't work out was the shape of the puzzle she was looking at. What was the common denominator between a sick girl from Seattle, and a serial killer in Los Angeles, that would cause the same guy to involve himself in both situations?

Unless he's involved at a much deeper level, Susan considered. The cult leader in Mexico had been killed under mysterious circumstances, and this guy seemed to know far more than he should about the strange killings going on here in town than he should have.

Susan shook her head. *No, that's not right.* Grace had specifically said that she'd enlisted additional help—presumably the man she was tracing—only after they'd gotten back to the States. And it would be too much a case of sheer, blind luck for her to stumble upon a potential suspect in the killings this quickly. Nothing came that easy, not for her.

She sighed, noting absently that she was starting to sound a lot like Rob. Part of her was inclined to abandon this avenue of investigation. After all, she didn't have much more to go on than sheer gut instinct. It was possible there was no connection at all between the two situations, he might be just some kind of perverse curiosity seeker.

But then again, he might not.

She resolved to give it one last shot. If her hunch paid off, and she could find him where she believed he might next show up, then she'd take it to the next level. If not, then she'd let it go and try somehow to justify the plane fare to Seattle.

The door to Gate 14 opened with a rush of noise from the waiting plane. Susan grabbed her bags and started toward it, wondering if her shoulders looked as slumped as they felt right now.

We All Got Problems

"If you'll all please take a seat…"

The City Council was assembled behind a long table set just above the rest of the auditorium. The noise level was almost deafening, echoing off the old plaster walls that had been built in the twenties, a much quieter and more polite time, Raymond decided. He had arrived late, ten minutes after the meeting began, but from the state of affairs he suspected that he hadn't missed much.

Councilwoman Eileen Braverman continued trying to gavel the public meeting to order. She had the hard–edged look of a school teacher addressing an unruly class. "If you will *please* all be seated, we can begin," she said into the microphone. "Everyone will have a chance to be heard."

After a few moments, the crowd settled down into a dull murmur. "Thank you," she said. "Councilman McClintock, if you're ready to begin, could you open?"

"I am, thank you," McClintock said. He was the elder member of the council, Raymond guessed sixty, maybe sixty–five. "Ladies and gentlemen, members of the Council, this public meeting has been convened so that we can address the concerns in the community concerning the recent events downtown. To allay your concerns where we can, to listen to your suggestions, and to help you to better understand what is being done to address this problem."

Raymond looked around the room and shook his head. Why were people so reluctant to use words like *death* or *murder* or *serial killer*, choosing instead to fall back on bureaucratic terminology, such as *the recent events*, or the *problem*. They seemed to believe that speaking of it in such terms diminished the horror of it, and made it less personal, less intimate; transformed it into something that could be dealt with in line–item budget reports and open hearings.

Sometimes, Raymond believed that predisposition was every bit as much *the problem* as anything under discussion. But he hadn't come here today to speak. He had come to listen.

McClintock was continuing. "We've also invited Chief of Police William Darrow to handle any specific question on police activity downtown, though of course he will be limited in what he can say; after all, we don't want to compromise any ongoing investigations.

"Finally, I would just like to add that every possible step is being taken to control, contain and eliminate the problem at its source. Police patrols in the downtown and East Hollywood areas have been doubled, and decoy units have been deployed. We've logged over two thousand calls to the I–Tip hotline, and we believe some of them may prove extremely useful to the ongoing investigation. In short, everything that can be done, is being done. So with that, we'll open up the floor to take your questions. We'll begin on the left." He pointed to a tall, slender African–American man standing at a microphone along the northern wall. Raymond vaguely recognized him as a community activist. "Yes sir, will you please state your name, and your question."

"My name is Lawrence Munroe, I'm the director of Peace in Our Streets, and there's something I don't understand. This killer, whoever he is, has killed eight homeless people so far, is that right?"

"It is."

"Okay. But see, I live in East LA, and between the crack houses—and the police know where they are, don't tell me they don't—between them, the pushers, the pimps, the gang fights, and the robberies, the muggings, we get two, three, sometimes four dead people a week just in my part of town. We've been trying to get more police and more attention to our problems, we've filed petitions, we've had rallies, and in all that time, nothing ever got done. Not one new patrol officer assigned to an area with children and schools and homes. Now a few homeless white folk get killed in a bad part of town and they get the attention that we as taxpayers and citizens have been trying to get for years."

"Surely, Mr. Munroe, you're not saying that homeless people deserve less safety than anyone else, are you?"

"No, sir, I'm not. But where does it say they require *more* safety? They're in the street, Councilman, and that's not a safe place, they know it same as you do. Now, I'll give you that not all of them are there by choice, but how much can you really *do* for these people? I'm not against the homeless, I understand they got problems, but we *all* got problems, and I don't see how it helps anybody to take police away from one area where they're needed and send them in after this one guy. Hell, we got a pusher works the projects downtown killed that many people before he turned sixteen."

There was some cheering from the back of the room at this. Several of the council members conferred away from the microphones before nodding to Braverman. "If you're saying there has been an increase in crime due to the diversion of police forces, I don't think that's the case, is it, Chief?"

The police chief shook his head. "We haven't seen any such rise."

"I'm not talking about a rise," Munroe said, his frustration evident. "What I'm talking about is what we have to deal with every day, day in and day out, and I'd like to see a little of this same police enthusiasm employed in my part of town. Otherwise it looks like favoritism, since as I understand it, most of the victims of this guy have been white. That makes it sound like you're saying that homeless white people deserve more attention and more police than hard work-ing, tax–paying African–American people with homes and families."

With that, he returned to his seat. Others in the audience stood and applauded, shouting their agreement. Braverman gaveled for quiet.

"I don't think it's in anyone's interest to turn this into a racial issue, Mr. Munroe," McClintock said.

"Sure as hell ain't in yours," Munroe said, quietly but not entirely to him-self. There was some laughter at this.

"Can we have the next—" Braverman started, when Chief Darrow held up a hand to interject.

"Before we move on," he said, "just let me say for the record that if anyone here knows the location of a crack house, tell us, because despite what the ques-tioner suggested, believe me, we do *not* know where all of them are. When we find one, we shut it down. That's all, I just wanted to clarify that."

"Thank you, Chief Darrow," Braverman said. "Can we have the next question?"

The meeting lasted for well over two hours. Raymond Weil stayed for all of it. Listening.

He listened to the homeless advocate who vowed to go on a hunger strike unless more resources were invested in finding the man responsible for the murders.

He listened to a spokeswoman for the neighborhood in which two of the murders had taken place, who complained that the extra police presence and questioning of citizens constituted a breach of civil rights and unnecessary sur-veillance of innocent civilians.

He listened to the elderly man who demanded to know why his tax dollars were being spent to save those who could not be saved when that same money could be better spent moving the homeless elsewhere, away from the areas were decent people lived, and he listened to the young woman who jumped the agenda and tried to accuse the police chief of sexual harassment before being rushed quickly off the stage.

For two hours and twelve minutes, he listened to impassioned pleas and earnest jeremiads, to spokesmen and spokeswomen, advocates, activists, priests, neighbors, social workers, counselors, lawyers, psychiatrists, psychologists, Desert Storm veterans and retired police officers. They were as disparate a group of people as could be hoped for at a public meeting like this, and for all the talk and all the debate, Raymond found himself depressed by the realization that every statement made reflected the universal constant of enlightened self–interest more than it reflected any attempt, however marginal, to confront and solve the problem under discussion.

But Raymond knew that meetings like this rarely produced results or solu-tions. They were held to facilitate two things: to allow an increasingly nervous and angry community to vent its frustrations in a non–violent way, thus forestalling additional complications, and on the off–chance that such a gathering might prove an irresistible attraction for the man responsible for the crimes that had brought together such an unlikely chorus.

After all, what performer doesn't seek out the reaction of his audience so that he can bask in the realization that he has achieved his intended effect?

But nowhere in any of the faces of those speaking did he get any sense of culpability. Each one of them had a valid reason for being here. By the one–hour mark, even the audience had grown bored, shrinking from several hundred to one third that, of which at least half a dozen were almost certainly undercover police. Still, he was determined to see it to the end. That was his policy. Whatever he did, he would see it through to the end. No excuses, no exceptions.

By two hours and thirty minutes, the number of speakers queued up behind microphones had shrunk to just two apiece. Even the council members were restlessly whispering to each other during the statements, eager to adjourn and return to their families.

Then the man in the denim shirt got up at the microphone that had been set up at the back of the room. "Yes, sir," councilwoman Braverman said. "Your name and your question?"

"My name is Michael Hardesty," he said, his voice low, almost soft, barely carrying even through the amplified PA system.

"And what's your question, Mr. Hardesty?"

"Well, it's actually more of a statement than a question."

"It wouldn't be the first one tonight," McClintock said. The council members on either side of him smiled or laughed tiredly. "Go on."

"Well, I just don't think anything that's being said or done here, any of the preparations you folks are taking, are going to make any difference."

"And why is that, Mr. Hardesty?" Braverman asked, pouring a glass of water and trying gamely to show interest between sips.

"Because I just heard that the guy you're looking for has killed another guy about two blocks from here. Not only that, they say he did it at the exact moment this meeting started."

The impact of the news was immediate and electric. People were on their feet, shouting over one another to be heard. The council members were conferring heatedly as Chief Darrow moved away from the table, frantically calling for confirmation on his walkie–talkie. "What the hell do you *mean* you didn't think I should be interrupted onstage?" he shouted into the police radio. "Goddamnit, get me an escort and get me there *right now*."

The man in denim stood quietly in the midst of the confusion, seemingly unaffected by it all, except for the faintest trace of a cold and strangely lifeless smile.

Raymond was on his feet, pushing through the crowd. He stumbled, barely catching himself before he could fall between two rows of seats.

When he looked up again, the man was gone.

Damn it! he thought, and hurried outside.

He caught up with the man on the sidewalk outside city hall. "Hey, you!" The man turned. "Yeah?"

Raymond slowed, approached cautiously. "How is it you could know about the murder before Chief Darrow?"

The man smiled again, this time the smile genuine. "What, you think I did it or something?" He jerked a thumb at the cab parked curbside. "I got a police scanner in my cab. You wanna see it? I was driving by about five minutes ago when the cop who found the body called for backup. I knew this meeting was going on, and I figured what the heck, I could get one hell of a reaction by being first in with the news."

Raymond frowned, looking at the police scanner clearly visible in the cab. "I see."

"Anyway, I better get back to work," he said, walking around to the driver's side of the cab. "I heard something else about this one that I was gonna mention, but I didn't exactly get a chance. It went kinda nuts in there, didn't it?"

"Yeah, it did," Raymond said. "So what was it?"

"I drive this neighborhood all the time. The address the cop gave was for an apartment building about two blocks from here. Nice place. They got a lady there who goes to the race track every Tuesday afternoon, a good tipper. Anyway, they gave this address, and said the body was in a fourth-floor apartment."

He looked at Raymond. "Don't you get it? This guy is supposed to kill only homeless people. But this time he hit inside somebody's apartment.

"He's moving uptown, buddy. And if you think *that* reaction was something, just wait until *this* news gets out."

A Quiet Guy

Susan had noticed that in the movies, funerals generally took place in the rain. The reality, in the fourteen funerals she had attended since coming to Los Angeles (three personal, eleven related to stories, the consequence of covering the crime beat) was that most funerals took place on hot, sunny days. They were also a lot less crowded than the ones in the movies; most people preferred to come to the service before or the reception afterward and sit in air conditioned comfort than stand around in the heat waiting for a box to be lowered into the ground.

The Rypczynsky funeral had even fewer mourners than usual. Under the thin white tarp, Mrs. Rypczynsky sat by herself in the first of four rows of wooden folding chairs, most of which were empty. From their appearance, the few others who did show up were friends of the victim from earlier years who had come out of a sense of years–old obligation, one or two who might have been friends of Mrs. Rypczynsky, and a couple more who were definitely police. Even if she hadn't recognized them from her years on the crime beat, she could've figured they were cops just from their bearing, and the way they were watching everything in the cemetery *except* Mrs. Rypczynsky and the ritual lowering of the box. It wasn't uncommon for killers to show up at the funerals for their victims. For some, it provided a sense of closure; for others, a vicarious thrill and the chance to experience one last time the death of their victims. Now that the killer seemed to be widening his selection of victims, Susan sensed an even greater urgency in their desire to find him.

Susan stood well apart from the funeral party, on a tree–lined hill that overlooked the cemetery, which covered half a dozen acres of prime real estate between Burbank and Sun Valley. She watched the proceedings through binoculars, scanning the surrounding area as the Catholic priest went soundlessly (from her vantage point) through the burial ritual.

So far: nothing. She'd stood and waited and watched for almost ninety minutes, since the funeral began, and thus far had nothing to show for it.

She flexed a shoulder, grown sore under the weight of binoculars, purse and camera, as below, an electric winch began to crank, the coffin edging down into the open ground below. The priest had gone to Mrs. Rypczynsky and was holding her hand, offering comfort. The police officers and others behind her began to move away, each taking last looks but for considerably different reasons.

Dead end, she thought, and started to turn away, then decided to give the grounds one last look before leaving.

The winch had stopped. The coffin had settled. The few mourners were returning to the cars, limos and taxis lined up at the curb. The groundskeepers started toward a tarp–covered mound of dirt, which would momentarily be piled back into the open wound in the earth.

And something glittered on the edge of the trees at the top of the next hill.

Someone was standing there, in a dark jacket and pants, watching the scene through binoculars of his own…binoculars that had caught the sunlight for just a moment, long enough for Susan to lock in on his location.

Gotcha.

She yanked up the camera and took a quick shot, even knowing that it would probably be unusable given the distance and the shadows around him, then hurried down the hill toward the other collection of sheltering trees. She glanced up. As she feared, he was already out of sight; but she knew there were only two ways out of the cemetery: back the way the others had gone, to the parking lot, and back through the complex that housed the administration and reception buildings.

She quickened her step, cresting the next hill and coming down again.

She caught a glimpse of him again, moving fast on foot, heading for the cul–de–sac that led to the administration building. She didn't know if he'd seen her, but she couldn't risk assuming he hadn't. She walked faster, breaking into a run as she hit the bottom of the small hill.

A car engine started.

She got to the street just as a beige Ford shot away from the curb. *Not so fast*, she thought, and brought up the camera, snapping off one picture of the license plate before the car turned and disappeared down Chandler.

She lowered the camera, nodded to herself, then started quickly back the way she'd come, hoping that she hadn't jiggled the camera, that the lens had been in focus, and that she'd gotten a clear shot of the license plate. *Just give me one break, God, is that really so much to ask?*

From the license plate she had finally gotten a name and an address. The name of the person who owned the car—who might or might not be the person who was actually *driving* said car at the moment she saw it, that would have to await a DMV photo before she could verify the face involved—was Raymond Weil, age fifty–one.

The address was no address at all. 11713 Moorpark Street, Suite 10, was not a suite at all, but rather, as she had feared, a mail drop. It was a tiny rental box office with maybe fifty boxes stuck into an anonymous, whitewashed room, perfect for receiving illicit communiqués and mail–order porn.

A man was there as she entered, picking up his mail. She glanced at him, then moved to the small door at the back of the room, which she assumed led into the management office. She knocked once, then again. No answer.

"Looking for the manager?"

She turned to the man behind her, who stood with a handful of parcels postmarked Sweden. "Yes, I'm trying to find the owner of one of these boxes."

"He's not here. He only comes in around ten in the morning to deliver stuff, then he leaves."

"Great," she said resigned to coming back again the next day.

"Though if it's important, you can probably find him at the bookstore next door. He owns both places. It used to be just one big store, then he put up a couple of walls and parceled out this part of it as a separate business."

"Thanks, I appreciate the information," she said, heading for the door.

"Listen, once you're done, if you want to get a cup of coffee or a drink or something—"

She nodded to the wedding ring on his left hand. "Doesn't that get in your way a bit?"

He smiled. "Not if it doesn't get in yours."

She gave him her biggest smile. "Did I mention that I'm a reporter?"

His smile froze in place. "Well, I've…got to go."

He did.

Susan stepped back out into the bright sunlight and walked to the bookstore next door. It was painted a garish red, beneath a gold and purple sign that proclaimed this *The Psychic Life Bookstore*. The strong aroma of incense drifted out the front door onto the sidewalk. Sandalwood, she guessed.

Inside, the store continued the red, purple and gold color scheme. Crystal pendants and earrings hung beside copper rings and bracelets in mirrored glass cabinets beside the cash register. Most of the store was taken up by bookcases crowded with old and new volumes on shamanism, personal power, chakra maps, color readings, the Tarot, ESP, UFOs and other New Age attractions, each wrapped in covers even more colorful than their surroundings. A separate section contained CDs with Celtic music, Mantra lullabies and Eastern meditation music.

A young blonde woman sitting behind the cash register looked up and smiled as Susan approached. Everything about her screamed college surfer girl doing part time work so she could afford to buy a yet another new wardrobe. *Probably got a name like Sapphire or Cherisse or Fawn or—*

"Hi, I'm Dawn, can I help you?"

Close enough. "I'm looking for the manager."

"Mister Meyer? He's on his break right now. Is it important? Maybe I can help you—"

"No, thanks, I really have to talk to him."

"All right, I guess…he's in the back. Go past the tarot section, it'll be the first door on your right."

Susan nodded and continued deeper into the musty store. She found the door and knocked. "Yeah?" called a voice from inside.

Susan stepped into the tiny back office. The walls were plain white, unadorned except for a cat calendar over the metal desk and chair that took up most of the room. A pastrami sandwich with quarter–sliced pickles and macaroni salad sat half–finished on the desk, in front of a thin, frail looking man in his sixties. There was a sleeping dachshund at his feet.

"Mister Meyer?"

"You got him," he said. "There some kind of problem?"

"No, no problem," she said, and pulled out her business card. "I'm Susan Randall, with the *Trib*. Can I ask you a few questions?"

"Depends on the questions," he said. "Listen, you want half a pastrami sandwich? I always tell them to cut it lean and go easy on the meat, so naturally every time it comes fatty and big enough to choke a horse."

"No, thank you," she said.

He shrugged. "More for Munchkin, then," he said, and dropped a small piece of fatty pastrami in front of the dachshund at his feet. The dog stirred long enough to swallow the piece and go back to sleep. "Bad for my heart, but he loves it. Doesn't even mind the mustard. So, what can I do for you? Are you writing an article about my store?"

"No, I'm—"

"Because it's got quite a history, let me tell you."

"I'm sure it does, Mr. Meyer. But we'll have to do that one another time. I'm here about the mail box office next door."

"I got nothing to do with whatever comes in there," he said, waving a dismissive hand in front of his face. "Anybody who rents a box, they sign a waiver says I'm not responsible for anything they get through the mail."

"I'm not here about any of that," she said. "I'm here specifically about one of your customers. Raymond Weil, box ten."

Meyer nodded to himself. "Yeah, well, I guess I shouldn't be surprised. His line of work and all, it draws people, you know?"

"And what line of work is that?"

"What, you don't know?"

"In your own words, please."

"Well, you know, he *helps* people. I suppose he makes a good living at it, always dresses very nice, though he doesn't say much about it. Doesn't say much of anything, really. A quiet guy."

"How exactly does he help people?"

"If you want details, I can't help you. I don't know. All I know is what I hear from the occasional client of his who comes here, or somebody curious like you…he comes around and buys books once in a while. Sometimes I think he really uses them, other times I just think he's trying to keep me happy, but I got no problem with that.

"Basically, what I hear," he paused long enough to take another bite of pastrami, "is that he fights evil."

"Fights evil."

"That's right." Meyer chewed with his mouth open. She figured he didn't even know he was doing it.

"Fights evil how?"

He smiled. "How should I know? That's what I hear. But don't take that too much to heart. I mean, me, I fight evil by giving kids like Dawn a decent job and single—handedly keeping the incense business going. My brother, Alex, the dentist, fights evil and gingivitis." He dropped another piece of pastrami in front of the nearly motionless dachshund. "Munchkin here also fights evil, by making sure I don't eat so much pastrami that I have a heart attack and fall over dead right here in my office."

"Mr. Meyer," Susan said, "that's a very cute answer, but I suspect you know a little more than you're telling."

He shrugged again, and looked away. "I said I don't know, I meant I don't know. I hear, I see, I suspect, I guess, but I don't actually know."

"And what do you hear, see, suspect or guess?"

"He's a strange guy," Meyer said. "I mean, there was this woman came in here about three, four months ago, said there was something evil living in her house. I said I fully understood, that I had an out—of—work nephew living with me too. But when she started to cry, I gave her Ray's phone number. From what I hear, he helped. He consults with people. Makes them feel better."

"How?"

"I told you, I don't *know*. Look, Ms. Randall, the people who come to a store like this, most of them aren't...well, they're not like you and me, you know what I'm saying here? We got a lady comes in every other week to buy a new crystal for her cat, because she says the cat talks to her through the crystals, but each one only has a shelf life of fourteen days. She's crazy, but on the other hand the crystal market has not been good lately, so who am I to question it?

"Some people who come through here are troubled. And we got other people coming through who say they can ease that trouble. It's that whole yin and yang thing, one person needs, another person comes along who provides. We got psychics, palm readers, guys who can help you straighten out your aura, or get rid of your migraines by sticking needles in your feet." He shrugged, and added, "Usually there's money involved."

"So you're saying...what? That he's a con—man?"

"There are no con—men in this store," he said firmly. "Only people who believe in different things. The girl at the front desk believes she'll meet a nice man while she's working here and they'll set up a little place by the beach where they can sell incense and skateboards and live happily ever after. Some people who come through here believe in devils and monsters and UFO aliens with an unhealthy interest in their lower colon. Some people believe they're possessed, or that God speaks through them. And some people believe they fight evil. Or at least that's what they tell me." He shrugged. "What they *really* believe is between them and God. Who am I to get in the middle of that?"

"I see." She glanced over her notes, trying to decide how best to proceed. "Is there any way you could give me his address or phone number, so I can ask him some questions?"

He shook his head. "That I can't do. Private information. You want that, you have to get a court order."

"Is there any way you can get word to him, tell him I'd like to speak with him?"

"Yeah, I suppose I could, but I only see him every couple of weeks. On the other hand, he checks his mail every other day, if you want to leave him a note."

"That would be great, thanks," she said, pulling out another business card. She hesitated, then put it back into her purse, substituting a post-it note from Meyer's desk. She wrote only her phone number, her first name, and *Please call me, I need your help.*

She handed Meyer the note, thanked him for his help, and started out the door.

"One thing," Meyer said. "When you meet him, just remember that he's…sensitive."

"Sensitive as in psychic?"

"Sensitive as in a pain in the ass. Sensitive as in touchy. Maybe this guy does some good, maybe he doesn't, either way his bedside manner is zero. He can be impolite, rude, sometimes even—"

"Even what?"

"It's nothing I can put a name to."

"Are you saying he's dangerous?"

"I don't know. Maybe. There's certainly something you see there in his eyes that I sure as hell wouldn't want to mess with. Like I said, he's…different. Try not to let anything he says or does bother you, it's just the way he is. But if he gives you any trouble, you call me, all right?"

"I will," she said, and smiled. "Thanks."

The phone call arrived in her private voicemail early the next day. It was carefully, deliberately neutral, with just the faintest hint of an accent. *This is Raymond Weil. I got your message. I can be reached at the following number. Please set a time and a place. I will be there.* His only other request: *Come alone.*

She called the number and left a message suggesting they meet at seven o'clock that evening, and gave the address of a coffee shop around the corner from the *Trib.* Just to err on the side of caution, she told the receptionist where the meeting was to take place, and left all the pertinent information about Weil—which amounted to very little—in a file on her desk, where Rob could find it and call the police if she didn't check in by ten.

Are you sure you want to do this? Rob had asked.

It's a brightly lit coffee shop, with a lot of people around, in the middle of the evening. What can he do?

Yeah, I guess you're right. Which is probably why, just as a for-instance, there's never been a hit against a mob guy in a crowded restaurant before, huh?

She couldn't decide when Rob was more annoying: when he was wrong, or when he had a point. But she felt strongly that she had to go ahead with it. She'd come too far and worked too hard for this meeting to back out now. Something in her gut told her this was important, and she always tried to listen when that particular voice spoke to her.

Wearing the red scarf she'd described in her message, she sat in a corner window seat of the coffee shop, watching the street outside. It was dark, most of the day shift—workers, businessmen, secretaries and the occasional agent or unemployed actor—long gone, clearing the way for the night shift of young couples gathering to decide which movie to see, students lumbered with textbooks sucking down coffee to keep from falling asleep as they ran through the history of the Ottoman empire, and aspiring writers pounding away on laptops because writing in a public place made them feel they were actually doing something of consequence, or because they hoped someone in a position of power would wander in, notice them writing their fourteenth spec screenplay and ask to produce it.

You're getting cynical, Susan thought. *Also long-winded. What would Mrs. Tuvalle in fourth grade grammar think of a sentence like—*

"Susan?"

She glanced up, startled, to see Larry Dixon standing over her. "*Larry?* What're you—"

"I asked the receptionist where you were," he said, smiling. "I told her I had to get some important papers to you ASAP."

He was dressed casually for a work day, in a blue sweater and tan slacks, a combination carefully selected to complement his blonde hair and admittedly very blue eyes. He was what her mother would have called a good catch. As a junior partner in one of the biggest film/TV agencies in Los Angeles, he spent more on lunches than she earned in a year on the *Trib*.

Sometimes that prompted him to forget that what she did was still important enough to take precedence over his convenience.

This, she suspected, was about to become another such instance.

"What are you doing here?" she asked, glancing furtively through the window to the darkened street outside. *Come alone*, Weil had said, very specifically and very firmly.

"You haven't returned any of my calls, so I figured if the mountain won't come to Mohammed—"

"You're not Mohammed, and I'm not a mountain," she said. "And I'm here to meet someone."

"Oh? Anyone I know?"

"No, it's—" She glanced down the street. Someone was coming. The silhouette matched. *Damn it...*

"Look, Larry, you picked the worst possible moment to pull this, and I don't have time to explain. Would you just trust me on this and please go somewhere else?"

"I just—"

"*Now?*"

He looked up sharply at her, with that look she'd seen too many times. *He's offended,* she thought. *Great, one more thing to deal with. But I'll have to deal with it later.*

"All right," he said, rising. "I thought it might be a pleasant surprise, maybe a chance for us to catch up a little, but if that's how you feel about it, then...I guess we'll talk later."

"Absolutely."

The man approaching the coffee shop passed under the light of the street lamp outside. It was definitely Weil. He hadn't seen her yet.

"Okay," Larry said, "fine, then." He turned and headed out the door just as Weil was entering. The older man scanned the clientele in one long sweep before settling on Susan's face. He approached and stood beside her table. He wore a plain black suit jacket, tan pants and a gray shirt, unremarkable and almost certainly inconspicuous by design. In the bright light of the coffee shop, his eyes were an even deeper blue than she had remembered. He had a face that looked as if it had been carved out of stone by a sculptor unafraid of making occasional mistakes, then left outside until the wind and rain had softened the imperfections into shadings of character, thought and reflection.

"You're Susan." It was less a question than a statement.

"Yes. Raymond?"

He nodded, studying her curiously for a moment. "We've met before." He sat across the table from her, his eyes never leaving her face. His expression was just as she had seen it that night, distant but intensely focused, eyes that seemed at times almost metallic.

"Yes, I remember now," he continued. "You were in the hospital with Cheryl."

"That's right, Mr. Weil."

"Raymond will do," he said, and frowned. He leaned in, studying her closely. "The same hospital room the night we worked there," he said, half to himself. "I hadn't expected there to be any chance of contamination, but...have you been having any bad dreams since then? Lost time? Unaccountable mood shifts?"

"No," she said.

"You're sure?"

"Positive, at least no more so than usual."

He sat back, seeming to accept her answer. "Good, that's a relief," he said. "So, your note mentioned you needed help."

"Yes, and that's true, insofar as it goes, but it may not be in quite the way you might have been expecting. Mr. Weil—Raymond—I'm a reporter with the *News–Tribune*, and—"

He was on his feet before she got out the next word. "Then I think I should be going. Good evening, Ms. Randall."

"Wait, look, I'm sorry if I wasn't entirely straight with you—"

He didn't listen, was already halfway to the door.

This night just gets better and better, she thought as she grabbed her purse and hurried after him.

She stepped out the door, saw him heading east on the sidewalk and quickened her pace to catch up with him, determined not to let him pull a fast fade on her again. "Mr. Weil, I just want to talk to you."

"About what?" he called back without slowing. "And more to the point, what on earth could *I* possibly want to talk to *you* about?"

"The work you do. I was told you help people. Isn't that right?"

"You shouldn't believe everything you're told, Ms. Randall. Good evening." He continued briskly away.

Susan stopped, planting her feet. *Screw it*, she thought, *if he's going to bolt I may as well go out with a bang*. "I want to talk to you about the murders."

He stopped, turned to her. "The murders? And why would you want to talk to *me* about them?" There was something in his voice, not dangerous, but concerned. Evasive.

"I know you have an interest in them," she said. "I know you visited Mrs. Rypczynsky's home the day her son was killed. I know you had more information about the killing than anyone was supposed to have. And I know you were at her son's funeral."

He stepped toward her a pace. "That was you, at the funeral, who followed me to my car. I didn't get a good look, but it *was* you, wasn't it?"

She nodded.

He took another step toward her. She hadn't realized until this moment how much larger than her he was. He moved like a man who even at fifty–one worked out regularly to stay in peak physical condition. "You know far more than you should about things that *do* not concern you, and *should* not concern you for your own good. Not if you want to stay alive."

"Is that a threat?" she asked.

He smiled. It was a thin, grim and tired smile. "No. Not a threat. Only an observation."

"Look, Raymond, I've gone through a considerable amount of time, effort and expense to find you. All I want is an hour of your time to talk to you. What's so wrong with that?"

"Words have power," he said. "More than you will ever know." With that, he turned and started away from her again.

She called after him. "Okay, thirty minutes,"

He continued walking.

"You know, I was told you were sensitive," she called again, "I didn't know sensitive meant pain in the ass."

He didn't reply. Only kept walking.

"I was told you help people. Here I give you a chance to help me, and maybe help a lot of other people, and you walk away. So I guess that really is just a line with you, isn't it? But I guess it works better than 'What's your sign?' or 'Come here often?' and it's probably every bit as sincere."

He paused at that one, and for a moment, it looked almost as if he might turn back to her, if only to answer the charge. *Do whatever you have to,* her college journalism teacher had told her long ago, *compliment them, piss them off, whatever it takes, just keep your subject talking.*

Then, as if reconsidering, he continued on his way. He crossed the street, got into the now–familiar Ford, and drove off without another backward glance.

Shit, she thought. *Shit, shit, shit, shit, shit.*

On top of everything else, I went through all that with Larry for nothing, and now I'm going to have to go have another one of our Talks.

As Weil's car disappeared around the corner, she turned and walked slowly back to her car, trying to decide what she had done that had made God hate her so utterly and completely.

Dinner at Le Dome the next night with Larry was quiet, but it was the *kind* of quiet that always set Susan's teeth on edge. Pointless small talk thrown out onto the table in place of what neither one of them felt like talking about because talking would turn into arguing and neither of them had any desire to be thrown out of the restaurant mid–dinner.

They generally waited until dessert for that one.

"Anyway," Larry said after a long silence, then paused as the waiter poured another cup of coffee. *Anyway* was how Larry always set aside *old* unpleasant business to make room for *new* unpleasant business. "I know things haven't been going as well between us lately as we might like," he said. "And I have some ideas about that."

Susan nodded. As a literary agent with aspirations of becoming a producer, Larry always had *ideas about* one thing or another. *I had an idea about casting on this one. I had an idea about some changes in the script.* She wondered what his idea would be this time: counseling? meditation? a trip to Aspen? nerf bats at twenty paces?

"I was thinking maybe we should start seeing other people," he said.

She stared at him over her coffee. "This by you is a way for us to get closer, to start dating other people?"

"Sometimes you don't appreciate what you have until you measure it against someone else," he said. She knew from experience, having seen him practicing naked in front of the mirror, that this was the same tone of practiced earnestness he used when he went in to sell a property he didn't much believe in to a studio that didn't much want it.

"I see," she said. She couldn't understand why it was that when she sat down to write, she could pour out pages and pages of material without effort, but when it came to moments like this, she never knew what to say. "If that's what you want—"

"It's not so much an issue of what I want, *per se*," he said. "But you haven't exactly been going out of your way to keep the relationship alive lately."

"You pulled back first," she shot back.

"At least I call."

"You call because my number pops up on your Palm Pilot every day at two o'clock, just like your other calls, because you can't be bothered to think about it on your own. And the reason you call at two is that it's after lunch and before the rest of the day's meetings, and it always lasts for exactly ten minutes because that gives you twenty minutes to make a couple of other calls, and get a coffee before you go into the next meeting at two–thirty. It's all very orderly and efficient and it has nothing to do with being actually *involved* with someone."

"You're shouting," he said.

"I'm not shouting," she said. *"This is shouting. Can you tell the difference now?"*

Heads turned at several nearby tables. Larry leaned in, lowering his voice as far as possible. "Look, Susan, I really don't want to make a scene. I thought you'd be happy to have the space to see other people."

"It's not like there's a chain around either one of us, so I don't exactly see what you're supposed to be freeing me from. It's obvious that you want to see other people, and you think you can get out of any guilt associated with that by making it a contractual kind of understanding that we can *both* do it, even though I don't *want* to do it, *didn't* do it, and haven't *been* doing it, even though I could."

She stood from the table. "Look, Larry, you want to go screwing around, it's okay with me. You're right, we haven't exactly been close lately. Maybe it's my fault, maybe it's your fault, I don't know, and right now I don't care. You just...do whatever you have to. Now if you'll excuse me, I'm going home to get some work done."

"At least let me drive you—"

"I can get a cab," she said, already heading for the door.

Once outside, she crossed the street and found a taxi waiting at the cab stand in front of the Beverly–Wilshire hotel. She got in, gave the driver her address, and settled back to watch the night glide by.

I am seriously messed up, she decided, then added, *So what else is new?*

Two Tylenol, three hours and a cup of chamomile tea later, Susan was in bed, trying to find the right combination of position, breathing patterns and mental distance that would allow her to get some sleep, failing miserably in the attempt.

She glanced at the clock. One fifteen a.m.

Crap, she thought, and closed her eyes.

Then opened them again as the phone rang.

If it's Larry I'm going to kill him, she thought as she grabbed for the phone and pulled it over to her. "Yeah?"

The first thing she heard was the sound of traffic at the other end of the line. *Pay phone*, she decided.

"It's Raymond," the voice announced.

She sat up in bed. "Mister Weil," she said, glancing again at the clock. "It's late—"

"I know. But if I waited until tomorrow, I would almost certainly change my mind and this conversation would never happen." There was the creak of a phone booth door closing behind him, and the sound of traffic diminished. "I'm at Paty's Restaurant in Toluca Lake, do you know the place?"

She nodded, then realized that he couldn't hear a nod. "Yes...yes, I've been there before."

"It's open all night," he said. "I'll be here for the next half hour. If you show up during that time, we can talk. If not—"

"I'll be there."

"Good, then I'll see you in twenty nine minutes or less," he said, and hung up.

She kicked off the blankets and hurried to the closet. *Could my life get any more screwed up?* she wondered as she dressed frantically, finally deciding that not only could it get more screwed up, it almost certainly would before the night was out.

"Do you believe in God, Ms. Randall?"

She stared at Raymond across a formica table in the empty back section of Paty's. Toluca Lake was a quiet bedroom community between Burbank and Studio City that was named after a lake that no one she knew had ever seen, but whose existence everyone pretty much accepted as an act of faith. The only other customers were four bikers seated in front, who paid them no attention. She took another sip of coffee, trying desperately to get more than three neurons to function together at the same time. *Come on, fellas, work with me here*, she thought.

"I don't know," she said at last. "I guess I do. I mean, I haven't really given it a lot of thought."

"So you're saying that on a day–to–day basis, you give more thought and more consideration to what you're going to wear than you do to the question of the existence of a supreme being, which could have profound ramifications on the way in which you live your life."

"No, that's *not* what I'm saying. It's just that it's almost two in the morning and I wasn't prepared to have a big theological discussion over coffee and Danish pastry."

"That's Streudel, it's German."

"Whatever."

He smiled, and set down his coffee. "Do you pray?"

"I guess it's all in how you define the word pray. Sure, sometimes we all say, God, just get me out of this and I'll never do it again. But I don't see what any of this has to do with the killings. I came to you for an interview, not a sermon. If you're interested in proselytizing—"

"I'm not," he said, his voice calm and deliberate. "I'm only trying to open up a dialogue. That first requires that we establish what common ground we do or don't have. So far we've established that you're a little fuzzy on the whole God thing, but that's all right, we believe what we want to believe. Or what we *allow* ourselves to believe."

"I suppose the next obvious question is do I believe in the devil."

He shrugged. "You can call it that. Or you can think of it in terms of evil as a concept, if that makes you more comfortable."

"I'm not the issue here," she said.

"Aren't you? You've been trailing me for some time, you must have been drawn to my work in some way, responded to it."

Susan ran a hand through her hair, no longer caring if her frustration showed through. "Raymond, I still don't even know what your work *is*. That's what this conversation was supposed to be all *about*."

"And so it is."

"Good," she said.

"So…?"

"Yes?"

"*Do* you believe in evil? The kind of evil that transcends all human boundaries?"

She tapped her fingers on the formica table. *This is pointless*, she thought. *He's just winding me up. I should get up and leave and forget the whole thing.*

"Susan?"

"The only evil I've seen has been totally and completely human," she said, continuing in spite of herself. "I once saw a fifteen–year–old mother so messed up on drugs that she threw her six–month–old kid out of a fourth–story window because she thought wolves were coming up the stairs at her. Another time I interviewed a male prostitute who knowingly infected almost two dozen of his clients with AIDs because he figured that if he had to go, so did they. When I was still a junior reporter on the crime beat, I was assigned to cover one of Charlie Manson's parole hearings. He came in, and sat down not five feet away from me. Never said a word, let his lawyers do the talking for him. But once during the hearing he looked at me. Just once, but it still took me nearly a week of showers before I finally felt clean again.

"I've seen a five–year–old kid crippled in a drive–by shooting, women so badly beaten by abusive husbands that you couldn't even recognize them, and drunk drivers who end up killing someone, then act as if it was the victim's fault because they can't face their own problem, thereby guaranteeing that they'll go out and do the same damned thing all over again as soon as they're back on the streets.

"So yes, Raymond, I do believe in evil. But the only evil I've seen, the only evil I believe in, wears a human face. I don't know whether or not there's a hell somewhere else, but I have seen an *awful* lot of people trying to create a home-made version right here.

"Does any of that answer your question?"

"To a degree," he said quietly.

"Good, because it's the middle of the night, I'm tired, and I don't even know what I'm doing here. So why don't you tell me. What *am* I doing here, Raymond? Why did you call me and drag me clear across town like this? Was it just so we could play *Name That Theology?*"

He looked away, and for a moment she thought he looked tired, as if the weight of the world was on his shoulders. "You're here because the other night, as I left, what you said was…well, it was very rude, to start with. More than that, though, it reminded me of someone else. Someone who used to challenge me, as you challenged me. And I thought she might approve…" His voice trailed off, his gaze fixed at a point somewhere far beyond the walls of the restaurant.

After a moment, he pulled himself back, and focused on her. "I try to *help* people, Susan. Sometimes I succeed, sometimes I fail, but at least I try."

"And what do you help them deal with?"

He paused for a moment, seemed to be choosing his answer carefully. "Intangibles. Concepts. Good. Evil. And a few of the things in–between."

"Uh, huh," Susan said. She hesitated, then gathered up her purse. "Well, it's been fun, Raymond, but I came here to talk to you about these murders, and if that's the best you can do for specifics, throw words around like one more new age feel–good pyramid–hugger, there's really nothing I can—"

"What do you know about demonic possession and demonic obsession?"

She stopped, wondering idly if he was playing with her again. "I saw most of *The Exorcist* once. I was twelve, and the first time that head spun around I was gone. Does that count?"

He allowed a small smile. "I'm not entirely sure," he said. "Please, Ms. Randall. Sit."

She hesitated, then did as he asked. "Go on."

"I cannot give you the details of what I do because it is always different, and the specifics are private. To talk about them in any detail would be to violate my word to those involved, and expose them to public embarrassment. Sometimes I am paid for my services, and sometimes I serve *pro bono*. This is one such case."

"The murders."

"Yes.

"So your theory is that the killer is possessed? Or that he *thinks* he's possessed?" She deliberately left out the third possibility: Do *you* think he's possessed, which was the more psychologically interesting question, but she'd take that one up later. "I don't mean to sound callous, but you don't need to be possessed to go around killing people."

"I know, and that is a sad statement, is it not?" He sipped his coffee. "At first, I agreed with you, that this was just another serial killer. Understand that I am very cautious about these things. Later, however, I began to realize that there was more going on than appeared on the surface."

"Such as?"

He studied her for a moment before replying. "I'll tell you what," he said. "You're a reporter, you believe only what you can see and hear, you have your own resources, so let me give you an assignment. Check around the neighborhoods where each of the killings took place. In every case, you will find signs of desecration at a nearby church or synagogue. Desecration committed the same night as the victim was killed. Investigate it for yourself, you'll see that I'm right."

She made a note on her pad. "I will," she said. "What else? I mean, I thought that when people got possessed, they mainly sat around spewing up green stuff and quoting Milton in the original Latin. It's all about tormenting that one person."

"Check your history," he said. "Possessed people attack other people. They are violent, clever and extremely strong. In South America there have been cases of entire villages eliminated by one possessed individual. Medieval textbooks record similar incidents. As for that movie, which got many things right and many other things wrong, you must remember that the only reason she was in that bed was that she was tied down, because if she hadn't been tied down she would have torn apart anyone who got between her and her target."

"Wasn't the girl in that story the target?"

"No. And that was one of the areas where they got things right. Possession, true possession, is an attack on both a spiritual and psychological plane. But in nearly every case, the possessed person is not the actual target of the attack; he or she is rather the *means* of the attack. The actual target may be someone close to the possessed person, a relative or friend, someone whose faith is being tested. Or a priest whose skill, courage and resolve is being tried.

"There is always a reason. Sometimes that reason is nothing more than a show of power, the residents of hell issuing the statement 'We are still here.' Other times the reason is something more profound. There is a logic behind these murders. They are too deliberate to be otherwise. Discovering that reason will lead us to the target, and that in turn will help us overcome this attack."

"Is this similar to the Danny Harold Rolling case? That's the only other case I can think of in which someone claiming to be possessed went around hurting other people." Susan had read about the case some years before. Danny Rolling, aka Gemini, was a serial killer in Gainsville who believed that at times of stress a demon named Gemini took over his body and used it to commit murders.

Raymond shook his head sharply, seemingly annoyed by the question. "There is no comparison. Look, there is no question that many cases of so–called possession can be traced to multiple personality disorder. The specific case you are referring to involved an individual diagnosed with a particular kind of dissociative disorder known as possession disorder or possession syndrome."

"I don't see the difference."

"The difference is that in the Rollings case, the killer used the idea of possession to escape his responsibility for crimes so heinous that they exceeded his ability to rationalize them."

"And in this case?"

"In this case, I believe the situation is real. The severity of the case, whether it is demonic possession, or obsession, or something else, I don't yet know."

"Again, what's the difference? Like I said, I'm a little vague on this stuff."

"In true cases of possession, the person is possessed all or nearly all the time, making it difficult to operate in society. Yet our killer seems to pursue his activities without anyone paying much attention.

"Obsession results from someone, either young and suggestible or emotionally disturbed, who has immersed himself in demonic literature, until he begins to act out what he reads. He can sometimes become a conduit for forces beyond his control. There are other variations beyond that, such as demonic influence, in which the victim does not know what he is doing as he is doing it, but in most such cases, it comes down to one of those two."

"And what's your angle in all this? What do you do?"

"I try to help."

"Are you a priest?"

He smiled again, ruefully this time, and looked away. "Not as such, no."

"Then what do you—"

"I think we've talked enough for one night," he said, rising. "As you said, it's late. The sun will be coming up soon."

She glanced at her watch. It was nearly four. Had they really talked this long? It seemed as if they'd barely started.

"You will want to conduct your own investigation into what I've said, and

I have work of my own awaiting my attention," he said. "We will reconvene later."

"When?"

"In the fullness of time." He extended a hand. "Good morning, Ms. Randall."

She shook it, and watched as he left the restaurant.

As she returned to her car, she ran through the conversation in her mind. She began to wonder if in the final analysis this was really a lead worth pursuing. *He doesn't have anything concrete, and this pseudo–exorcist nonsense is just that. Although...*

She stopped under a street lamp and pulled out her notes, reviewing his comments concerning the desecration of churches and synagogues. She dimly remembered hearing something about at least one church being vandalized, but at the time she didn't think too much about it; these days it seemed churches were vandalized on a regular basis. In the final analysis, she realized that it might not make any difference what Raymond believed about the killer. What mattered was, what did the *killer* believe about *himself?*

Though she had chosen not to say anything about it at the time, in truth she put no more stock in what Raymond was selling than she did in faith healers, aura readers or the kind of people who wore pyramid hats because it made them more receptive to the Martian bozo–beams. Call it what you want, she didn't believe in demonic possession, obsession or influence; or, for that matter, in demonic speeding, littering or direct marketing.

Still, if there *was* a killer out there who believed he was possessed, and here was someone who believed in that paradigm and was using it to figure out the identify of the killer, it was within the realm of possibility that the latter might lead to some useful information about the former. They were, after all, both playing by the same rules.

Assuming that really is *what the killer believes*, she reminded herself. *Killings like these are a Rorschach test, you can read into them whatever you want.*

She shoved the notes back in her purse and stepped into her car. The night's adrenaline was wearing off, rapidly being replaced by the morning's fatigue. She'd think about this when she got to the office and had a chance to verify some of Raymond's story. If any of it checked out, then it might be worth staying close to him a little longer.

At the very least, it might make an interesting sidebar story or personality profile. *When a city is traumatized by crime, it brings out all kinds of people who want to help. One such person is Raymond Weil, a man who believes in the unbelievable...*

As she started the car and drove off, she realized that she hadn't seen Raymond get into his car. *Probably parked down the street and hoofed it from there so I couldn't ID the car, or maybe he lives somewhere in the area.*

Doesn't matter, she decided, and continued on, hoping she could get a few hours sleep before going to the office, but doubting it.

The clock read 4:48 A.M.

The clock was the only light in Steven Banks' bedroom.

The clock was the entirety of his world. It was all he could see when he awoke on his stomach, ankles taped together, hands tied behind his back, palms facing up, up to where—

Don't think about it, his mind screamed at him.

Look at the clock.

Steven hated dentists, so he would always stare up into the light above the dentist's chair when he had work done, try to disappear into the light, to escape from the reality of what was being done.

Look at the clock.

Look at the light.

Disappear into the light.

4:49 A.M.

Pain slashed across his open, exposed hands, slashed across his palms, left to right.

The LED numerals swam in front of his eyes, blurred by tears. He thought he would pass out. Prayed he would pass out.

Why are you doing this? he wanted to scream, but the gag across his mouth caught the sound. *I didn't do anything to you! I don't even know who you are!*

The news shows he had seen about killers said that to stay alive it helped to talk to them, get them to see you as a person. But he couldn't talk, couldn't tell the man who sat straddling his back that he worked in the accounting department at Macy's, that his father loved to go bass fishing twice a year even though he couldn't really afford the trip to Michigan on an Army Sergeant's pension, that he was thirty–two and earned a reasonable living and he was dating a very nice girl from the sales department and he hadn't even slept with her yet and he hadn't done anything to anyone that he felt he should have to die for, this wasn't right, it wasn't fair.

He wanted to say all those things, but the man who crouched above him had no interest in hearing him, or seeing him as a person.

He saw Steven as meat.

And the only thing you can do with meat is to slice it.

4:50 A.M.

He screamed into the gag as the blade sliced across his palms. Meat. Soft, fleshy meat.

One slice per minute.

How long had it been going on? He couldn't remember anymore, was sure he had blacked out somewhere after it all began. How long would it continue?

Until he ran out of palm.

And then…?

He thought he heard a sound above him in the darkness, a high, keening sound that could have been a laugh, could have been a sigh, could have been one voice, could have been many.

Get it over with, please God, just get it over with.

He counted the seconds, knowing 4:51 was coming, coming soon, any moment now.

He blinked away the tears, desperate to escape between the bright red numbers that filled his sight, to fall through them, fall away, anywhere but here, anywhere but here.

Look at the clock.

Look at the clock.

Look at the clock…

Kicking a Police Officer in the Nuts

"What can I do you for *this* time, Ms. Randall?"

The voice at the other end of the phone had the same tired, frustrated tone she'd come to expect lately when she called the LAPD's news liaison office. Officer Leanne Mathias was the latest warm body rotated into that position. Under the best of conditions the career lifespan of a PR person with the Los Angeles Police Department was about six months; since the serial murders had begun, with the consequent increase in demands for material and access, that figure had been cut nearly in half.

"I'm looking for the duty roster printout on crime reports for the following days," she said, and listed the dates immediately after each of the murders.

"Can you make my life easier and narrow that down a little? I mean, this is a big town, and a lot happens every night. Do you want personal injury, property damage, narco, vice, domestic abuse, *all* of it? Because if you do that's going to take me a long time and with everything that's going on right now it'll be hard for me to justify investing that much time and effort."

Susan tapped her pencil against the desk. Last night's attack by the LA Slasher—he had a name now, thanks to this morning's *Times*—had the LAPD touchier than usual. "I guess just property damage will do."

"Public, private or both?"

"Both. In particular, I'm looking for any churches, synagogues or religious–themed properties that might have been vandalized."

"You want this faxed, mailed or is somebody gonna pick it up?"

Susan glanced at the office wall clock. The Police Chief was holding a press conference at two o'clock, three hours from now. "I'll be there anyway around one–thirty, can you have it ready by then?"

"I've got a lot to handle right now. Is it important?"

"Could be."

There was a long–suffering sigh from the other end of the line. "All right, I'll see what I can do, but no promises."

"Good enough," Susan said.

Click and disconnect.

"Hey, Susan, how about the LA Slashers as the name of a new hockey team?"

She looked up at Leo, who was leaning over his cubicle in her direction. "Stinks on ice," she said.

"That's a good one, Susan. An all serial–killer hockey team *would* stink on ice. But you know as well as I do that we'd sell out the front row in ten minutes."

She went back to her notes.

"So how come *we* didn't come up with a name for this guy?" Leo asked. "Why let the *Times* name him? I mean, it'd be one thing if he was just the Slasher, now he's the *LA* Slasher, so even if he leaves town and goes to work somewhere else, we'll always get the rap for him. Every time he appears in the news, bang, property values will go down, just like when they named that big earthquake in '94 the Northridge Quake instead of the Transverse Ranges Quake, which would've been great since no one knows where the hell that is. But they had to go ahead and call it the Northridge Quake, and boom, anyone who owned property in Northridge couldn't sell it for almost a year afterward. On the other hand maybe they named him the LA Slasher because the *LA Times* liked the symmetry."

I am going to kill him, she thought. *Someday, maybe even someday soon, he is going to lean over his cubicle just like that, just like he's doing right now, and I am going to reach down his throat, yank out his lungs and his vocal cords, and use them to beat him to death.*

"I think we should've been first to name him," Leo continued, because continuing was what Leo did best. "We could've named him the Nightstalker, or the Killer Angel. Hell, we could've printed a mail–in ballot and let the whole *town* pick out a name. We'd set it up so the only way you could vote would be to buy an issue, so you *know* our circulation would go right through the roof. I mean, he's *our* killer, so why shouldn't everyone get a vote on his name? This is a democracy, right? Christ, they showed the headline with his name on CNN this morning. That could've been *our* headline, *our* front page. *That's* publicity, you know?"

That's it.

Susan tossed down her folder and stood. "The Nightstalker was Richard Ramirez," she said in a voice loud enough to be heard clear across the newsroom. "It was also a TV show starring Darren McGavin, and *The Killer Angels* was a book about the Civil War by Michael Shaara. So right off the bat the best thing you can do is to plagiarize somebody else, which for you is about par for the course."

"Just a minute—"

"The only *original* idea is the ballot and that is so demented, so utterly reprehensible that only the lowest form of life could even *conceive* of it."

She was aware that the newsroom had gotten very quiet around them, but she was long past caring. "Leo, you are sick, annoying, irresponsible, insensitive, callous, and not only am I tired of *you*, I've read your stupid features and I'm tired of reading more about you and your views than I am about the person you're supposed to be writing about, and if it wasn't for the fact that Rob's a *damned* good editor who rewrites your crap into decent form because he thinks he *has* to, because the publisher thinks you're a valuable addition to the staff, you'd be out on your ass right now because the truth is you can't write for shit, Leo.

"Now I'm going to lunch and I want you to stay out of my face for the rest of the day or I will not be held responsible for the consequences."

She grabbed her purse and notebag and headed out of the newsroom, past a stunned Leo, feeling sick at her stomach in spite of the rather substantial applause she heard from around the room.

I'm going to get a bill for that one, she thought, *but I don't care. It had to be said.*

So why does it always fall to me to say these things? Why doesn't anybody else ever jump in?

Because you're a pain in the ass, she thought back, answering her own question. *But just remember: that's what makes you a good reporter.*

Yeah, great, but that isn't going to help when Rob hears about this. He's going to just shit.

She rubbed at her temples, which were starting to throb, announcing a headache about to land. *Well, there's always the Chicago Tribune,* she thought ruefully.

Lord knows it'd certainly be a lot safer than this town right now.

By two o'clock, the pressroom at the LAPD headquarters downtown was jammed with reporters, recorders and television cameras. As if her day hadn't already gone badly enough—including getting into an argument upon arrival with a new reporter from the *Los Angeles Reader* over sitting rights to her usual chair—her heart sank as she read over the report given her by the public information liaison on her way in.

Duty rosters and overnight crime statistics were public information, gathered, collated and published every day. Since there was no reason why the owners of vandalized public buildings would withhold that information—as opposed to a woman who decides not to press charges against an abusive husband—if the kind of desecrations Raymond described had taken place, they'd be in the daily logs.

And, in fact, there were two such reports, each discovered the morning after the first two murders: obscenities painted on the side of a Baptist church less than half a mile from the first murder, and dog excrement found smeared over the front door and mezuzah at a synagogue two blocks from the second murder.

That was, however, the full extent of it.

She flipped through the report a second time, in case she'd missed anything, but found nothing else that even came close.

He almost had me believing it. She knew she should not be disappointed; most leads a reporter receives go nowhere, but somewhat to her own surprise she'd wanted this one to go *somewhere*, to know that Raymond was more than just another flake, con man, or publicity seeker. Maybe he'd thought that she wouldn't actually do the legwork, that she'd just take him at his word that these desecrations had taken place. But Susan came from the same journalistic school of thought as the reporters challenged by Senator Gary Hart to follow him around if they thought he was committing moral indiscretions, a challenge he would later regret to the tune of a devastated presidential campaign. *If you don't want the press to chase the bone, don't wave it in front of us or you'll get bit.*

There was no question in Susan's mind that Raymond was sincere, but sincerity and the truth were not always the same thing. The report in her hand demonstrated pretty effectively that in this case, as with so many others, they remained two vastly different things.

Too bad, she thought, and folded the report into her notebag as Chief Darrow entered and approached the podium.

"Good afternoon," he said. "I'll keep this brief, since obviously we all have work to do. Subsequent to the first reported attack by the individual now apparently, and *unfortunately*, designated the LA Slasher—"

Susan looked to the reporter from the *Los Angeles Times* seated two rows in front of her, and decided that he looked even more smug than usual. *Great, now even the police are using it.*

"—we have received more than two thousand phone, mail, fax and email leads. Every one of them is being followed up with interviews and, if merited, further on–site investigation. We are coordinating with the FBI's Special Crimes unit and we have allocated the maximum amount of resources, time and personnel to the task at hand. We have achieved some progress in the course of the investigation, and we expect to continue moving forward. Toward that end we ask for your continued support and the support of the citizens of Los Angeles in passing along any information that could be of use in our investigation.

"I'll now open up the floor to questions."

That's it? Susan thought. She'd heard her share of vanilla statements before, but…didn't they have *anything* new? Anything at *all?*

The reporter from the *Times* was the first one with his hand in the air. *Bastard*, she thought.

"Chief Darrow, the Slasher began going after homeless victims, attacking them in the open. He has now changed his strategy and seems to be going after hardworking average people, attacking them right in their own homes. But according to the psychiatrists we've interviewed, serial killers are noted for sticking to one particular *modus operandi* when it comes to victims. How do you account for this shift?"

"We don't know that there's been a shift or a change," Darrow said. "For instance, we don't know if there's just one person involved, or if there are multiple killers involved, each with his own obsession. We do know that so far all of the victims have been male, which reinforces our conviction that the suspect's overall M.O. has not changed. The suspect has always gone after targets of opportunity, and the increased police presence in the downtown and Hollywood areas may have removed those targets of opportunity, forcing the suspect to take chances. This, we believe, is a sign of desperation. Taking those chances makes it increasingly more likely that he will make a mistake. When he does, we will be there.

"Next question."

Susan's hand shot up alongside everyone else. Chief Darrow pointed to the new reporter from the *LA Reader* who had tried to appropriate Susan's chair.

"When the LAPD cracked down on prostitution along Hollywood and Sunset Boulevards last year, the main result was to drive the trade north, up into the valley along Sepulveda and Vanowen, bringing a level of crime to those areas that had not been present previously. Are you saying, and should I tell my readers, that because the LAPD has so far failed to identify or apprehend this individual downtown, it has deliberately endangered the lives of middle class residents uptown out of a blind hope that this might force him to make a mistake?"

"Just a minute—"

"Because it sounds like you're putting the protection of the criminal, unemployed underclass above the needs of families and decent neighborhoods. If you hadn't chosen to close off one avenue, forcing him into going uptown to find his victims, and if you had instead concentrated on finding the person or persons responsible, is it not possible that Steven Banks might be alive right now?"

"If you're saying that the LAPD is somehow responsible—"

"It's a matter of priorities—"

"Our *priority* is saving lives."

"But you can't save lives until you know who this guy is. All you're doing is redirecting him into middle class neighborhoods so that now the whole *city* has to live in fear. By making him range further afield to find his victims, you've pretty much ensured that no place is safe."

"Susan?"

She turned at the voice that came from behind her to the right. Sergeant Mike Devereaux stood in the aisle, nearly filling it. "Mike? What—"

"I need to talk to you."

"Right now?"

She looked from Mike to where the police chief was starting to lose his temper with the reporter from the *Reader*. "I won't even dignify this line of inquiry with an answer," he said.

"Right now," Mike said.

"Just let me ask one question—"

"I mean it, Susan. It's important."

She looked back at the podium, too late, as another round of hands went up and the next question went to a stringer from CNN. *Damn....*

"All right, all right, just a second." She gathered up her belongings and stepped carefully out of the row of seats, trying not to walk on anyone.

"This had better be worth it," she said as they walked up the aisle. "I'm missing the press conference."

"Nothing new is going to be said," he shot back, adding "Don't worry, you can read about it tomorrow in the *Times*."

Susan bristled but kept walking. "Mike, does freedom of the press extend to kicking a police officer in the nuts?"

"No."

"Just checking."

They didn't stop until they were in the parking lot outside police head-quarters. "Good enough," he said.

"Fine, now would you like to explain to me why you dragged my ass out of there? I mean, what the hell are you up to?"

"I was going to ask you the same thing."

"What're you talking about?"

"Damn it, Susan, you should've checked with me before you asked for that report about the churches. I didn't hear about it until just a few minutes ago. You set off alarm bells all the way to City Hall."

Susan paused before saying anything else, her instincts kicking in. *Play this careful*, she thought. *I think he thinks I know more than I know.*

"Why wasn't there anything in the report about them after the first two incidents?"

"They were deleted from the published logs about two weeks ago, when the brass figured out there was some kind of connection. Those first two must've gotten cross–referenced to civil and that's why we missed them. Look, Susan, it's the only lead we've got. They've put special undercover units on twenty–four hour rotation to patrol churches and synagogues and any other religious–oriented buildings in the vicinity of the murders. Yeah, some public records got changed, but that's because we didn't want anyone else figuring out the con-nection and scaring him off. This is our best chance to nail the guy."

"That's why you pulled me out of there before I could ask a question," she said. "You were afraid I'd ask about this and blow the whole thing wide open."

"That's right."

"So you want me to sit on it."

"For now. I'm asking you as a personal favor. I've done for you, now you have to do for me on this one. How the hell did you crack this, anyway?"

"You know better than that, Mike. I can't reveal my sources."

"All I'm asking is, did it come from inside the department? Because right now my ass is on the line. They know I know you, and if this gets out they're going to blame me for it."

"In that case, no, it didn't come from inside the department. I have plenty of other sources."

"I got your word on that?"

"Cross my heart and hope to die."

He studied her for a long moment, then decided she was telling the truth. "Okay," he said. "Good. I can at least tell them that much. Maybe it'll get them off my back a little. Christ, you don't know what I've been through over this."

"I still haven't agreed not to print this, Mike. I have pressure on my side to deal with too, you know. Last time I sat on information regarding these murders the *Times* came out with it first. My editor was not a happy man."

He sighed and leaned against a squad car. It lowered measurably under his mass. "Okay...what do you want?"

"*Quid pro quo.* I do for you, you do for me. Tell me something I don't know."

"Those shoes don't go with that purse."

"Like I said, tell me something I *don't* know."

He nodded toward a diner across the street. "You want some coffee?"

"Love some."

"Okay, here's the deal." Mike was wedged into the booth behind a table that had been built for smaller men. It nudged against his stomach, which parenthesized itself around the table edge in a way Susan found oddly fascinating. Mike seemed not to even notice. "You got two basic kinds of serial killer: organized killers and disorganized killers. Under that you've got four main categories: you've got your thrill killer, your lust killer, your visionary killer and your missionary killer. Each of them gets off on it, but in different ways.

"Your thrill killer is in it for the adrenaline, he gets off on the hunt. He likes the danger, he likes the pursuit, it's as addictive as getting high. It makes him feel smarter than the people he's killing and the people who are chasing him. This guy kills for the same reason other guys skydive or race cars or spend thousands of dollars flying down to Pamploma so they can run with a bunch of *other* nuts trying to avoid getting gored by several hundred angry bulls charging down the middle of the street. It makes his heart go piddy–pat.

"A thrill killer goes completely fucking nuts when he's in the midst of his work. He enjoys killing, so this type is probably the most sadistic of them all. We're talking here the kind of guy who stabs somebody eighty–seven times and only stops because the knife breaks off in the victim's spinal column, then he bites, claws, kicks and scratches whatever's left. So your average thrill killer falls into the category of disorganized killers.

"Our guy, however, is very organized, very methodical. He takes his time. Thrill killers also usually try to torment the police with notes and clues, most of which don't mean anything. In all this time, we haven't heard a word from the Slasher.

"A thrill killer looks for victims wherever he can find them, male or female.

"A lust killer, on the other hand, usually targets one gender or the other because he's in it for the sex. Sometimes that sex takes place while the victim's alive, sometimes after they're dead, sometimes at the moment in–between, at least that's where the real connoisseurs say it's the best. I'm not grossing you out with this, am I?"

"No, not at all" she said, her stomach tightening, the taste of bile nipping the back of her throat. She sipped at the coffee and let it burn going down. "Go on."

"Some lust killers are disorganized, others organized, but obviously sex is key to the whole thing for them. The more he tortures someone, the more aroused he becomes. But over time, they need more and more violence to become aroused. Now, so far, our guy has killed only males, so that fits. But none of them have been sexually assaulted, there's been no trace of semen or saliva found in inappropriate locations, no escalation in the way attacks are conducted, and there hasn't been any indication that the victims or the perpetrator are gay or bi. So that theory goes up in smoke."

"That still leaves two categories."

"Correct. Now, visionary killers hear voices in their head, instructing them to kill. They're psychotic, unpredictable, often suffering from multiple personality disorder. In most such cases, the main personality is the one who feels victimized, because he believes he has no control over these murders, it's *them*, the voices in his head, the other minds living in his body. Invariably he tries to communicate this, to inform others of his distress or innocence. Conversely, the other personalities or voices may try to communicate in order to gloat about being the ones actually responsible, not this weakling they inhabit. Either way, it's important for them to be understood. But so far, we've had zero communication with this guy, and there's nothing in the nature of the crimes that points to the visionary aspect."

"What about the desecrations? Wouldn't that fit into the category of sending a message?"

"Not yet, because there hasn't been anything actually communicated in them. There's been no message. Lots of damage and shit, but nothing written, nothing said. We don't know where they fit into the picture yet, we just know there's some kind of connection."

"But what if the desecrations *are* the message?"

"Still doesn't fit. It's a statement, sure, but there still isn't a message."

Susan considered her conversation with Raymond. "What if he's, I don't know, obsessed with the devil or something?"

"Then he'd say so. I mean that. Subtle these guys ain't. He'd write Satan Rules or Hail Satan or something equally screwy and obvious. The flip side is some nut who thinks the church has fallen away from the divine path, and needs to be brought closer to god, so this kind of desecration becomes kind of a Jesus–in–the–temple–bashing–moneychangers thing. The one side definitely doesn't want to be confused with the other, so if one of these guys *was* responsible, there'd be literal, written messages, threats, warnings, *something*. So far, nothing. Now, maybe you're right, and somehow the desecrations are the message, but I sure as hell can't interpret it yet, and none of the experts can either.

"So that leaves the missionary killer. This is somebody like Jack the Ripper, who murdered prostitutes because he thought he was sending a message to society. This kind of killer has a deep–seated need to rid the world of people he feels are immoral in some way. He's usually somebody with schizophrenic–level insecurities about himself and his own worth. He projects those traits onto others because if he can kill the evil in others, he can kill the evil in himself without having to admit he has it. Instead of being evil, he believes himself to be the hand of god, sending an important message: clear out the streets, clean up your room, save the whales, trust in Allah, whatever. He'll usually pick out one class of victims, which can be fairly easily identified by group: gays, hookers, IRS agents, pick a group and at some point or other *somebody's* decided they need to die. But there's been nothing to link the victims to any one group.

"At first we thought our guy fell into this category because the initial murders were all committed against the homeless. That definitely falls under the heading of 'Clean up the streets.' But then he shifted to ordinary, average, middle class men with decent jobs who, as far as we can determine, never bothered anyone in their lives. Which blew that theory out the door.

"And again, this kind of killer has to create some form of communication between himself and the world around him, otherwise his message isn't being conveyed, and the 'pure motive' behind his actions isn't being understood.

"Ninety percent of the time—I'm leaving out ten percent to cover the crackheads and drunks who don't have any idea what the hell they're doing—people kill for a reason. It may be a reason that makes sense only to *them*, but it's still a valid reason as far as they're concerned. This is true for the average person, and even more true for a serial killer because a serial killer is a creature of habit and obsession.

"An average human being doesn't just decide one day to go around killing people. Someone like this starts off a loaded gun just waiting for a trigger. Maybe he was molested as a kid, and he's venting the rage now that he has the power to do to others as he was done unto. Maybe he liked torturing small animals and graduated up the evolutionary chain to human beings. One way or another there's always a reason, and the murders always reflect that reason.

"But we don't have a reason with this guy, Susan."

"So what you're saying is that after over two months of investigation, you don't have anything at all on this guy."

"That's not what I brought you over here to tell you."

"Then what is it?"

"You're smart, work it out."

She frowned, staring silently down at her coffee for a moment before looking up again. "It isn't that you don't have enough information to place him into any of the categories, you're saying the killer doesn't *fit* any known category. That we may have an entirely new kind of serial killer on our hands, something no one's encountered before. Someone who isn't playing by any of the usual rules."

"Exactly. Everything we've got is designed to help us catch killers who fall into the known categories. Whoever this guy is, he's operating outside of everything we know. His logic is nothing we've seen, he's unpredictable and, until we figure out what we're dealing with, the horrendous thing is that he's almost certainly uncatchable, until and unless he makes some kind of stupid mistake. But he hasn't made any so far, and I doubt that's going to change any time soon."

"So once again, Los Angeles is on the bleeding edge of social innovation," Susan said. "Literally, this time."

Mike nodded. "Some of the psychiatrists we're working with want to write a book about this guy. "Me, I just want to put a bullet in his brain."

It was almost eight o'clock when Susan returned to the *Trib* to check her email, write up her notes and pick up any waiting messages. She liked writing in the office after hours, because most everybody was gone for the day, leaving just a skeleton crew on duty in case somebody shot a President or sank an aircraft carrier. Rob was usually out by six.

Tonight, he was still there when she came in.

"You want to talk about it?" he said, nodding toward Leo's empty cubicle.

"Not really."

"Okay, then let me rephrase: let's talk about it."

He pulled a chair over to her desk and sat facing her. "After you left, about a half a dozen people came into my office to tell me what happened."

"Typical."

"I disagree. They came specifically to tell me that they thought you did the right thing. Apparently Leo is not much beloved among the staff."

"Good."

"I disagree again. *Not* good. If you've got a problem, you need to take it up with that person privately. I can't have the office getting disrupted or politicized into camps, your side vs. his side. And believe me, there are plenty of other people who are on his side. They just don't come to me because they know that I brought you in and I tend to cut you a lot of slack. Sometimes, I think, too much slack."

"Rob, the guy has been a pain in the ass for three months, ever since he got moved downstairs from the other office. He rides me from the moment I get in until the moment I go home, and he thinks it's funny. Whatever I may have done or said to him in two minutes doesn't come anywhere *near* the grief he's given me day in and day out for the last three months."

"That's probably true. It's also true that for the most part, only a few people were aware of it because he talked only to you. He didn't turn it into performance art."

"So you're saying it's okay to behave like a jerk if nobody notices except the person you're being a jerk to."

"*To whom* you're being a jerk."

"Whatever."

"No, I'm not saying it's okay. I'm *saying* that you should have come to me three months ago when all this started."

"I can't go running to you for help every time I get in a situation like this, I can take care of myself."

"Nobody's saying otherwise. But I'm the editor here, Susan. Part of my job is ensuring that our dysfunctional little family goes through every day with the minimum possible level of conflict. Writing is your job. Politics is mine. I try not to get in your way, and in return I'm asking that you not get in the way of me doing my job, however well–intentioned your motives. All right?"

"I guess," she said. "So what happens now?"

Rob stood. It seemed to Susan that he was standing more slowly these days. "I called Leo into my office before he left for the day. He confirmed that you two have been at it for months now, and since it doesn't seem like that's going to change anytime soon, I'm moving your cubicle across the room so you won't be in each others' face every day."

"*Me?* Why do *I* have to move? He's the one who—"

"Because you're the one who made the noise. If you'd come to me on the QT, I could've found an excuse to move him somewhere else. Now, if I do that, it'll look like favoritism, which is understandable because that's exactly what it *would* be. Is that what you want?"

"It's just—"

"Is it?"

She frowned, then sat back in her chair. "No."

"Susan, look…the truth is, you're a hustler in the best sense of the word: you go out and you fight for stories, you don't take no for an answer. You're relentless, impatient and a pain in the ass; you've got the kind of fire in the belly that doesn't come along very often. In short you're a *good reporter*, and you're ten times the writer Leo will *ever* be. You know it, I know it, and *he* knows it. I can see that when he talks about you. He knows that twenty years from now, you'll be on the AP, or you'll jump over to CNN, hell, maybe someday you'll end up on the *Washington Post* or something. Twenty years from now he's still going to be doing the same stupid feature articles about the latest flavor of the month actor or some rich old lady who's given UCLA a million dollar grant in memory of her dog Pumpkin. The kind of ephemeral, trivial stories you read and throw away two seconds later.

"The point is you're *going* somewhere, and he isn't. So he pinks you. It's the only thing he *can* do. Now I'm not saying that should make you like him, or understand him, or want to have his babies, or take him out for lunch. But you should know what's behind it, and that in the final analysis it doesn't mean anything, it's strictly schoolyard stuff. And you may as well get used to it now, because for every one that comes through like you, there are thirty like Leo. Guys like him can't destroy what you are, only you can do that by letting them get to you, push you into making mistakes.

"What matters is that twenty years from now, when you come back here to visit the old place, you can show your kids where your desk used to be. And you can show them where Leo's desk still *is*. At that moment, all of this will seem unimportant, and trivial, because that's exactly what it is."

She looked up at him, and he was smiling at her. "What's the first rule of reporting I taught you when you came here to work?"

"Rob—"

"What is it?"

"'Don't fight the rabbits, the lions will get you.'"

"Case closed. Agreed?"

"Agreed," she said, rubbing tiredly at her face. "When do you want me to move?"

"Anytime in the next few days will be fine. Just call down to the front desk, and they'll send up some guys to take care of it. I'll even try to get you a window seat."

"The window on that side faces a wall."

"I know," he said. Still smiling, he picked up his jacket and started toward the door.

"Hey, Rob?" she called after him. He stopped. "Listen, I know you put up with a lot on my behalf, and I just want you to know it's appreciated."

"All part of the job," he said, continuing away. "'Night."

"Night."

Alone in the newsroom, Susan touched the keyboard, and her computer flared to life. After talking to Rob, she decided she was too tired to write up her notes. She'd just check her email and leave.

There were fourteen messages waiting. To her dismay, all of them were spam, as far as she could tell from the headings. The junk emails always tried different hooks, never the same twice, but they were always painfully obvious in their attempts to draw her attention.

Make millions surfing the web!

I have the information you requested!

Important news on your financial history!

Do you want to know who I am?

She highlighted them one at a time and pressed delete.

Make millions surfing the web!

Gone.

I have the information you requested!

Gone.

Important news on your financial history!

Gone. Then, finally, the last one.

Do you want to know who I am?

Gone.

She looked up again at the screen.

Do you want to know who I am?

She blinked at the screen for a moment. She was sure she had erased it. She highlighted the email again and hit DELETE.

Gone.

She looked up again.

Do you want to know who I am?

Great, she thought. *Some new spam engine that keeps throwing out email until you open it and read it. One more computer science student with too much time on his hands and I have to pay for it.*

She hit DELETE a third time.

This time it was gone and stayed gone.

The computer screen read NO WAITING MESSAGES.

Satisfied, she reached to turn off the computer just as the phone rang loudly at her elbow, startling her. She picked it up. "Randall."

"Were you able to verify my information?"

She recognized the voice. "Raymond?"

"Yes."

"Yeah, it checked out. I kind of went around the horn to find *out* that it checked, but…listen, can we meet somewhere to talk? Maybe tomorrow morning?"

"Cantor's Deli. Breakfast."

"What about your place? Maybe you'd be more comfortable in your own surroundings, and I can get a sense of—"

"No. My home is private. Cantor's Deli. Seven o'clock tomorrow morning."

"*Seven?* Could we possibly do it at eight or nine, or—"

He was already gone.

Doesn't this guy ever sleep?

Susan racked the phone. With a tired sigh, she gathered up her belongings and headed out of the newsroom.

I'm starting to sigh just like Rob, she thought distantly.

God's Periscope

Since 1931, Cantor's Delicatessen had been in business on Fairfax north of Beverly Boulevard, a part of town often referred to as Little Israel, shot through with bookstores offering titles in Hebrew, Kosher delis, and every Friday, *Hassidim* in their heavy coats and hats *en route* to temple, making their way on foot through the north–south flow of cars passing through on their way to Farmer's Market or CBS. During that time, it had seen one world war and several smaller ones, and had been the deli of choice for stars during the forties and fifties. It was still struggling to hold onto some of that image, despite the wear and tear that had settled into the old place, prompting many of the new breed of stars to seek out better or livelier prospects.

But the only place that offered better corned beef was Art's Deli, on Ventura Boulevard in the valley, and Susan always came for the corned beef.

"You're having that for breakfast?" Raymond asked as plates were deposited on their table.

Susan dug into her sandwich. "If I have to come clear across town to get here at seven in the morning, I'm having something I can't make at home. That leaves sweetbreads or corned beef, and I'd rather stick an ice pick in my ear than eat sweetbreads."

Raymond smiled and turned a fork to his scrambled eggs.

He smiles but he never laughs, Susan thought. *Not once, not in all this. Not that there's anything particularly funny about serial killings, but I'm doing my best here to get through to him.* Each time she'd seen him, she had come away with the vague but undeniable sense that under the brusqueness there was something profoundly sad at his center, something he kept guarded and close to his heart. *Even when he smiles he looks like someone just killed his cat.*

"So, how should we proceed from here?" he asked.

"Well, I'd like to interview you, if that's all right. A more formal interview than the last time we met."

"I did not agree to speak with you so that I would see my name in the paper. I'm not a publicity seeker. I would prefer to remain anonymous."

"I understand and respect that. But we seem to be in the position of working together, so obviously I'd like to know more about you. This is going to require a bond of trust between us, and that has to start somewhere. I'll treat anything said between us as background for my articles. No names. Worst case scenario, if anyone asks, I'll say I got my information from an unnamed source, and I always protect my sources. I won't do anything beyond that without your express permission, and you obviously don't have to answer any question you don't want to answer."

He hesitated for a moment, then nodded. "All right."

"Do you mind if I record this?"

He shook his head. She removed a mini–recorder and placed it discreetly on the table, close enough to catch his voice but without being so constantly in sight that it would make him self–conscious. *As if that's possible*, she thought.

"I'd like to start with your background," she said. "At first I thought your accent might be German, but now that I've heard it a few times I'm guessing it's Austrian."

"Vienna. I came to America with my father when I was fifteen. He married an American woman, an editor in New York. I've only been back a few times. I'm surprised it is still noticeable."

"Just barely," she said. "You really have to listen for it. And there's a vaguely European syntax that slips into your voice every so often."

"You're very observant. Have you ever been to Vienna?"

"No, the only reason I know…" She paused, and laughed. Was she really going to tell him this? *What the heck, we're trying to build bridges here, after all.* "When I was young, I caught just about every childhood illness known to modern science. Measles, mumps, chicken pox, you name it, I got it. So I was stuck at home a lot watching television because there wasn't anything else to do. At three o'clock, one of the local stations used to run old Universal Studios monster movies from the forties, and I fell in love with Turhan Bey's voice. He was in *The Mad Ghoul*, and *The Mummy's Tomb* and *Ali Baba and the Forty Thieves*, and he had this *voice* that made my pre–pubescent little brain melt right out my ears. He was suave, and elegant, and as I later learned, born in Vienna. And that's how I recognized your voice."

"I'm flattered, I think."

"You're welcome. So," she said, feeling vaguely silly at the revelation, "were you raised here?"

"Mostly. We traveled a great deal."

"Married?"

He paused here. "No. Not anymore."

"Kids?"

"One daughter. Claire. She…passed away, some years ago."

"I'm sorry."

He nodded, looked down at his plate. She decided that he had the deepest eyes of anyone she had ever met. *If God had a periscope, and he raised it behind someone's eyes, so he could see through them into this world, I think that's what it would look like.*

"How did she—"

"This is one of those topics that I would prefer to leave for another time," he said.

"I understand," she said.

"And you? Is there a husband? Children?"

She shook her head. "I've had sort of an on–again off–again—mostly off—relationship with a guy named Larry Drake, he's an agent with Carlton–Hauser–Shain–Ifmann, but it just…I don't know, I guess it just isn't there. He's a jerk, but then I haven't met a guy in this town so far who wasn't a jerk. No offense meant."

He smiled. "None taken. So he is well–to–do, then?"

"Yeah, I suppose you could say that. But that doesn't matter much to me. I suppose it should, but it doesn't. It never has. I've always figured, you can only ride in one car at a time, only eat one meal at a time, sleep in one bed at a time—well, maybe Larry can handle more than that—but the point is, how much money do you really need? And in the end, do you end up owning the money, so it lets you do what you want, or does the money end up owning you?"

He considered her for a long moment. "You're very young to be having thoughts that old."

"Is that a compliment?"

"I think so."

She smiled, then looked away, returning to her notes. "I'd like to ask you about the young girl, Cheryl Stearns, who was in my hospital room the first night we met. What's your connection? Her mother said you were helping, but didn't specify how. Does that situation have anything to do with this one?"

"Not as such, no," he said. "Cheryl had run away from home about six months before her parents called me."

"How did they find you?"

"Through other people. That's all I can say for now."

"The first thing I did was to direct them to some associates in Mexico who were able to positively identify her daughter and locate her inside the compound owned by the cult in Churubusco, about an hour's drive outside Mexico City. I had some small involvement with the operation to remove her from the compound and return her to the United States."

"And that's when she got sick on the plane coming back."

Raymond nodded. "A sickness of the soul. She was spiritually oppressed. You can also say psychologically oppressed, if you wish, the distinction between them is a fine one. Either way, the leader of the cult, who had named himself *San Juan de los Deos*—Saint John of God—had by strength of personality and deception intruded forces into her soul that had nothing to do with either Saint

John or God. She was young, and vulnerable, and like all the others who had been brought to that compound, she did not have the will to resist."

"She had the guts to run away, and travel halfway across the Western Hemisphere, that sounds like a pretty willful person to me."

He shook his head. "Too many people mistake *force* of conviction with *strength* of conviction, confuse *volume of voice* with *content of character*, teenagers in particular. As a result, they blur the lines between rebellion and identity. There is no question that they feel their beliefs strongly, but those beliefs are often built on the shallowest foundation, untested by the real world, and adhered to because their whole self–image is tied up in it.

"In short, beneath the shouting and the incidents of leaving home there is great insecurity. That is why runaways so often fall under the control of cult leaders or pimps or drug dealers. They want *others* to believe in who they are, but are often unable to believe in *themselves*. This makes them vulnerable to someone with a stronger will, a more profound and magnetic sense of self.

"When she was taken out of the compound and put on a plane by the individuals hired by her parents, the leader was furious. He lashed out at her, invoking forces that struck at her on a level that is both subtle and frightening."

"What kind of forces?"

"All I can say is that when she got on that airplane, she was no longer entirely alone. There was something with her, *inside* her, that was fighting for dominance; something that preyed on her lack of confidence and the weakness of her will, which had been further diminished by weeks of hard work, little food and less sleep.

"In time, it would have killed her."

Susan felt her cell phone go off against her hip in vibrating mode. *Not now, why the hell do people always call at the worst possible moment?* She let it go, didn't answer.

"But it didn't kill her," she continued.

"No."

"Why?"

"As I said, such things are often matters of will. On her behalf, I set my will against the will of that which had taken up residence within her. I was fortunate in that it had only just begun its destruction of Cheryl from the inside–out; if there had been more time for it to harm her, and further weaken her condition, there's nothing I or anyone else could have done to save her. We were also helped by the apparent death in Mexico of the cult leader responsible for unleashing it."

"What happened there, anyway? Mrs. Stearns said some of the local villagers killed him."

Raymond shrugged. "Mexico can sometimes be a dangerous place. Things happen. I can only be happy that they did happen, because otherwise the process would have been considerably more…difficult."

"How did—" She stopped. The phone was vibrating again. Frustrated, she pulled it out of her pocket. "I'm sorry," she said, switching off the recorder. "Only a few people have this number, and if they're calling, it must be important."

At least it'd better be, she thought as she flipped open the phone, *or someone's going to die.*

"Yes?"

"Susan?" It was Rob's voice. "Where are you?"

"Cantor's, look, can I call you back or—"

"They think they've got the killer."

"What?" She looked up at Raymond, who caught the tone in her voice. "Where? How did you—"

"It's on the TV right now. All the local stations just started picking up the feed, CNN should have it any time now. I figured you'd like to know."

"Thanks, Rob, I'll get back to you," she said.

"Now look, don't do anything—"

He probably said *foolish* or *dangerous*, but she had already snapped the phone closed. It would've been a pointless request anyway; he knew how much this story meant to her.

"What is it?" Raymond asked.

"We have to find a TV."

"I think I saw a small one by the cashier's desk."

As Raymond tossed down money for the bill, she stood and hurried to the desk. The set was dark. "Can you turn that on for a moment?" Susan asked.

The clerk behind the cash register barely noted the request. Without taking her nose out of a copy of *People* magazine, she reached around the counter and switched on the set.

The TV warmed up with what had become a familiar sight on Los Angeles television: another high-speed chase captured by a news helicopter as it roared down the Golden State Freeway. The live feed from the copter-mounted video camera revealed a cherry red pickup pursued by half a dozen Highway Patrol and LAPD squad cars.

"—heading North along the 405," the traffic reporter was saying, "where a massive pursuit is just now passing the Getty Museum and continuing into the Valley at speeds frequently in excess of one hundred miles an hour.

"The pursuit began about thirty minutes ago after an unidentified homeless man was attacked by a knife-wielding assailant just half a block from the last attack by the LA Slasher. Eyewitnesses' reports confirm that the attacker had sliced the palms of the victim and was moving in for the kill when he was approached by police officers. The suspect managed to escape into the red pickup we're seeing right now.

"While police sources have not yet officially confirmed that this suspect may indeed be the LA Slasher, unofficially we continue to receive indications that *they* believe they've found him."

"I've got to get out there," Susan said, moving toward the door and out. "I'm sorry, maybe we can pick this up later—"

"It's not him."

"You don't know that, not for sure."

"It doesn't feel right to me."

She was heading for her car at a trot, calling back to Raymond. "I understand, but I have to check it out just in case, be there when it goes down."

She climbed into the car and snapped on the radio, punching up the news radio stations. "Call me later," she said as she gunned the engine and raced away, heading up Fairfax, mentally diagramming the best way to get over the hill and into the valley without using the freeway, which would be cut off by barricades at the on-ramps, a lesson the LAPD had learned after the O.J. Simpson chase had led to a freeway crowd of massive proportions. *West to Sepulveda then punch it and hope the police in the area are all busy with this chase.*

She swerved around a stalled BMW—a happy sight in almost anyone's eyes—and shot left across the next intersection just as the light turned red. With luck she could catch up with them not too long after the chase ended and the suspect was in custody, wherever and whoever that would end up being.

Assuming he wasn't dead by that point.

As Susan had suspected, the chase led north along the 405 until it cleared the narrow divide between the Santa Monica Mountains and reached the valley, which offered the first opportunity for the suspect to jump off onto surface streets. When the radio placed him going east on Ventura Boulevard, Susan turned off Sepulveda and headed east on Mulholland, ready to grab any of the canyon roads—Laurel, Coldwater or Benedict—as soon as she got a sense where the police were going to box him in.

"—suspect has just run over a tire strip set out by police officers on Whitsett," the radio anchor reported.

It'll be Laurel, she thought, and turned north just as the canyon road came up.

By the time she hit Ventura she could hear the wail of sirens, and followed it until she caught sight of the convoy. The red pickup was riding on the rims and throwing sparks. The suspect was driving erratically down the middle of Ventura, past trendy shops and restaurants, fighting to maintain control of the car and stay ahead of his pursuers. Then the need for speed overrode common sense and he jammed the accelerator, knocking one car aside and plunging out into the intersection, clearly hoping to jump onto the 101 and lose his pursuers in the east-west morning traffic.

But that hope was dashed as the car spun out of control and flipped over next to a shopping center on Moorpark. The fugitive climbed out of the wreck and ran out into the middle of traffic, barely avoiding the rush of oncoming cars as he plunged into the parking lot.

Susan cut left into an alley behind Moorpark as the convoy of squad cars took up positions on the street, closing off access to all other traffic. She ditched the car and ran through a donut shop to come out into the middle of the shopping center.

Clutching his ribcage, the fugitive staggered into the open parking lot as people came running out of stores and supermarkets, drawn by the sirens.

"That's him!" somebody yelled, pointing at the fugitive.

Another voice joined in. "I saw it on TV! That's the killer!"

First one, then another moved to follow him, circling warily. Then someone rushed out and shoved him back, retreating into the crowd as the suspect turned, began to run.

Now others were running toward him even as the police were running into the lot.

No, Susan thought, as they fell on him. They dragged him down and he disappeared beneath waves of fists and feet. They shouted and cursed and pounded and kicked and there was a flash of blood and a cry of pain and suddenly the police were running into the crowd, shoving them aside, reaching down and pushing away and dragging out as the fugitive staggered twice then fell again as police shoved him to the ground, yanked his arms behind his back and handcuffed him. Men cursed at him and women cried out at him from behind the black uniforms that restrained them.

Susan pressed through the crowd of bodies, flashing her press ID and looking for officers who might recognize her. One did and raised an arm to let her pass. She reached the middle of the lot just as the police yanked him to his feet and led him toward a waiting squad car.

"Who are you?" she called.

He continued on to the squad car, throwing a glance to her without answering.

"Why'd you do it? Are you the LA Sla—" she couldn't bear to use the *Times* jargon—"are you the killer?" she called.

"I never killed anybody!" he yelled back. "I'm not saying anything else until I talk to a lawyer!" An officer standing beside the waiting car popped the door and helped him in, making sure his head didn't hit the hood on the way in.

"At least tell me your name!"

He hesitated as the door started to close, then shouted out "Lee...Lee Garrison!"

As the squad car drove off, Susan turned to see reporters from other newspapers and TV stations arriving at the scene. They pushed through the crowd until they got to her. "Did he say anything?" asked a reporter she recognized from the *Times*.

She considered for a moment, then answered, "Beats me, I couldn't hear a thing."

With that, she hurried to her car, for this moment at least feeling curiously positive about the universe and her place in it.

Having worn out his welcome at the cashier's desk at Cantor's, Raymond Weil drove to a bar further down Beverly where he knew there was a television. He watched the pursuit end along with a handful of patrons who sat mesmerized by the images splashed across the television that hung on the wall at one end of the bar, a wall that was covered with the photos of actors who had come in over the years for a quick drink. The news copter footage was shaky, but for a moment he thought he saw Susan there among the crowd. If he'd had any doubts about her determination or strength of will, that one shot had resolved the question in her favor.

There was applause as the squad car drove off with its handcuffed passenger. "How about that, they got the bastard," somebody said.

"Hope he gets the chair," somebody else chimed in.

"Shit, I hope he doesn't live long enough to *get* the chair," a third man said, "which won't happen because of the liberal judges we got these days. I say just turn him loose with the other animals they got in prison and let them take care of him. Now that'd be justice."

"You got that right."

Raymond estimated that the last speaker was in his twenties. He wore a T–shirt and jeans, his sandy hair long and not recently washed, with a bike chain that went from belt loop to wallet.

"Give me five minutes with the son of a bitch, and I'll take care of him myself." He looked to Raymond. "You know what I'm saying?"

Raymond smiled thinly. "Of course." He set down two dollars and change for the coffee and pulled on his jacket.

"What do you mean 'of course'? What kind of answer is that? You don't think I could take this guy? Is that what you're saying?"

"Obviously you believe it, and I suppose that is what matters. What else is there to discuss?"

"I don't believe, I *know*," the young man said.

"Of course," Raymond said, starting toward the door.

"If he were here right now, or if that bastard came into *my* house in the middle of the night, you know what I'd do? Man, I'd kick the shit out of him. By the time I got through with him he'd wish he'd never been born."

Raymond paused at the door. *Don't get into it*, he told himself. *He's had too much to drink. Just let it go.*

"That's the problem today," the sandy–haired man continued, "people got no guts. He'd come at me, and I'd get him with one of those, you know, kung–fujitsu flip–kicks, and he'd be on the floor crying like a little girl before I even started to kick the shit out of him. I think—"

"*I* think that you do not know what you are talking about," someone in the bar said. Raymond was vaguely annoyed to realize that it was his own voice.

The young man whipped around to look at him. "That so?"

"Yes, that's so. Let me explain something to you. If you were sufficiently unlucky to wake up one night and find yourself alone with this individual, you would not 'kick his ass.' You would see his eyes, and you would see something no living man should ever see in this world. You would then spend the next few minutes, however long he chose to keep you alive for his own purposes, begging for your life until finally, in his own time and at his own whim, he chose to take it from you."

"You're saying I'm a coward?"

"When the zebra runs from the lion, it does not run because it is a coward. It runs because it understands that there are hunters and there are prey. The lion is a force of nature; it cannot be bargained with, cannot be reasoned with, cannot be stopped except by its own death. This individual is also a force of nature. You, however many beers you may consume before lunch, are *not*. That is the end–all and the be–all of both the equation, and this conversation."

With that, he turned and walked out the door.

"Yeah, you better run, old man," Jerry Levin yelled at the closing door.

The other guys in the bar were laughing and hooting. "He sure dissed you, Jerry!" somebody yelled.

"Shut up!"

"Gonna call you the Zebra from now on."

"I said shut the hell up!" He slid off the barstool and stood, slightly unsteadily. "Sonofabitch, who the hell does he think he's talking to, anyway?' Thinks he can get away with that? Give me a fucking break."

"Go get him, Jer!" someone yelled as he headed for the door.

"Damn right I will."

He stepped out onto the street just in time to catch a glimpse of the old man heading away down the street. "Hey, you!" he called.

The old man didn't turn.

"Hey! I'm talking to you, you piece of shit!"

He picked up his pace, coming up behind the old man as he turned the corner into a small alley. *Got you now*, he thought, running up to the alley. "Yeah, you better run 'cause I'm gonna kick your ass!"

He started to turn the corner.

Two powerful hands reached around the corner and grabbed him, hurled him against the alley wall. He hit the bricks hard. He tried to bring his fists up but he was too slow, as the other man slapped him across the face twice, hard, fast. *Jesus he's fast, how the hell can an old guy be that fast?* he managed to think before he was thrown across the alley and slammed into the opposite wall hard enough to make his head ring.

Then he was lifted up by his shoulders. The man had powerful hands, muscular and lean and they dug into his shirt and the flesh underneath, pinning him against the wall. Jerry's vision cleared a bit, and on a slow, cellular level he began to realize he was looking into the eyes of someone he should never have messed with.

"Do you remember what I said about lions and zebras?" the man asked, his voice low and deadly.

Jerry nodded.

"And which of us, right here, right now, in this alley, do you think is wearing stripes?"

Jerry didn't answer. He didn't need to. He had once looked into the face of a lion at a zoo, and those same eyes were at this moment burning into his own. He glanced away.

After a moment, the man released him. Jerry slumped to the alley floor, his knees weak. Then the man turned and, without a backward glance, walked out of the alley.

The guy is freakin' insane, Jerry thought.

He's going to kill somebody someday.

Sergeant Mike Devereaux waited with half a dozen of the other lead officers assigned to the Slasher case as two of the primary detectives came out of the interrogation room. "So how's it going in there?" he asked. "He confess yet? What've we got?"

Thomas Firelli, the primary who had drawn the first Slasher case, glanced back at the interrogation room as his partner headed for the men's room. "We got shit," he said.

"What're you talking about?" Mike asked over the other officers, who refused to believe what they were hearing. "Christ, Tom, we got two eye witnesses who put him on the scene, with a knife in his hand, going at it."

"You don't believe me, go check it out for yourself. He's in there now giving a statement with his lawyer. May as well, it'll all be public in a few hours anyway." He shook his head. "I need a drink."

He continued down the hall as Devereaux looked to the others. "Okay, you guys wait here, I'm gonna find out what the hell is going on," he said, and entered the observation room.

Inside the interrogation room, seated at a long table on the other side of the mirrored glass, were Garrison, the suspect, along with his attorney, a rep from the DA's office and two other detectives. A table microphone picked up the conversation and relayed it to the observation room.

"—with the understanding that in exchange for his cooperation my client will plead guilty to the lesser charge of aggravated assault and felony evading rather than attempted murder. Is that correct?"

The rep from the DA's office nodded. "We just want to get this clarified as quickly as possible so we can properly redirect our tactical response to the ongoing investigation."

"Very well," the attorney said. "As we stated, we can prove beyond question that my client was out of state for at least two of the previous murders. We can produce video of his attendance at his cousin's wedding in New Jersey the same night as the second murder, and a traffic ticket given when he was in New York the night of the fourth murder. We can also provide testimony as to his locations the other nights which will—"

"We've stipulated to those points," the DA rep said. "Can counsel please get to the issue at hand?"

"Of course. As my client has indicated, he was accosted by a panhandler as he emerged from McGilly's, a pub on Melrose, where he had consumed a legally acceptable amount of alcohol."

"I had three drinks," Garrison said, defensively. "*Three fucking drinks!*"

Counsel put a restraining hand on Garrison's arm. "As I said, a legally acceptable amount of alcohol. When the individual in question demanded money, my client did not provide the funds requested. At this time the subject became hostile—"

"I work for my money," Garrison said. "I work goddamn hard for it, too. Not only do I have to bust my ass to take care of my family, now I got—we *all* got—some fucking nut going around killing people because of assholes like this guy, living in the street, trash attracting trash, violence attracting violence, and I got to pay the price? I got to live in fear of some freakin' nut slicing me up every night because now he can't get to one of *them* and he's pissed about it? And on top of that he asks me for money? For *money?* No way! That's what I told him: No fucking way! And he pushed me around! I got a legal right to defend myself!"

"Lee," the attorney said. "Let me go on."

Garrison waved dismissively at the detectives and pulled out a cigarette. "Go ahead."

"The problem occurred when my client, acting in his own defense, pulled out a knife—"

The DA rep jumped in. "A concealed weapon."

"We've already stipulated to the fact that it was a concealed knife of *legal* length. Mr. Garrison was attempting to defend himself from what he considered a valid threat to his personal safety. As your own forensics experts have confirmed, the knife wounds found on the subject's palms are standard defensive wounds that are in no way similar to the careful and premeditated carvings inflicted on victims of the so-called Slasher."

"Then why did your client run?"

"The record will show that my client has one prior conviction for assault. In his panic concerning the possible consequences of a repeat appearance before the court he fled the scene hoping to avoid capture. He has subsequently realized the error of his actions, as I feel his cooperation here today clearly demonstrates.

"That said, we would now like to discuss pressing charges against the individuals at the shopping center who assaulted my client and violated his civil rights prior to the arrest."

That's enough, Devereaux decided, disgusted.

He stepped out into the hall, where the other officers were still waiting. "Is it true?" one of them asked. "He isn't the guy?" They looked to him, hoping he would tell them that it wasn't true, that they'd finally nailed the sick sonofabitch.

Devereaux shook his head. "It isn't him." Groans came from all around him, and someone slammed his fist into a nearby locker. "Come on, look, what're the odds we'd get him this easy? It's trial and error, people, that's the line of business we're in. Sooner or later, it's his error and we get to have the trial. That didn't happen today, big fucking deal, we're still the good guys, he's still out there, and we've got work to do. So let's get to it."

He waited as the others slowly dispersed, until finally he stood alone in the hall. What he hadn't said, what the others knew without him having to say it, was: *The public got a taste of blood today, they got excited, they got their hopes up. For a minute they thought they could relax. When they find out otherwise, they're gonna bounce right to the other extreme.*

If we thought things were bad before, now this is going to get really *ugly.*

Susan's new desk was a flurry of paper and boxes. With the phone cradled against one shoulder, she dug through the piles, frantically trying to find her notes while quietly cursing the receptionist who decided it would be a nice surprise on her last day of work if she helped Susan move her stuff to the new cubicle that had been assigned to her on the other side of the newsroom. Unfortunately, the about–to–be–married receptionist had done the move *for* her, in the hours before Susan got in, and now she couldn't find anything. She was even denied the satisfaction of complaining about it since it had been painfully well–intentioned.

She upturned a box labeled PAPER—as if her entire life was not a constant onslaught of paper, such that every box she touched, including one day her own coffin, should simply be marked PAPER—looking for something to write on while an editorial assistant at her feet worked to reconnect her computer. She kept an eye on him, privately convinced that he was taking the opportunity to glance up her skirt.

"We've got listings for seven L. Garrisons in the greater Los Angeles area," the reference director downstairs was saying on the phone.

"Is there any way you can narrow it down any more than that? I'd rather not have to make seven calls and get six wrong numbers, maybe seven if this guy's unlisted." She looked down at the editorial assistant, who had positioned himself perfectly to see not just the parallel and serial ports in the back of her computer tower, but was almost certainly maneuvering himself to get a view of her own. "How's it going down there?"

"Almost there," he said, glancing up and smiling.

I'll bet, she thought. *And I'm wearing heels today so wipe that grin off your face while you still have one.*

"On the other hand," the reference director continued, "you could end up making just one or two wrong–number calls before finding the right one. Statistically, it could be anywhere in the list of—"

"Bill, don't get mathematical with me, just give me the numbers."

She started to write them down on a scrap of paper when the soon–to–be–married receptionist buzzed her line. "Just a second, Bill." She punched the second line. "Randall."

"It's Mike Devereaux. You got a second?"

"For you, Mike, anything. Just hang on." She clicked back to line one. "Bill? Let me get back to you."

She reached for line two again, smiling in spite of herself, anticipating what-ever news Mike was bringing. Despite having to change cubicles, despite the mixed–up boxes and over–eager receptionists and Leo smirking on the other side of the newsroom and an editorial assistant who was going to have to marry her if he got any more personal, these were the moments she lived for. The thrill of the pursuit, pushing herself to make the deadline, being the first person to find out who this guy was, and the knowledge that her article would be the first one to break open the story was more than enough to compensate for—

"It's the wrong guy, Susan."

"What?" She couldn't move. He couldn't have said what she thought he said. "What happened?"

As he recounted Garrison's statement, she sank lower and lower in the chair, the energy and joy of a moment earlier leeching away until she no longer cared if the editorial assistant saw things only her gynecologist and god were ever sup-posed to see. How could this be? "You're *sure* this checks out?"

"Positive."

"Damn."

"Yeah, that's pretty much how I feel about it. He's been transferred to County General, but he'll be out as soon as he can post bail on the assault and evasion charges. Anyway, I thought you'd want to hear the bad news before you locked down the next edition."

"I appreciate it, Mike. It's crummy news, but I'd rather pull it than go out with something that's wrong."

"Sure," he said. "You okay?"

"Fine, Mike. Just fine. If you get any more good news, I'll be up on the roof. You think a four–story drop is good enough to be fatal, or should I go across town to a taller building?"

"You could always jump off the *Times* building."

"No thanks, the metaphor's too obvious." She looked down to see the edi-torial assistant gesturing at her. "Listen, Mike, I have to go. Stay in touch."

"Will do."

She hung up and swiveled away from the desk so she could look to where Brian was untangling himself from the web of cords, plugs and cables. "What's the prognosis, doctor?

"You're all set, Ms. Randall," he said. "I had kind of a hard time reaching the modem plug, but I think it'll be okay."

"I appreciate the help, Brian. Thanks."

As he nodded and headed away, she discreetly checked south of the border to see if he'd gotten too excited by anything, but failed to notice anything amiss. Or atwitch, for that matter.

Get real, she thought. *You're fifteen years older than he is, he was almost certainly too busy down there to look at anything that didn't come with a UHL rating, and why the hell did that guy have to turn out to be the* wrong *guy?*

As she switched on the computer, she gazed wistfully in the direction of her previous cubicle, which now sat empty awaiting a decision from Rob as to which damned soul would draw the short straw and end up berthing next to Leo. She had been in that cubicle for nearly two years. Everything had been just fine while she had been in that cubicle. Now there was only Leo to soak up whatever good mojo still emanated from it.

On top of that, she hadn't head from Larry since that night they'd had dinner and he'd expressed the desire to return to his Cro–Magnon roots as a sexual hunter–gatherer. *Well, what did you expect? You told him to take a hike. He did. What part of that escapes understanding?* In truth she wasn't sure she wanted to hear from him, under the circumstances.

Except of course that *not* hearing from him indicated pretty clearly that she was more emotionally expendable than she had considered herself to be.

I wonder which stairwell door leads to the roof, she thought absently, then looked up as her computer beeped at her. She watched as her desktop wallpaper with the *Trib* logo appeared, relieved to see that everything seemed to be in order, having feared that the hard drive had been jostled in the move, deleting all the files she hadn't backed up for the last six months despite the ticker she'd put in the system's calendar to remind her every few weeks.

She clicked on her email icon. A window snapped into view, announcing YOU HAVE THIRTY–SEVEN WAITING MESSAGES.

She scrolled down the list of messages, seeing pretty much what she'd expected.

More spam.

Is your account really secure?

SusanRandall@newstribune.com, use the web to spy on your competitors!

Pursuant to our phone conversation last week.

Start your own web–venture on the net!

Do you want to know who I am?

She stared at the last entry in the list. She'd deleted it three times before, why was it still being sent to her? Normally spammers changed subject headers every day, sometimes every few hours, to get past the email filters.

She highlighted the messages and did a group delete.

For a moment, she had NO WAITING MESSAGES.

Then with a small incoming mail beep, a lone email reappeared on her screen.

Do you want to know who I am?

She frowned, realizing that it was probably going to keep appearing in her mailbox until she opened it and sent back a sharply worded *unsubscribe* message. Resignedly, she clicked the message number.

If this downloads a virus into my computer someone's going to die, she thought as the mouse hourglass turned, retrieving the email.

With a pleasant chime, the email appeared on her screen.

Oh my god, she thought.

> You don't know me but I thought I would drop you a line. I would say I would give you a hand but mine have blood on them. But you've heard that before haven't you? Nothing new under the sun as they say. Or in front of the moon. I have a shadow. Do you? My shadow says hello to your shadow. You may not think you have one but we all do. My shadow has been very busy. The Slasher is a stupid name but at least they got the S right.
>
> You may think I destroyed those people and that's right but I destroyed them with my mind. I thought them dead.
>
> I have been reading you and I think you are my kind of person even though you have fallen into bad company. Perhaps we should talk some time.
>
> So you will know this is me the number of the beast is 1127686705.

Susan stared at the monitor for a long moment before she could get her body to move again. Her heart was pounding so loudly that she could barely hear the usual roar of the newsroom in full swing.

Can't be. It's got to be a hoax.

She picked up the phone, dialed Mike Devereaux. "I've got a favor to ask," she said.

"Shoot."

"I've got a number in front of me, 1127686705, does that mean anything to you in relation to the murders?"

"Not offhand," he said. "Let me check around. What's up?"

"I'm not sure yet. Let me know what you find."

He hung up. She looked again at the message.

> You have fallen into bad company.

Was he watching her? *Does he mean Raymond? Or does he mean the police?*

Or was he simply playing mind games with her, to keep her off balance?

The phone rang at her elbow, startling her. She realized that she'd been reading and rereading the message for almost twenty minutes. "Randall," she said, unable to take her eyes off it.

It was Devereaux. "You got lucky. I figured I'd go back in chronological order, and I hit it the first time out."

"Hit what?"

"The last victim was born November 27th, 1968. 11-27-68."

"What about the rest?"

"The last five digits of the victim's social security number. So how'd you get this? We haven't released this information to the press yet. Or anybody else, for that matter."

"Let me get back to you," she said, and hung up.

She looked at the message. It could be real. And it could just as easily be a hoax. Granted, it contained information that hadn't been released to the public, but it *was* stored somewhere in the LAPD's computer system, otherwise how could Devereaux have located it so quickly? A determined hacker could easily crack the database, especially in a case like this, which always brought out the whackos, flakes and murder–groupies. Six months earlier, during yet another showdown between the U.S. and Iraq over weapons inspections, the *Trib's* political writer Mike Durang had come within an inch of being fooled into believing that he was getting regular inside information from a source deep within Saddam Hussein's military headquarters...only to discover it was a high–school student who was cutting and pasting discussions from the Iraqi chat–channel on AOL.

So it *could* be a hoax.

But it could also be the real thing.

The question was: what should she do about it?

If this were the movies, she'd engage in a dialogue with this person, whoever it was, without telling her editor or the police, in order to make sure she had the exclusive on the story. Then she'd set up a meeting, thinking she could talk him into surrendering to the police, only to end up facing the business end of a chainsaw until Harrison Ford showed up at the last minute to beat the crap out of the killer.

But this wasn't the movies, she wasn't stupid, and as much as the idea appealed to her, Harrison Ford wasn't going to come calling anytime soon.

She also didn't want to get everyone excited if it turned out to be a hoax. She would need more information before she could legitimately ring the alarm bell.

She resolved to send just one message back, neutrally worded. If he replied with something that would confirm that he really was who he said he was, she would notify Rob, Rob would notify the *Trib's* legal staff, and they'd bring in the police to handle the rest. That was the only option that made sense. One message back was safe. It wasn't like he could kill her through the email. Bedsides, so far all the victims had been male. In theory she had nothing to worry about.

Yeah, and once upon a time everybody thought he was attacking only homeless people. Don't get stupid.

She hit REPLY, hesitated, then began typing.

> Message received. Sounds good but I'm still unconvinced. Can you give me something else? I wouldn't want this to be just a fib. I think fibbers should go to church. What do you think? Been to church lately?

She nodded to herself. The church desecrations had been expunged from the logs, so even a hacker probably wouldn't have access to that information. With any luck, if he really was the killer, that would prompt him into saying something that would confirm his involvement.

She hesitated just a moment longer, then sent the email, realizing just as it went that while she'd been composing the note she had been humming "Me and My Shadow."

She settled back in her chair, content to wait and see what happened next. She felt that she had made the right decision.

The next decision she would have to make was: what, if anything, should she tell Raymond? He'd called earlier, and she'd intended to call him back, but she didn't think she should tell him anything about the email until she talked to Rob, and she wasn't ready for that conversation yet. She'd give it 24 hours, then tell him.

She looked back at the message.

My shadow says hello to your shadow.

On reflection, she wondered: *was* Raymond the bad company he had mentioned?

Or was Raymond *her* shadow?

Raymond watched the evening news as a police spokesman explained that despite stories to the contrary, the subject of the highway pursuit was *not* wanted in connection with the Slasher murders. Which was just as he had expected. This would not be so easily resolved, certainly not by a car chase on national television. The Other was too subtle for that. When the time came, it would be a struggle on many competing planes. Spiritual. Psychological. Physical.

Of the three, he feared only the first two. Whether he lived or died was beyond his control. He had to be careful, though, not to let the Other consume his soul by causing him to abandon his cause, or his faith.

For the devil prowls the world, seeking to devour the innocent.

Someone would die again before too long. The Other would have to make sure everyone concerned understood that he was not so trivial a creature as the man they apprehended. And blood was the only language that could always be relied on to communicate that message.

He stood and stretched, his muscles sore from the rigors of the day. He needed sleep, he decided. As he switched off the television, he looked at the phone.

Susan hadn't called back. He had waited, but she had not called, as she'd promised she would. *Perhaps I was wrong about her, perhaps—*

He shook his head. *You're tired. You need to sleep.*

Yes, he thought. *But not quite yet. There is still much to be done.*

He shut down the lights in the front room and continued deeper into the small house, turning off lights as he went, until he reached the back room. There he stood before the body that lay without moving on a small bed. "I'm here," he said.

There was, of course, no response.

Prepared to Roar

Susan entered the lobby of the *News–Tribune* an hour and a half earlier than usual. If the email she was expecting had come in, she wanted the maximum amount of time to deal with it. On her way in, she stopped by the reception desk, where a temp was taking calls and opening mail.

"Any messages for me?"

The temp blinked at her. "And you are…?"

"Susan Randall."

"Oh, right…yeah, there were some…I think." She flipped through the piles of paper, magazines and pink message slips that covered her desk. "Right, here you go."

Susan took the messages, filtered out the ones that didn't belong to her, and handed them back.

The receptionist smiled and shrugged. "Oops."

I'll bet she thinks that little move is cute, Susan thought, and continued into the newsroom, reading the message slips as she went. She could understand the necessity of hiring from the bottom of the work force barrel while they looked for someone permanent, but she expected that being a carbon–based life form was the absolute minimum requirement.

She put the messages down on her desk—one from Raymond, another from Mike Devereaux, one from her car company asking if she wanted to extend her lease, still nothing from Larry—and switched on the computer. The list of email messages appeared a few moments later. At the top of the list was the one she'd been anticipating.

Re: Do you want to know who I am?

She tapped a key and opened the email.

I go to church but I don't think you'd approve of the way I leave it. They will find another one today if they are smart enough to look in the right places. He has blonde hair. You will know it was me because now his face ripples when you touch it. I think we should meet soon. I will tell you where and when.

She read the message twice before she sat back in her chair, noticing for the first time that every muscle in her body was tensed so tightly that they hurt.

It's him, she thought. *My god it is him.*

"Rob!" she called as she stood and hurried across the newsroom to his office. "Rob…we have to talk and we have to talk *right now*."

"Susan Randall, please."

"I'm sorry," the receptionist said, "she's in a meeting. Can I take a message?"

Raymond hesitated, then said, "No, that's all right, I'll try back later."

He hung up the phone, then slowly crossed to the closet, pulling out a jacket. He didn't know if she had decided to write him off, or if she was simply busy—either way it was already nine a.m. and he couldn't simply wait around all day for her to call. He had his own sources and his own methods; the investigation would go on, with or without her help. He tore out a newspaper article announcing the funeral for one of the latest victims scheduled for later this afternoon; he had to be there in case the Other made his presence known.

Raymond slipped the article into a shirt pocket and turned at the sound of someone knocking at the front door. *On time, as always*, he thought.

He opened the door and admitted Karl into the front room. He had his oversized medical bag with him, and nodded to Raymond as he entered. "I thought you'd be gone by now, I was just about to use the key." Karl had been raised in Moscow most of his life, emigrating shortly before the fall of the Berlin Wall, a history evident in his heavily accented English.

"I was delayed," Raymond said. "I was just leaving."

"Then it's time for the day shift to go to work, yes?" Karl began unpacking his bag, laying out a line of silver needles with loving care. "I will take this from here. You go on to your work, I will attend to mine." With that, he continued into the back room, with its waiting, motionless patient.

Raymond stepped out of the house and walked toward his car. Karl knew what had to be done, he had been doing it for a long time now, and there was no one better suited to the task. Raymond would only get in the way.

"Do you know why this individual would want to contact you, Ms. Randall?" The detective from the LAPD special crimes unit, Lieutenant Simon Trask, sat in the conference room on one side of the long, polished, dark wood table that dominated the room. Susan, Rob and the *Trib's* legal counsel, Herb Barnett, sat on the other side of the table. Trask was a thin, severe looking man, in direct contrast to Herb, who was round and balding and knew more bad jokes than Susan had ever heard.

"Specifically," Trask continued, "why you in particular? There are several hundred journalists covering this story. Why you, and not the *Times*, or the AP, or CNN?"

"He said he liked my work," Susan said. "Who am I to get in the way of his one show of good taste?"

Trask noted her response with the same unreadable expression he had worn since arriving twenty minutes earlier. She had turned over the emails, offered full and complete cooperation, and yet he still looked at her as if she were actually the guilty party. *All part of the act*, she reminded herself; it was their game face, the one they wore all the time to convince suspects to confess. It was understandable; Susan knew that in many cases the person who suddenly came in with apparently good information was actually involved in the crime, whether directly or indirectly, and hoped to use that inside information to misdirect and confuse the investigation.

Nonetheless, she felt happier for having legal counsel present during the discussion.

"I don't want to be seen as beating a dead horse, Ms. Randall, but I want to pursue this a little further. You must understand that to date, the suspect has not attempted to contact anyone: not law enforcement, not the media, no one. This is a significant divergence from his pattern to date. It would help if we could determine what made him change tactics, what drew him to you in particular."

"I wish I could help you, Lieutenant, but right now your guess is as good as mine." She was deeply conflicted about whether or not to mention Raymond. It was altogether possible that the killer contacting her had nothing to do with Raymond. She also couldn't fight the feeling that she would be getting him into trouble if she mentioned his name. Besides, for the time being at least he was only a source, and she always protected the identity of her sources.

"Is it possible—I'm not even asking if it's *probable*, is it just *possible*—that the person who sent you this email is someone you know? A serial killer works from a very complex viewpoint, one that is extremely personal when it comes to people he likes, and totally depersonalized when it comes to victims and the rest of the world. So I can't help but wonder if there's some kind of personal connection."

"If there is, I sure don't know about it," Susan said.

Herb Barnett leaned forward. "I don't think that any further questioning along these lines is germane to the investigation, Lieutenant," he said. "It's altogether possible that Ms. Randall was totally at random. It's also possible that half the crime reporters in town got this email, and she's the only one with the integrity and honesty to let you guys know about it. Either way, I don't think that it's fair or appropriate to question her personal life or personal connections."

Lieutenant Trask nodded absently, but didn't change expression. "Have you received any further communications from this individual?"

"No, none. I checked my email about five minutes before you got here, nothing. Do you still think it might be a hoax?"

"We have to consider every possibility. We're currently logging several hundred phone calls a day. Most of them are tips that go nowhere. Others are accusations, somebody doesn't like the way his neighbor looks at him, and calls us to say it's the killer. We've had two more people beaten because somebody thought they might have been the Slasher. In at least one of those cases the problem was caused deliberately by someone with a grudge against the victim. People are scared, they're panicking, and there are plenty of other people out there who'd like to take advantage of that and fuel the fire. So you'll understand that I have to approach everything right now with a dose of healthy skepticism."

"What about the body he described in the last email? He said the victim was blonde—"

"If there's been another killing, we certainly haven't heard anything about it yet. Until we do, that comment goes into the *interesting but not yet significant* pile."

"Something I don't understand," Rob said. "You've got this email. Why don't you just backcheck the email address and find out who owns the account that sent it?"

"We tried that as soon as we got her call," Trask said. "The individual sent both pieces of email using an anonymizer, a second party server that lets you log on anonymously, create any kind of address you want, and send it out through their server. Unless you register using your real email address, any email you send can't be traced back beyond that point."

"But he had to register under *some* kind of email address, even if it was fraudulent, right?" Susan asked. Trask nodded. "So what was that address? I mean, that should tell you something about his mindset if nothing else."

"The email address logged with the anonymous server was Susan Randall, at newstribune.com. So we end up going full circle."

He paused then as his cellular phone rang. "Just a second," he said, and snapped it open.

As he talked quietly with whoever was on the other end of the line, and Herb and Rob conferred beside her, Susan considered what the hell it might mean, if anything, that he had chosen her address to use as his own. For some reason, it chilled her to think that he had logged her name into an email service without her ever knowing about it.

Trask closed the cell phone and slipped it into his jacket pocket. "I'd like permission to set up an email tap, so whatever comes into your mailbox gets routed to us first."

Herb Barnett shook his head. "Not possible. Inappropriate intrusion into the fifth estate. Ms. Randall receives emails related to other stories she's writing, and to give the LAPD carte blanche to view those emails would compromise those sources and amount to a fishing expedition."

"We wouldn't be looking at any unrelated emails," Trask said.

Barnett smiled. "I have a five–year–old at home. He always promises he won't lick the chocolate off one of my wife's cakes if we leave it out on the counter before dinner, and every night I get cake with tongue marks on it." He shrugged. "I'd rather not put that temptation in front of the LAPD. If we get another email contact, we'll forward it to you immediately."

"An email tap is a lot of work," Susan said. "What would make you ask about that when you're saying it could still be a hoax?"

"I just got a call from downtown," Trask said. "We found another body. Turns out a guy who owned a car wash in Burbank didn't show up for work today. When they went to check in on him, they found him dead in his bedroom. His face was slashed. And he was blonde, just like in the email. No one else could have known that but the killer.

"Congratulations, Ms. Randall, you've just won the psycho lottery."

Leo Dexter was putting on his coat, getting ready to meet a contact at Universal Studios for lunch—apparently someone had closed a deal for Travolta to star in a remake of *Willy Wonka and the Chocolate Factory*, and he wanted to set up the first interview with Travolta to break the news—when the temporary receptionist entered, carrying a pink message slip. She wandered over to Susan Randall's empty desk—her *old* desk, he reminded himself with a thin smile—and looked around, confused.

"Mr. Dexter?"

"Yes?"

"Do you know where Susan Randall's desk is? I checked the roster and it's supposed to be right here, but it's empty."

Leo nodded and smiled paternally, thinking, *It must be terribly difficult going through life with an infirmity like that. To be born and discover to your horror that you have a tiny piece of brain lodged in your skull....*

"She's moved," he said. "If you need her I think she's in the conference room with Rob and some others."

"I know, but I was told they're not to be disturbed. But this message sounds kind of important. He told me to write down what he said, word for word. It's about a meeting."

Leo hesitated. It would be the easiest thing in the world to point to Susan's desk across the room and put the poor creature standing before him out of her misery. But he had caught a sense of what Susan was into, and had shaken his head in disgust. Susan's career represented the ultimate triumph of luck over ability, always getting the breaks that fortune denied other, more seasoned reporters.

But luck does have a way of changing from time to time, he thought.

"Tell you what," he said, "why don't you give me the message? I'll make sure she gets it as soon as she's out of her meeting."

"You're sure it's not a problem—"

"No problem at all," he said, smiling.

She handed him the message slip and raced back to the front desk, where he was sure the phone bank was approaching melt–down. When she was gone, he unfolded the message slip.

Urgent from the man with the Hands. I will give only one interview. To you. Tonight, six o'clock. Your safety is guaranteed. I need to talk to someone. The address given belonged to a low–rent part of town known for cheap bars, motels that rented by the hour, and tiny apartments in serious need of refurbishing, repainting and delousing.

In the end, he's just like everybody else, Leo thought. *He wants publicity. He wants to see his name in the paper. He wants to be famous. He needs to talk to someone, and he doesn't care who that is as long as he gets what he wants, no one does. I can give him that moment in the spotlight just as easily as Susan. Moreso, in fact. He can rant all he likes, I won't challenge him like she would. I'll just take down the conversation, thank him very kindly, run the whole thing, and turn everything over to the police. When they get him, it'll be courtesy of Leo Dexter, who will ask for repayment by having the first post–arrest interview with the killer.*

There was, to be sure, a certain level of risk involved. He couldn't ask for police escort because that would prompt them to ask how he got this information, and he'd lose the interview to Susan. He had handled himself in dangerous situations many times in the years before he'd been relegated by middle management to a position beneath his abilities. He felt reasonably sure that he could handle this one as well.

He would bring a pocket recorder, in case he missed anything. It would also give his story play on the other media. He could visualize the tape and a transcript playing on *Nightline* the next day. At last he would have the exposure he needed to get off this beat and onto something more rewarding, with greater attention, money and prestige.

He would also bring a gun.

Because Leo was many things, but he prided himself on the fact that he was most definitely *not* stupid.

Never go into the lion's den unless you're prepared to roar, he thought, and headed out for lunch.

The funeral for Steven Banks went just like all the others. Lines of waiting limos, cars and taxis, rows of seated mourners, of which an ever–growing proportion were almost certainly undercover police, and an equally expanding number of reporters, isolated from the bereaved by groups of police and security guards. Raymond watched the proceedings through binoculars, keeping low and near the trees that covered the cemetery. He couldn't hear what was being said, but he didn't need to.

He'd heard it all before, too many times. Too *damned* many times.

As he watched, he was annoyed to find his thoughts returning frequently to Susan. There was no question in his mind that there was a demonic influence involved in these murders. But with every passing day, he became less sure that he could ever convince her of that. Perhaps that was why she had fallen out of contact; perhaps she had written him off as a nut who saw devils under his bed at night, and decided that spending her time with criminologists and psychiatrists and psychologists would be a more fruitful means of pursuing her investigation.

And can you really blame her? he thought. Fifteen years ago, before he had seen the things he had seen, would he have believed any of this? *No, I wouldn't.*

It was the reasonable reply. Unfortunately, it didn't do a thing to improve his mood.

Raymond peered through his binoculars as the minister finished his service and closed the bible in his hands. Then a young woman with auburn hair stood and, carrying a single rose, approached the coffin that sat closed beneath the white tent. *Girlfriend,* Raymond thought sadly.

As she reached the coffin, she hesitated, and spoke to the minister, who looked with uncertainty to the attendants from the funeral home. He couldn't read her lips, but her meaning was clear from her expression and the way she kept glancing at the coffin. *I'd like to see him, please, just one last time, to say goodbye.*

There was some discussion among the attendants and the minister, then one of the attendants nodded and moved to the coffin, which had not yet been sealed in preparation for delivery into the ground. He turned several screws at either end of the coffin, and gently popped the lid.

The young woman screamed. Raymond could hear it halfway across the cemetery.

What the hell...?

Mourners rose, shouted, raced toward the coffin or ran away in fear. There was movement and confusion and suddenly police were there, blocking off access to the coffin and the grounds.

Raymond struggled to hold the binoculars still, desperate to see what was inside the coffin that could have triggered this reaction. But he was at the wrong angle, the view too shallow to see inside.

Reluctantly, he stepped out of the shadow of the covering trees and ran further up the hill, knowing that he was exposing himself to possible discovery. *I just need one more minute, just one.*

He peered through the binoculars again and focused on the coffin. The young woman was on her knees, sobbing, in front of it. He looked past her.

Inside the coffin, a crown of thorns made of glittering razor wire had been shoved onto the head of Steven Banks.

Then he heard a second commotion, and swung the binoculars around to see several plainclothes police officers pointing to the hill where he stood.

Damn!

He moved back and away, retreating as fast as he could toward the opening in the fence where he had secreted his car, hoping that he had enough of a lead to get away. He couldn't afford to answer any inconvenient questions right now.

He could hear them shouting as he reached his car and climbed in, starting the engine before he'd even closed the door. He guided the car off the shoulder and onto the road, flooring the gas. He was already rounding the corner when he looked back and saw the plainclothes police coming up over the hill, then disappearing from view as Raymond turned a corner in the road and aimed for the freeway.

He was there, Raymond thought as he drove. The body had been on display during the memorial services earlier, after which the coffin was closed in preparation for burial. The only way the crown of thorns could have appeared on the body was if someone had slipped into the preparation room and placed it there during the forty–five minutes between services.

He was there. He was there and I missed him. He had been somewhere amid the crowd of mourners and attendants and others, and Raymond had not seen him. How many other times had they been in the same place, at the same time, and just missed encountering each other? And for each missed opportunity, someone else would have to die.

He cursed under his breath, annoyed that he had been seen. They might decide he was nothing more than a macabre curiosity seeker, but he couldn't risk attending any more funerals. They'd be watching now, and security would be even tighter. He gripped the steering wheel hard, realizing he had missed a crucial opportunity, not knowing when he might have another chance to get this close.

It wasn't like the Other was sending out invitations, after all.

Leo stopped the car in front of the address written on the pink message slip. It was not an area he found himself visiting very often, a four–block neighborhood on the border between East LA and Hollywood where you didn't want to linger if you didn't live there. It was already dark, most of the residents having retreated for the evening behind chain link fences and locked doors. There was the smell of food in the air, and the flicker of TV screens past barred windows and thin curtains.

The house at the indicated address hunkered low behind a chain link fence that was missing a gate. The grass had already turned a faint yellow–brown, and the windows were covered by drawn blinds that obscured the rooms within.

You're out of your mind, Leo thought, fully aware that there was fear not far beneath his determination. For a moment he reconsidered the whole idea of going into that house. But he had taken reasonable precautions. The gun nestled in his jacket pocket, loaded and cocked, even though he knew that carried risks of its own. Better to nick himself in the leg than be carried out in a body bag, he had decided. And he had left a message on his voice mail that indicated where he had gone. For additional safety he'd told a friend to dial that number and punch in his access code if Leo didn't call in by seven thirty. The message instructed his friend to call 911 and send the police to the scene immediately.

He had covered every base he could think of.

But he still hadn't gotten out of the car.

She'd be halfway in the front door by now, he thought, and decided to stop thinking and do something for once.

He switched on the tape recorder, climbed out of the car, closed and locked the door, and started up the walk toward the small house.

At the door, he knocked. Twice.

He waited.

There was no reply.

He knocked again, then peered in through a space between the window and the blinds. The window was dirty, nearly impossible to see through, and the room beyond was dark.

Nothing moved inside the house.

For the first time it occurred to Leo that it was quite possible that the temp receptionist had gotten the address wrong.

When he cautiously tried the door, and found it unlocked, he began to suspect that this was, indeed, the wrong address, that he was standing on the threshold of an empty house. He wasn't sure whether to be irritated or relieved, and decided to go for both.

He started to turn away, then decided that it wouldn't hurt to look inside, just to be sure.

He pushed the door open and, one hand on the gun in his jacket, moved a few inches into the house.

"Hello," he said.

There was no reply.

"Anybody home?"

Nothing.

Okay, we're done, he thought, and started to turn away.

Then he stopped at a sound.

He paused, and listened. Yes, he was sure of it now, there was definitely something moving inside the house.

He squinted into the darkness.

He could almost see what it was.

They've Got Something

Susan knew something was wrong when Rob called her into his office the moment she arrived; knew that whatever was wrong was serious when she saw Lieutenant Trask waiting there with him. But she couldn't have imagined the first words that Rob would say when the door closed.

"Leo's dead."

She could imagine a car accident or a mugging in the middle of the night as Leo left a strip joint or a massage parlor, could imagine him falling downstairs or having a heart attack or choking on a chicken bone, but she *couldn't* imagine what any of those could possibly have to do with *her*. Then Trask explained what they had managed to reconstruct of the last hours of Leo Dexter's life: the 911 call from a friend when Leo had failed to check in by seven–thirty, the squad car that arrived minutes later, scouring the area and finding nothing, until the smell of blood prompted them to pull up the floorboards, where they found what was left of him.

Trask left out most of the details concerning the condition of the body, what had been done to it, and how, and with what level of enthusiasm. But what he left in, combined with what she knew of the prior murders, was more than enough.

I'm going to throw up, she thought.

She looked out the window to the newsroom, which was filling as other staffers arrived. They glanced furtively at the closed glass door, at the expression on Susan's face, and looked quickly away again, none of them venturing near. *They can smell blood*, she thought, and fought the bile rising in her throat as the phrase conjured up images of Leo's body under the floorboards.

Leo was an asshole. He had proved that in the way he lived his life and the way he went to his death. He wanted to undercut her, to use her resources for his own benefit. But he didn't deserve what had been done to him. No one did.

Susan nodded to the newsroom. "Do the others know?"

"Not yet," Rob said. "I wanted to talk to you first."

"We've held off releasing his name to the press until we can notify his next of kin," Trask said.

Susan turned away again, looking out the window to where Leo's desk sat conspicuously empty. She couldn't remember him ever being late for work. No matter what Rob had or hadn't told the others, if they hadn't gotten at least a sense of the problem by now, they didn't deserve to be called journalists.

He screwed me again, she thought, anger finally burrowing out from under shock and grief. All her carefully worked out coordination with the police was eliminated in one night because Leo had swooped in and stolen the lead. Worse still was the realization that if he had not intruded, had not kept the message to himself, the police might have had the information and the opportunity needed to catch the killer.

Now, instead of being in a jail cell awaiting trial, the killer was free, and he was angry, and there would be even more murders. In his stupidity, his jealousy and his ambition, Leo had ensured not only his own death, he'd all but guaranteed that he would not be the last victim.

"There's something else we need to consider," Rob said. "A big unanswered question. Did this guy kill Leo out of rage and frustration when he realized it wasn't you? Or was he intending to kill you all along, and settled for Leo as a consolation prize when he couldn't get to his primary target?"

"I don't know," she said.

"What's your gut feeling?" Trask asked.

"Right now, all I feel is numb."

Rob nodded distantly. "Yeah, I know how you feel. I'm right there with you."

He walked across the office until he stood in front of her. "So I'm hoping you'll understand my reasons for what I'm about to do."

"Rob, don't—"

"I'm taking you off this story for a while, Susan."

"You can't do this to me, not now—"

"This isn't a discussion. We've got a serial killer out there who's taken out one of my writers, I won't let him take out another."

"Leo was stupid—"

"Yes, he was. But that doesn't change the fact that he intercepted a message that was meant for *you*. You've drawn his attention, and from where I sit that's unacceptably dangerous. If we take you out of the line of fire for a while, with luck he'll lose interest and go somewhere else."

She could see that Rob had dug in his heels, and looked to Trask for support. "Lieutenant, I'm the only person this guy's tried to contact. If we can keep him talking, maybe we can draw him out, get him to make a mistake. Isn't it worth the risk if we can help nail him?"

Trask shook his head. "Before you got here, I asked Mr. Klein to check your email, determine if any further communications had been received."

She shot Rob a look, but before she could protest he jumped in. "It's a company computer, a company account, you know all email on that account is company business and subject to examination. But I give you my word that nothing was read that shouldn't have been."

"Doesn't matter in any event, because there was nothing waiting for you," Trask said. "He has not attempted to make any further contact with you since last night, and I do not believe he will make any such attempts in future. As far as he's concerned, his pipeline to you has been compromised; he knows that if Leo Dexter got that message, then anything else he sends might be diverted. If I genuinely thought he might attempt further contact, I might consider leaving you in the loop. But I simply don't think that's going to happen now."

"But what if it *does?*"

"If it does, if he in any way tries to initiate contact, you are to notify us at once, for your own protection," Rob said. "Lieutenant Trask has assured me that if that happens, he will assign you round–the–clock police protection. Meanwhile, you're off this story, at least for now. I suggest you take a few days off, get out from under, clear your head. I'll assign someone else to write up whatever pertinent facts the Lieutenant wants us to release, and rotate the police beat coverage for a little while, just until we can cool you off in this guy's head."

"We've put the other papers on notice in case he tries the same thing some-where else," Trask said.

She pulled her hair back from her neck, suddenly tired. "He won't. This was aimed at me."

"Then as far as I'm concerned, my decision was definitely the right one," Rob said. "And it's final. I value you as a reporter, as a member of my staff, and as a friend. I won't risk losing all three of you."

She met his look, and recognized it; it was the look that said she could sooner change the course of a river than alter his decision. "Okay," she said, at last. "Anything else?"

"No," Rob said. "That'll do it."

Susan rose and stepped out of the office. The newsroom was unnaturally quiet as she headed for her desk. Behind her, Rob stood in the doorway, and called out to the rest of the staff. "If I can have your attention, there will be a general meeting in twenty minutes. We'll use the big conference room, and this is mandatory attendance, people."

Then he stepped back inside with Lieutenant Trask, closing the door behind him.

"What's all that about?" Susan looked up as Sandra Mitchell, one of the *Trib's* staff photographers, crossed the room to her.

"I...think Rob needs to be the one to talk to everyone, not me," she said, then paused to look at her old desk, now empty, next to Leo's, which was now just as empty.

What did it all accomplish? she wondered.

What the hell were you thinking?

Rob and Lieutenant Trask looked out the office window as Susan walked to her desk, picked up her papers, and continued out the door.

"She took that better than I'd expected," Trask said.

"She's a good reporter. Maybe one of the best I've got. That makes her a professional."

"Then we won't have a problem with her?"

Rob hesitated before saying, "Probably not." Sometimes being a professional and presenting a problem were different things, and sometimes they weren't. Rob didn't know for absolute certain which way this would cut—Susan was her own person, and damn the consequences—but he wasn't about to tell Trask that.

"Then I'd better get back to the office." Trask rose, picking up his briefcase. "You need anything else from us?"

"Not at the moment, Mr. Klein. We have a lot of work to do, and I should get to it"

"I should imagine so," Rob said, rubbing at the back of his neck. He was already bone tired, and the day had barely begun. "Especially since I hear the killer was a lot more vicious than before."

Trask stopped at the door. "Where did you hear that?"

"You know better than that, Lieutenant. The reason I'm asking is, when somebody like this gets messy, sometimes he gets sloppy, too. That's what you've been waiting for, isn't it? For him to get sloppy, to make a mistake?"

"So?"

"So did he?" Rob asked. "Did he make a mistake?"

"I'm afraid I can't comment on that," Trask said, opening the door.

"Funny thing about *no comments*," Rob said. "I mean, don't you think it's kind of funny how *no comment* almost always ends up translating into *it's true* a few days later?"

"At this precise moment, Mr. Klein, I can't think of one damned thing about this case that can even remotely be called funny," Trask said, walking out of the office.

Rob settled behind his desk, watching Trask move through the newsroom. *They know something, all right. But what? And how?*

Then he looked across the room, and saw the others starting to file into the big conference room, where he would have to break the news about Leo in just under five minutes. He sighed.

You died badly and you died stupid, Leo, he thought. *Let's just hope some good comes out of it.*

Sergeant Mike Devereaux filed into the ready room along with the other officers and detectives assigned to the Slasher case, settling into one of the small desks that had been arranged in neat rows extending from the dark wood podium at the front of the room. A green chalkboard ran the length of the front wall, the other walls covered with maps, photos, and posters announcing blood drives and urging contributions to the police fund. When he'd been told to report to the meeting, he was also instructed not to tell anyone who wasn't directly involved with the investigation.

Something's up, he thought. *Maybe we've finally got something.*

A moment later, Lieutenants Trask, Pierce and Firelli entered, taking up position at the podium. Devereaux could feel the energy in the room jump as they came in together. *Yep, they've got something, all right.*

"We'll keep this brief," Firelli said. "As most of you know, we had another serial murder last night. What is not generally known, and which will not be repeated outside this room by anyone who does not want to lose his badge, is that we have a recording of the killer's voice."

There was a stir among the officers seated and standing along the back wall. Firelli waited until they settled down to continue. "The victim, Leo Dexter, a reporter with the *News–Tribune*, was carrying a micro–recorder. He was wired for sound, and the recorder was active at the time of his murder."

Goddamn, Devereaux thought.

Firelli pulled out a micro–cassette recorder and held it above his head. "This was found on the body. It had apparently gotten tangled up in his jacket pocket during the struggle, which may be the only thing that saved it from discovery. It also muffles out some of the sound. But we were able to pick out a few things."

Trask picked up the thread. "We're going to play this for you now. Even aside from the problems mentioned by Lieutenant Firelli, the sound quality isn't great, about what you'd expect from a recorder hidden inside someone's jacket. We want you to listen to this voice very carefully. It's one of two ways we may have to identify the killer."

Two ways? Devereaux wondered. He was about to ask what the other way was when Firelli pushed PLAY.

For a few moments, there was silence, just tape leader. Then a CLICK as the recorder had been moved into RECORD, followed by the sound of a car door opening and closing, and footsteps on a sidewalk. Devereaux could just make out the sound of traffic in the background.

He strained to hear, and was momentarily startled by the sound of a knock, clear, hard and loud. There was a pause, then from the tape, a voice calling, "Hello?"

They looked to Firelli. "This is the victim's voice."

There was a long pause, then another knock.

A long moment passed with painful slowness.

"Anybody home?"

Another long pause.

Then Devereaux heard something moving. He leaned forward in his desk, straining to hear. It was something between a scraping and a dry, whispery sound.

Dexter's voice shuddered on the tape. "Oh my god—"

Then: sudden movement, a flash of sound he couldn't identify, and the thud of someone hitting the floor.

The tape warbled inside the machine, as if it were being knocked around, jerking back and forth across the recording heads with each impact.

"The next few minutes are dead, so I'm going to fast forward past that," Firelli said, as he scanned ahead. "We believe this is when the body was moved such that the recorder was in a position to begin picking up sound again."

He clicked on PLAY.

For a long moment, there was just the static hiss of dead tape. It filled the room, every officer utterly silent, straining to hear.

First there came the sound of something hard hitting something soft, followed by a wet scraping noise.

Devereaux felt his stomach lurch. He had heard that sound before, when he was a kid, working part time in his father's butcher shop. It was the sound of a large blade striking deep into dead meat, then moving across bone to pare away the flesh. The sound was slow, deliberate, methodical.

Then: a voice.

He closed his eyes, fighting to separate the voice from the surrounding sounds. It was a dry, thin voice, somewhere between a rasp and a lover's whisper. There was a hollowness to it, and a slight echo. It could almost have been two voices, speaking as one.

It was repeating something, over and over. Devereaux caught only parts of it. It took three times before he could put it all together.

Hello, Raymond, the voice was saying, over and over.

Hello, Raymond.

"Hello, Raymond," Firelli said, and switched off the recorder.

Devereaux was the first one to speak. "Who the hell is Raymond?"

"We don't know. One possibility is that we're dealing with a case of mistaken identity. It could be that he saw Dexter and mistook him for someone else."

"The other possibility," Trask said, "is that there are two people involved in this. Raymond could be an accomplice. We won't know what it means for a while yet. What matters is that we have a name we didn't have before, and we have his voice. We've sent a copy of the tape to the FBI voice identification lab in case they can add anything to what we've got here. They'll also digitize the tape and enhance it on the off chance that they can pick out any other background noises, like another person moving in the house, or anything that can lead to an identification. They'll also do a stress test on the voice, to see what they can find out there."

"We'll keep one other copy of the tape here for any of you to review at your convenience, but I'm sure you'll understand why we can't risk making any additional copies. The fifth estate has not exactly been our friend in this, and we can't afford any leaks that might scare our subject into going underground.

"Which brings us to one additional lead," he continued, pulling out a box containing several dozen sheets. "An intruder was sighted yesterday at the funeral for one of the victims. For those of you who haven't been briefed yet, there was also an...*incident* at that funeral involving the body of the recently deceased which convinces us that our suspect was present at the services. The two may be separate events, and they may not.

"This is a composite drawing made in cooperation with the two officers who sighted the intruder."

One of the officers looked up from the drawing in his hands. "Are you saying this is the Slasher?"

"Negative, we are not prepared to say that at this time," Trask said.

"At this time?" Devereaux took one of the drawings as they passed his row. "Does that mean you think it's *possible* that he's our guy?"

"All we're saying for now is that he's wanted for questioning in connection with this case," Firelli said. "Two other investigating officers have seen the composite drawing and can place this individual near at least two other funerals. He has also been seen loitering at or near the scene of three of the murders within twelve to twenty-four hours after the fact. If any of the rest of you can identify this individual in connection with any of the other murder locations, please notify either myself or Lieutenant Trask after the meeting.

"It's possible that this individual could be involved. He could also be a murder groupie, or have some other, personal connection to the crimes. So we need to determine, *quietly*, whether this individual could be the subject of our investigation, or an impediment to same."

"Distribute the composite to the lead officers under each of your commands," Trask said, picking up the thread. " Instruct them to approach this individual with caution. We don't know if he is armed or dangerous, but under the circumstances we would suggest taking reasonable precautions."

"That's all," Firelli said. "Hit the streets and stay alert."

The meeting broke up into pockets of excited conversation as Devereaux studied the composite drawing in his hands, committing every line and shading to memory, trying to move it from a two-dimensional sketch to a face he could recognize if he saw it on the street, or across the counter in a restaurant.

Devereaux estimated that the man who stared back at him from the sketch was in his early fifties, with salt-and-pepper hair, and a face that had seen rough times.

It didn't look like the face of a murderer.

But then, *most* murderers he had seen looked nothing like what a murderer was supposed to look like. *If they all looked like Charlie Manson, our job would be a hell of a lot easier. Depressing thing is, most serial killers look like they should be teaching grade school.*

And some of them do.

When he looked up again, he realized that he was the last person still in the room.

He stood slowly, easing his mass out from behind the desk, and carefully folded away the sketch of the man who just might possibly be the Slasher.

It was getting dark by the time Susan returned to her apartment, her legs sore from walking. Whenever things went badly, she would go up to Brand Park, north of Glendale, home to the Brand library with its Taj Majal–style architecture and several carefully preserved Victorian–era houses that had been relocated there over the years. It was one of the few places left in Los Angeles where you could go and pass time and without having to spend money shopping. She would walk until her anger and her recriminations and her confusion had been walked off.

In the last four hours, she had walked the length and breadth of the park, and had still not quite gotten it all out.

I need a hot bath, she thought, pulling off her shoes and dropping them by the front door.

As she passed through the small living room, she noticed the answering machine light blinking at her. She hesitated, then pushed PLAY.

"Hi, Susan, this is Larry. I'm up in San Francisco on business and I just heard about what happened to that guy at your paper, it's all over the news. I was just calling to—"

The phone was momentarily muffled by a hand placed over the speaker. She could dimly hear someone else's voice. A woman's voice. Then the sound cleared.

"—anyway, I'm just calling to see if you're okay. I'm going to be in and out for a while—"

I'll bet, Susan thought.

"—so it's better if I call you than if you call me."

Better so I won't interrupt you or have the wrong person answer the phone in your room.

"I'll be checking messages later at my place, so if you get this and want to talk, you know where to find me."

There was some fumbling with the line, then it hung up at the other end.

And now my day is complete.

She took the receiver off the hook and set it down by the phone, not interested in taking any further calls, live or on her machine, for at least the next two hours.

The world can wait, she decided, continuing on toward the bathroom and pulling off her clothes as she went. *It can also go fuck itself.*

Susan opened her eyes at the sound of someone knocking at her front door.

She sat up in the darkened bedroom, blinking at the clock. It was 7:30, less than an hour after she had come out of the tub, more wrinkled but considerably less pained than she had gone into it. She had intended to lie down for just a minute, to rest her eyes.

The knocking continued.

She pushed herself upright and stood, pulling on a robe. "Just a second," she called, padding out of the bedroom and into the living room, turning on lights as she went, then pausing to peer out the peephole before responding further.

She could just make out Raymond standing on the front porch.

"Raymond?"

He glanced up at the peephole at the sound of his name. "Are you all right?" he asked.

"Well...yeah, sure..."

"I heard about what happened, and I called to convey my sympathies. When the operator said your phone was off the hook, I thought I should stop by and make sure everything was all right."

"I'm fine. I just took the phone off the hook for a bit so I wouldn't be disturbed."

"Good," he said. "Can you open the door?"

She started to protest, then realized, *He wants to make sure nobody's standing behind me with a gun at my back.* For the barest moment, she found that strangely cute.

She popped the deadbolt and swung wide the door. "I'm fine, Raymond. Really."

He stepped in and glanced around briefly before nodding, satisfied. Then he turned to her and noticed her robe. "I'm sorry. You were asleep?"

"No, just...resting."

"Ah. I ask because all of your hair has moved to one side of your head, and that usually only happens when one is sleeping on it."

She smiled. "Okay, you've got me, I was napping. And don't apologize. Well, except for that bit about my hair. I appreciate the concern."

"It was not a problem." He stood in the middle of the room, looking just a little bit awkward being in her home with her in her bathrobe. "Well, I should go."

"No, it's okay. Look, you drove all the way out here on my behalf, I should at least make you a cup of coffee."

"It's not necessary—"

"If it were necessary, I probably wouldn't do it. Now sit. I'll be out in a second."

She crossed back into the bedroom, closed the door and quickly changed into a pair of slacks and a pullover shirt. She came out to find him standing in exactly the same place he'd occupied when she left. There were some times when he could be brusque and painfully to-the-point; yet at other moments there was something very formal and Old World about him. Almost courtly. She decided it gave him an air of strength and a kind of odd innocence, both at the same time.

"You have a nice place," Raymond said.

"Thanks." She crossed into the kitchen, searching for two clean cups and the coffee beans. "I've got Starbucks and Gevalia, any preference?"

"No, either would be fine, thank you."

"Then it's Gevalia," she said, dumping a half-cup of beans into the grinder.

After a moment, Raymond called again from the other room. "Actually, I lied."

"Lied about what?"

"When I said I had no preference."

She turned to find him in the entrance to her kitchen. "I was thinking perhaps it would be better if you got out of here for a while," he said. "If what I have heard is correct, you have had quite a day. You should not be alone at a time like this."

"Why not?"

"Because you will find yourself turning to guilt over the death of someone you did not like, running through the details over and over to see what you missed, what you could have done to prevent this from happening."

She stiffened, and turned her attention to the grinder. "And what makes you think I'm doing any of that?"

"It's what I have done under such circumstances," he said. "I was fortunate to have people who came and removed me from that state. Got me out into the world, to see that it still continued, because if the world could somehow continue, even knowing all the things in it that could go so terribly wrong, how could I do any less?"

She looked back at him, and decided there was truth behind his eyes. "I don't know...it's been a long day, Raymond."

"You need do nothing but sit. I will drive, I will take you to a place where there is good food, and I will return you home again before ten. I take it you have not yet eaten?"

"No, but—"

"Then we will go."

She hesitated, but the long walk at Brand Park had left her famished, and it wasn't as if this was the first time she'd gone to a restaurant with him and returned unmolested. *Besides, look at him, he's smiling as if someone* didn't *kill his cat this time, how can I say no to eyes like that?*

She stopped the thought at its source. *He's twenty years older than you, Susan, and he thinks there are demons walking around in the world in human form. Get a clue.*

Nonetheless, if she didn't eat something soon, she'd fall over. She glanced at the silent phone, now back on its hook. *And I'm not exactly drowning in other offers.*

"Okay," she said, brushing coffee bean grit from her hands. "Should I change?"

"Not at all. We won't go anywhere fancy."

"Good." She grabbed a jacket and headed for the door, which he held open for her, and stepped outside. As the door closed, she shot back a thought, *And screw you too, Larry.*

When Raymond said they wouldn't be going anyplace fancy, she had assumed they were en route to the nearest Hamburger Hamlet, or another deli. She hadn't anticipated a drive south into East LA, and a tiny, hole–in–the–wall Chilean restaurant. It was clearly a mom and pop operation, just a few small checkered–cloth tables in a rental space sandwiched between a bail bondsman and a pawnshop.

"You come here a lot?" she asked as they stepped through the door, a small bell announcing their presence. There were no other customers in the place.

"From time to time," Raymond said. "On special occasions."

She started to ask what made this a special occasion when the owner of the restaurant and his wife came out of the back, rushing toward Raymond with arms outstretched. The owner was Hector, a large man with a broad, smiling face and a loud voice; his wife Anna was a small, thin woman, more reserved but no less warm in her reception.

When Raymond introduced them he spoke in nearly flawless Spanish. Susan knew a smattering of the language, it was nearly impossible to grow up in Los Angeles without picking it up, but Raymond spoke it with a natural ease.

From the moment of their introduction, everything was a blur of food and music and wine and laughter. The couple were joined by their children, who ranged from about ten to late teens, who wandered in and out of the back room. Plates of home–cooked bread appeared on the table as if by magic, followed by crisp breaded cutlet and shredded beef with onions, peppers and tomato sauce, served alongside steaming bowls of black beans and white rice. Susan could pick up only a little of the exchanges between Raymond and the rest, but there was clearly affection here. They also seemed to be giving him a playful hard time about her presence; she got the impression he didn't come here with women very often.

When they brought the coffee and flan, Hector pulled Raymond aside and they spoke quietly in another corner of the restaurant. Hector had his hand on Raymond's shoulder, and his eyes burned with earnestness as he spoke. At one point, Hector pulled a crucifix on a chain out from beneath his shirt, and kissed it.

Susan glanced off to one side, and saw Anna watching the two men talking, her eyes moist. "What are they talking about?" Susan asked.

Anna, she had discovered, knew a little English, not much but more than Hector, enough at least to understand the question. She looked back at

Raymond, then at Susan. "Mano de los deos," she said.

Mano de los Deos? "Hand of God?"

Anna nodded. "Si. Hand of God."

And that was all she would say of the conversation.

At the end, Raymond reached for his wallet, but Hector waved off his attempt to pay for the meal. Raymond insisted, still in Spanish. Hector stood his ground. Susan got the impression that this was a common occurrence, one which had assumed a role of tradition between the two men. Finally, Raymond was persuaded to close his wallet, and Hector retreated to the back of the restaurant with a shout and an expression that was nearly radiant in victory.

Before she knew it, they were out the door again and heading for Raymond's car. She checked her watch; it was nine–thirty. Even with traffic she estimated they would be back by ten, as he had promised.

"Did you enjoy the food?" he asked.

Susan groaned. "I couldn't eat anything else right now if my life depended on it."

Raymond smiled. "Good."

"So let me guess: these are some of the people you've helped, right?"

"Yes, but not in the same way as now," he said. "It was—" He hesitated for a moment, then continued. "It was another life. I was a different person then."

"Do you know what they call you? The Hand of God."

"Do they?" he asked, and for a moment, his face seemed troubled.

"What? Is that significant?"

"Probably not," he said.

They continued past small houses on either side of the narrow street until they reached his car. As she climbed in and closed the door, she turned to face Raymond. "Three things," she said. "First: thank you. You were right, I need-ed to get out from under."

"It was my pleasure. And number two?"

"Number two—" she frowned and looked out the window. "Rob took me off the serial killer story today. He thinks with everything that's happened, it's too dangerous right now, and I should take a break."

"Perhaps he's right."

"Maybe. Maybe not. What do *you* think?"

"I think you have to do what your conscience tells you is right."

"I'm glad you feel that way," she said, "because that's number three. He took me off the serial killer story, but he didn't take me off *you*. I thought from the start that there was something interesting in your story, and I still do. So I'd like to stick around for a while."

"And the fact that I am looking into this situation, even if you are not, therefore keeping you close to what is going on without your having to violate the instructions from your editor is—"

"A happy coincidence," Susan said.

Raymond started the car and flipped the turn signal to pull out into the street. "Give me tonight to think about it," he said, pulling away.

"You've got a deal," she said, and rolled down the window. She closed her eyes and let the cool night air play over her face as he drove.

He didn't reach her apartment—being sure to walk her to her door before driving off again—until ten–fifteen.

Susan found she didn't care one bit about the extra quarter–hour delay.

Sometimes I Just Get Toast

The answering machine caught Raymond's message a little after eight a.m. *Meet me at St. Mary's at 28th and B Streets at nine. Dress casual.*

Susan was up, showered, dressed and tearing down the streets into the heart of downtown Los Angeles by 8:45. *Doesn't he know anyplace in the Valley?* she wondered as she hurtled down Hill Street paying only moderate attention to the colors in the traffic lights.

St. Mary's was a Catholic church built in the 1920s, when the neighborhoods surrounding the downtown area were quiet, peaceful little enclaves where people used to say hello to their neighbors as they walked to the corner store for groceries and a two–cent seltzer. Now many of these same neighborhoods were known for alleys littered with makeshift coke pipes made from spoons and soda cans, shooting galleries covered in used, broken needles, and the occasional drive–by shooting. Every day was a struggle between the forces of destruction and the residents who fought to clean up the streets, determined to make this a better place for their children.

Susan stepped into the otherwise empty church, heels echoing on the old hardwood floor. The scent of incense, old paint and Bible paper hung in the air. She thought the stained glass windows didn't quite fit their frames, as if they had been broken and replaced several times, and a moment later a slight breeze moved past her cheek in confirmation. She stepped past the rows of pews, their backs stained a darker black at regular intervals where generations of faithful had knelt and rested their closed hands to pray.

She checked her watch. He was supposed to be here, but where could he—

"The kitchen's out back."

She turned at the voice of a Hispanic nun who stood in the doorway behind her. "I assume that's what you're looking for," she continued.

"I'm not sure…I'm supposed to meet someone here."

"The kitchen's the only place where you can meet anyone right now," the nun said. "It's out that door and around the corner, in the back."

"Thanks," Susan said, and stepped out the back door into a small courtyard which led to a long, whitewashed building behind the rectory. Inside she found rows of folding tables and chairs, where groups of homeless people sat or stood lined up at the kitchen window, plastic plates and trays in hand. Another nun moved down the length of each table, depositing pints of milk at each chair.

When a clutch of homeless moved aside, she spotted Raymond seated across the table from three men, and moved toward him. He glanced up at her approach and nodded to the chair next to him, but didn't interrupt his conversation.

Of the three men, Susan guessed the oldest was in his seventies. Grizzled and bearded, he chewed at his corn bread open–mouthed, without modesty or front teeth. The two on either side of the old man were in their thirties; the one on the left looked as if he had been on the streets for only a few months; the one on the right had skin that had been leathered and darkened by years spent outside, his eyes a pale yellow–white against his weathered face. His clothes were street– and soot–blackened to the point where she couldn't tell what colors they had once been.

Raymond introduced them from left to right in the same tone she might use when introducing the board of directors of a Fortune 500 corporation. "Susan Randall, I'd like you to meet Jim Polachek, Alex Stein, and Will Kramer."

They nodded at her, and she nodded back, feeling slightly out of place and self–conscious in her freshly laundered and pressed clothing.

"I've been looking for Mister Stein here for quite some time," Raymond said. "Jim and Will here were able to help me locate him."

"He was sleeping in an alley just around the corner from where the first murder took place," Polachek said at the left. "He told a buddy all about it, and I told Will, and Will told Ray, didn't you, Will?"

Will Kramer, at the far right, barely nodded, his eyes fixed at a distant spot far away from anything Susan could see.

"Mr. Stein was just telling me about what happened that night," Raymond said, turning back to the old man. "Please, go on."

"I want another piece of corn bread," Stein said.

"Of course. Jim, can you give him yours? I'll tell Sister Margaret to give you another."

"I suppose," Jim said, reluctantly handing over his small piece of corn bread.

Stein took it and gnawed at it with satisfaction. "It's good corn bread," he said. "Sometimes I just get toast. Sometimes I get no toast at all. But mostly I get toast. It's cold. But at least it's toast."

He gnawed for a moment longer, then set it down on his tray. Susan noticed his hands were shaking. "It was warm that night, Mr. Weil."

Raymond nodded. "Yes, I remember."

"That's how I figured something was wrong. I was sleeping, see, down this alley off Vermont, well sort of an alley, it's really more of a...what do you call it? You know, where you got a narrow space between two buildings?"

"A breezeway?"

"Yeah, that's it, a breezeway. So anyway, I was sleeping, and I woke up because I thought I heard something. I'm good at that. You got to be on your toes if you're gonna live in the streets, let me tell you. Never know who's gonna be coming after you, and if you ain't paying attention, well…

"Anyhow, like I said, I woke up, and the first thing I thought is, It's cold. I mean, *cold* cold. I could see my own breath in front of me, like it was the middle of winter. But the sign on the bank across the street said it was, like, 68. Same time as that happened, I thought I saw a shadow."

"What kind of shadow?"

"I dunno, just a shadow. Something or somebody moved between me and the light across the street. Then it was gone. I thought, well, that's that, I can try to get back to sleep now, even if it is pretty damned cold, but then—"

He stopped, and looked to one of the men beside him. "I can't, this is crazy—"

"It's okay," Polachek said, "just tell him what happened."

Stein picked a piece of corn bread off his tray and chewed at it. "There were these…insects."

"Insects?" Raymond asked. "What kind?"

"I don't know, how the hell am I supposed to know? I'm not some kind of bug doctor. I mean, sure, some of 'em I recognized, you can't mistake a cockroach, no sir, no mistaking them, but there were all kinds of insects, everywhere, all over the alley, all over me, on the walls, on the ground, it was like they just came out of nowhere, they—"

"Mister Stein," Susan said, "I hope you won't mind my asking, but…had you been drinking that night?"

He stopped, and turned to her without meeting her gaze. "Yes, ma'am. I drink when I can. When I got the money, or when I can find half a can in a trash bin, but that's hard, you know, because lots of folks throw away half–finished cans of soda, or those little bottles of Perrier, but hardly anyone ever throws away half a can of Bud, you know? So yeah, I drink, and I drank that night. But the last drink I had was a long time before any of this happened."

He looked to Raymond. "On my mother's grave, Mr. Weil, I was sober as a judge when I woke up that night."

"I believe you," Raymond said. "Go on."

"I don't think I ever been so scared like I was that night," Stein said. "I mean, they was everywhere, you know? In my hair, on my face, in my pants legs, everydamnwhere. I was like to scream, but something in me said no, no, something's wrong, don't scream, don't do anything, there's something out here, something real bad and real close and you *don't* want to draw its attention.

"But somebody else, somebody else yelled, down around the corner. Then all the insects were gone, just like that. Then I heard something moving in the street, something heavy–like, and a cutting sound, and these…I don't know, like thumps, like something soft slamming into brick, and it was *really* cold now, Mr. Weil, I mean it was so cold I couldn't keep myself from shaking."

His jaw was trembling now, whether from memory or fear or a physical ailment, Susan couldn't tell, but he was caught up in *something*, that much was certain.

"Then…see, this is the part that makes me think maybe I'm losing my mind a little, because Mr. Weil, I looked up and I swear to god the bricks were bleeding. Right out between the cracks, out of the mortar, out of the lines in the plaster, I saw blood. And that's when I lost it. I couldn't stay in that place one second longer, no sir, I just…I screamed, and I mean *loud*, and I ran out of there and I started running and I didn't look back, not once, just kept running until I fell about two blocks further on. Next thing I knew it was the next day, and I heard about this guy getting killed not twenty feet from where I was sleeping."

"Did you tell the police what you had seen?" Raymond asked.

Stein nodded. "Tried to, anyway."

"What did they say?"

He glanced to Susan, meeting her eyes this time when he said, "They listened for a bit, then they said, 'Must've had a lot to drink last night, huh, buddy?'"

Ouch, Susan thought.

"It's okay," Stein said, looking away again with a shrug. "If somebody told me a story like that, shit, I'd think they were drunk or crazy or both. But I wasn't drunk, and I'm not crazy. I know what I saw."

"I know you do," Raymond said, standing. He reached for his wallet and pulled out three twenties, handing one to each of the three men. "Twenty as promised for the information, Mr. Stein, and your finders fees."

They tucked the money into their pockets. The man on the left, Jim, was the next one to stand. "I think I got some other people you might be interested in talking to, Mr. Weil. If you're still looking."

"I am. By all means, tell them I'd be happy to meet them. Good day, gentlemen."

Putting a hand behind Susan's back, he led her out of the kitchen into the courtyard.

"*Gentlemen?*" Susan asked. The church bell was tolling above them, echoing across the courtyard.

"They're fellow human beings. Respect costs nothing, and earns considerable dividends. These are men who are practically invisible to the rest of the world, unacknowledged except in campaign speeches, ignored on street corners, cursed and spit at for the crime of being underfoot, unemployed, displaced from the institutions where they could receive the treatment they need, beaten up and sometimes killed simply because they *are*, because they're in our line of sight, reminding us that there is a too–fine line of caprice and circumstance between where *we* stand, and where *they* stand."

"I don't need a lecture on the state of the homeless," Susan shot back. "I've put in my time in soup kitchens and places that make this look like the Hilton. That's not what I was referring to. I mean, come on, Raymond, these guys are hustlers. They were feeding you a line. They'll say anything they think you want to hear if it means separating you from twenty bucks apiece."

"You saw his face. Do you really think Stein was lying, just making the whole thing up?"

"I don't know," she said. "Maybe. I've seen street people who could give ten people ten different sob stories and make each one sound absolutely true, if it got them some money. And even if he is telling the truth, or what he *thinks* is the truth, consider the source. He's probably an alcoholic, he admits he was drinking earlier, and who knows what else he was taking, given his story. I mean, blood, insects, shadows…I'm surprised he didn't see pink alligators dancing the fandango."

Raymond stopped at a wooden bench in the courtyard and sat heavily. "All right," he said. "Suppose instead of all this, Stein had actually seen the murderer in action. Had seen the murder, right there in front of him, and gave you an eyewitness account: height, weight, hair color, clothing. Would you publish that? Would the police consider it a valid lead?"

She sat beside him. The bench was as hard and inflexible as Raymond seemed to her sometimes. "That's not the same."

"*Would* you?"

"I don't know."

He shot her a look.

"Okay, possibly. *Maybe*. And maybe the police might take down that information as one of a *number* of leads that could cumulatively point to the guilty party. His testimony would still be considered shaky by the DA's office."

"But he would still be called to testify, right?"

"I suppose. But again, we're talking apples and oranges. An eyewitness account of a crime, as opposed to—"

"As opposed to something beyond your experience."

"If you want to put it that way."

"Then where is the problem? In the testimony of the witness? Or in the limited extent of your experience that prevents you from accepting it?"

"That's a specious argument, Raymond. We all have a certain shared understanding about what is and isn't real."

"Do we?" He pointed to a statue of the Virgin Mary that stood in the center of a fountain at one end of the courtyard. "Several billion people believe that woman over there gave birth even though she was a virgin, that this child grew up to cure lepers and raise the dead, and that one day she bodily ascended into the sky long before NASA ever thought about such excursions. You look at that, and then tell me again about how we all share an understanding of what is and isn't real."

"You're talking theology again, Raymond. That has nothing to do with what we're dealing with here."

"No? I have a friend, a man I met once in New York, who says that in the final analysis, everything that happens comes down to mathematics. From population growth to relationships, it all comes down to the math, to the physics of the brain, to the random movement of subatomic particles whose existence cannot be proven, only accepted on principle. If I say that in the final analysis everything comes down to theology, how is that any different?"

"That's a rhetorical question, isn't it?" she said.

"Susan, if you go outside this courtyard and down that street, just a few blocks, you will find muggers, gang members, violence, drugs, prostitution…evil works through these things just as well as anything you might see in a painting by Hieronymous Bosch."

"Evil didn't create those problems, Raymond. Those problems create the evil you're talking about."

Raymond shrugged. "Well, there we have one of those unprovable chicken and egg questions. Which came first, the devil or the desire? At the end of the day, all I know is what I have seen, and what I believe. What concerns me is that important leads are not being followed because they are not believed."

"And you still think this all stems from somebody who's possessed."

"It fits with everything Stein mentioned. The sudden cold, the insects, the blood, the desecrations."

"Of which only the desecrations can actually be proven, and those can be explained in a lot of ways that don't involve demonic influence."

"I know, I know," Raymond sighed. She thought for a moment that he sounded a lot like Rob. *Do I bring that out in people?* she wondered.

He sounds so sure. But that's because he's going at it backwards, starting with a theory and making the facts fit the theory instead of starting with the facts and forming a theory that explains them.

"Well, we've done all we can here, we should go," he said brusquely, rising.

She stood, following him out of the courtyard. *This day didn't exactly get off to a rousing start*, she thought. Despite herself, she had been looking forward to spending the day in his company. Maybe it was the voice, maybe it was that he was old fashioned enough to open doors and escort her home as if it were a pleasure and an honor not a responsibility, and maybe she found something vaguely appealing about anyone who could be on this much of a crusade in a world where getting involved in other people's problems was considered passé. There was something of a knight errant about him that she found curiously appealing, especially in a town like Los Angeles, where it seemed some days as if everybody was out for himself.

Now she felt only vaguely annoyed, a headache starting to form behind her right eye.

Well it's still early, things can only get better, right?

Luanna Miller knocked at the door of her managing editor. In the two months she had been with the WNYN news team, she had only initiated two previous stories. One of them, an investigative piece into over–billing welfare patients by a local hospital, had gone nowhere. The other, an expose of a former football player who was using his new business venture as a front to sell coke, had earned her a fair amount of attention, credibility, and most of all, a new crop of sources.

One of them had called her, and arranged for a meeting in the parking lot outside the LAPD headquarters downtown. It was a long drive on short notice, but the piece of paper she held in her hand might just be worth it.

She studied the composite drawing of the man police were searching for in connection with the Slasher murders; the man who might, in fact, *be* the killer. Her source would not commit to that part of it, but he hadn't ruled it out, either. So it was *possible*.

Either way, the police were looking for this guy. She knew that the Powers That Be at the LAPD would be furious that this had leaked, but after all, the FCC had clearly mandated that it was the responsibility of a television station using public airwaves to operate in the public interest, necessity and convenience.

It was in the public interest for this guy to be found. The more people who saw this picture, the faster the LAPD would get hold of him for questioning.

As far as she knew, none of the other stations had this picture yet, but it was only a matter of time. Nothing ever stayed secret for very long in this town.

Better for WNYN to be the first station to break the story than the last.

Her editor's voice came through the closed door. "Come in."

She opened the door and entered, smiling.

With luck, they could have this on the air by the 6:00 news.

The hand–painted sign over the entrance to the tiny, red–and–yellow storefront on Sunset Boulevard announced MUAD EL–KHADALLI, PSYCHIC READINGS. Two narrow windows overhead indicated a small second floor apartment, where the owner of the store probably lived. This part of Sunset was as close as LA got to a tenderloin district, not far from where Hugh Grant had gotten popped for solicitation; an area populated by strip joints, leather stores, fetish shops, discount outlets for Doc Martins head–stompers, and one of the few remaining gay bath houses in Los Angeles.

Susan and Randall waited as Muad finished with his client, a heavy–set woman who carried a nervous–looking cat in her purse and wanted to know when she was destined to meet a fellow vegetarian who did *not* believe in reincarnation, the odds of which Susan placed at about zero.

Once she and her cat had departed, Muad turned the door sign from OPEN to CLOSED, and shook Raymond's hand. He was a thin man, with a pronounced Middle Eastern accent and a mustache that threatened to explode into a beard at any moment. She guessed he was either Palestinian or Syrian.

"How are you, my old friend?" Muad asked after Raymond had handled the usual introductions.

"Good. What do you have for me?"

Muad looked at Susan, amused. "You hear how he is? Some people will sit and talk with you as if they are actually interested in hearing how you are doing. They will make polite conversation, yes? With this one, it's always 'What do you have for me.'"

Raymond's expression didn't change. "So...what do you have for me?"

"See? As I told you." Muad sat tiredly on the bench that ran along the store-front window, which was decorated with astronomical symbols and charts and faux-psychic graffiti. He folded his arms and looked out at the street. "I don't know what I have," he said at last. "Something is happening. And that something is becoming a bigger something every day. You go out in the street, and you can feel it. You go sit in a restaurant and have a cup of coffee, and you can smell it. It's the people. Every day they get wound tighter, like a watch. Tense. Angry. And something more."

"What?"

"I don't know."

"Is that your opinion as a psychic?" Susan asked.

Muad turned to look at her, then jerked a thumb at Raymond. "My very attractive friend, as my not *quite* as attractive friend has already probably told you, I am no more a psychic than you are. But I do a good business. Also, I listen. I have sources. And people come to me."

He looked back to Raymond. "They tell me their dreams, they tell me what they are afraid of, they tell me things they don't tell their analysts, their wives, their husbands. And every day since the killings start, people come to me, and they say to me, 'Muad, I'm having nightmares.' They say to me, 'Muad, last night I had a terrible dream, what does it mean?' And I listen to this...*horror* that they describe, visions of death and fire and something stalking them from the shadows, and I tell them it's just—how do you say?—a *metaphor*, that it doesn't mean what you and I and anyone with any sense *knows* it means. I tell them it means good things are coming their way, that the death they see is just a symbol of the subconscious which always interprets change as the death of the old ways, as the tower of destruction is a symbol of change, not death.

"But I know better. Muad knows. But I also know that if I tell them the truth—that what they see in their dreams is like a canary in a mine shaft, that they are reacting to something the soul feels but cannot express in words, a sense that is telling them to get as far away from here as they can—they will not come to me any more. They will find someone else who will tell them that everything will be fine in the morning."

"What else?" Raymond asked.

"Little things, nothing I can point to and say, 'Go there, see this, talk to that person.' One strange thing, though. I have a number of wealthy clients, mostly women. They come to me because…well, because I am a handsome man and I cannot be resisted, but in addition to that, they come for what I can offer: someone who can appreciate them and nod and smile and help them feel good about themselves.

"Most of their husbands own big houses in Beverly Hills; they own planes, boats, major corporations. Last night, almost every one of them had a similar experience. Their security systems shut down, all at once. Half the security systems in Beverly Hills were completely out, non–functioning, for almost an hour."

"Why wasn't this in the news?"

"What rich man wants to call the newspaper and say, 'My security system isn't working?' You may as well hang out a sign that says 'Rob me.' The security company isn't volunteering anything because they want to protect the security of their clients, preserve their peace of mind. Sure, some people have probably heard about it, but no one's going to confirm it because everyone has a vested interest in saying everything's fine. They say it is a *non–repeating phenomenon*, that it will not happen again, and no one should worry. Who is Muad to say otherwise?"

Susan glanced over to see Raymond sitting quietly in a too–soft sofa, looking past them, deep in thought. "What is it?"

"I'm not sure," he said. "A thought, perhaps. Susan, how many homeless were killed?"

"Five."

"And then the killer began attacking average, middle–class citizens."

"Yes."

"How many victims to date?"

"Six."

Raymond shook his head. "Not six. Five plus one. Your associate was an afterthought, an anomaly, something that came up separately."

"Okay, assuming you're right, you've got five homeless and five middle–class victims, what are you…"

Her voice trailed off. Raymond nodded as he saw a look of understanding come into her face. "He's going to flip again," she said. "He's working his way up. Five poor, five middle class, and now, he's going to go after the rich."

"Exactly."

"And you think the massive failure of these security systems has something to do with it."

"Don't you?"

"One person couldn't do all this."

"That wasn't what I asked," Raymond said. "Don't listen to what your logic tells you cannot be. Follow your heart, because that listens to the logic of what *might be*, in spite of our logic. Does it tell you there is a connection?"

She reluctantly nodded. "Yes."

Raymond stood slowly, then turned to Muad. "I need to speak with Saddig."

Muad looked pained. "Not today. Today is not a good day. He is...nervous."

"All the more reason."

"Perhaps tomorrow. Come back tomorrow, and we can—"

"Now."

Muad appeared ready to continue the debate, but even he could tell that Raymond was not about to be talked out of seeing whoever it was he wanted to see.

"Go on, then," Muad said. "He's downstairs, same as usual."

"Thanks," Raymond said, and glanced to Susan. "I'll be right back," he added, and walked through a curtain into the back of the store.

As the curtain closed behind him, Susan turned back to Muad. "Who's Saddig?"

Muad paced to the curtain and back. "You remember I said that many people come to me, and that I do well at this, yes? So do you not wonder how I keep them, how I continue to do well even though, as I told you, I am not a psychic?"

"You're a good talker, I figured that was the secret."

He smiled, acknowledging the compliment with a nod. "You are a kind and generous soul," he said, "and in most cases, you are correct. But from time to time, even my nearly infinite charm is not sufficient, and something more is needed. I cannot always get by on my good looks, you know."

"I'm astonished," Susan said, playing along. "But that still doesn't answer my question. Who's Saddig?"

"Saddig is my brother. I brought him with me when I left Syria to come here four years ago. Saddig...he is the one who is psychic."

"So why isn't he helping you run the business, and taking some of the burden of flirting with all the pretty women? Why isn't he up here?"

Muad glanced back at the curtain that led to the back of the store, and the basement stairs beyond. "My brother," he said, very quietly, "is...not a well man."

Raymond edged down the narrow wooden steps that led into the basement. Very few stores or homes in Los Angeles had basements, due to the fear of earthquakes. But some of the older buildings, like this one, still had them. Raymond knew that was important. Saddig didn't like the light. The windows were painted black, the only illumination coming from a small night light at the top of the steps: a glowing miniature basketball that read BOSTON CELTICS 1998. He continued down the stairs, making his way down the steps more by touch than sight.

He stopped as his feet touched the dirt floor. The basement was cold, damp, and smelled of old clothes. "Saddig?"

There was silence, then something rustled in the shadows. "Yes?"

"It's Raymond."

"I know."

He caught another sense of movement, then the familiar silhouette of a man glided into the soft glow of the night light, stopping a few feet in front of him. Saddig was naked except for a pair of jogging pants, his hair a dark and unkempt tangle, his face drawn and pale. Raymond always thought his eyes looked wider and larger than they should have been, or could have been. They were the eyes of a man who had seen too many things that, once seen, could not be unseen again.

"How are you, Saddig?"

The answer that came back to him was thin and reedy, more an exhalation than a voice. "Tired."

"I'm sorry to hear that," Raymond said gently. "I'm sorry to disturb you. I hope you understand that I would not do so unless it were important."

Saddig looked at him but said nothing. Not for the first time, Raymond noticed that he hardly ever blinked.

"Did Muad tell you what has been happening?"

"The murders."

"Yes."

"He does not tell me. He believes these things disturb me. But I felt them."

"What else do you feel?"

"There is something out there."

"What can you tell me about it?"

Saddig looked away, his expression blank, lips moving quietly in the dim light. Raymond strained to hear what he was saying. "...and they came and they hurt Saddig and Muad was angry and they came to help him came to get him but Saddig was all purple, he was all purple and he couldn't hear them—"

"Saddig?"

He roused slightly, and finally focused on Raymond. He cleared his throat. "Sometimes it is angry," he said. "Sometimes it..." His voice trailed off. "When they had me in the other place, there was a man there. In the next cell. He would laugh, all night, all day. But the laugh was...wrong, somehow. One day, the guards came and they killed him, because that was the only way to make the sound go away, because it did not have any business being in this world. Do you know that sound, Raymond?"

"I think I do."

"That is the sound it makes when it is not angry."

"What else can you tell me?"

"It is not here for long. It has come and it will go when it is finished."

"Finished doing what?"

For the first time, Saddig looked away, looked down at the dirt at their feet. "I don't know."

"It's using someone, isn't it?"

Saddig nodded, then looked past him again. "Saddig looked, and Saddig saw, then Saddig went far away, far away, far away, where the white couldn't hurt him, where the white couldn't find him, where he couldn't hear the green…"

"Saddig? Saddig, listen to me, can you tell me who it's using?"

For the first time in a long while, Saddig blinked, his gaze returning to Raymond's face. "No. He is moving, all the time moving. It likes that he is moving. It likes him because he is empty, because the foundation was there and he was so easy to move into, and because…" He frowned again, looked back to Raymond. "Because no one sees him."

"What do you mean, no one sees him?"

"I don't know."

"Could you find out more if you tried?"

Saddig didn't answer.

"Could you?"

There was another long pause, then Saddig said, in a soft, low voice, "I like it dark. I like it dark because no one can see me unless I want them to. No one can hurt me."

Raymond let it go. *If you pushed harder to see, it would know you were here. It would see you. And it would hurt you.*

"I understand," Raymond said. "Is there anything else you can tell me? Anything at all?"

"All I know…is that there is something out there, right now, walking the streets. And it knows your name."

Saddig paused. "And it knows hers."

Muad was pouring tea into two small green cups. "After Saddig disappeared, I searched for him for two years. Then I found him in that…that *place*." His face darkened with the memory of it. "An *institution*, they said. A house of torture, I say. Lunatics, murderers, rapists, pedophiles, all locked up together, preying on each other. Saddig always had problems. But he was able to get by. Then they put him in that place, and by the time I found him, by the time we got him out…he was not the same person anymore. Something in him died in that place. And something else was born. And I do not think it was a fair exchange."

"Did Raymond have anything to do with—"

"I cannot talk about it. I'm sorry." He handed her a cup and sat across from her. "Promises were made. You understand."

"I think so."

Muad sipped at his tea. "Is the tea all right? I think it may be weak."

"It's fine."

"Good," he said, and let the silence return for a moment. "How long has he been down there?"

Susan checked her watch. "Twenty minutes." She set the cup down on the table between them. Outside the window, the pre–rush–hour rush–hour was beginning, cars choking the Sunset corridor as they tried to beat the very congestion they were causing. "So what can you tell me about Raymond? I get the impression you've known him for some time."

"Ten years." He studied her for a moment. "You like him, yes?"

"He's an interesting man. That's all."

"But you want to understand him, yes?"

"Yes,"

"Don't bother. Cannot be done."

She smiled. "He's that complex a person?"

"No. I said he cannot be understood. I *meant* he cannot be understood by *you*."

"Why not?"

"The people who come here mostly come alone, but sometimes they bring with them a friend, sometimes a brother, sometimes a sister…a boyfriend or a girlfriend or a husband or a wife. I call them come–alongs. As in, 'I have an appointment with my psychic, I know you don't believe in these things, but you might want to come along just to see how he works.' My client sits *here*, and the come–along sits *there*, and listens, and does not believe."

"Why should they? You said it yourself, you're not a psychic."

"It is not the point that they do not believe in me. I do not believe in me either at times, but I have somehow managed to convince myself that I exist. What I am saying is that they do not *believe*. In anything. They are like a radio that has unplugged itself from the wall, and demand to know why they cannot hear music."

He pointed at her. "You have unplugged yourself. You do not believe. And so you will never be able to understand him."

Susan's cheeks flushed with annoyance. "Where do you—"

Then Raymond came back through the curtain. "I think that's enough for one day," he said. "We should go." She thought he looked considerably paler and more tired than he was when he left.

Susan stood, picking up her bag. "What did he say?"

She caught a look pass between Raymond and Muad, then without looking at her, Raymond said, "Nothing that I could possibly repeat."

"Thank you for your time, Muad. If I need anything else, I'll be in touch."

With that, he stepped out the storefront door. Susan paused before following, and looked to Muad. "So after all this, he's not going to tell me?"

"That is not what he said. He said he could not *repeat* it. There are some things which, if I said them to you, I do not think you would wish to repeat them to another person, in polite company. As it says in the Bible, it is not that which goes *into* the mouth of a man that defiles him, it is what comes *out* of the mouth of a man that defiles him."

"In other words, he's either being polite, or he thinks I can't handle it."

Muad smiled. "It is as I told you," he said. "You will never understand."

Without bothering to respond, Susan walked out the front door, hurrying to catch up with Raymond.

We'll just see about that, she decided.

The long drive back to the parking lot at St. Mary's, where she had left her car, was conducted mostly in silence. She tried several times to start a conversation, only to be met with non–committal grunts or nods. Raymond's body might be in the car, but it was clear to Susan that his mind was somewhere else.

Probably still in the basement with Saddig, she thought.

It was almost six o'clock when they reached the parking lot, which was starting to fill with other cars for evening services and Bible study classes. "Well, thanks, it's been interesting," Susan said.

Raymond didn't answer. He was staring, preoccupied out the front windshield.

"You okay?" she asked.

"I don't know," he said at last. "I'm beginning to think it was a mistake to bring you into this."

"Raymond, I was covering the story long before I ever met you."

"I mean into *this*, into this side of it," he said. She noticed that whenever he became intense, his Austrian accent increased noticeably. "In a situation like this, there is much to be said for not being noticed by the powers that are at work. I anticipated that I would be noticed, it was only a matter of time. It is like the spider at the center of the web, if you step on the edge of the web, no matter how carefully you walk, the vibrations travel to that which waits at the center. But I had not stopped to consider that, in noticing *me*, it might also notice *you*.

"When I heard about what happened to your associate, I thought, perhaps it was a random selection, it could just as easily have been someone else, at another newspaper. But now, I have reason to believe that it has noticed you, that it knows your name.

"This," he said, slowly and pointedly, "is not good."

"So what're you saying? That I should stay home and lock the door and not go out again until this guy is captured, assuming that ever happens?"

"Would you do it?"

"No."

"Then it would not do me much good to say it, now would it?"

"Okay, here's something I don't understand," Susan said, "First, to be brutally honest with you, I still haven't seen one bit of evidence that corroborates your theory. *Everything* we've seen so far can be just as easily attributed to gossip, hysteria, or at the very worst someone who *thinks* he's possessed, which is a far cry from someone who really *is* possessed, which I don't believe in anyway.

"But just to give you the benefit of the doubt for a moment, if everything you're saying is true, the demonic influence, all of it, and if you're the only person who knows what's going on, then why doesn't this person just kill you and save himself a lot of trouble?"

"As I told you, this is a battle on several different planes. The physical is only a part of it. We are being played with in a game where we do not know what the stakes are, only that they are high. And with any game, there are rules. In chess, you can only capture or disable the king by surrounding him with hostile forces, you cannot simply kill him by taking him off the board."

"And you're saying that in this game, you're the king, is that it? Raymond, do you have any *idea* how grandiose that sounds? I mean, aren't we being just a little center-of-the- universe here?"

"Yes, we are all taught that we are fundamentally unimportant, aren't we? Taught that one person does not matter, that only groups, cities, nations count for anything. To believe the contrary, that the disposition of one soul could be of consequence, *that* is supposed to be unimaginable, egotistical, narcissistic. I say that the real problem is that we've forgotten how *important* we are, as souls, as individuals. *That* is the grandiosity of society, *that* is cultural ego at its finest, *that* is—"

"Raymond...please. I'm getting a headache here."

"All right," he sighed. "Look, all I am saying is that in this world, just as in the natural world, there are rules. In an exorcism, why doesn't the demon simply use the body to strangle the priest? Then it could remain in the body as long as it wants, do whatever it wants. It would be the simplest thing in the world, but it is not done. Why? Because the true battle is being played out on another level."

"I know, I know...'the person who's being possessed is not the actual target.' You covered that in Demonic Logic 101."

"What I'm trying to say is that murder is not the point of this, Susan. Whether a man dies today or tomorrow, we all die, we are all mortal. The devil does not care when you die, gets nothing out of it. A soul that is heaven-bound gets there whether he is killed or dies peacefully in his sleep. The murders are only a means to an end. We must determine what that end is before it is reached, and stop it if humanly possible."

"And you're saying that I could become one more of those means-to-an-end, is that it?"

Raymond shrugged, rubbed wearily at his eyes, and Susan felt a pang of guilt for hammering at him. They were both tired, and she knew that neither of them should really be having this conversation right now. *Well, he started it,* she thought, though it didn't do much to assuage her guilt.

"I'm just saying that I'm concerned for your well being, that's all. If a problem comes, it will not come straight-on, it always comes from the side. They come at you through other people, from the direction you least expect, because the devil never comes at you out in the open. You should be careful." He looked at her, and she could see that his concern was genuine.

"I'm always careful, Raymond," she said, more quietly this time. "The police have guaranteed that if I get even a whiff of trouble, they'll assign me round–the–clock protection."

"I hope that is enough," he said, and started the car. "I'll call you later, all right?"

"Sure." Susan started out of the car, pausing at Raymond's voice.

"You know," he said, "I cannot quite decide if having you along is good for me, or bad for me. Sometimes, I think, I annoy you as much as you annoy me. But most of the time, I think I very much appreciate the company. It's been a long time since I've had anyone challenge what I believe. I find the change of pace…invigorating."

Susan smiled. "I'm not sure, but I think I've just been complimented."

"It's been a long day. I'm tired. I don't know what I'm saying."

"And there we have something in common," she said, and laughed. "I'll talk to you later, Raymond. Good night."

"Good night."

She closed the door and walked to her car. He waited until she had climbed in and started the engine before driving off into the darkening streets.

She shook her head. He was, at times, an infuriating combination of pleasant and troubling qualities. *That's because he's a fanatic,* she chastised herself. *Fanatics can be perfectly charming, pleasant people until you challenge their belief that giant, radioactive panda bears are living in their basement, and then they get hostile. Remember what you're dealing with here.*

It was a valid point. But on the other hand, it was possible that Raymond had at least one valid point of his own. The murders had gone just as he'd said: five homeless, and five middle–class. She had to reluctantly agree that Leo was probably an aberration, a hiccup in the itinerary.

So if that were true, given what they had learned from Muad, then it was indeed possible that the killer was about to move further uptown. And there wasn't anyplace further uptown than Beverly Hills.

She hesitated, then pulled her cell phone out of her purse and dialed Mike Devereaux's number. She stayed on hold as she moved her car out of the parking lot and started north, back toward Silverlake.

Finally, Mike came on the line. "Susan? That you?"

"Yeah."

"I thought you got pulled off this story."

"I was. I just had a thought, that's all."

"Yeah, I know your thoughts," he said. "They're always trouble. But go ahead anyway."

"Well, I was thinking about the murders, and so far there have been five killings downtown, and not counting Leo there have been five killings right smack in the middle of the middle–class, so it occurred to me—"

Mike Devereaux's voice cut in abruptly. "Oh, shit."

"What? You got the same idea I did, or—"

"We had the TV on in here and the WNYN news just came on. You got a TV near you?"

"No, I'm in the car, why?"

"Shit," he said again at the other end of the line. "God*damn* it."

Jerry Levin looked up at the TV set above the bar as the news anchor—another clean cut, male model type whose job was simply to read what was put in front of him as if he'd done the work himself—cut to a composite drawing that looked very familiar.

"Hey, Johnny, turn the sound up," he yelled.

The bartender looked around for the remote control, found it, and pointed it at the television as the anchor's voice came through.

"—with sources close to the investigation saying that he is wanted for questioning in connection with the Slasher murders. They have not positively stated that this is the Slasher, but our sources have not ruled out the possibility either. Anyone who may have information about the man in this picture is urged to contact your local police or this station."

"That's him," Jerry said. "That's the guy that roughed me up. Goddamnit, I knew something was wrong with that guy."

"Hey, you hear that?" Johnny called back to the rest. "Jerry here saw the Slasher."

"No shit!" somebody yelled back.

Jerry stood and slapped a dollar on the bar. "Gimme some change, Johnny. I'm gonna make a phone call."

Johnny punched up NO SALE on the cash register, pulling out two quarters and five dimes. "You calling the police?"

"Hell no," Jerry said. "I'm calling the station. I'm gonna be on TeeVee."

"Well, if they say yes, have 'em come here for the interview," Johnny called as Jerry headed for the pay phone. "We could use the free advertising."

Jerry dropped coins into the phone, got directory information, and dialed the station. *This'll teach that son of a bitch to try and push me around*, he thought. *He's gonna find his ass in a whole world of hurt.*

Halfway home, Raymond stopped at Dawson's Mega–Pharmacy to pick up the supplies he knew Karl would need for his work. It was nearly as big as a supermarket, and about as poorly laid out. He was halfway down aisle three, heading past the feminine hygiene department when he felt something was wrong. He glanced up at the security camera, which normally scanned back and forth across the aisles, and now seemed to be pointed in his direction, looking at him. He glanced up at it, and at his movement it looked away, went back to its scanning.

Probably just got stuck, he thought, pushing away the oddly insistent feeling of concern that was building inside him. *Susan's right, you're starting to think everyone in the world is after you.*

He picked up the last of his supplies and moved to an open cash register, smiling absently at the cashier as she hurriedly rang up his purchase without once glancing up at him. When he handed over the money, he noticed her fingers were trembling.

She's nervous. Why?

He turned as a security guard pushed through the crowded pharmacy. "Can I talk to you for a second, sir?" he said, one hand uncomfortably near his gun belt.

Raymond looked around. The wary attitude of the heavy–set guard was drawing attention. "Why?"

"I'd rather not say right here, please come with me to the office."

"Not until I know why I'm being detained. I didn't take anything."

"Nobody's saying you did, sir, but I'm asking you again to come with me."

Raymond started to protest, then stopped abruptly when he saw his face splashed across several rows of tiny TVs on the hardware shelf. A crowd of people that had gathered to watch now turned in his direction, recognizing him. He saw fear in their eyes, and fear in the eyes of the guard.

"It's him!" someone yelled.

"Sir, please come with me *right now*," the guard said. He put a hand on his gun, and his expression told Raymond that he was now more afraid of the growing mob around them than he was of Raymond.

Several men charged toward him. Raymond had seen the look in their eyes before, seen it in the expressions of the crowd that had taken down and beaten the previous suspect.

He was not going to get out of here in one piece.

Raymond moved fast, faster than the guard expected. He threw back an elbow into the guard's chest, sending him to the ground and knocking the wind out of him. He knocked a hardware display to the floor, blocking the men who ran toward him. With the front door unavailable, he ran back the way he had come, plunging deeper into the store, racing for the rear exit, the pursuing mob forced to narrow into the aisle to follow him.

"He attacked the guard!" somebody yelled.

Someone else called, "Get his gun! Grab the guard's gun!"

"Get the son of a bitch!"

Shit.

He ran through the back entrance and across the loading dock, running fast, his breath coming sharp, chest throbbing, legs pumping with everything he had. He jumped three feet to the alley behind the store, nearly colliding with a dumpster before he caught his balance.

He ran for the corner. Once he was around the corner, he'd be safe, could get to his car before the crowd could double back and catch up to him. Just a few more feet and he'd be—

An explosion of pain shot through his arm, spun him around and slammed him against the alley wall. He looked back long enough to see one of the customers with the guard's pistol, taking aim again.

Raymond staggered as another shot whizzed past his head, chunking into the brick and sending shards flying at his back.

They always come at you through other people, they always come at you from the direction you least expect, he thought through the pain. *Can't let it end like this, I can't, I can't.*

The gun spoke again, and it was the loudest sound in the universe.

What Is, Is

Susan raced home as fast as she could drive, which was considerably above the speed limit. She snapped on the set as soon as she got in the door, too late to catch the report, but she knew from Mike's description that it was Raymond.

What the hell do I do now? she thought. Except for the mail drop, she didn't have an address for Raymond, didn't even have a phone number to call and warn him. Every time they'd spoken, he'd been the one to contact her.

She found Muad's Psychic Readings in the phone book, but there was no answer at the other end and directory information had nothing listed under Weil. She picked up the phone again to call a friend in the Pacific Bell downtown office when she froze at a sound, the sound no woman alone in an apartment ever wants to hear.

The sound of glass breaking in a back door.

She grabbed the cell phone and was dialing 911 even as she ran for the front door, stopping for only the barest second when she heard another sound, a voice.

"…Susan…"

She hesitated, recognizing the voice. "Raymond?"

She edged back toward the kitchen.

Raymond stood in the open back door, one arm hanging useless at his side. Blood dripped from his arm to the checkered linoleum floor. "…didn't mean to break the window, I slipped, I…I've been shot…"

He slumped against the door frame and slid to the floor.

Susan realized the 911 operator's voice was coming through the cordless phone. "Ma'am? Hello? Do you require assistance?"

"Yes," she started, but Raymond held up a hand.

"No," he said. "No police…please don't…"

"I'll call you back," Susan said, and hung up. She hurried to Raymond, who was pressing his good hand tight against the wound, staunching the blood. "How bad is it?"

"Bullet passed through…no arteries hit, but it hurts…"

"I have to get you to a hospital."

He shook his head. "Too many questions," he said. "They will have to report it to the police...don't want anyone to know where I am. Take me home."

"But you need help."

"I know," he managed. From the floor he looked up into her eyes. "Please, I know what I'm doing."

Susan hesitated, then nodded. "All right, but let me at least try to bandage that up first. Are you sure you can walk?"

"I got this far," he said, reaching up. She helped him stand. "Got to the car, drove off, then started to pass out, realized I couldn't make it all the way...your place was closer. I'm sorry, I didn't mean to—"

"It's okay. You can explain how this happened on the way. Just tell me a cop didn't do this, because if a cop shot you and I help, I'm in for felony evading."

"No, not a cop," he said, "at least, not yet."

She helped him into the bathroom, wondering how she was going to explain any of this to anyone.

Raymond's home was a small Tudor–style house in Woodland Hills, just north of the Ventura Freeway. She pulled up into a narrow driveway that led around behind the house. As she turned into the garage in back, the headlights illuminated colonies of lovingly tended and cultivated rose bushes that crowded the back of the house and lined the driveway on both sides. She had never imagined Raymond as the kind of man who spent his free time tending roses.

What the hell am I doing here? she asked herself.

You're here because he needed help, because he didn't want to go to a hospital and he would've died on your floor and that would almost certainly be a violation of the lease. Because he asked for your help, and you've always been a sucker for guys in need. And because this might help you to understand him, despite anything Mr. I'm–A–Fake–Psychic says to the contrary.

That doesn't change the facts. I'm a reporter, I'm not supposed to get personally involved in these things.

Yeah, but on the other hand, Rob told you to take a few days off, remember? You're off–duty.

Terrific, this is some way to spend my vacation.

She came around the other side and helped Raymond in through the back door.

"Straight ahead," he said, "then left."

Just as they reached the living room she heard a door open behind them. A tall man stood in the doorway, short–cropped black hair above a pair of wire framed glasses. He wore a dark vest over a plain white shirt, the sleeves rolled up past the elbow.

He stopped at the sight in front of him. "Raymond?"

He's gay? Is that why he didn't want me to know where he lived, because he was afraid I'd find out he was gay?

Will someone please tell me why the good ones are always gay?

"Over here, quickly" the man said with a pronounced Russian accent. He spread a quilt over a nearby sofa to avoid getting blood on the leather upholstery. Before she could speak, he began cutting away the shirt where it was most heavily covered in blood.

"He needs a doctor," Susan said.

"I am a doctor," he said. "Karl Malenkov. I take it you are Susan?"

She nodded. "Then you know about—"

"Raymond keeps me informed about all his comings and goings, in case anything goes wrong. This is the first time anything's gone quite this badly, however." He appraised the injury with a quick glance. "You bandaged this?"

"Yes."

"Good job. You may have kept him from losing the arm." He frowned as he examined the wound. "He's lost a lot of blood. Keep an eye on him, I'll be right back, just let me make a phone call and get my bag."

He hurried into a back room as she moved closer to Raymond, who looked at her through half-open eyes. "Thank you," he managed.

"It's all right. You're sure he can handle this?"

"He'll do fine." He closed his eyes as a ripple of pain shot through his arm, then focused on her again. "You...do not have to stay, Susan, if you do not—"

"I came this far, I'd like to see this through."

If Raymond intended to argue, he didn't have the chance. Karl came back into the room with his medical bag and an IV setup. "I've called a friend at the hospital, someone we can trust. He's bringing some blood right now."

He glanced over his shoulder at Susan as he began to work. "You may want to wait in the other room."

She nodded and stepped into the den. As she left, she heard Raymond say something to Karl, but couldn't make it out. She heard only Karl's whispered reply. "It's too late to worry about that now. What she sees, she sees; what is, is."

The den was paneled in dark wood, with sofas and a recliner in rich, brown leather. A fire burned in the fireplace. One wall was covered entirely by shelves filled with books, most of them old. She recognized several different translations of the Bible, the Apocrypha, and other religious texts alongside the Talmud, the Bhagavad Gita, the Egyptian Book of the Dead and the Koran. One complete shelf was crowded with books on possession, but the only one she recognized was the Malachi Martin text.

The shelf below it was more disturbing, containing books on guns, bomb making, terrorism, anti-terrorism, and tactics for modern chemical, biological and conventional warfare.

A host of New Age magazines, cult-watch publications and supermarket tabloids were spread out on the coffee table, with articles cut out or outlined in red felt pen. The sofa that sat alongside the coffee table sagged toward one end, and there was a worn depression on the arm at the other end.

He's spent a lot of time sleeping on this sofa, she decided. She could easily imagine him laying out here, feet up on the arms of the sofa, reading through his books and his magazines late into the night, searching for the hidden signs and portents that would tell him where the Devil was at work, slowly falling asleep with his papers draped over his chest.

There was a fine patina of dust on the end tables and chairs, adding to the sense that this was a place that had once been a cordial, comfortable, even happy place to live...but was now little more than an expanded office. She didn't feel that he actually lived here anymore, that he just came here to sleep, eat and research. The only place that wasn't lightly coated with dust was a small desk with a computer and monitor, the rest of the available desktop covered by newspaper articles and letters.

She crossed to the fireplace, where a collection of framed photos were carefully arranged on the mantel. She saw Raymond as a younger man, she guessed in his thirties and forties, fishing with a young girl she assumed was his daughter. He was a handsome man, she decided. Another photo showed him at a beach carrying the same girl piggy–back as another woman looked on smiling. *His wife?* Susan wondered. *So maybe he isn't gay. Or maybe he changed his lifestyle later, and that's why they split.*

She continued down the row of photographs, and stopped abruptly at a picture taken in a desert somewhere. It showed Raymond in combat fatigues, holding an M16 in one hand, his other arm around a man in traditional Middle Eastern garb, both smiling for the camera. It took her a moment to recognize the other man in the picture as Muad.

There were other, similar photos: Raymond in a South American jungle, camped out with other men in camouflage combat fatigues, but without the usual American armed forces logos or identification patches...a blurry shot taken out of a helicopter with Raymond pointing to something on fire down among the trees below...and most confusing of all, at the far right was a picture that had been taken in a church or monastery somewhere, in which Raymond wore the dark clothes and collar of a Catholic priest or novitiate. He stood alongside another priest, an older man, who had the same kind of sad eyes she had seen so many times in Raymond.

What the hell is all this, anyway? Who is this guy?

Muad's words came back to her. *You will never understand.*

She left the mantel, and walked back across the den. Karl was still working in the living room. She heard a soft moan of pain, and cringed at the sound.

A hallway between the two rooms led off to what she assumed were the bedrooms. She hesitated, then stepped quietly down the hall.

The first bedroom was almost certainly Raymond's. Even though it was tastefully appointed in dark woods and mirrored cabinets, it had the same sense of disuse as the den. Books were stacked in all four corners of the room, and piles of unopened mail sat on a side table. The king–size bed was neatly made, with corners tucked military–tight, but the depression in the center told the story of Raymond coming home, kicking off his shoes, exhausted, and falling asleep on top of the bedspread.

She moved deeper into the hall, pausing at the next door, which was partially closed. *Partially closed is also partially open, so it's okay to look.*

She gently nudged open the door and peered inside.

She was not prepared for what she saw.

A woman lay without moving in the single bed of what she guessed was once his daughter's room. Her hair was an auburn that had gone to gray years before, combed out straight to cover the pillow. She recognized the woman's face from one of the pictures on the mantel, but older now. A vase of freshly cut roses sat next to the head of the bed, near an IV drip that spiraled into her arm, and a heart monitor that beeped steadily beside the bed. Trays of medications, syringes, and other medical equipment were carefully arranged on folding tables around the bed for easy access. The only other sound in the too–warm room was the regular sigh of a breather unit attached to a tube that ran down her throat.

"Ms. Randall?"

Susan started at the voice behind her. She turned to find Karl at her elbow.

"Please come with me." He started back toward the den. Susan took one last look into the room, then followed.

"I think he will be all right," Karl said once they had reached the den. "You can go if you like, or—"

"Why does everyone seem to want me out of here as quickly as possible?" Susan asked. She nodded toward the far bedroom. "Is it because of her? Who is that woman?"

"Ms. Randall—"

"Who is it?"

Karl ran a tired hand through his hair. "Elizabeth Weil. Raymond's wife."

Susan stopped, looked back down the hall at the door. "But…I thought he wasn't married anymore."

"That's correct."

"Then what's she doing here? Is she all right?"

"She is in a coma. She has been for several years now. The hospital did not give her the care she required, and there was a bit of a scandal with some of the orderlies taking certain liberties with the patients, enough so that Raymond did not feel safe leaving her there. It made more sense to have her here, at home, surrounded by familiar things."

"So do you live here, with Raymond?"

"No, I help take care of her. I come by three, four times a day. My office is not far from here, so it's not a burden. I check her condition, and give her the medication she requires. Every other day I bring along a physical therapist to ensure that she gets enough movement to keep her limbs from atrophying further."

He smiled thinly. "My job is to give God a hard time on her behalf."

"I didn't know doctors made house calls anymore."

"I would come by seven, eight, ten times a day, if necessary. He is my friend, she was my friend, and I owe them more than I can ever explain."

"So what happened to her? And what about those pictures on the mantel? I recognized him in the Middle East, in South America, and several other places. He knows Syrians, he knows Chileans, I'm guessing you're Russian—"

"Born and raised in Minsk," he said.

"Mix that in with some of the reading material out here, and I'd guess he's either former military intelligence, or an ex–mercenary, except for that other photo of him dressed as a priest. Or was that just one of his covers?"

"Those are all...very long stories, Ms. Randall."

She crossed her arms. "Is he going anywhere, anytime soon?"

"No."

"Then neither am I. After all this I think I have a right to know what's going on."

"Perhaps." He sat at one end of the long sofa, and indicated for her to sit at the other end. "I suggest you make yourself comfortable," he said.

"This may take a while."

What the Doctor Said

I met Raymond for the first time quite by accident. I was a staff doctor in the Soviet army, stationed with the 14th armored infantry brigade in Afghanistan. For most of the previous week, we had sent scouting parties to locate the bases of Afgani rebels so that the targeting information could be relayed to the artillery divisions. When we received word that one of our patrol units had taken enemy fire, we airlifted out as many survivors as we could. But nearly half a dozen wounded soldiers were still pinned down.

I was assigned to a rescue party sent to extract them from the hot zone and make sure they returned to base alive for further medical attention. When we arrived, we found that all but two of the soldiers were dead. We were already on the ground when our helicopter was hit by an rebel shoulder–mounted rocket, leaving us stranded. After that, there was a great deal of shooting, at the conclusion of which I and three non–commissioned officers were taken prisoner.

We were brought into their camp, and treated very badly by our captors. My friend, Sergeant Feyodor Samoyan, was beaten nearly to death when he tried to escape. I could understand only a little of what they were saying, but even so it was clear that they intended to execute all of us by firing squad.

It was then that I noticed another man talking to the Afgani rebel leader. He looked like an American or a German, but he was not in a uniform from either country, which meant he had to be one of the mercenaries who had come to organize the Afgani rebels. They were having a very heated discussion, after which the American walked over to me and kneeled at my side, his back to the rebel leader.

"My name's Raymond," he said. "Do you understand English?"

I nodded. "Yes, a little."

"Good. Then listen to me very carefully. Tafiq over there is about ten seconds away from having all of you shot, then arranging for your bodies to be carved into pieces and fired across the skirmish line by cannon as a warning to the rest of your unit."

"He sounds...upset."

"He is. His brother is in that tent back there, badly wounded in a battle with your advance unit, possibly dying, and Tafiq's looking for someone to take it out on. I may be able to persuade him to take another approach, but I'll need your help."

"What do you want?"

"I saw you carrying a field medical bag. You're a doctor?"

"Yes."

"Good. If you can save his brother, I think I can convince Tafiq to let you go, and guarantee you safe passage back to your unit."

"What about the others with me?"

"He won't let them go, but he won't kill them, either. He'll hold onto them and use them to barter for the release of some of his men."

"Doesn't matter, I can't work on him," I said. "He is an enemy soldier."

Raymond frowned, looked off into the hot sun. "All right," he said, "What about this. If he were captured by your forces, given that he's an officer, and the brother of one of the main rebel leaders around here, would you give him medical treatment?"

"Of course. According to the Geneva convention, I am required to give a prisoner any medical attention necessary to keep him alive."

"There you go."

"But the Geneva convention also prohibits me from being forced into working for the enemy while a prisoner of war."

"You're a very stubborn man."

I shrugged. "I'm Russian. It goes with the territory."

"My *point* is that if you're standing there with his life in your hands, and you're deciding his fate minute by minute, then in a sense, isn't he your prisoner?"

I will confess that I stared at him for a very long time. "I have not met many Americans before this," I said. "Are they all like you?"

"I'm American only by upbringing, I was born in Austria."

"Somehow, that makes me feel better," I said.

Then he smiled, a very big smile, I thought at the time, and I agreed to the job.

"But what if he is so badly wounded that I cannot save him?" I asked.

"Then leave me a note, and I'll make sure it gets to your next of kin. I'll even tell them where to find your body."

I spent the next six hours working, at the end of which I was able to save Tafiq's brother. Afterward, the Afgani rebels wanted to renege on the offer, but Raymond was able to persuade them to keep the deal. He personally escorted me to neutral territory, where my people were able to pick me up.

I never forgot the experience, or the debt I owed him. After the fall of the Berlin Wall, I made it a point to seek him out. It didn't take long; my contacts in the former Soviet military were able to help me contact him, and really, mercenaries are fairly easy to find, because after all, they depend on others finding them to give them work.

We arranged to meet at a little café in Mexico City, where I was able to properly thank him for saving my life, and ask him why he had so extended himself on my behalf.

He said, "Something about you said that you were a good man, and I hate to see a good man die without an equally good reason."

Over the next few days, I learned quite a bit about him, about the missions he had worked in Israel, Iraq, Chile, Cuba, even my own country. He was quite modest about it all, a trait that continues to this day. But I am a good listener, and the beer in Mexico City on a hot day can loosen the tongue of any man on the planet.

Mostly, though, he talked about his wife, whom he loved, and his daughter, Claire, who was the alpha and the omega of his existence. He could have easily taken advantage of the distance between them to…dally, as you say. He was a handsome man, in a glamorous profession, he could have had anyone he chose, at any time of his choosing. But in all the time I saw him, he never seemed to have any interest in such things. He was married, and he was faithful, and that was that.

I found him to be a man of tremendous contradictions. He was for sale to anyone who wanted to hire him. Politically, he didn't care which side you were on as long as the check cashed. Now, you might think that is a very callous attitude. But on the job, he brought in his own unique set of morals. He would not allow the execution of civilians, did not permit torture or abuse; he conducted himself as a professional soldier, and when those around him did not, he…*encouraged* them to mend their ways. And Raymond can be most persuasive when he chooses to be.

I asked him, one day, how he could justify this contradiction. He said, "Karl, the plain and simple truth is, the world is going to hell. You know it, and I know it. Left, right, centrist, it really doesn't matter, it's all about power, about manipulation. The corporations own two–thirds of the planet and will own the last third before the century's out. There's nothing moral at the core of any of it. I can't control that, I can't change that part of the world. Hell, I wouldn't even know where to start. All I can do is control my own actions, live by my own ethical code, if I can call it that without you laughing at me."

So I asked him if he believed in God. He thought about it for a long time, and then finally said, "No. I've seen too many good, decent people die, and too many mean, despicable bastards live to be ninety years old to even *consider* the idea that there's any kind of justice in the world. If there is a God, he's an absentee landlord. He's not paying attention, and I don't think benign neglect is a god–like quality in anybody's book. It's cruel and it's malicious and I can't accept it."

That, mind you, is the condensed version. The full reply went on for well over an hour and several very large pitchers of beer.

Over the years, we kept in touch when and where possible. A card would come in the mail from Chile or Syria, sometimes we would talk by phone. I think that on some level it amused him that I would be grateful for what he did, but more than that, it was an affirmation for him that he had done the right thing, that there was still some measure of gratitude in the world.

Then, about five years ago, something happened. To this day, he has not spoken of it to me in any detail. I can only tell you what little I know.

He was on an operation in Bolivia. It was one of the last jobs he had intended to take before retiring. He always spoke of buying a little house by the sea in Washington or Oregon, and spending the rest of his life fishing and sleeping. This job would have put him within inches of having the money he needed to retire.

He and the rest of his party had settled in on the outskirts of a tiny village. These were good men; he had worked with them many times over the years. They were like brothers. After they had set up camp, several of them went into the local village to buy supplies. They found the villagers nervous, even frightened, but not about their operation.

Two nights before, the village church had been desecrated. The next morning, several of their young men had disappeared from the village. They said that one of them returned the following night, walking down the middle of the street, crying out in words they did not understand. They said that when he entered one of the buildings, everything in the room flew around, crashing into walls, shattering on the floor, and that where he walked he left footprints of blood.

They tried to restrain him, but apparently he had the strength of a mad beast, and was able to escape back into the woods. They could not find him again after that, but they could hear him, deep in the trees, calling out to them by name, whispering secrets about the villagers that he could not possibly have known. They said he had been taken by the Devil, and was beyond hope, beyond redemption.

They told all this to Raymond's people, and they in turn told Raymond, who did not believe in God or the Devil. But he *did* believe in dangerous madmen, so he set a patrol on watch at the encampment.

I do not know the specifics of what happened after that. Raymond has never spoken to me about that part of it, and I doubt he ever will. All I know is that the next morning, some of the villagers were drawn to the encampment by smoke rising from the area.

They found all the other mercenaries dead. Some had their throats cut while they slept. Others had been shot in what was apparently a terrible firefight of some kind. There was blood everywhere. The encampment had been burned to the ground. It was as if the night itself had turned on them, striking out at the group with a fury that cannot be described. Whether they were attacked by outside forces, or whether for reasons unknown they began firing on each other, I do not know for certain, but I have always suspected the latter.

Raymond was nowhere to be found.

It was not until two days later that he staggered out of the forest, badly wounded, fevered, and nearly dead from knife wounds, loss of blood and infection. They cared for him as best they could while they waited for a doctor to arrive. I don't know what he said in his fever, he has never told me, but apparently it was enough to drive nearly everyone out of the house where he was being kept; enough to cause the local priest to say a prayer of exorcism over the empty house when he had gone.

He barely made it back to the States, where he spent the next six months recovering. Despite my calls and letters, he would not tell me what happened, would not even tell his wife what happened.

But whatever happened that night in Bolivia, he was never the same thereafter.

Even after his recovery, my letters continued to come back unopened and unanswered. I spoke with his wife, who said that he was spending all his time with people she characterized as "crackpots, fanatics, phony psychics and renegade priests." He began to fill his library with many of the books you see here now: books on the Bible, religion, demonology, and possession. I thought at times that he was preparing to attack God and the Devil with the same planning, tactical precision, and military intelligence he would have used to invade a village or take on an armored unit.

He would disappear completely for days at a time, only to return pale and shaken by something he had seen or done. But instead of being put off by whatever it was he saw, it only made him more determined to pursue the path he had chosen: to somehow avenge the deaths of those who had served with him, and called him friend.

Elizabeth tried to put the best face on it, but all of this put a terrible strain on their marriage. Finally, shortly after Claire went off to college, Elizabeth filed papers for a formal separation. A year later, when the divorce came through, Raymond did not contest it. The only thing he kept was this house, the house Claire had grown up in, the house in which he had, for a while, known happiness. Even after Elizabeth was gone, he carefully tended the rose bushes that she had planted around the house, because they were hers, and because she had asked him to.

I think it was about six, seven months later that I got what was probably the most surprising phone call I had ever received from Raymond. He said, "Karl, I have joined the church."

For a moment, I could not even speak. Was this *Raymond?* The same Raymond who once told me he did not, *could* not, believe in God? I told him it was a terrible joke to play on a man of my age, but he insisted he was telling the truth. Even so, I told him I would not believe it until he sent me a copy of the papers recognizing him as a novitiate in the Catholic Church.

The day they arrived, I spent all that afternoon getting quite drunk, convinced that the world was surely on the verge of apocalypse.

Raymond stayed in the church for almost two years, during which time he somehow managed to apprentice himself to a priest named Father Louis Delmonico, who had spent many years inside the Vatican working with their chief exorcist, Monsignor Corrado Balducci. Delmonico had been personally involved in three cases of demonic possession, of which he was the formal exorcist at one of them. Raymond immersed himself in church lore and doctrine concerning demonology, read every available case study of possession and demonic influence. The church was uncertain about his interests, because the Catholic Church only reluctantly recognizes the possibility of possession. But as I said, Raymond has a way of convincing people to let him go his own way, even when they are absolutely determined to do otherwise.

By this time, I had met an American woman from Los Angeles during her vacation in Moscow, and we fell very much in love. We married, and I moved here with her. It was strange, to think that having started so far apart, Raymond and I would end up living not ten minutes from each other, in the same city. He says it is the American way of things. I say it is fate. And sometimes I think the truth is more on my side than on his.

During this time his letters and occasional phone calls became livelier, as if he were starting gradually to find himself again in his work. We even met for coffee a few times after I came to Los Angeles, to talk about the old days. I thought, Well, he has had a hard time, but he is coming out of it now. Soon he will be the Raymond I remember, and God had better be prepared to answer some very tough questions.

Then his world fell apart a second time.

During Spring break, Claire had gone to join her mother at the new home she had leased after the divorce. At that time, June of 1996, Elizabeth was living in San Francisco.

Do you remember what happened in June 1996 in San Francisco, Ms. Randall?

Yes, I can see from your face that you do.

A young man, Steven Jason Lloyd, walked onto the wharf at Pier 39 on a Sunday afternoon. The pier was crowded with tourists and locals who had come to enjoy what had turned out to be a sunny, warm, pleasant day.

According to the survivors, this disturbed young man stood at one end of the long pier for a long time, facing the sea, then took a high–powered rifle out of his bag and began shooting. He walked along almost casually, firing into the crowd as he went, moving slowly toward the end of the pier. The terrified crowds could not get past him without being shot, and there was no other way off the pier except to risk diving off into the sea.

Fourteen men, women and children died that day, before he reached the far end of the pier, turned toward the police cars that were finally arriving on the scene, and used his last bullet to take his own life. In his bag, and in his small apartment, they found demonic literature, a videotape and writings in his own hand explaining that he believed himself to be a tool of retribution against society, that the Devil was speaking to him and working through him.

Elizabeth and Claire were both on Pier 39 that day.

Claire was killed instantly in the attack. Another bullet struck Elizabeth in the head, almost killing her. The doctors managed to save her life, but she never came out of the coma.

When Raymond heard the news, he went…well, to be honest, I think he went a little insane, but who of us would not? He left the church, and stayed at Elizabeth's side until he was sure she would live.

When he wasn't at her side, he would become furious. He began drinking, lost his temper, got into fights…I think he blamed himself. On some level, even to this day, I think he believes that if they had never divorced, Elizabeth would never have been there that day; or that if he had been there with her, he could have stopped that man from killing as many people as he did.

Most of all, though, I think he decided that staying within the church was not a solution, it was only an evasion, an escape from the responsibility to do what he felt only he could do.

After a few months, when her condition had stabilized and showed no signs of changing, Raymond arranged for her to be transported here, to the home they had shared for so many years.

She has been here now for three years. Every day, he goes in and he talks to her for an hour in the morning, and an hour in the evening, and who knows how many times in–between. He brings fresh–cut roses from her garden, knowing the smell will fill her room. He plays her favorite music for her. He believes that some day, she will wake up. Perhaps then, he can settle his quarrel with the Universe.

Until then, he has his work.

I suppose you could say that he has declared his own personal war. His world was destroyed twice by whatever is out there, and he intends to balance out the scales by whatever means necessary.

You can ask, is it proper for me to tell you these things? They are not secrets. They are known to Muad, whom you met, to me, and to others. Raymond does not speak of them only because he cannot speak of them anymore, because the pain is too great. But I think you should know, because it may help you to help him.

You can ask, do I believe in these things? Do I believe in what he sees, the forces he claims are out there, on the edge of our perception, tearing at our souls where we cannot see them?

I will tell you: I do not know. I have not seen what he has seen. I know there is a God, and if there is a God then there is a Devil. I know that in the Bible it says the Devil walks to and fro upon the earth, and up and down in it, which would seem to imply that he is with us always, here, beside us, every moment, right now. And I know that Raymond believes.

For me, that is enough.

He has chosen a difficult path, and he has chosen to walk it almost entirely alone. That would demand my respect, and my help, even if his friendship did not. I only hope that you can help him now, so that his path will not be quite so solitary.

Ah. That is the doorbell. You will excuse me. I believe that Raymond's blood has just arrived.

Face Down in the LA River

"You've got to call off the dogs, Mike. You've got the wrong guy."

Paying no attention to the lunch time crowd, Mike Devereaux sat across from Susan at Pinks Hot Dog stand on La Brea Avenue just north of Melrose in Hollywood, eating the first of three chili dogs with onions, relish and mustard that he had brought to the open–air benches squeezed in between the stand and the neighboring businesses. The chili dogs were a Pinks specialty, a three–alarm heart attack on a bun that had been sought after and lined–up–for since the place had opened in 1939.

But the pinched look on Devereaux's face at this moment had nothing to do with the chili. "Susan, we've been working this case now for almost five months. In all that time, with the Mayor's office and City Hall and the press leaning on us every day, day in and day out, we finally got one good lead, the guy in that picture. And now you want me to go back into that hurricane and tell them we have to forget the whole thing and start from scratch all over again?" He shook his head. "Do you *want* to find me floating face down in the LA River? What the hell did I ever do to you?"

He started on the second dog, having practically swallowed the first in one angry bite.

The only reason he's biting the chili dog like that is because he can't bite me, *as much as I think he'd like to right now.*

"I've been working with Raymond as a…collaborator and consultant," she said, which was mostly true. "He's been covering some areas on my behalf when I couldn't be there myself. That's why your people saw him at that funeral."

"Yeah? Then why'd he run?"

"He came in through a break in the fence, he was afraid he'd be arrested for trespassing."

"So what kind of consulting–and–collaborating work are we talking about here? I mean, does he just carry your pencils and write up your notes, or is he some kind of expert?"

"He's…an investigator."

"With a license?"

"He's working on it."

Mike's face got that pinched look again. The second hot dog was gone. "So this investigator in training, does he have a theory about the Slasher?"

"Yes."

"You want to share that theory with me?"

Susan hesitated. "Not yet. It may not pan out. If it shows even a hint of promise, believe me, you'll be the first to know."

"I better be." He picked up the third chili dog, examining it from all sides as though working out what plan of attack would let it angle into his stomach and land snugly alongside its companions without causing a gastronomical eruption of Krakatoan proportions.

"So that's it, then?" she asked. "You'll tell Trask and the rest to let it go?"

"On your word?"

"I'll vouch for him, Mike."

Down went the third chili dog. Susan felt curiously sea sick.

"Before I say yes or no, there's just one other thing," Mike said, dabbing away the traces of mustard and chili that had somehow avoided capture. "We got an audio tape of the killer talking while he took out Leo Dexter."

"What? You're kidding."

"Clear as day."

"What does he say?"

Mike sat back with what Susan first interpreted as the contented look of a man who had just filled in all the corners and was basking in his inner radiance, but which turned out to be the expression of the proverbial cat that had just eaten the equally proverbial canary.

"He said, 'Hello, Raymond.' You got an explanation for *that* one, Susan?"

She sat forward and took a bite of her turkey dog, hoping her attempt to buy time before answering would not be quite as obvious as it felt right now.

What the hell is going on here? she thought as she swallowed.

"Well, Mike, you have to remember that I've been consulting with Raymond for a while now. The killer went out of his way to contact me, rather than the other papers. That means he probably checked me out, and in the process of that he either saw me meeting with Raymond, or heard his name some other way."

Mike drummed his fingers on the table.

"Then, when he killed Leo, he may have thought it was Raymond coming in my place, as he's done for me elsewhere, out of a desire to protect me. And it was dark, I hear, so it's reasonable to assume that it was a case of mistaken identity. He said 'Hello, Raymond,' because he thought Leo *was* Raymond. After all, a person wouldn't say hello to himself, would he? I mean, that *would* explain it, right?"

He gave it another moment, then sat back, folding his massive arms across his chest. "Maybe. But the thing is, I know you, Susan, and you *know* I know you, and I can tell you're holding something back."

"A reporter—"

"Don't give me that *reporter has a right to protect her sources* crap right now, Susan. I'm cutting you some slack so don't make me feel like a chump, okay? Look, all I'm telling you is that whatever the hell's going on, you damned well better be real careful. We're dealing with a dangerous nut that could make the Zodiac killer and the Unabomber nervous. I don't want to see you get hurt, and I sure as hell don't want to see my face ground in the dirt if I listen to you and get screwed at the end of the day.

"If you say I should go in there and front for you, well, okay, I'll do that, even though every cell in my brain is saying don't do it, just yank the guy in for questioning and screw loyalty. But so far you've never lied to me, and as much as I don't want to honor that right now, I guess I kind of have to."

"I appreciate that, Mike."

"Don't. You remember what I said before about blowing up your car if you fouled me up on something?"

She nodded.

"Just remember: that offer is still open."

She nodded again. His expression was dead serious. "I understand."

"Good." He stretched then let his hands fall at his sides. "So is this guy gonna press charges against whoever winged him?"

"No, not at this time, anyway. He understands the panic caused by that police sketch."

"Then he isn't going to sue the LAPD either, right?"

"Right."

"Well, that's some good news, I guess." He stood from the picnic bench, stomach rumbling. "Oh, man, I got to hit the bathroom before I go back to the station. If the dogs weren't bad enough, the thought of going into Trask's office and falling on my sword for you took care of the rest of it. Oh, man..."

As he started away, Susan stood. "One more thing, Mike."

He stopped, looking distressed on every level she could think of. "One *more* thing? Just how much joy do you think I can *handle* at one time?"

"Just a little quid pro quo," she said, "since you're putting yourself out on a limb on my behalf. I may have a lead for you."

He studied her for a moment. "Is this the thing you started to tell me when all hell broke loose?"

"Yes."

"Go on."

"I have reason to believe that the next victim will be someone with a lot of money. Beverly Hills level money."

"So we're talking here rich white folk."

"Exactly. On top of that, if you run a check on the personal security systems around there, you'll find there was a glitch that disabled the whole network for about an hour a few days ago."

"Who could do something like that?"

"I don't know," she said, "but it's an interesting question, isn't it?"

He nodded. "Yeah, it is. Thanks."

Then he turned and continued off to the men's room, walking faster with each step. As she watched him disappear through the back door of Pinks, she remembered what Raymond had said to her in the car.

I anticipated that I would be noticed, it was only a matter of time.

But I had not stopped to consider that, in noticing me, it might also notice you.

I have reason to believe that it has noticed you, that it knows your name.

If the killer had indeed noticed her, and knew her name, then maybe there was some reasonable way in which he might have seen Raymond, known his name.

But if that were the case, then he would also know what Raymond *looked* like.

And Raymond looked nothing like Leo Dexter, even in a dark room. Which, despite what she had just told Mike, totally eliminated the mistaken identity theory.

So why had he said Hello, Raymond?

He could've had an accomplice, she thought. *Could be just a coincidence, with both having the same first name. It's possible.*

And it could be that the killer knew the tape was there. It could be that he was deliberately saying hello to Raymond to mock him, or foul him up with the police.

She tried to find a third possibility, one that would be somewhat less distressing than the previous two, but failed.

She rubbed at her temples, a headache coming on with the guilty realization that she had fed Mike a load of cow flop so high she was surprised he didn't get a nosebleed from standing on it. If she couldn't explain that tape reasonably to herself, by what right did she lead Mike astray?

As she reached her car, she decided that she had to learn more about Raymond. She was putting a lot at risk right now, and she needed to expand her level of comfort.

But that would be later, after she had pretty much the same conversation with Rob, in which she expected no level of comfort at all.

Carefully balancing a bag of groceries, Karl opened the front door and stepped into Raymond's house. When he'd finally left the night before, he'd noticed that the refrigerator was poorly stocked, and decided to pick up a few of the essentials Raymond would need during his convalescence.

After unloading the groceries, he stepped into the den and found Raymond sitting at the corner desk, staring at the computer monitor.

"I thought I told you to stay in bed," Karl said.

"I got tired of being horizontal. Thought I'd try vertical for a change."

"So what're you doing?"

"I jumped online to do some research. Do you realize there are now over fourteen web sites dedicated to this killer and his activities? Here, take a look at this."

He pulled a page out of the printer and handed it to Karl. It was covered with sketches of the crime scenes based on police reports, and in the center of it, a poem dedicated to the Slasher.

You avenge the patriarchal crimes
That have become part of our times
Now these men know how it feels
To be a woman beneath society's heels.

"This is a joke, right?" Karl asked.

"It's a fringe lesbian site that considers all men potential rapists. They think the patriarchal system is corrupt because men created it, and seem to feel that men should experience what it's like to have their power usurped and made vulnerable. Naturally they abhor violence, because violence is patriarchal, but if it's going to be done, better us than them. They figure this guy is advancing the feminist agenda by making males feel victimized for a change."

"That's terrible."

"Yeah, and the poem's not too good either." Raymond switched off the computer and rubbed at his eyes. "Believe it or not that's the least offensive of the bunch. There's a whole national network of websites dedicated to serial killers, talking about the romance of serial killers, the power of serial killers, their sexuality and how they're rebels against society.

"You know that doctor up in Vermont, who sold his house and his practice so he could set up shop in a poor part of town and treat people who couldn't afford a regular doctor?"

"Sure."

"You know how many sites people have made about him? Three. Three for a guy who saves lives every day, and fourteen for this…animal. And of those three, two were so-called Pro-Life sites that suspect him of providing low-cost abortions to women who couldn't afford them elsewhere."

Raymond stood carefully, favoring his wounded arm, which Karl was pleased to note was still in its sling. He'd imagined Raymond slipping it out at the first opportunity just to annoy him. "When did we learn to value hate over everything else, Karl? When did that happen?"

"I don't know. I sometimes wonder myself. The other day, at the hospital, we had a gunshot victim come in. It was another one of those road-rage situations. He'd accidentally cut somebody off, and the guy chased him down, jumped out of his car, ran over and shot him.

"I wish I could say I don't understand it, but in part, I do. Sometimes, when I'm driving, and some idiot does something stupid like make a left turn from the far right lane, there's this…anger that jumps out in me. I can actually see myself getting out of my car and pounding the shit out of him. I once talked about this to some of the other residents at the hospital, and each of them said that every day, they feel more and more the same way. You go from perfectly benign, happy...to murderous rage in about ten seconds. And it just burns you all day long. When I think of it, a part of me is ashamed, and a part of me still wants to go find that person and kick his teeth in."

"You're right, Raymond. It's pandemic rage. And I'll tell you the truth, when I think about it too long, there are days I find myself thinking that as a people, as a race, we're not worth saving."

He waited for a reply, but instead Raymond stared quietly ahead, lost in thought.

"Raymond?" Karl asked after a moment.

Raymond finally stirred. "Yes?"

"Are you all right? You went away on me."

"Did I? Yes, I suppose you did. Just thinking about what you said. Give me a minute..."

He turned away and went back to the computer, working with one hand.

"You'll be using the other hand for a few more days, until the injured one's strong enough to sustain any kind of weight," Karl said.

"Mmm," Raymond said, preoccupied.

Karl recognized the look, and realized that Raymond was somewhere else, and wouldn't come back until he had worked out whatever it was he was obsessed with. He picked up his bag and walked down the hall to Elizabeth's room, glancing back one last time to see Raymond at the computer, tapping slowly, painfully, on the keys.

"By the way," Karl called, "I got word from Susan, she thinks she's convinced the police that you're not the killer or an accomplice, so your face should be coming off the Most Wanted list sometime today."

"Mmm," Raymond said, and continued typing.

The WNYN News video crew had taken over an hour to set up their shot at Murphy's Pub. Jerry Levin had endured makeup and suggestions about the best color shirt to wear on TV from the other patrons, who alternately gave him a hard time and cheered him on. The owner of the bar kept a wary eye on the video monitor and without great subtlety continued to move a sign with the name of the bar back into view of the camera every time the lens edged away from it.

Finally Jerry was led to a stool that had been carefully lit and arranged for the most flattering appearance, settled in, and waited for the on–site reporter—someone he recognized from the Saturday night news team, not one of their main anchors but one had to take what one could get—to launch with his first question. The interview would be distilled to its fine points and aired on the evening news.

Jerry ran through his lines. *He was a big guy, and scary. I mean, scary. He came in here picking a fight, and he defended the Slasher. I mean, he seemed like he knew what the guy was thinking. The way he talked about the killer, I should've known they were the same guy, you know? And then when I went outside, he jumped me, right out of nowhere. Well, sure, I fought back, fought back real good. I used to box in college, see, and I know how to take care of myself, see these arms? But he kept coming at me, calling himself some kind of lion, and I'm pretty sure he was reaching for a knife, but I cold–cocked him good, and I got out of there fast. I didn't think too much of it, heck I've always got somebody trying to prove they're somebody by trying to mess with me, but then when I saw that picture on your news, hell, I knew that was the guy, and the responsible thing was to come forth and tell what I knew.*

That's Jerry Levin, L–e–v–i–n.

He glanced up as the reporter was abruptly called to the back of the bar by the man who had introduced himself to Jerry as the producer on this story. He didn't know what a producer did, but he assumed it was important. The producer had one ear glued to a cell phone as he spoke to the reporter.

He sat on the bar stool under the hot lights, feeling his makeup start to melt and fill in his pores, nodding at the other partons who kept referring to him as Our Star, for a full three minutes before the producer and the reporter returned from their conference at the back of the room.

"Interview's off," the producer said.

"What're you talking about?"

"The office just got word from the LAPD, the guy in the composite drawing is no longer considered a suspect or wanted for questioning. So at this point, until we hear otherwise, this is a non–story. Sorry, Mr. Levin."

He nodded to his crew, and they began turning off lights and packing up equipment.

"Wait a minute," Jerry said as another technician reached into his shirt and fished around for the remote mike. "Look, I'm telling you, this guy is dangerous."

"Then we'll just have to wait until he does something to prove it," the reporter said, and walked away.

"Hey, Jerry," someone called from the back of the bar. "You're an asshole!"

This is my life, he thought as the last video light winked out over his head. *This is just my fucking life.*

Susan finished repeating the same information she'd given Mike over lunch, and sat back, waiting for Rob to react.

He didn't reply for a long moment, studying her closely before he spoke. His silence reminded Susan of her grade school vice–principal, whose office she had visited on more than one occasion. Mr. Claremont always sat in stony silence for at least a minute before telling one of his charges how much trouble they were in, and how disappointed he was in their behavior.

Keep this up and you'll never amount to anything, he'd told Susan repeatedly. And he was almost right.

"And this…consultant…is the same guy you were chasing down in Seattle?"

"The same," she said, waiting for the hammer to fall.

Robb nodded silently for a moment. "Well, I guess that makes the trip one hundred percent legitimate and deductible," he said. "I guess that's a good thing."

She let out a breath she hadn't realized she'd been holding, relieved that he wasn't going to hang her by her ankles from the third floor as an example to the rest of the staff.

"The irony is, I guess if you'd still been hanging around, you might've gotten a copy of that composite drawing and told the police who he was, saving them and everybody else a lot of grief."

"It's possible," Susan said, then caught herself. "You're being awfully conciliatory," she said. "Why?"

Rob sat back in his tall leather chair, not meeting her gaze. She thought he looked even more tired than usual. "I'm putting you back on the story."

"Like I said: why?"

"Well, for starters, it's been a few days now, and there's been no further indication that the killer's showing any kind of special interest in you. But mainly…I need your input, and your opinion, and I can't exactly ask for that if you're not on the story."

He opened a drawer in his desk, pulled out a photocopy of a typed letter, and handed it to her. "This came in by fax a few hours ago. I need your opinion: Based on the prior emails, do you think it came from the same source I think it came from? If so, then I have to decide what to do about it. I think I've made up my mind, assuming you think it's genuine. I don't think you're going to like it, but I'd like to at least hear from someone who's willing to argue with me."

As she examined the letter, her breath caught in her chest. The words, the whole tone of voice was instantly familiar. "It's him," she said, "no question."

"That's what I thought. I made some informal calls, and every other newspaper and TV station in town had that letter show up in their fax machines at roughly the same time. I don't think there's much question that someone's going to run it, possibly all of them. I wouldn't commit to that option until I heard from you first on its authenticity, but—"

"Rob, you can't. You can't run this. If you do—"

"If I don't, it's going to look like every other paper in the county is ahead of us again. And there's always the chance that one of our readers might recognize the style of writing, just like the Unabomber's brother recognized that excuse for a term paper. It could be a public service."

"It could also be the most blatant example of throwing gasoline on a fire in the history of modern journalism."

"I know," he said. "But I don't see a whole lot of other choices."

She shook her head, and looked back at the letter in her hands. *This is going to be bad*, she thought, as she read it over again.

> *You all know who I am. And you all know why I'm doing what I'm doing.*
>
> *The streets are filled with filth and human trash. The city wouldn't take out the trash, so I took it out myself, one at a time, to show the rest of you how it was done. But I forgot that you're lazy. You saw me doing it and felt you didn't need to do it yourselves. You were happy about it. You enjoyed seeing the filth in the streets being afraid, as they made you afraid. You liked seeing them bleed. But you couldn't let them see you enjoying it. So you turned against me to protect the filth, to protect your precious self-image.*
>
> *So I turned against you too. Sought to remind you that a knife cuts in two directions. You are either for me or against me. My knife doesn't care either way, as long as it drinks. As long as it strikes deep at your hypocrisy. You don't care about them and they don't care about you. They would kill you in a second if they could, and take what's yours. You know it. I know it. Why are you lying to yourselves?*
>
> *So I'm giving you all another chance. The only thing worse than gutter trash is rich trash. The ones who keep you down in the dirt, who grind your face in the street every day because they can, because they own you, because the law won't touch them. The law cares only about the rich. If you want proof, just see how they react when my knife begins to drink from the rich. They will pull out every stop to find me then, and only then, because they don't care if you die, only if the rich die.*
>
> *You know who I am.*
>
> *I am all of you. I am what you truly believe, deep in your hearts. I am the fear and hatred you hold for those who fear and hate you, and would kill you if they could.*
>
> *You made me in your image. I'm only doing what you don't have the guts to do yourselves.*

"Christ," Susan whispered.

"At least Lieutenant Trask will get what he wanted. Between this attempt to make contact, and the explanation of his motivations, they have enough information to start profiling the guy."

"They can stick him into one of their little boxes all they want," Susan said, "call him an organized killer, a disorganized killer, whatever, it doesn't matter. He's playing with us. He knows there's just enough truth in this to draw blood all over town."

"If we don't print it, somebody else will. I have a publisher, stockholders, and a board of directors to answer to."

"Then print just a few excerpts."

"These murders have been chewing up everybody in town for months; our readers want to see the whole thing, and if they can't get it from us, they'll get it somewhere else. Hell, the *San Francisco Chronicle* not only ran the full text of the Zodiac's letters, they printed photocopies of the damned things so everybody could see his penmanship."

"I'm not disagreeing with you on principle, Susan. I'd rather not give this nutcase a forum. It's always a mixed blessing. But it's newsworthy, it could help the investigation, and I can't justify *not* printing it to the people who stand above me on the food chain."

"You're giving him what he wants."

"Maybe I am. That's a real possibility. And maybe I'm giving him just enough rope to hang himself with. The only thing I *do* know for certain is that this story is going to start heating up in a big way. It needs your experience, your commitment, and your opinions. You can run it your way. What you print in your stories is up to you, same as always. You can even disagree with me in print for running this letter, I'm fine with that. Assuming you want back on the merry–go–round."

She didn't hesitate before answering. "I'm in," she said, handing back the letter.

"Don't you want to keep a copy?"

"Why? It'll be on page one tomorrow morning, I can get it then. Besides, I don't think I'll forget that anytime soon."

"You want your old desk back?"

She looked through the window to the newsroom, and shook her head. "No, I'd feel...awkward over there. I'll stay where I am.

"Just one other thing," she added. "This guy stands foursquare for destruction. He's smart, and he's dangerous, and he loves to inflict as much pain as possible when he works. So what do you think prompted him to send this letter? Do you really think he had some sudden desire for self–expression? Or did he send it because he figures the aftershocks will make his whole campaign considerably more efficient?"

Rob looked down at his desk. "I don't know, but you're right...on some level, however much I justify this, I feel like an accomplice."

"Good," she said firmly, and stepped outside, closing the door more loudly than she had intended.

As she reached her desk, she found her hands were shaking, and there was a message on her desk from Mike Devereaux.

Just got copy of the letter sent from Times. Re: killing the rich folk, you were right. How'd you know?

She reached for the phone to return his call, then cradled it again. She would give herself ten minutes to compose herself, and get back into a professional mindset

Because right now, the only thing she wanted to do was yell at anyone, anything, everyone and everything.

A River
of Flame

For Susan, it was not a question of *if* trouble would follow the letter, only *when*. She didn't have long to wait.

The trouble started three days after the Slasher's letter appeared in every local news outlet in Los Angeles county.

Three days after road blocks and cordons and increased police security had been put into place throughout Beverly Hills, Malibu and Brentwood, patrolling the streets and questioning anyone found in the area after dark.

Two days since panicked residents of multimillion dollar estates in Pasadena, Glendale and other parts of the Valley demanded to know why such protection had not been extended to include their neighborhoods, unimpressed by the police logic that thus far the Slasher had not struck anywhere north of the mountainous ridge that separated the Valley from Los Angeles proper, or improper.

One day since protesters had shown up at City Hall in the hundreds, demanding to know why such vast amounts of money were being spent to protect the rich, monies that had *not* been spent in these amounts to protect the poor or the middle-class. The protest had begun peacefully but quickly turned sullen when mounted police officers arrived to break up the crowd.

Orders led to pushing, pushing led to shoving, and when a startled horse stepped onto an elderly woman's leg as it backed up, snapping her ankle, something snapped in the crowd as well.

Grand total, as reported in the *Trib*: two officers injured, over two dozen civilians—mostly protestors, some bystanders, and one reporter with a local radio station—injured by rubber bullets, pepper spray and batons; seventeen windows broken, two fires started, three cars tipped over (including one squad car), nineteen charges of police brutality, and nearly fifty arrests.

The next day, Friday, was the day the real trouble started. The news cameras were not there to capture how it started, only what followed. It would take Susan most of the following week to piece together how things actually got rolling.

The day started out hot and dry, the kind of bitter heat that only came when the Santa Ana winds blew west over the desert and swooped into the Los Angeles basin, sucking all the moisture and all the patience out of anyone fool-ish enough to go out in the hundred degree–plus heat. The killer had not struck since publication of his letter, presumably waiting for the tension to hit critical mass as everyone waited for the other shoe to drop.

According to police reports, at 2:30 p.m. a homeless man was caught shoplifting at a neighborhood grocery store at Third and Normandy owned by a Korean man. The owner of the store knocked the items out of his hands and pushed him outside onto the sidewalk. The shoplifter fell, picked himself up again and began swearing at the owner. The owner swore back. A crowd gath-ered, a crowd that by subsequent reports had never much liked the owner, believing that he kept his prices unreasonably high in order to gouge the neighborhood.

The homeless man shoved the Korean. The Korean shoved back. Someone in the crowd yelled and pushed the owner back against the door. A beer bottle was thrown out of the crowd, smashing against the back of the owner's head.

The Korean man's college–age sons left their post in the store and rushed out into the street, pushing and shoving at the crowd that had gathered. Fists followed shoving, and bricks followed fists. The police who arrived on the scene quickly discovered that they were considerably outnumbered by the angry mob, who were now smashing the front glass of the store and moving on to those on either side.

According to police archives, the 1992 Los Angeles riots that followed the Rodney King verdict began in earnest when one African–American man was shoved to the ground and allegedly manhandled by police. The King verdict provided the gunpowder; the single incident that followed, one of many poten-tial sparks, was the one that triggered the actual fighting that became the worst riot to that time ever to hit Los Angeles.

The 2000 Los Angeles riots began when the Korean store owner came out of his shop with a gun, and fired one shot into the face of the man who had hit him over the head with a beer bottle.

Santa Monica Boulevard was a river of flame.

Smoke blackened the sky over half of the downtown district, clearly visible from the top floor newsroom of the *Trib*. Crowds of reporters and staff gath-ered to look at it, stunned into silence or the occasional profanity as reports came in over the wire, the radio, and TV. Those few who had ventured out on behalf of the *Trib* were on strict orders to phone in every half hour on the half hour.

The police scanner crackled with frantic instructions and requests for back-up, adding personal counterpoint to the helicopter–camera scenes playing on the television:

A toy warehouse on Wilshire engulfed in flames, fire fighters arriving on the scene only to be pinned down by sniper fire.

Intersections where anyone driving an upscale vehicle—a BMW, a Mercedes, a Jaguar—was stopped, dragged out of his car, robbed and beaten, the car trashed and set afire by the crowds that had gathered to watch the show.

Supermarkets and department stores and electronics shops being looted, hundreds of people streaming in through broken windows and out again, pushing shopping carts piled high with stereos, TVs, food, Nike sneakers.

A black minister standing in the middle of Vermont Avenue, calling to the crowds to stop, being jumped and beaten by four gang members armed with tire irons and bricks.

Vans crowded with looters taking advantage of the diversion of police forces to stream uptown, driving right into the front windows of posh jewelry stores on Rodeo Drive and Cañon and Beverly, smashing their way in and jumping out to grab whatever they could find before backing out and doing the same to the next store.

Store owners on rooftops, armed with shotguns and rifles, protecting their property from looters.

Hundreds of police in riot gear, outnumbered and outgunned, no longer trying to stop the violence, only hoping to contain it and let it burn itself out.

Trash fires in the streets.

Graffiti on torched buildings, FUCK THE RICH.

Civilians caught in the wrong place at the wrong time.

Blood caught on video and relayed by satellite to stunned news anchors and viewers in a hundred million homes across the country.

Then the long night: stores that had been looted twice already ravaged again for anything that might have been missed... civilians staying home or sleeping in offices rather than risk the streets...stores isolated by gunfire and mobs left to burn, turning the night an ominous red...news helicopters circling the destruction like fireflies, the images constant, unremitting, viewers riveted to television screens, pointing to familiar landmarks and street signs now deserted, strewn with glass, or awash in fire.

The police came with the dawn, taking advantage of the looters' exhaustion to pour in with riot equipment, tanks, tear gas, rubber bullets, plexiglass shields, batons, shotguns and additional forces from neighboring sheriff's departments, seizing territory from rioters too tired to riot further.

With the police came the field reports, interviews with victims, with store owners, with rioters and looters who gleefully displayed their new stereos, microwave ovens and projection TVs with the pride and clear conscience of lottery winners. News anchors flown in from New York and Seattle and Atlanta and Washington followed field reporters as each battle zone was cleared of gunfire, reporting back to their constituents from notepads crowded with body counts and multimillion dollar damage estimates.

Print and media editorials would follow. Psychologists and urban planners and celebrities and clergy would be interviewed, offer theories, solutions, warnings, Jeremiads. Ted Koppel would dedicate an entire week's worth of *Nightline*s to an attempt to answer the question, "LA: What Went Wrong?"

But Susan never considered it much of a question.

What went wrong is that we printed that goddamned letter.

All this, she thought with disbelief as she finally left the Tribune building after camping out there for most of the preceding two days. *All this, because of one lunatic with a knife, who knew how to push everyone's buttons.*

She knew she shouldn't be surprised. It wasn't the first time this sort of thing had happened as a result of one person. It had happened with the Martin Luther King murder, the Rodney King beating; it had happened in Newark and Los Angeles and Tampa and it would happen again. But never had she seen it so obviously, and so effectively manipulated into being by one person.

What's the saying? Big oak trees from little acorns?

I wonder what the rest of this tree is going to look like.

A War
of Souls

"So when do you think something's going to happen?"

Susan looked up as Rob took the seat across from her in the small kitchen that was adjacent to the *Trib*'s newsroom. It wasn't much to look at, a collection of multicolored plastic chairs and tables in a white room with a refrigerator, a microwave, several honor–system snack boxes, and the single most important item of all to any working journalist: a massive coffee brewer that pumped out caffeine constantly throughout the day and most nights. When the streets were paralyzed during the riot, several members of the staff camped out here in sleeping bags because it kept them close to the emergency stairs, and the coffee machines, in inverse order of priority.

Susan put down the draft of her latest attempt to frame the riots so they made sense—a nearly impossible task—and sat back. "Haven't we had enough *happen* lately?"

"I'm not talking about the riots, Susan. It's been over a week since the letter, and nearly two weeks since the last murder. Since then we haven't heard a word, and there hasn't been another murder, attempted or otherwise. Where is he?"

"Rob, do I *look* like his appointment secretary?"

"That depends. Have you read the part of the employee handbook that prohibits writers from smiting their editors?"

"No."

"Than I see no resemblance whatsoever."

He got up from the table and fished around in the refrigerator for a cold drink. "I was talking to Rudy Miles, assistant to the Mayor this morning, and he thinks the killer has moved on."

"Wishful thinking," Susan said.

"Maybe. But on the other hand, he got what he wanted. He made millions of dollars worth of trouble, and said what he came here to say. Rudy thinks the killer will lay low for a while, maybe even a couple of years."

"I'm glad to find out that Rudy knows so much about serial killers," Susan said dryly, "based on his long years of experience in real estate."

Rob found the Coke can he was looking for and returned to the table, snagging a bag of roasted peanuts on the way back. "Serial killers do take breaks sometimes, when the need to kill has been satisfied. Zodiac, the Unabomber, John Wayne Gacy, even Jeffrey Dahmer took some time off, a couple of years worth in some cases." He popped the Coke can. "Hell, once they'd stocked the kitchen with parts, why go shopping for a while?"

"You are, without question, the most tactless human being I have ever known," Susan said.

"Thank you. Anyway, since the topic came up, I thought I'd see what you had to say on the issue."

Susan absently tapped a pencil against the formica tabletop, cupping her chin in her other hand. "He hasn't gone away. I just think he's waiting as long as possible before dropping the other shoe so he can get everyone wound up to the max. LAPD's getting budget pressure to step down the Beverly Hills patrols, and I think they're going to do it. They can sustain that kind of massive police presence for only so long before the costs get completely out of line, especially with no immediate threat. I mean, are they going to keep those roadblocks and squad cars in place indefinitely, tying up resources needed elsewhere? You know how shorthanded they are these days. I'd be surprised if they didn't step down the patrols at least fifty percent by the end of the week. They won't tell anyone that, of course, they want the killer to think the patrols are still out in force, but on a simple dollar basis, they have to cut back sometime soon."

"So maybe that's what our guy is waiting for," Rob said. "Lay low until the LAPD can't afford to field this level of surveillance, then move in to pick up where he left off."

"That's one possibility. But his reasons could have nothing to do with any of this. For all we know, his apartment was burned down during the riots, he could've been shot, hell, he could've been killed in a traffic accident on the Ventura Freeway this morning for all we know. That's the worst of it: we have absolutely no idea what's going on, where he is, or what he's going to do. He's in complete control, which is probably what he wanted from the start. We have to wait on his pleasure. When he feels like picking up where he left off, he will. Meanwhile, anybody who says they know what's going on in his brain is full of it, me included."

"What about this consultant of yours, Raymond? What does he think?"

"I don't know. With everything that's been going on with the riot, I haven't talked to him in a couple of days. He's been convalescing, and I figured he didn't need the distraction. I was planning to stop by this afternoon and see how he was doing. Maybe he'll have an idea or two for me."

She glanced at her watch, then stood, gathering her papers. "Which reminds me, I'd better get these changes typed in or I'll miss deadline, and my editor is a pain in the ass about these things."

"Good for him," Rob said, rising. "Sounds like my kind of guy."

He accompanied her back to the newsroom, the sound of rapid keystrokes coming from every cubicle as reporters hurried to pull together stories before the three o'clock deadline. The newsroom was usually a loud, boisterous place—put that many high–verbals in one room and you're going to have noise—but by mutual, unspoken agreement, the place quieted down considerably the closer it got to three o'clock. At 2:59 she could always feel the relief in the room as forty–seven reporters hit RETURN almost simultaneously, sending their articles down the Ethernet links to the printing complex.

She had fifteen minutes; barring interruptions, that was more than enough time to plug in the small changes she had made in the kitchen.

But she knew there ware always interruptions.

"One last thing," Rob said as they reached her cubicle, providing said interruption.

"What's that?" Susan glanced at her computer screen and tried to turn off the clock in her head that was already counting down the deadline. *Fourteen minutes fifty seconds, fourteen minutes forty seconds...*

"I was wondering, how much do you actually know about this Raymond Wiley—"

"Weil, with an e–i–l." *Fourteen minutes twenty seconds, fourteen minutes ten seconds...*

"Right, Weil. You're investing a lot of time and effort into this guy, consulting with him on a regular basis, and I think it might not be a bad idea, when you have some time, to find out a little more about him, so you know who you've gotten into bed with, so to speak."

Rob was about to continue when he was paged for a phone call over the intercom. "I better take that, it's probably the Mayor's office again. Catch you later."

He headed for his office as Susan sat at her desk, staring at the console. She'd intended for some time now to follow up on what she'd learned about Raymond, but there never seemed to be enough time in the day. Rob was being gentle about it, but she had dropped the ball, and she knew she was being reminded about it. *Always make sure your source is legitimate, sane, credible, and doesn't have an axe to grind or an agenda to promote. Do your homework.* He had drilled those principles into every one of his staff over the years, and that caution had paid off in the relatively few retractions they'd had to print because of an ill–informed or malicious source.

Thirteen minutes twenty seconds, thirteen minutes ten seconds....

She started typing, resolving that as soon as she hit RETURN at 2:59, she would modem a request for information about Raymond down to the research department. They'd correlate and compare results from a dozen search engines including AltaVista, Google, DejaCom, InfoBot and Webcrawler, as well as searching other newspapers, magazines, and the *Trib*'s own archives for any relevant matches. She'd have the results by tomorrow morning, organized by date, keyword and relevance.

But that was for later; she glanced at her watch and started typing, knowing she had just under twelve minutes to make fifteen minutes worth of edits.

The phone rang at her elbow.

She snatched it up on the second ring, cradling it against her shoulder as she typed. "Hi, whoever this is, I'm on deadline, can I call you back?"

"It's Larry."

She closed her eyes. Larry had the worst sense of timing of anyone on the planet. "Look, Larry, this isn't—"

"I quit the agency."

"You what?"

"I gave them my notice this afternoon."

"Why? I thought you were happy there."

"I was. But now I have a chance to do my own thing. I just got picked up by Paramount as a producer. They know I can get the stars they want, they like my take on stories, and they made me a three-picture deal for more money than I could earn at the agency in five years. So I thought I'd see if you wanted to get together and celebrate my good news."

Ten minutes fifteen seconds.

"Larry…" She sat back, speechless for a moment. "God damn it, Larry, you can't just pop in and out of my life at your convenience because you've got good news, or you want to celebrate, then turn around and ignore me the rest of the time, or go off to San Francisco with somebody else."

"Susan, there's no point in dwelling on the past."

"Yes there is! What the hell does that even *mean*, 'there's no point in dwelling on the past?' Maybe they should try that one at murder trials. 'Yes, my client killed three nuns and a baby duck, but let's not dwell on the past.' It's just a way of ducking responsibility for your actions."

"I just called you to see if you wanted to do dinner, I don't think that merits my being called a murderer."

"I didn't call you a murderer, Larry, that's just a metaphor. Don't you even *try* to turn this around and get me on the defensive. Christ, half of LA was in flames a week ago and you didn't even call to see if I was okay, because that would have meant showing some interest in me. Instead, when something goes good for *you*, now you call, because in the end that's what matters to you: you. You are at the center of your own universe, the first thing you think about when you get up and the last thing you think about when you go to bed and I don't want to hear from you anymore, Larry, okay? I don't want to—"

It took her a moment to realize that she was talking to a dead line. He had hung up on her.

She slammed down the phone. "God *damn* it!" she said, loud enough to draw stares.

I've got eight minutes to meet a freaking deadline, and I've got a dead line of another kind and thanks for the pun God you're a real pain in the ass some days and this is just not fair, it's not right, I don't need this right now.

She pushed it to the back of her mind and tried to focus on the words on the monitor in front of her, wiping at her eyes, refusing to recognize what was making it hard to read the text.

The sky was already starting to darken over Woodland Hills when Susan pulled up in front of Raymond's house. The horizon was indigo blue with a brilliant strip of red at its lowest point, spectacular sunsets born of smog, fog, and unspecified particulate matter being among the few benefits of living in Los Angeles.

She felt guilty that she had not come by more often, but she knew he would understand. They both had their obsessions and their work, which in this case were the same thing. She tried to push away the headache that had come to rest behind her eyes since Larry's call. *No reason to drag my emotional baggage in through the front door,* she told herself.

She climbed out of the car, headed up the walk to the front porch, and knocked. For a long moment, there was no answer. She knocked again, and peered past the window. The house was dark inside. She was about to turn around and leave, assuming he was taking a nap or had gone out, when the door opened and Raymond stood in the entrance, dressed in slacks and a pullover shirt, his hair disheveled, rubbing sleepily at his face.

"I'm sorry," he said, "I was sleeping, didn't hear the door."

"It's all right," she said, "I'm sorry, I didn't know you would be asleep this early. I can come back—"

"No, no, it's all right. I did the same to you, and turn about is fair play. Come on inside."

She followed him into the house, closing the door behind her.

"Are you okay?" he said.

"Yeah, I'm fine, why?"

"Well, you look a little upset."

"Tough day at the office," she said. "I really don't want to talk about it."

The curtains were drawn throughout the house, the television providing most of the light in the den. He switched on lamps as he went, and Susan noticed that the television was tuned to one of the countless documentaries about the recent LA riots.

He caught her glance and nodded toward the TV. "I keep watching it, over and over…all of it, all the news reports, the analyses, the recaps, what went wrong…"

He gestured to a chair, and she sat as he eased himself back onto the couch. His arm was out of the sling, but he still moved gingerly. "How are you feeling?" she asked.

"Better. It seems I don't heal as fast as I used to, which is damned inconvenient. But I've finally gotten to where I can use it pretty well now. No reason to avoid going back to work."

She smiled and glanced back at the television. "I'm surprised you can watch that," she said. "I can't even look at the footage without getting angry. It's like watching a train wreck in slow motion, except that this one could have been avoided."

Raymond settled gently back on the sofa, using a pillow to prop himself up at one end. "Do you really think so?"

"Well, yes, don't you?"

"No. Not anymore. This is exactly what he wanted. And this is what he *would* have gotten one way or another. If the newspapers and TV stations hadn't gone out with that letter, it would've been something else."

He turned to her from the television, and it seemed to Susan that his eyes were impossibly tired. No longer a steel gray, more the gray of mist and sadness. "I've figured it out," he said quietly.

"Figured what out?"

"The message." He pointed to the television. "For the last six days, ever since the riot, I have been sitting here, watching every report, every comment, every frame of footage. I have listened to the interviews, the experts, the politicians, the clergy, the commentators, the average man in the street. I would read the papers, end to end, and watch the reports on TV until I fell asleep, then start all over again when I woke up. The meaning has been burned in me with a clarity I find startling, revelatory."

He was more awake now and building up a head of steam, but it was one that Susan found vaguely troubling. His voice had an almost fanatical sound to it, as if he had been the recipient of revealed truth captured between commercials. She had seen many of the same reports, read many of the same articles, and if there was a revelation to be found there, she had most certainly missed it.

"So what's the message?" she asked.

He turned back to the television, pointed at the images of fire and destruction that paraded across the screen. "Look at what he has done. Look at how he has set us against each other. When it was all downtown, when only the displaced were being victimized, the average middle–class guy on the street was fine with it all. Oh, sure, it was tragic, but tragic in the way that something happening to a small village halfway around the world is tragic: it's distant, it's uninvolving, and if those people didn't want to be victimized they shouldn't have been there in the first place. Most people see the homeless as threats, as the criminal element, which is sometimes true and sometimes not, but it was easy to say that the murders would help clean out the streets, that the victims had it coming."

Susan flinched inside, remembering Leo's comments during the first phase of the murders. *The downtown renovation and gene–pool–cleaning project*, he had called it.

Raymond continued. "Then the murders shifted, and suddenly it was the average middle–class man who was the target. *Now* it's a crime, *now* it's important, *now* we have to demand accountability from the police, from our elected officials. The poor and homeless who had been targeted first laughed because they figured it was our due, that it was right and proper for us to know the terror they had known. The second phase of the murders threw that anger into stark relief, just as it brought out our own ugliness. We blamed the homeless for being the kind of victims that could attract a killer like this. It brought us face to face with our own base hypocrisy, because *now* the killings represented a real tragedy because now it was *us* being killed, not them.

"The loop was closed and the noose tightened around our necks as soon as the killer announced he was moving further uptown. We saw the special treatment the rich received, that they have *always* received, only now it was right there, in our face; treatment the average hardworking taxpayer had not received. Why should they get extra protection and round the clock police presence at our expense? What makes them special? I'll bet you a hundred dollars right now that there isn't a bar in this town where the news of the killer's new target wasn't greeted by someone saying, 'Better them than me.' Who feels sorry for the rich? Who worries that they're not being kept safe? They can take care of themselves, they can afford it, it's not our problem."

"So you're saying it's class warfare? That this guy is trying to foment revolution on a class basis?"

"No, that's—"

"Because that makes a weird kind of sense. Look at Charlie Manson, and the Tate–LaBianca murders. The whole reason those murders happened was because Charlie wanted to foment open warfare between the races. In just the last few years there have been plenty of killers and cult leaders and extremists who believed that their actions would start a war, send a message that would start a revolution pitting one class of people against another." She found herself getting excited, sparking to the idea. "It fits, you know, it starts to really—"

"Susan—"

"What?"

"That's not it," he said. "That's not it at all. The division by class is just a handy way of packaging the message. You're looking at the ribbons and the box, not what's inside the box."

She sat back, arms folded, growing impatient despite herself. "All right then, Raymond, you tell me: what's inside the box? What's the message?"

"The purpose is to bring out the worst in us; to make us hate ourselves and everyone around us; to see us drown in our own self–interest and hypocrisy; to force us to recognize that we are of the pit and always will be; to see ourselves as creatures of dirt instead of beings of light; and in the end to convince us that we are baseless and worthless and undeserving of salvation."

"Don't tell me we're back to that again—"

He picked up a Bible on the sofa beside him. "Romans 8:35. 'Who shall separate us from the love of Christ? Shall tribulation, or distress, or persecution, or famine, or nakedness, or peril, or sword? Just as it is written, For Thy sake we are being put to death all day long; We were considered as sheep to be slaughtered.'

"The Devil feeds on despair, Susan. The cry of a soul in torment, a soul that does not choose redemption because it believes itself unworthy, is the sweetest song imaginable."

He pointed again to the scenes of carnage playing on the television: civilians turned looters, mothers and children gleefully carrying food and electronic equipment out of the burned husks of neighborhood stores, paramedics pinned down by sniper fire watching as a wounded pregnant woman dies because they cannot get to her without being shot themselves, neighborhoods tearing themselves apart, beatings in the street by gang bangers, by street kids, by police.

Raymond's voice was still and quiet in the room. "Who, seeing all of *that*, could imagine that God could love such creatures?

"This is a war of souls, Susan, and every soul the Devil can deny God, every soul he can snare through hopelessness and despair, is a victory. How many victories has he won in this city, I wonder? How many souls—"

"Raymond, *stop*." She stood, walked to the television and turned it off. "I mean, *listen* to yourself. Can't you hear how this sounds? There's *nothing*, nothing in any newscast, nothing in any article, that has *anything* to do with what you just said. That's what you see because that's what you *want* to see. That came entirely from inside of you.

"I just don't understand you, Raymond. One minute you're making sense, and I think you're really onto something, and the next you're back on this...this—"

"Bullshit?"

She paused. "I was looking for a more polite word."

"Don't bother."

Raymond eased himself slowly out of the couch until he stood before her. "Susan, I've been absolutely straightforward with you from the beginning. You know what I believe, I've never lied to you about that. If you didn't accept that, if you don't believe that—"

"I can't, Raymond. I've tried, really I have, but as far as I'm concerned the whole demonic influence thing is just one more manifestation of the Twinkie defense, a way of dodging responsibility and I'm up to here with people ducking responsibility for their actions."

On some level she knew she had crossed arguments, that she was arguing with Larry who was *not* in the room just as much as she was arguing with Raymond who *was*, but she had reached critical mass.

"I mean, it's absurd. 'No, I didn't kill these people, it was the sugar in the Twinkie that made me go nuts and kill the Mayor of San Francisco...no, it wasn't me shot those kids while they sat in their cars fooling around, not good old Son of Sam, it was my dog talking to me made me do it...no, huh–uh, not me, it was the Devil made Steven Jason Lloyd shoot up a pier in San Francisco..."

She stopped, horrified.

Raymond wasn't looking at her.

What the hell is wrong with you how could you say such a thing Christ the woman's comatose not twenty feet down the hall.

"Oh god, Raymond, I'm sorry, I didn't—"

"I think you should go now." His voice was low, barely above a whisper.

"It's just...I had this argument with Larry and I'm still upset and I didn't mean to—"

"Now. Please."

She nodded and moved past him, heading for the front door. She glanced back once before leaving, to see him still standing where she had left him. He reached down slowly, the slowness of an old man who seemed suddenly very small and very tired and very much alone. He picked up the remote control, and switched on the television again.

She stepped outside, closed the door, and walked back to her car, eyes burning for the second time that day.

Some days I wonder why I even get out of bed, she thought. *Some days I truly do wonder.*

Who Are You Now?

There were times Susan hated the blank screen almost as much as she hated her life, and today she could easily accommodate both at the same time.

She looked at the accumulated crime stats for the previous evening, an inglorious and unremarkable collection of muggings, domestic disputes, car thefts and drivebys.

She looked at the monitor's blank screen, which was waiting for her to type words that would somehow make sense of the statistics, arrange them such that they seemed newsworthy when in fact they were anything but; or when all else failed, find some way to thematically weave them together into an article that might, just possibly, maybe, *might* not suck.

She looked at her life.

Stick with the monitor and the stats, she decided. *You'll have better luck whipping those into shape.*

She hadn't slept well the night before, her conversation with Raymond running ceaselessly through her mind every time she closed her eyes and tried to sleep. In the few moments when she managed to push it away completely, her conversation with Larry took center stage. She had spent the night angry with herself, angry with Larry, and angry with the fact that she couldn't get to sleep, which in turn only made it that much harder to get to sleep, which made her that much angrier, and the spiral took her into the dawn and the damned mourning doves who seemed to think daylight was such a particularly wonderful thing that they had to yell about it right outside her bedroom window.

The "Larry Thing" as she had come to refer to it was now officially old, dead news. No one who hung up on her once was ever given the chance to do it a second time. In the vernacular of some of the younger and sprightlier editorial assistants, she thought, *I have so moved on.*

Raymond, however, was a different situation. She had been the one to overreact, she was the one who had misspoken about as poorly as anyone since Prime Minister Chamberlain returned from a trip to Germany to announce that Hitler and his Beer Hall Buddies posed absolutely no threat to Western civilization.

He had done nothing to merit the comment; he was right, she knew what he believed, she had no business berating him about it just because she was mad at somebody else. She was determined to find some way to apologize, some way to make up for it.

Maybe a signed, personalized letter from the Devil saying, "You win," she thought.

Stop it right there young lady, announced the voice in her mind that always sounded like her mother. *This is exactly the kind of comment that got you in trouble in the first place.*

Yeah, but it's funny, and right now I could use a laugh.

She reached for the phone as it rang at her elbow. "City Morgue," she said.

There was a long pause at the other end of the line. "Ms. Randall?"

She recognized the voice. It belonged to Mitch Barkin, one of the *Trib's* crack team of researchers. "Sorry Mitch, it's me."

"I thought I'd misdialed for a minute."

"Yeah, sorry, it's just been that kind of day. What's up?"

"I've got the results of the search you asked for yesterday on Raymond Weil. Should I modem it on up?"

She sat back. She'd almost forgotten about it. *Maybe I'll find something there that can let me make up to him,* she thought. *Or at least find something that'll help me avoid any land–mines in future.*

"Sure, yeah, that'd be great," she said. "Send it on up, thanks. Find anything interesting?"

There was another long pause. "Well, I suppose that's one way of looking at it."

"What do you mean?"

"Maybe nothing. Sending it up now."

She hung up and waited for the Ethernet link to pop the file into her system. A moment later the screen filled with a list of references the research division had turned up under Raymond's name, most accompanied by links to the original source material.

She scanned down the list, looking for the references whose one–line descriptions seemed the most promising.

One link took her to a small article in the *Detroit Daily News*, dated two years earlier. *Missing Area Man Reunited With Family.*

> Citing a nervous breakdown as reason for his seven day disappearance, Detroit car salesman Francis Daly returned today to his anxious family. Police reports filed last Sunday stated that Daly had been briefly seen in the Farmington Hills area accosting strangers, brandishing a knife and screaming incoherently.

Susan skipped over the rest of the report, which mentioned Raymond nowhere, and studied the captioned photograph. *Francis Daly (l) seen here with his wife Jennifer and family friends Father James Richards and Raymond Weil.*

She copied the image into Photoshop and enlarged it. The man on the far right was definitely Raymond, smiling but looking very tired. She noticed that his right hand was bandaged and his jacket didn't go with the pants he was wearing, which was not at all Raymond–like. His taste in clothing had so far been impeccable.

So…what? He lost it in a struggle? Maybe with this Daly guy? And got injured in the process.

She looked back at Daly. Enlarged, his face was filled with relief at being back, but there was something more, a haunted look, eyes hollow, the appearance of a man who had looked into Hell and somehow, luckily, returned alive.

They chose to call it a nervous breakdown, she thought. *Kind of makes you wonder what they might've called it if they thought nobody would decide they were crazy.*

Another link took her to an article in the *Soldier of Fortune* web archive. The piece was twelve years old, an interview with half a dozen mercenaries about their life, their work and their adventures. The garish writing style made it practically a recruitment ad for would–be mercenaries.

She scrolled down until she got to a picture of a younger and more dashing Raymond, who was standing somewhere in a desert alongside another mercenary, both in combat fatigues, carrying heavy–duty weapons. They were smiling broadly for the camera, faces tanned dark from long stretches in the sun.

> Ray Weil (above right) seen with his frequent collaborator in covert activity Lee Hannibal, have traveled the world over in search of action, and found more than their share of it. Pictured here after a successful operation in the Sudan, the details of which unfortunately cannot be discussed, the New Zealand–born Hannibal said, "You can't do this kind of work unless there's someone at your back you trust implicitly. I figure I've only got another five, ten years in the business, and I can tell you right now that Ray here is the only guarantee I have of making it out alive, and the only guarantee I need. We know each other inside and out. Where I go, Ray goes, and where he goes, I go."

Interesting, Susan thought. *I wonder what happened to that promise later.*

Weil, the more soft-spoken of the two—not hard given the gregarious nature of his partner in mercenary pursuits—downplayed the danger and the action. "We all work in places and under conditions over which we have no control. You accept that going in. What we can control is how we choose to conduct our business. I have no patience with those who would use this lifestyle as an excuse for the kind of behavior that would get you tossed out of a real army."

She skimmed down the rest of it, but found nothing more interesting than the kind of posturing and self-aggrandizement she'd come to expect from the kind of testosterone-poisoned men who thought it was great fun to go uninvited into someone else's country and shoot things up. At least Raymond seemed not to play into that mentality, and for some reason that pleased her.

She noticed a small note from Mitch Barkin appended to the list. *Decided to check the national crimewatch list to see if they had anything on Weil, and thought you might find these of interest. MC.*

She scanned down the entries with growing dismay and unease. They included a variety of minor—and some not so minor—incidents involving weapons charges, assault charges, invasion of privacy, trespassing, illegal firearms possession and concealment, and a charge of aggravated battery later dismissed "in the interest of justice" which implied that the victim never showed up or decided not to press charges.

But it was the final two entries that were the most troubling. The first involved an investigation in Atlanta for attempted murder that had apparently stalled out for lack of evidence. The complaint had been signed by the owner of a New Age bookstore who, she noted, was later arrested himself on drug and pandering charges.

The second was an outstanding warrant issued after Raymond apparently jumped bail while awaiting trial on charges of assaulting a police officer in Seattle in 1997.

No wonder he wanted to keep a low profile, and didn't want to press charges against the man who shot him. That's why he didn't want to go to a hospital, and kept telling me, no police. If they did a wants-and-warrants on him, this would show up in no time.

For some reason, even though she knew Raymond had been a mercenary, he had never come across as a violent man. Or even a *potentially* violent man. But mild-mannered accountants didn't generally become mercenaries.

She began to wonder if she really knew Raymond at all.

She scanned down the list to the final item, a link that pointed to *La Grande Libertad*, a South American human rights publication. She clicked on the link, which took her to the main web page where she had to choose between the Spanish and English Language versions. The link then automatically took her to a page concerning American and other covert activities in South and Central America.

Central to the article was a photograph of a burned out encampment in Bolivia. The picture appeared to have been taken by a helicopter. She could see the blurry remains of several bodies scattered around the encampment. As she read the article—which was primarily a vehicle for anti–American sentiment, conspiracy theories and demands for tighter government control over the kind of people who were allowed to enter the country—she slowly began to realize that she was looking at a picture of the camp where Raymond's group had been attacked and wiped out.

> How can we hope to improve the condition under which our people must suffer when the government allows criminals to turn our lands into cemeteries, our churches into slaughterhouses? As this picture shows, these people cannot be trusted. If they would do this to each other, how much more willingly will they murder and abuse our own people?

> These renegade soldiers entered our country with the help of bribed officials, and sought to interfere by force with the agricultural industry of Luis Estefan Morcilla.

She recognized the name. Morcilla had been linked to one of the largest cocaine cartels in South America. *Agricultural industry indeed*, she thought.

So somebody paid Raymond to take out Morcilla's drug plantation? Or maybe Morcilla himself? Could it have been our own government? The Bolivian government? Or maybe a competing cartel? Karl said it didn't make a difference who hired him, which makes sense if he was working for another cartel. Neither side has the moral high ground, all that matters is taking out the target, which on the other hand does eliminate one more source of trouble in the cocaine market.

> The leader of this terrorist group has been identified as Raymond Weil, a known mercenary for sale to the highest bidder. He is wanted for questioning by the Bolivian Policia Nationale on suspicion of having murdered his cronies before fleeing the country. These criminals turn our country into a war zone with the silent complicity of corrupt local politicians.

She read the article twice, looking for more specifics, but if they were there, they were buried beneath the weight of pseudo–Marxist propaganda.

Karl had said Raymond was the sole survivor of the mission to Bolivia. He had *not* said that Raymond was the prime suspect in that mass murder.

Maybe he didn't know.

Then again, maybe he did.

She began to realize that though she had been told a lot of things about Raymond, and had suspected more, she actually *knew* very little. And as she reviewed the list of references, she decided that she needed to find out who this person was, really.

She turned back to the article in *La Grande Libertad*, searching for a list of the other mercenaries killed in the expedition, then scrolled back until she came to the *Soldier of Fortune* article. Lee Hannibal, the New Zealander who had said *where Raymond goes, I go*, was not among the list of casualties.

She picked up the phone and dialed down to Research. Mitch answered on the second ring. "I've got another job for you," she said, and gave him Hannibal's name. "If this guy is still around, can you find him?"

"I'll find him," Mitch said. "Just give me a few hours, I've got about half a dozen other requests ahead of you."

"That's fine, thanks."

She racked the phone, staring at the picture of Raymond and Hannibal taken in the Sudanese desert. She studied his face, the face that she had come to trust, to rely on.

When you introduced me to Hector at that South American restaurant, you said that you'd helped Hector once upon a time. You said you had been a different person.

Who were you then?

And maybe more important, who are you now?

Samuel Klein drummed his fingers impatiently against the steering wheel of his new Porsche. He had been sitting for ten minutes at the corner of Rodeo Drive and Lexington waiting for the police officer checking IDs to get within striking distance of his car. During those ten minutes, he could have been sitting in his hot tub at home. He could have been drinking a Margarita, ordering up a new suit from Hugo Boss, watching television, or on the phone discussing which director to hire for the new film he was producing for Columbia with his partner Jacque Jarvis, assuming said partner wasn't in detox, in Aspen, or screwing any of the half dozen "escorts" he kept on the side.

Instead, he spent those ten minutes staring at a little rat–dog in the back of Mrs. George Hamilton's Mercedes as it barked and snarled and snapped at him through the safety of the rear window. Its eyes bugged out impossibly as it yapped at him, almost knocking itself over each time it barked.

Jump out the window, come on, just jump on out so I can run you down you furry little creep.

Finally, the Mercedes moved, and Beverly Hills Police Officer Lou Montana, badge number 8171, checked Samuel's driver's license, peered through the window at him, and waved him on so he could drive the hundred and fifty feet remaining to his front driveway.

How much longer are we going to have to put up with this bullshit? he wondered. *Christ, nobody's heard boo from this guy in two weeks, and even if he did stick his nose into this part of town, even if he did manage to avoid getting seen and picked up, I paid good money for the best damned security system on the planet. He isn't getting anywhere near me.*

He could never understand hysteria. It's why he had never been tempted by the lottery. Everyone knew that the odds of winning the lottery were about the same as being hit by lightning. The odds of going down in a plane or hijacked by terrorists were even smaller, which is why he resented having to sacrifice his personal freedom and convenience at airports. Why should everyone in the country accept a one hundred percent chance of being inconvenienced to protect against a threat that was statistically and mathematically infinitesimal? And the delays were even the more infuriating and unjustifiable given the stupidity of some of it. Metal detectors, sure, he could more or less get behind that one. But who thought up the questions that every single person had to answer before being allowed on a plane? Who actually thought that a trained terrorist would fall for any of them?

"Did you pack your luggage yourself?"

"No, I asked Ahmed the Bomb Builder to do it for me since he's so much better than me at cramming a lot of material into a very small space."

Give me a fucking break.

He ran through the math as he pulled up into the driveway. He enjoyed playing with numbers, which was fortunate because in Hollywood, it was all about the numbers.

Okay, let's assume it takes 30 seconds to go through all those questions. Leave out the mouth–breathers and the space cases who run the bell curve up to a full minute, let's assume the best and say 30 seconds. On a busy day, LAX handles an average of 180,000 people. Obviously most of those people are being asked the same questions simultaneously, so let's just take the raw numbers. 30 seconds times 180,000 people comes to 1500 man–hours per day, 534,000 man–hours per year, 22,250 man–days per year.

And in all those man–minutes, man–hours and man–days, has anyone, once, answered yes to any of those questions?

He climbed out of the Porsche and stepped up the long walk that led to the front door. *Of course not. And we lose 22,250 days out of a calendar year that only has 365 days in it to begin with.*

Someone explain to me how that makes sense.

He unlocked the front door and stepped inside, punching in his security access code at the panel beside the door.

"*Access Four: Service porch door open,*" the panel announced in its flat, synthesized computer voice.

"Maria?" He checked his watch. 5:23. His housekeeper was usually gone by 4:30, walking the eight blocks down to Wilshire where she caught the bus back to East LA. "Maria, you still here?"

He stepped into the service porch/laundry room, where his shirts had been ironed and hung for tomorrow's meetings. The rear patio door swung gently open in the wind next to the security panel where she would enter in the maid's code each day when she arrived for work.

He closed the door and stepped back into the hall. "Maria?"

A door closed somewhere in the house.

"Goddamn it, Maria, I've told you before about leaving the door open. Maria?"

He heard footsteps behind him.

He turned.

It wasn't Maria.

Down South American Way

Susan turned off the 5 freeway in Orange County, forty–five minutes south of Los Angeles, looking for the address she'd written down on a Post–It Note: 427 Brighton Way, home base for Hannibal And Associates Personal Protection, Lee Hannibal's retirement business. She would have preferred to conduct her interview by phone, but he made it clear in the brief conversation they'd had earlier this morning that he didn't talk business over the phone. She could come see him in person, and take notes, but no tape recorders were allowed.

"And if you try to sneak one in, trust me, I'll know."

She continued along the main road that would take her to the address he'd supplied, and found herself driving deep into a rural area noted more for farmland than corporate offices. Every other house she passed seemed to have an incrementally bigger American flag in the front yard, and every car wore at least one and usually more conservative bumper stickers, announcing *Grab Steering Wheel In Case of Rapture*, or *Guns Guts and Glory Made This Country Great*.

She was well and truly behind what many in Los Angeles referred to as the Orange Curtain.

The address led her to a sprawling ranch set off by itself along a rural road. She pulled in through an old wooden gate and drove up to a two–story house that overlooked exercise and training yards before climbing out and gingerly walking across the gravel–covered driveway to the front door.

A young woman who introduced herself as Lee's assistant, Jennifer, led her down a hallway covered with combat photos, decorations, citations and still more American flags, stopping finally at an office at the back of the house. Lee Hannibal—broader in the face and older than he'd been in the picture from *Soldier of Fortune* but no less robust—rose from behind an oversized wooden desk and crossed to her, hand extended.

"So you're a journalist and a friend of Ray's?" he said. Despite his years in America his accent was still strongly rooted in New Zealand.

"That's right."

"I'm amazed. Those two don't usually go together. Here, sit."

She sat across from Lee in a dark brown leather corner sofa that looked as if it had been dragged cross–country numerous times by elephant caravan. "I understand you were his partner, is that right?"

"I don't know that you'd say partner, exactly. We worked together a lot, sure, but we always negotiated our own fees separately, and he was free to go his own way any time, same as me. Sometimes a job didn't need both of us, sometimes it did, and sometimes it needed a team. He had his guys, I had mine, and it was just one of those things that worked real well for a long time, you know?"

"Is that why you weren't there in Bolivia?"

His expression froze, and in his eyes she could see him clicking through any number of possible, non–committal answers before finally deciding on, "So you heard about that one, eh?"

"It's the main reason I'm here. I'm hoping you can tell me something more it."

"Well, it's hard, because like you said, I wasn't there. My daughter, Susie, was about to graduate High School, and I'd missed so much of the rest of her life while I was running around the world, I just didn't want to miss that, you know? I told Ray if he really needed me I'd be there, but he could see where my heart was, and he said not to worry about it, he had it covered.

"He called up some of his other mates, got them in on the job, set the whole thing up himself. The way I heard it, there were some pols high up in the Bolivian government who wanted that Morcilla guy out of business. Apparently he'd made some threats he shouldn't have made against a bunch of people high up on the food chain, killed some people he shouldn't have killed, and they took it kind of personal. They knew they couldn't move against him themselves, the Bolivian army was full of informers at the time, so they arranged for an outside team to go in, find him, extract him, and turn him over. After that, it wasn't anybody's problem but Morcilla's."

"You mean they would've killed him."

"Probably. Or held him hostage, arranged some kind of swap for protection, whatever. Remember, this guy was a stone killer. Word on the street was that he'd personally whacked about thirty of his competitors, not counting half a dozen assassinations of minor officials he'd paid for out of cocaine profits. Not a nice man even by American standards. But he put a lot of money in the hands of the locals, so they were real protective of him. That's why they needed someone from the outside. That way they could also deny any involvement if things went pear–shaped during the operation."

He pulled a cigar out of his shirt pocket. "You mind?"

"Not at all." She did, but as long as he was talking, he could ignite his nose hairs and it was fine with her.

"So what happened down there?" she asked as he lit the cigar. "What went wrong?"

"What Raymond says happened is something you'll have to get from Raymond. What I can tell you is what I think happened, *based on* what he told me."

He took a long draw on the cigar. "You ever been in one of those charismatic churches? You know, the evangelical ones, holy rollers they used to call 'em, everybody speaking in tongues, that sort of thing? Real popular in some places, especially when they can't get TV and don't have anything better to do. Start talking in tongues when you're in one of those churches and they treat you like a bloody celebrity.

"Well, there's a flip side of that, especially the further South you go. Out of the blue somebody will fall down, start having seizures and talking in pig–latin, acting crazy, and the locals will say he's possessed by el Diablo. Suddenly everybody knows your name, suddenly you're real important, because if the Devil wants your soul, well, your soul must be worth stealing, right? And when it's over, no matter what you said or did, it wasn't your fault, now was it?

"Half the time the person's just plain crazy, really thinks he's got a devil inside him. The rest of the time it's sheer manipulation, because down South American way it's the next best thing to being a rock star."

He brushed the ashes off the end of the cigar and considered the glowing tip. "Now for every punter who suddenly decides he's el Diablo, there are twenty–five other guys ready to worship him, follow him around, or use him for their purposes, to further their own agenda. That's the flip side I was talking about. Whether you talk for god or you talk for the devil, either way you've got clout.

"If you've done your homework then I suppose you heard about the two guys who had this happen right about the time Ray's team showed up."

Susan nodded.

"Kind of a coincidence, isn't it? I mean, nobody down there wanted Ray's group hanging around. Then suddenly this happens. The way I figure it, either that whole business was a setup to keep everybody looking in a different direction, make sure the villagers stayed scared and stayed *inside* and didn't get in the way, or somebody took advantage of a situation that happened with perfect timing. Maybe it was one of those Devil–loving groups out to flex a little muscle. Or it could've been some of the local guerillas tired of American Imperialists interference in local affairs, or some thugs on Morcilla's payroll looking to win brownie points with the boss. Either way, it gave them the perfect opportunity to move in on Ray's operation without anybody getting in the way for fear of pissing off el Diablo.

"Whoever they were, they waited for night, then went in and tore the place apart."

Susan looked up from her notes. "I was told that most of the gunshots that killed Raymond's team came from their own weapons."

Lee snorted. "You think they've got a forensics lab right there in the middle of the jungle capable of doing a ballistics test on spent ammunition? Come on. They were ambushed."

"Is it possible that some of them were in on the deal, and switched sides? Sold out the rest?"

Here Lee paused. "I don't know. It's possible, I suppose, if there was enough money involved. Doesn't happen often, but it has happened. I didn't work with them as much as Ray, but if he trusted them, then they were good soldiers. Maybe they got caught in a crossfire. If there was enough confusion, in a small space like that, you could get some collateral damage from friendly fire. That might explain it.

"But for that theory to work the situation would have to be pretty intense. These people are trained to look out for each other. That's their first instinct in a firefight. You're talking something that could scare them so badly that all their training would go out the window, and I can't even imagine what that would be."

He stood, motioning toward the back door of the office. "Here, let me show you something."

She followed him outside, to the rear of the compound. Barbed wire, water–filled trenches and foliage had been used to construct hostile environments. "This is where I train my students in how to be mercenaries. It's a three–week course. Ninety percent of them drop out after the first few days. The only people who make it through are the ones who come here hard, who don't panic. If you try to run through this mess or bull your way through, it'll cut you to pieces. You have to go slow and be patient. Lots of people think it's all about looking tough and running around in some kind of testosterone cloud, making a lot of noise and blowing shit up, but in the end it's about being quiet.

"The best mercenary gets in and gets out and nobody even knows he was there. You try to avoid a fight where possible. You're not an adventure hero, you're a freelance soldier, and you have to act like one. Ray believed that right down to his socks, and I feel the same way."

"So what happened between the two of you? When did you stop working together?"

He stepped toward one of the trenches, looking down into the water. "After Bolivia. He was never the same after that."

"How so?"

"Well, it's just…after he got back to the U.S., he went a little wiggy, you know? He went off."

"Are you saying he had a nervous breakdown?"

"I'm not a doctor, but…yeah, something like that. He completely dropped out of sight for a while. It totally messed him up. I hear he got treatment at some hospital up in Santa Clarita. The Mathias Clinic, I think. When he finally pulled himself together I figured he'd get back on track again, but that's when he started calling me and some of the other guys we worked with. He'd call day and night, trying to get us in on this devil–chasing stuff. They said no. It didn't sit well with them, you know? And a lot of them thought it was strange that of all those guys who died in Bolivia, only Ray survived somehow. I didn't think anything about it, I mean, if anyone's going to survive that kind of situation it's Ray, but this is a business that feeds on money, guns and paranoia, and something about the whole thing felt wrong to the other guys, so they just walked away."

"And what did *you* tell him when he called?"

"What *could* I tell him? I said no. Aside from the fact that it was crazy, I mean, where was the money? Most of the stuff he does is pro bono. I know he's gotten a few bucks here and there in the years since Bolivia, but it can't be nearly enough to pay expenses let alone show a profit. By now he's probably gone through his retirement fund and he's running on fumes."

"Then you've kept in touch?"

He grimaced and looked away. "Not really. I mean, once or twice a year I get a phone call or a letter. Maybe a Christmas card. I know he thinks he's into some really deep shit, but I just can't get behind it. Sometimes I think he's really lost it. And that's sad, because we used to be friends, and it's hard when suddenly the guy you knew isn't that same guy anymore."

At the sound of approaching engines, he turned and looked down the road at half a dozen cars, jeeps and off–road vehicles. "My students," he said with an ironic smile. "The next generation of freelance soldiers reporting for class."

"Then I should let you go," she said. "I appreciate you taking the time to talk to me."

"It's all right," he said. "I just hope he's doing well. And tell him that when you talk to him, okay? Last time I heard from him, about six months ago, he said he was on top of something big, that he was going to straighten things out once and for all after Bolivia."

She nodded. Six months ago was shortly after the murders started. "Did he say how?"

"Nope. We both kinda learned not to talk about some things, you know what I'm saying?"

"I do," she said as the arriving cars pulled up into the long, circular driveway. "Well, I should be on my way."

"One thing," he said. "You want to know what happened down there, what I think *really* happened?" He looked away from her, into the distance. "I think he saw something that he couldn't unsee afterward. I think he saw the darker part of himself, of you, me, everybody. What he saw wasn't inhuman, it was our own *inhumanity*. Whatever he's trying to kill out there, I think he's just trying to kill the evil in himself. If he can make whatever it is something outside us, something he can track down and defeat, then he can be free.

"But none of us are free that way, you know? We carry the evil inside us, every day. For Ray, that evil is now outside: it's the devil, or demons, or the supernatural; one way or the other it's been made manifest, and he's out to destroy it, without understanding that he's really just hunting himself."

White On White

Mike Devereaux had never exactly considered himself a *Better Homes and Garden* or *Interior Design Magazine* kind of guy. He couldn't tell Pembroke furniture from mission furniture from baroque or American Provincial, didn't know the difference between faux wall painting and rag wall painting, had no interest in learning the different styles of curtains, sinks, loveseats, or bedroom sets.

But Mike knew that the object in front of him was the most elegant white sofa he had ever seen. It was a contemporary high–back sofa with white–on–white brocade, white plush down pillows and roll–over arms that swept forward in an elegant curve. The sofa back and the two outer cushions were spotless.

The center cushion was covered in blood.

The victim's face had been shoved into the center cushion as his throat had been cut, the soft down inside absorbing all of the blood, turning the cushion a dark red.

As with the previous victims, his hands had been slashed and lay at his sides, the blood from each creating small pools of blood on the white carpet as dramatic counterpoint to the single large pool on the sofa.

The officer standing vigil at the door poked his head inside. "Lieutenant just radioed in, said he should be here in two minutes."

Mike nodded absently and continued looking around the room. The victim's wallet lay untouched on the coffee table next to his keys, and the walls were decorated with pictures of the victim standing alongside movie and TV actors. *Guy must've been an agent or a producer*, he decided.

He kept an eye on the door, making sure none of the other officers, especially the rookie who got the call, came anywhere near the victim until Trask arrived. His job was to secure the scene, keep a low profile, and wait for Homicide to come and do its thing. To that effect he'd sent away two of the other cars that had arrived, hoping it would draw less attention. There wasn't much point to an extensive police presence at this stage anyway; from the appearance of the body he estimated that the victim had been deceased since the middle of the night. The killer was long gone.

He glanced back to the door as Lieutenant Trask entered. They nodded to each other as Trask moved slowly into the living room, studying the crime scene.

"Nothing's been touched," Mike said. Trask would know he wouldn't allow anything to be touched, ever, when he was on the job, but it had to be said for the record.

Trask put on a pair of white latex gloves and approached the body. Except for the sofa and the body, the house was utterly pristine and undisturbed. *Must've knocked the victim out fast, without even much of a struggle, then got to work.*

"Was this wallet here on the coffee table when you got here?"

"Yep. Like I said, nothing's been touched."

Trask knelt on the floor next to the body, gently moving it to inspect the throat wounds. Mike looked away.

"Same as the rest," Trask said, letting the body settle back into place.

"Which rest?"

Trask looked up, and for the first time Mike noticed that his face was pale. "This is the third victim we've found today."

"Christ. What're you saying, that this guy killed three people in *one night*?"

"Three *minimum*. The day's young, we may still hear about more." He edged over to the coffee table and carefully nudged the wallet open, looking for ID. "We're playing this close to the vest for now, not even talking about it on the radio in case someone's scanning. That this guy could come into expensive estates, right under our noses, without setting off any alarms and kill people three times in one night...nobody's going to feel safe."

"Maybe they shouldn't," Mike said. "So who else got nailed?"

"First one we found was Gerry Damrock."

Mike straightened. "The head of RoadDust Pictures? Jesus, I just saw him on TV the other night at some charity thing. He was gonna produce that new *Starfire* movie with Costner and Schwarzeneggar."

Trask nodded. "Script sucked anyway. My wife has a friend who's a casting director, and she said it was lame. I'm telling you, ever since *Waterworld* and *The Postman* it seems like Costner couldn't find a good script with a hunting dog and a Ouija board."

"So who was number two?"

"Samuel Klein, another producer. Both had big buck deals in place."

So I wonder who this is? Mike wondered as Trask used a pencil to slide credit cards and a driver's license out of the wallet.

Then he passed another photo on the living room wall. The victim was standing next to a young woman at a party. "Hey, I know her," he said. "Oh, Christ...Susan."

Trask looked at the name on the driver's license.

"Victim's name is Larry Drake."

"What're you trying to do, kill me here?"

"I know I'm asking a lot," Susan said, "but it could be really important." She'd found a contact at the Mathias Clinic, an intern who had previously worked at Cedars Sinai Hospital and helped keep her informed about the movements of Jimmy the Arm Borzini when the mob leader had been treated there for heart failure and every two–bit mobster in the country was hoping he'd die so they could split up his territory.

"Okay, okay," Carlos said at last. "I'll get you whatever I can find on this Raymond Weil guy, but remember, he was here several years ago. I'll have to go into the archives, and I'm not supposed to be there. And I won't give you anything juicy. Just the medical information and the kind of counseling, that's all. If this backfires, I'll probably get fired but I don't want to get sued on top of it, you know?"

"I understand." Susan looked at her watch. "Look, I'm going to be in and out of the office for the rest of the day, so if I'm not here you can either call me at home and leave the information on my answering machine, or fax it to me at home. All right?"

"Will do. I'll be in touch."

Susan hung up the phone and put away her notes. This wasn't the sort of investigation she felt comfortable doing, but ever since leaving Raymond's house the other day she had gathered just enough information to be troubled. It was not uncommon for journalists to secure the medical records of elected officials and others—everything from Michael Jackson's latest plastic surgery to the psychiatric report that brought down Senator Edmund Muskie in '68 and the report on the heart palpitations of Senator Bill Bradley—but she had no intention of using any of this information in print, only to help put her mind at ease.

I hate doing this, but I need to know who I'm working with. I need to know that I can trust him.

Next on the agenda was a discreet phone call to the Seattle Police Department to inquire about the charge that Raymond had assaulted a police officer and then jumped bail. *I can say I'm writing a piece about the risks police officers take while performing in the line of duty, then back into any outstanding cases, see what I can find out—*

"Susan?"

She looked up from her notes, startled, to find Mike Devereaux standing in the doorway of the newsroom.

"Mike? What're you—"

"Do you know a...I mean, do you have a friend named Larry Drake?"

"Yes, I mean, we've been going out for a while but what...did something happen or—"

"I'm afraid he's dead, Susan."

Susan felt a cold hand close around her heart. "No, that's not possible, I mean, I just *talked* to him the other day. There has to be some kind of mistake."

"There's no mistake."

She thought he might have said *He's been murdered*, thought he might even have said *We're pretty sure it's the Slasher*, but he suddenly seemed to be speaking to her from down a very long, dark tunnel, his voice impossibly far away, and then everything around her kicked slantwise and went black.

I Will Never Eat Pasta Again

Susan could remember sitting up on the sofa in the kitchen, could remember a lot of people standing around and making sure she was all right, but couldn't remember how she got from there to the parking lot.

She could remember Mike apologizing, saying that they had found a total of five victims since the night before, and that maybe it was over now, because that was five in each category and there wasn't any more categories left.

She could remember Rob driving her home, but couldn't remember anything he said on the way.

She could remember going into the bedroom to sleep, but couldn't remember actually arriving at her apartment.

So this is shock, she thought distantly as she opened her eyes. *I always wondered what it was like.* The bedroom clock showed 7:15 P.M. It was dark outside her window. *I always close the curtains when it gets dark because the next apartment can see in if I don't but the curtains are open so I must not have closed them so I must have gotten in and it was still light so I should get up and close them but I don't want to get up.*

She still couldn't quite accept that Larry was dead. Yes, they had argued, had split up, and he was a jerk, but she had never wanted him dead, could not even imagine him dead, let alone—she forced herself to say the word—*murdered.* He had always been energetic, full of life, had been intense even when being intense had equated being a pain in the ass.

She couldn't bring herself to believe that if she picked up the phone right now, and dialed his number, that he wouldn't be there today, that he wouldn't be there tomorrow, or the next day, or the week after that. That he was just...gone, erased from the planet.

This was the second time the killer had struck at someone she knew.

And she didn't care at all for the proximity.

Be reasonable. Everyone knows there's only six degrees of separation between any two people on the planet. You're a reporter. You meet more people in the course of a year, work with more people, than a hundred people in other jobs. It was inevitable that something like this would happen.

Yeah? That so? Well, if you're so smart then how come it never happened before now? How come it only happens after Raymond says this guy knows my name? Huh? You got an answer for that, smarty-pants?

Stop being so self-involved. The killer probably didn't even know about Larry. He just wanted somebody rich, and Larry fit the bill. So there goes your theory, up in smoke. What do you say to that?

Tell you what: I'll get back to you. I think I have to go throw up.

She sat up, fighting nausea. *I hate throwing up. I will not throw up. I refuse.* She ran to the bathroom and vomited into the toilet.

Ten minutes and two cups of mouthwash later, she emerged from the bathroom feeling slightly better, if a little shakier around the knees. *I will never eat pasta again, ever.*

She switched on the hall light, blinking against the sudden brightness, and padded out into the living room. *Milk. Milk will help. Milk is our friend.*

On her way toward the living room she passed the small side room she used as an office, and glanced at the phone.

Not today, not tomorrow, not the day after.

Then she noticed the message light was blinking on her answering machine, and there was paper waiting in the fax machine out-tray. She hadn't heard the phone ring, but under the circumstances, she doubted that she would have heard a thermonuclear device exploding on the front lawn.

Her first inclination was to wait until later to play the messages. She wasn't sure she could handle anything else right now. But on the chance that whatever it was might be important, she padded into the tiny office and hit PLAY. *You've always been too damned responsible for your own good,* she thought glumly.

"Susan, it's Rob. Just got in after dropping you off. I figure you're probably asleep by now—you were pretty whacked when I dropped you off—but I just wanted you to know, when you get this, that if there's anything I can do, or if you just want to talk, or get a cup of coffee, please don't hesitate to call. You've got my home number. Call anytime, day or night."

He's such a sweetie, she thought, as she waited for the next message to cue up past the beep.

"Susan, are you there?" There was a long pause. She recognized Raymond's voice. "I just heard the news. I wanted to pass along my condolences, and see how you were doing. I have to run some errands in your area a bit later, so if it's okay I thought I would stop by, see if you are all right. Again, I'm sorry for your loss. If you need anything, let me know."

Another pause, another beep, another familiar voice.

"Hey, Susan, it's Carlos at the clinic. I got that information you were asking about. I'm sending it over by fax. Once you've read it, destroy it, okay? I don't want anything around that can get into trouble, you know? Thanks."

The last message clicked off. She glanced at the tray with its waiting faxes, started away, then grabbed the papers and continued on toward the living room, depositing them on the sofa as she headed for the kitchen.

Maybe tea would be better. Chamomile tea. Maybe some dry toast. Yeah, I think I could handle that.

She popped two pieces of thin wheat bread into the toaster and set a pot of water to boil, then returned to the living room. She sat on the sofa by the window, the papers beside her on the next cushion. She could just make out the logo for the Mathias Clinic.

I should really read those later, when I'm feeling more up to it, she thought.

Then again, what else do I have to do until the water boils?

She picked up the papers, re–filed them in correct page order, and began flipping through the pages.

```
Patient: Raymond Weil.
    Diagnosis at time of referral: Acute depres-
sion, anxiety, stress. Observation of patient
indicates possibility of post-traumatic
stress-related breakdown. Medical history indi-
cates no prior episodes.
```

She flipped through pages of EKG, ECG, CAT scans and other medical tests, all of which appeared to be normal. A medical log entry caught her attention.

```
    During the course of drug treatment this date,
patient continually referred to the "other," indi-
cating that said "other" was of spiritual or
demonic nature, and responsible for the death of
many individuals who had recently assisted in his
work. When asked to define or describe this
"other" patient refused and became sullen and
depressed. Potential exists for patient having
reassigned responsibility for deaths caused in the
recorded attack in Bolivia to a larger power, non-
human, to assist him in dealing with it, result-
ing in depersonalizing the enemy forces.
    Possibility also exists for diagnosis of
response as indicative of a psychotic break, with
patient projecting his own perceived failure and
guilt for the death of his comrades to a nonhuman
"other" in order to reduce cognitive dissonance
over these feelings of guilt and remorse and
responsibility.
```

She flipped pages.

    During midnight shift patient Weil assaulted
orderly. Minor injuries only, bruises and two
cuts. Patient shows no recollection this morning
of last night's incident. Recommend modification
of drug treatment therapy to include Prozac.

She flipped pages.

    Patient appeared confused & disoriented
throughout morning sessions. Reduced medication
and requested additional blood and pharmaceutical
test in order to determine possible drug con-
traindications.

She flipped pages, stopping at the final entry.

    Panel convened to discuss condition of patient
and make additional recommendations for treatment.
All attending physicians and nursing staff have
witnessed patient talking to himself at various
times during the day, during which he stated he
was concerned for his safety from the "other."
Patient has shown substantial mood swings indica-
tive of bipolar disorder, and inability to remember actions he clearly has taken.
    Pending further tests, staff agreed to a tenta-
tive diagnosis of possible multiple personality
disorder.

She stared at the words. *Multiple personality disorder.*

She fought down the tightness that had her by the throat. She had already been through so much today, was already so upset, so frayed, so close to the edge emotionally; she didn't know how much more she could handle without going off the deep end. *Still, they said the diagnosis was tentative. Possible. Pending further tests. They didn't know for sure. He could've been reacting to the drug treatment itself.*

She looked again at the words. *Multiple personality disorder.*

    Upon being informed of this tentative diagno-
sis, patient responded angrily and demanded to be
released on his own recognizance. Because patient

checked in voluntarily, and staff has no evidence
that patient is a risk to himself or others,
release is being facilitated.

Susan closed the file and for the second time today, felt the world skidding sideways around her.

He got just as upset when I mentioned the Danny Rollings case. She fought to remember what he had said. *"The killer used the idea of possession to escape his responsibility for crimes so heinous that they exceeded his ability to rationalize them."* But wasn't that exactly what was hinted at in the medical file? Hadn't even Lee Hannibal hinted at something similar?

Raymond said it himself. The majority of so–called cases of possession can be attributed to multiple personality disorder.

He referred to the killer as the Other, the same way he referred to whoever attacked his group, but they can't logically be the same thing.

He knew about the slashed hands.

He knew all about Larry and me.

He's attacked a police officer, assaulted at least three people.

At dinner with Hector, Raymond said he was a different person back then.

Hannibal said what Raymond saw in Bolivia was his own inhumanity.

The doctors said he was projecting his own problems onto others, giving it demonic form.

Raymond seems to know what the killer is thinking, knows the message he's trying to send, even figured out his modus operandi, moving from homeless to middle class to rich people.

Hannibal said Raymond wasn't the same after Bolivia...said he thinks Raymond's been hunting himself.

And—

She fought to finish the sentence.

And for as long as Raymond was wounded, the killer didn't strike. Then Raymond gets better, says he's "ready to go back to work." And the killings start again.

She stared at the words. *Possible multiple personality disorder.*

God. Oh, god. It's him. He's been hunting himself. Hunting the evil in himself.

Since the beginning she had felt something was amiss in her dealings with Raymond, had felt progressively more uneasy with the passing of time and the accumulation of coincidences. She had denied it to herself even in the face of mounting—

She sat up suddenly at the sound of a knock at her door.

She crossed to the door, hesitated. "Who's there?"

"It's me." The voice was Raymond's.

Oh god...

"Did you get my message? I thought I'd come by, see if you were okay."

She backed away from the locked door. "I'm fine, Raymond. I'm just...I was sleeping."

You don't know for sure that it's him, you're being irrational, you're on edge because of what happened to Larry, said a voice in her head.

Maybe so, but maybe not, and I can't take that chance, not right now.

There was a pause from the other side of the door. "Are you sure you're okay?"

"Yes...yes, I'm sure."

Another pause. "Can you open the door?"

"No. No, I can't Raymond. I'm...I'm not dressed."

"I can wait."

"I don't think that's a good idea."

The next pause seemed to go on forever. "I think I should come in and check."

She could see the doorknob being tested on the other side of the door.

"Damn it, Raymond, I want you to stay away from me! You hear me? I want you out of here right now!" She grabbed the phone, dialed 911. "I'm dialing 911 right now!"

"Susan?"

"I know all about you!" she yelled. "I know about all of it, about the cop you assaulted in Seattle, the treatments, the MPD...you're not well, Raymond, you need help."

"Emergency Operator," a voice said on the other end of the line.

"Yes, I'd like to report an intruder," Susan said, loud enough to be heard through the door.

"You don't know what you're talking about," Raymond said. "Please, let me in, I can explain."

"I said go away!"

The operator's voice came through the phone, insistent. "Ma'am?"

"Just a second!"

There was another long pause, as if Raymond were considering his next move. Then she heard him move away from the door, down the sidewalk and into his car. She ventured a glance out the window just in time to see his car pull away from the curb and disappear down the darkened street.

"Ma'am, do you require assistance?"

"I don't think so...I'll call you back."

She hung up, then dialed Mike's number. He would have someone there as soon as she called in.

What have I gotten myself into? she wondered as the phone rang at the other end. *How do I explain to Mike that I vouched for this guy and now I think he, or another personality inside him, may be the killer?*

And the worst of it is that Raymond probably doesn't even know it himself. He's probably hurt by what I said, confused, doesn't understand why I'd turn on him like this.

He thinks he's hunting demons.
But he's just hunting himself.
Question is, what happens to anyone who gets between him and his Other?

Raymond hit the west–bound Ventura freeway doing 75, aiming for Woodland Hills. If he knew Susan half as well as he thought, she would be on the phone right now with one of her contacts in the police department. They would have someone at his house within the hour, and they would probably have been told about the Seattle warrant.

He had to get home fast, grab the few things he would need, and get out. He'd call Karl as soon as he got in the door, arrange for him to have a nurse assigned to Elizabeth around the clock.

It's all coming down around me, he thought.

No. Not yet. I've come too far to back out now. There's still work to do. We'll finish this. One way or another.

Going To and Fro in the Earth

At seven o'clock the next morning, Susan sat in the middle of the long wooden table in the main LAPD conference room downtown. She could feel the gaze of Lieutenants Trask and Firelli on her as she finished laying out her story for them. She told them all of it, from the first time she saw Raymond in her hospital room, to the incident at Mrs. Rypczynsky's apartment, all the way up through to her frantic call to Mike Devereaux, who sat at the other end of the room, his face a mask, unreadable.

There was a long pause when she had finished recounting her story for them.

Firelli was the first one to speak. "Ms. Randall, you have to appreciate our situation here. When we found what we considered good, independent information tying this individual to the murders, you gave us cause to reassess that opinion and remove him from the list of suspects. Now, based on really nothing more substantive than a hunch, on circumstantial evidence at best, you want us to go back after this individual again?"

He struggled for a moment to find his next words. "You'll forgive me for asking, but…is there any kind of romantic interest between the two of you?"

"No," she said, firmly. "No, that has nothing to do with anything."

"I didn't ask if your interest in this individual was relevant, I asked if there was any such interest. Your answer seems to indicate that there indeed was."

Susan opened her mouth to answer, then hesitated. Was there some truth to this? Yes, she had initially found Raymond a compelling, fascinating individual…contradictory and sometimes infuriating, but there had been a moment or two…

If you didn't care, if you hadn't been interested in him, why did you say all the good ones are gay when you thought he was living with Karl?

Shut up.

"Lieutenant Firelli, there is nothing romantic between myself and Raymond Weil. He was a subject of my work, and a source of information. Our working relationship never went beyond that at any time."

"I ask because this department has already suffered its share of embarrassments in this case, and in at least one instance that embarrassment can be traced directly back to you. I would very much want to avoid another if you should change your mind a third time."

"Look, I'm not saying for one–hundred–percent sure that it's him," Susan said. "When I first called Mike I was very upset. But there are some areas of concern that, when you add them all up, makes it pretty obvious that something's going on."

"And you believe that Weil—more correctly another personality inside Weil—is committing the murders, and that he himself is unaware of the crimes. That he—his dominant personality—is hunting down that killer not realizing that he's hunting down himself."

"I'm saying it's possible, based on what I've discovered. I know how it sounds, but it's not like this is the first time something like this has happened. The Danny Rollings case—"

Trask spoke finally. "I'm familiar with that case. And you're right, there have been other instances of possession syndrome that have turned extremely violent, even deadly. The problem is that we have absolutely no evidence on which to pursue this. We can't even pick him up and hold him to see if the murders stop because the Slasher has already hit five rich people, and for all we know he may be done."

"I don't think so," Susan said. "Raymond seemed to think there was more going on. He said that this would be a battle on many levels, physical, mental and spiritual. We've only really seen the physical. Maybe you can argue that some of it was also psychological, the way the killer used the murders to turn the town upside down. Either way, that still leaves the spiritual. Whether he was talking about someone else, or he was talking about himself without knowing it, I don't think we can afford to ignore the possibility that there's something big still to come."

Firelli ran a hand through his hair, clearly frustrated and at a loss. "Okay, here's the situation as I see it. Any way you look at it, this Weil character is a fugitive from justice. We've faxed the Seattle PD and they've confirmed that he's wanted for assaulting a peace officer and flight to escape justice. That's more than enough for us to issue a warrant without dragging the Slasher situation into this and looking like assholes a second time if it doesn't pan out."

"We've had a plain–clothes unit parked outside his house since we got the call," Trask said. "So far he hasn't been seen entering or leaving, though we have sighted the individual you mentioned who takes care of Weil's wife, and a nurse entering the premises. Once we get a judge to move on the search warrant, we'll go in and check out the place.

"Meanwhile, until we know what's going on, I think it would be prudent if we assigned you a police escort. Even if Weil isn't the killer, he's wanted for assault and evasion, and he might not look kindly on the fact that you've essentially rolled over on him." Trask looked to Devereaux. "I assume you have no other plans for the next few days?" he asked.

"Not a one," Mike said, never taking his eyes off Susan.

Mess me up on this and I'll blow up your car, he had said to her when she asked him to help get Weil's picture off the evening news, and the way he was looking at her he was almost certainly remembering that conversation.

Well, he can't exactly blow it up with himself inside it, now can he?

She glanced back at Devereaux, who at this moment looked big as a house and seemingly impervious. *On the other hand, maybe he can.*

Raymond awoke in his car in the parking lot of St. Mary's, early morning daylight streaming in through the windows. He was sore, and tired, and desperately in need of a shower.

He popped the rear driver's side door, eased out of the car, and walked across the parking lot to the church, which he knew would be open, the nuns and volunteers preparing breakfast for the next crowd of homeless. Sister Margaret would leave him alone; she knew him well enough to give him room when he needed it. He had certainly been there for her and the church when needed.

He could smell eggs and toasting bread as he crossed behind the long kitchen. In all the time he had seen people coming here for aid and food—the dispossessed, the hungry, the unemployed—he had never imagined that he would someday be one of them. But he had no choice. He was limited to the cash he had on hand, and he had to do everything possible to conserve his funds. If he tried to use his credit cards or an ATM, they would almost certainly give away his location, assuming they hadn't been closed already.

He stepped into the church, where he knew there was a large washroom in the back. Enough to scrub down his face before deciding what the hell to do next.

As he crossed the nave, he paused to look up the long rows of old pews to the cross at the front of the church. He moved to the last pew and sat heavily, exhausted physically and emotionally. *What did I do that was so wrong?* he asked in the direction of the cross. *My whole life is starting to fall apart around me. What did I do to deserve this? Didn't I try to help people? Didn't I try to fight the good fight on your behalf?*

In his thoughts, he heard Father Delmonico's voice, from the many mornings they spent talking after morning prayers at the seminary. *"Job's error was one of self-pity. He said to God, why are you doing this to me? What's the big idea, anyway?"*

"Did they actually use that kind of slang back then, Father?"

"Don't quibble. Anyway, Job said, in whatever *terms they used at the time,* 'What the heck were you thinking?'

"And God said, 'Who is this that darkens counsel by words without knowledge? You demand answers of me, your Lord? No, I *will demand, and* you *will answer* me. Where were you *when I laid the foundations of the Earth? Where were* you *when I filled the seas? Where were you when I created rivers? How does the wind blow? Can you send lightning? Can you create thunder?'*

"Sounds to me like He ducked the question."

"Not at all. What God's saying is that to understand the situation you're in, you'd have to go all the way back to creation before you could see the pattern that would make these seemingly random, cruel circumstances make sense. The human brain can't contain that much information. We can't see the pattern. So for us, it doesn't make sense. But that doesn't meant that it doesn't make sense for Him."

"So you're saying one thing is impossible for God, to explain the rationale for his actions and the universe around us? If that's true, then God is pretty limited."

"I didn't say that He couldn't explain it," Delmonico had said. *"I'm just saying that because of the complexity of the answer, it would take longer than the average human lifetime to explain it to us.*

"Wherever we are in life, that's exactly where we're supposed to be. God puts us in that place for a reason. Our job once we get there is to try and understand it as best we can, and learn what we can while we're there."

From practically the first day Raymond had arrived at the seminary, the tall, elegant, but fragile Father Delmonico had been his mentor and his sponsor, the one priest present who had not flinched when Raymond asked about demonic possession, because Delmonico had been places far beyond the walls of the seminary, and seen things the others had not.

After Raymond had confided to Delmonico what he had seen and done and experienced in Bolivia, they often spoke long into the evening, as they had this particular morning. Even now, all these years later, he could remember their conversation that day with startling detail. Not because anything extraordinary had been said, but because it was later that same day when they told him that Claire had died, and Elizabeth was in a coma.

He had left the seminary then, knowing in his heart that he would never return. He remembered looking back at Father Delmonico as he drove off, and seeing on his face not so much a look of disappointment as the expression of a man watching an unfinished piece of pottery he'd worked on for a long time being taken away before it could be properly seasoned and hardened.

Six months later, Raymond had called to check on his sponsor, only to learn that he had died of respiratory pneumonia after returning from what was described as "a very tough session in Venezuela."

It was an exorcism, wasn't it? And you couldn't handle the stress anymore, not at your age. And I wasn't there to help you. And now you're dead and I have one more life to account for when I can't sleep.

So now that you're on the other side, Father, does it all makes sense finally? Can you see the pattern now?

He shook his head. Despite anything Father Delmonico had said concerning the Book of Job and humility, Raymond was sure that when Delmonico got to wherever he finally ended up, he almost certainly had some very tough questions for God.

He leaned forward and pulled a worn bible out of the pocket on the back of the pew in front of him. It opened easily to the book of Job; it was always a popular source for sermons. He glanced down to 1:6-12.

> Now there was a day when the sons of God came to present themselves before the LORD, and Satan came also among them.
>
> And the LORD said unto Satan, Whence comest thou? Then Satan answered the LORD, and said, From going to and fro in the earth, and from walking up and down in it.
>
> And the LORD said unto Satan, Hast thou considered my servant Job, that there is none like him in the earth, a perfect and an upright man, one that feareth God, and escheweth evil?
>
> Then Satan answered the LORD, and said, Doth Job fear God for nought?
>
> Hast not thou made an hedge about him, and about his house, and about all that he hath on every side? Thou hast blessed the work of his hands, and his substance is increased in the land.
>
> But put forth thine hand now, and touch all that he hath, and he will curse thee to thy face.
>
> And the LORD said unto Satan, Behold, all that he hath is in thy power; only upon himself put not forth thine hand. So Satan went forth from the presence of the LORD.

Put not forth thine hand. In other words, don't kill him. Just take away everything he has, and everyone he loves, for the heavenly equivalent of a bar bet.

Raymond had lost his profession after Bolivia, had lost those few he called friends when he asked them for help in this cause, had lost Claire to the forces of destruction and despair, and now he was in imminent danger of losing his freedom and failing in his mission. Worst of all was the realization that he might now lose Elizabeth a second time. If he were captured by the police and sent to jail, she would be transferred to some other facility, probably a welfare operation, where there would be no one to look after her. Karl would do all he could to help, assuming they didn't arrest him as an accessory, but as a non–family member there was little he could really accomplish on her behalf.

Is this the true shape of the war between us? he wondered. *A war of pieces, of losses incurred until they cannot be tolerated anymore? And then what?* Until now he had thought he understood the form of the war that he had been engaged in; but until now he had been the pursuer. Until now he had been arrogant. Now he understood how fragile his position was, how ephemeral and easily destroyed the construct of his life had become.

He looked up at the empty church that surrounded him. The only refuge that would accept him.

"Wherever we are in life, that's exactly where we're supposed to be," Delmonico had said. *"God puts us in that place for a reason."*

He looked up at the statues of the saints, the statue of Mary, the stained glass images of the Apostles, all gazing heavenward, hands clasped in prayer and supplication.

"Our job once we get there is to try and understand it as best we can, and learn what we can while we're there."

Hands clasped in prayer and supplication.

Hands pierced by nails, bleeding.

Hands emanating light.

He had seen those images just recently. But where?

Perhaps the mutilations committed during the murders were as much a dese-cration as the subsequent attacks on the churches. Desecrating a holy image by cre-ating a perverse opposite.

Where had he seen these images of hands lately? He racked his brain, strug-gling to pull it out. *Where?*

Then he sat up abruptly and ran toward the kitchen, where the homeless and the poor were lining up for their morning meal, the only one they were like-ly to get. He ran to the bulletin board that lined one wall, pushing through the line of hungry people, ignoring their complaints, searching the multiple layers of handouts, church announcements, lost and found notices, flyers and—

Got it!

He yanked the flyer off the bulletin board, and his expression turned hard as he read the information it contained.

Today. It's today.

He shoved the flyer into a jacket pocket and started away, passing dirty, disheveled men who doubtless wondered at the abrupt change in this strange man, the cold determination, the sudden sober appearance that was not at all the same man whom they had seen run over in the heat of excitement.

Guns, he thought. *I'll need the guns and the ammunition from storage.*
All of it.

Susan paced in her living room, going from window to chair, sitting for a moment, then going to the window again before pacing back and forth again.

"You want to sit down for two minutes?" Mike asked. "I'm starting to get seasick."

"The way you eat? I've seen you eat three hot dogs at a time, Mike. Nothing short of a hydrochloric acid could get through your stomach lining."

He *hmmph*'d and continued reading the newspaper. She was sure it was his so—called sense of humor that had prompted him to bring a copy of the *Times* into her home. "You want to read the Metro section?" he asked. "Maybe it'll take your mind off things."

"I can't," she said. "I can't sit still long enough to focus on reading anything."

"Yeah, I kinda noticed that part."

"I keep running it through my mind. On the one hand, maybe Raymond is the Slasher. But if he's not—"

"Then you turned in somebody on the run from the law in Seattle, and you're still on the side of the angels. If you didn't pass along that information, you'd be guilty of harboring a fugitive."

Mike tossed the Metro section aside and fished through the paper for the sports section. "Speaking of food, you got anything to eat around here?"

"I don't know, let me check," she said, stepping past Mike and into the kitchen.

I don't want to do this. This isn't what I'd thought it would be.

His hands moved through the collection of guns, ammunition and supplies he had squirreled away. Inserting bullets into clips. Clips into guns.

I don't want to die.

The voice that spoke was not *his* voice, was not *its* voice, because it did not need words, it only crouched in the darkness of his thoughts and fed, and needed, and killed. The words that spoke to him now came again in the voice of his parents. *You opened the door, now you have to go through it. You made your bed, mister, now you have to sleep in it.*

He felt the other presence inside him start to move, to glide out of the shadows. In his readings and in his dreams and in his lusts and his rage and his determination he thought he had known what it was. He thought he understood it. Thought he could control it, contain it, direct it for his purposes.

Now he realized that he had never understood what it was.

Until this moment.

Until he saw it gliding up behind his tightly closed eyes.

It burns, dear God, it burns.

Susan's quick survey of cabinets and refrigerator revealed six individual packets of string cheese, some leftover Chinese food from two days earlier, cereal, skim milk, two Pepsis and a bag of pistachios. "Good news," she called back, "I've got what you probably think is a four-course gourmet meal right here."

She closed the refrigerator and stepped back into the living room, where Mike ignored her behind the newspaper.

"I said—"

She stopped, frozen at the sight of the newspaper.

"Let me see that," she said.

"What? I thought you didn't like the *Times*."

"Damn it, Mike, I'm not kidding, let me see that!"

He sat back, startled at the tone in her voice, and handed over the newspaper. She turned it over to the back page, which she had seen on her way in from the kitchen. It contained a full–page advertisement for an interfaith convention at the Staples Center that day. The ad promised a record attendance of ministers, priests, rabbis, reverends and lay people gathered under one roof to find common spiritual ground.

"What about it?" Mike asked.

"Look at it," she said. "I mean, really *look* at it."

He stared at it, clearly not understanding what it was he was supposed to be looking for.

Then she pointed to the logo of the organization, a drawing of two hands joined together in supplication beneath a cross.

Holy light poured up at the cross from fine lines that crossed the palms of both hands.

"Jesus Christ," Mike whispered.

"Cuts across the palms of the hands," she said, "just like the Slasher, only this is the God version of the thing. You said it yourself: the killer signed his victims using this exact symbol. But it's more than just a signature, it's part of the message itself. It's a mockery of a holy image.

"Raymond said this was a battle on several levels, the last being spiritual."

"Yeah, I know, but—"

"The killer started by hitting the three classes: poor, working class, upper class. You've got the whole secular world right there in a microcosm. Well, if you've hit the secular world, what's left but the spiritual? If your job is to send a message that will make people despair, make them feel that there is no redemption, no hope, what better way to dot the *i* and cross the *t* than to finish by striking right at the heart of the religious community?"

"Makes sense, if you sort of squint at it a little," Mike allowed. "But I have to tell you, nobody else is gonna buy into this theory. Which is all it is."

"Is that all you're going to say?"

"What am I supposed to do?" He studied the advertisement. "I don't want to call in the SWAT team when we've got nothing to back it up. You don't pull that trigger unless you've got something absolutely solid. I could get busted right back down to street patrol if we're wrong. Besides, a gathering like this always has private security and officers on watch in case of trouble."

"But if we're right—"

"If *you're* right, leave me out of this. I'm just supposed to be protecting your ass, remember?"

"Okay, if *I'm* right, we should at least warn them. Because there's trouble and there's *trouble*. This could be bad."

Mike hesitated.

"If this does go down the way I think, do you want to be responsible for the consequences?" she asked.

"Don't push it."

"*Do* you?"

He frowned at her for a long moment. His expression reminded of the time she had visited the underwater aquarium tunnel in Sea World in San Diego, where she stood eye to eye with a shark for several minutes, thinking, *If he could figure out some way to get through that glass, I'd be lunch right now.*

The shark never blinked.

Mike did.

"Get your stuff," he said.

More of What You Always Were

The parking lot at the new Staples convention center was jammed with cars beneath an electronic billboard that announced *Welcome Third Annual Interfaith Convention*. It was hot, and the sun bore down on the parked cars, windshields reflecting the light back into their eyes as Mike pulled into the lot.

It all looks so ordinary, she thought. *Do things like this really happen in the middle of the day, when everything looks this painfully normal?*

As soon as Mike swung the car around, parking behind the center, Susan popped the side door of the squad car, Mike right behind her. They hurried up the wide concrete steps toward a security guard standing at the back entrance. "I know this guy," Mike said. "Will Terenova. He's a cop, handles night shift. A lot of the guys also work security when they're off–duty to pick up a few extra bucks."

"Hey, Will!"

The guard turned, smiled. "Mike? What the hell are you doing here? I thought you didn't moonlight."

Mike stopped in front of him, catching his breath. *That's a lot of steps for a guy this big*, Susan thought.

"I think you got a problem, Will," he said.

The guard sobered instantly. "I didn't hear anything on the radio."

"We're keeping it off the radio until we know for sure what the hell's going on. We think somebody might try to hit the convention. Possibly armed."

"You got a description?"

Mike looked to Susan, who quickly described Raymond.

"Christ, Mike, that could be anybody in there. Most of the people I've seen today have been in their forties or fifties."

"You got the metal detectors up?"

"No. Who wants to scan priests and rabbis? This isn't a rock concert. We figured this would be a snoozer."

"Yeah, well, maybe our guy didn't know that. He could've decided to go in another way. Exits?"

"Covered."

"Check anyway."

The guard toggled the shoulder mike of his radio. "Status check. Everybody call in."

The radio crackled. "Door one, clear."

"Door two, clear."

"Door three, clear."

They waited.

Will toggled the radio again. "Door four, you clear? Macready?"

Silence.

"Shit," Mike said. "Where's door four?"

"Around by the loading dock. Fastest way there is to go around back."

"Okay, you go check it out, we'll go inside, scope things out. Go over to channel one and stay in touch."

"Right!"

The guard headed for the back of the center as Mike and Susan climbed the second set of steps to the entrance. They pushed through the glass doors into the carpeted lobby.

Susan could hear someone speaking on the PA system inside the huge main room. "The problem is not so much what we believe, as the doctrinal principles each denomination *wraps around* those core beliefs. If you set aside those doctrinal differences, we have far more in common than we might suspect."

They went to one of the main doors and peeked inside. The arena was packed all the way to the cheap seats in the upper balcony. The speaker at the podium was an elderly man in a dark suit similar to the thousands of other dark suits that filled the arena. While there were some young people present, what mainly greeted Susan was a sea of gray hair.

Mike's radio crackled. He snapped it off his belt and toggled the mike. "Will?"

"Door four's open wide. Got a couple of the other guys with me. We can't find Macready."

There was another long pause. The radio crackled again. "Shit."

"What?"

"We got blood."

"Call for backup!" Mike said.

"We're already doing it," Will radioed back.

"Mike?" Susan said. "What if he grabbed the guard's radio? What if he can hear you?"

Before he could answer they heard a heavy metallic chunk, then the sound of gears grinding behind them.

Susan turned to see the metal security grates lowering behind the glass doors.

Mike was yelling into the radio. "Get inside! He's sealing the place up! I repeat, *he's sealing the doors*! Damn it, get inside!"

The grates slammed into the floor, locking automatically.

Then the lights went out. Only the red emergency fire lights remained.

For just barest moment there was silence, broken first by a voice inside the arena. "I'm sure they'll have the lights back on in just a second," someone called from the podium.

Then: a gunshot echoed across the arena.

Followed by another one. Then a third.

Mike banged open the door, daylight spilling past him as people began screaming, rushing past them into the lobby, toward the main doors, only to discover them sealed. Panic turned into frenzy as they grabbed at the metal grates, trying to tear them open.

More people continued to pour out of the arena.

The lobby can only hold a fraction of them. The rest won't understand that there's no way out, they'll keep pushing forward, crushing the people in front of them.

More gunshots rang out.

With Susan behind him, Mike forced his way into the sea of people trying to escape the arena, struggling against the tide of bodies to see where the shots were coming from.

"There!" he said, pointing.

There was a flash by an open window for one of the upper spotlights. The sound of the gunshot followed an instant later.

"We've got to get up there," Mike said.

They backed out of the door and pushed through the mass of frightened people, heading for a stairwell door. A woman clawed at him. "What's happening?" she shrieked at him over the roar of cries and shouts.

Mike pushed past her and banged open the stairwell door. Susan followed rather than be crushed by the crowd that was now being sandwiched against the metal grates by those pushing from behind. More gunshots echoed through the arena.

Christ, she thought, *it's a shooting gallery up there.*

With only the red emergency lights to guide them, they hit the stairs at a dead run and climbed fast, past the loge section and the third floor balcony, aiming for the service floors. Mike was breathing hard, and it wasn't just the exertion. *He's scared*, she thought. Until this moment she could never imagine Mike scared of anything.

He's thinking he could get killed here.

With that thought, she realized that she was shaking.

I could just stay here and wait, she thought, climbing the stairs as fast as she could. *But it'll be a while before backup arrives, and they've still got to get inside. Mike may be scared, but he's still my best chance of getting out of here alive.*

And someone's got to watch his back. He may need me just as much as I need him right now.

She stayed close as he banged through the fourth floor door, nine–millimeter automatic up and ready.

A man charged around the corner at them.

"Freeze!" Mike yelled. "Police!"

The man stopped, panicked and breathing hard. He was wearing Staples Center coveralls. "Don't shoot!"

"Where's the control room?"

"Look, I just want to get out of here—"

"You're not going *anywhere* until I can open the goddamned doors! Now where's the fucking control room!"

He pointed back the way he came. "That way, then left up the stairs. Room 1215."

Mike ran past him without another word. Susan hurried to keep up with him as the employee raced down the stairs.

They ran down the long, carpeted hallway, past offices where other workers crouched behind desks and chairs. She heard more gunshots. The shooter was taking his time, drawing out the moments and the terror between shots. *How many is that now*? she wondered. *Eight? Nine? And how many more crushed or wounded in the panic to get out?*

"Stay down!" Mike yelled to the workers as he passed their offices. "Stay down!"

They hit the next steps and turned left, running toward the black double doors marked 1215.

Weapon up, clasped in both hands, breathing hard, Mike kicked open the door and lunged inside.

The control room was nearly the size of a basketball court, a maze of panels and computer control systems and cubicles. One whole wall was taken by windows where engineers could see the stage in order to hit their sound and light cues.

Another employee in Staples coveralls lay dead on the floor, blood pooling around his stomach.

Mike edged further into the room, Susan hanging behind, a second pair of eyes and ears alert for any movement. He reached the main control panel that ran most of the length of the room. "Shit!" he whispered.

"What?"

"System panel's been trashed. He disabled the automatic controls for the security doors after he closed 'em down."

At a sound, Susan suddenly looked up at the maze of computer panels that filled the rear of the room. "Movement," she whispered.

Mike nodded, signaling for her to wait where she was. He was sweating, eyes wide, scared but determined not to walk away. He edged slowly toward the rear of the room, checking each row of computer panels as he passed them.

As Mike looked down the first row, someone stepped out of the shadows farther down.

Raymond, Susan thought.

Then: *He's got a gun.*

She yelled. "Mike!"

And everything suddenly seemed to move in slow motion all around her. Mike turned, raising his gun.

Raymond did the same.

Mike fired.

Missed.

Raymond didn't.

The shot caught Mike at the hip and spun him around, slamming him into one of the control panels. The gun flew out of his hand. Mike moaned in pain.

Susan stepped into the main aisle, started to run for Mike's gun. Then froze. Raymond was pointing his gun right at her.

"Get down!" he yelled.

She dropped just as he fired past her.

She heard a moan, but couldn't tell if it was Mike or someone in the doorway. She looked behind her. There was no one there.

"Did you see him?" Raymond said.

Susan shook her head, numb.

"Get up," Raymond said, running toward her. He stooped to pick up Mike's gun and slipped it into his coat pocket, the other gun ready. "How is he?"

"I think he's unconscious…he hit the wall pretty hard. Look, please, he's bleeding."

Raymond hesitated, examined the wound with his free hand. "Didn't hit any arteries…he'll be okay for a while. We'll come back for him. Come on!"

He grabbed her arm, pulled her to her feet.

"Raymond, please, you've got to listen to me. Give yourself up. Those people—"

"—are going to die unless we can stop this!" he said. "I know what you think, but I'm not the one who's responsible."

"Then what are you doing here?"

"The same thing you are. Trying to stop it. Now come on! I'm going to need a witness."

He pulled her along, going out the door and across the empty hall. "There!" he said, pointing to an access door. There was blood on the door handle. "He escaped through there after I shot him!"

Could be anybody, she thought, *another employee he just shot, anyone, he's still chasing himself.*

They pushed through the door, which opened onto the series of catwalks and service panels that lined the upper decks of the Staples center. She looked down to the drop–ceilings that marked the various offices and rooms below them. *I could try to jump, I could try to—*

As if sensing her thoughts, Raymond took her arm, pulling her along.

"Careful," he said, and looked at her. "You still don't believe me. Why?"

"If you're not responsible then why did you shoot Mike?" she said. *Maybe I can talk him down, talk him out of this.*

"He shot first. I had to protect myself because if he couldn't stop what's going on, and there wasn't time to explain. I could just as easily have made it a head shot, but I didn't." He continued through the maze of catwalks, careful to keep her alongside him.

"He's here," Raymond whispered. "Do you feel him?"

"No, I don't." She shivered.

"It's cold. Do you remember what Stein said, when he was in the alley the night of the first murder? How cold it got? It gets cold around the possessed."

"It's just the air conditioning, or a draft."

"And you don't smell that?" he asked. "That rancid, fetid smell." He shook his head. "How much more proof do you want?"

She wanted to say, *I don't see these things, Raymond, I don't smell them, I don't feel this demonic cold you feel, because it's all in your head. You're hunting yourself, don't you understand that?*

And how much longer do I have until the other half of you decides to put in an appearance?

From outside, she could hear the wail of police cars racing into the parking lot.

"Listen to me, Raymond, there's no way you can get out of here in one piece. The best thing you can do is surrender. You can explain it all to them, and I'm sure they'll understand."

"How can I expect them to understand when *you* don't even believe me?" he asked, looking through the tangle of cables and catwalks, trying to decide which way to go next.

Then he glanced at an intersecting catwalk, and smiled. "We'll go this way."

"Why that way?"

"Look," he said. "See for yourself."

She looked to where he was pointing. In the glow of the red emergency lights she saw half a dozen roaches scuttling along the railing of one of the catwalks.

Raymond nodded. "Insects. Just like Stein said."

"They're just some roaches," she said, hysteria starting to creep into her voice. "There just some goddamned *roaches*, Raymond!" She was starting to laugh and cry at the same time. *Come on, damn it, you've got to hold it together here.* She pulled away and threw out her arms, turning and waving at the emptiness of around them. "This is California, Raymond, they're all over the place! Don't you understand? There are no devils here! It's just you and me and some *goddamned roaches*!"

A gunshot exploded in the darkness behind her.

The bullet slammed into the wall beside her, shards of brick and plaster slamming into the back of her arms and neck. Her knees went to jelly underneath her and she collapsed to the floor of the catwalk.

With an enraged yell, Raymond fired three times into the shadows around them.

He shot me. Numb, wondering how badly she was hit, she managed to put her hand behind her head. It came back wet with blood. *I'm going to die here,* she thought, surprised at how calm she suddenly seemed about the whole thing.

She looked up at Raymond, who stood above her, peering out into the darkness. Though she knew he was near enough to touch, in her dazed state he seemed a million miles away. She felt the world sliding away from her, and struggled to hold on. *Do not pass out, do not pass out, do not pass out.*

She struggled to sit up, fought to clear her head and answer the one calm question her mind had been able to form in the last few moments.

Where did the shot that hit me come from?

Was it Raymond?

Or did it come from out there in the darkness?

Was Raymond shooting, randomly, enraged?

Or was he shooting at someone out there?

Maybe it's a cop.

Maybe it's Mike.

Maybe it's someone else.

She looked up. Raymond was holding something in his hand, and speaking. She couldn't make out most of the words, could only catch a few fragments.

"I cast you out, unclean spirit, along with every Satanic power of the enemy, every specter from hell, and all your fell companions; in the name of our Lord Jesus Christ."

I don't believe this, she thought. *He's performing an exorcism.*

Then a voice came out of the shadows somewhere. A man's voice. "Please, don't hurt me anymore."

If Raymond heard the voice, he gave no sign of it. He stood above her, tall and straight. He spoke in a loud, commanding voice that roared through the room. "It is He who commands you, He who flung you headlong from the heights of heaven into the depths of hell...He who once stilled the sea and the wind and the storm."

The voice came again. "Please, help me. I didn't want this to happen."

Raymond continued. "Tremble in fear, Satan, you enemy of the faith, you foe of the human race, you begetter of death, you robber of life, you corrupter of justice, you root of all evil and vice; seducer of men, betrayer of the nations, instigator of envy, font of avarice, fomentor of discord, author of pain and sorrow."

She felt again as she did that first night in the hospital; felt something else in the room with them. A presence. An anger. But there was also the voice, trembling and frightened.

"Help me," it said.

Whoever it is, he's hurt, maybe dying, she thought. *I have to do something.*

With Raymond's attention diverted, continuing the exorcism, she forced herself to stand, still fighting for balance, made worse by the catwalk swaying underneath her.

He put Mike's gun in his jacket pocket, I saw him. She edged up behind him, hesitated, and made her peace. *I've always tried to live a good life. Never went out of my way to hurt anybody. I don't want to die, and I don't know what's on the other side, but either way, I'm okay with it. I can do this.*

She lunged at Raymond from behind, slashing at his jacket pocket. He turned to struggle, but with the paper in one hand, gun in the other, he would have needed a third to stop her before she ripped the jacket pocket, grabbing the gun.

"No!" he yelled, pulling back.

She raised the gun.

The catwalk swayed beneath her.

Raymond turned, reached for her.

Too late.

Something lunged out of the shadows, slamming into them.

God!

There was a flurry of limbs, a roar and a thrashing that shook the catwalk. Tangled up in the mass that crashed into them, Susan tumbled over the railing, twisting in midair then crashing through a drop–ceiling into a room below. She landed hard, but not as hard as she'd expected.

She lay there for a moment, the wind knocked out of her, pain wracking every limb. Tiny lights pinwheeled behind her eyes. Painfully, she reached out, felt for whatever she had landed on. *Insulation...rolls of ceiling insulation...storage room.*

She felt for the gun as her vision cleared, but couldn't find it.

Then there was the voice. The voice that belonged to whatever had lunged out of the shadows above, crashed into them and fallen into the room with her.

"I mean, we all play at it, like it's a game, you know?"

She blinked away the strobing behind her eyes, fighting to focus on the darkened room.

"You imagine what it would be like to do these things to people," the voice said, "all the people you hate, but you never really do it. Because you're afraid. Then, one day, something happens inside you, and suddenly you're doing it and you can't help yourself."

She could finally see him in the dim red glow of the emergency lights. Sandy hair. Average height.

He was bleeding profusely from the gut, a pool of blood that splattered the floor and walls where he had fallen beside her.

He was pulling himself forward. Inch by painful inch.

And smiling.

"You don't have any choice," he continued. "It's like you're being controlled from the outside, except it doesn't make you into something else, it makes you into more of what you always were. It's not my fault."

Then his face distorted. She blinked hard, trying to focus. It was as if there was another layer on top of his face and she was trying to see through it. And it was suddenly cold. Terribly cold.

"Hello, Susan," the voice whispered at her.

Larry's voice.

Not possible, she thought, *can't be*!

The voice came again, but this time it was a voice of dry, dead leaves and despair. *"Larry's in here. With us."*

The man continued crawling, his legs dragging uselessly behind him.

Oh God, oh God, what the hell is this?

Above them, somewhere in the darkness, she could hear Raymond continuing the exorcism. "I adjure you by the judge of the living and the dead, by your Creator, by the Creator of the whole universe, by Him who has the power to consign you to hell, to depart forthwith in fear."

Why isn't he coming down here?

Maybe he can't. Maybe he can't stop once he's started it.

The man continued pulling himself across the room, never taking his eyes off her. "Then one day something happens inside you," he said. "It's like all the self–preservation circuits in your brain get burned out, and you just don't care anymore if you live or die. Then you're just this toboggan riding a hundred miles an hour toward the target. Next thing you know it's all on the news about how somebody shot up a school or a McDonald's or a post office."

Slowly, she began to realize that he wasn't crawling toward her at all, as she'd first thought. His attention was to a point in the room past her.

She forced herself to turn, ignoring the pain that tore through her back to turn and see what it was he was dragging himself toward.

Weapons filled the room. Shotguns. Rifles. Handguns. Two boxes of Teflon–coated ammunition lay open on the floor.

And behind her, a series of pipe bombs had been attached to the load–bearing wall, spaced at regular intervals where the main support beams would be located.

The trigger mechanism for the bombs was waiting beside them.

The man was less than a yard away from the trigger.

The dead, dry voice came from him again, pulling her away from the cache. *"Larry always said you were a slut. You thought you were better than anyone else. Said you couldn't love anyone because you were too busy being in love with yourself, with seeing your name in the paper. You'd fuck anybody and fuck anybody over just for a byline. Leo said the same thing."*

He was two feet away from the trigger now.

Raymond's voice boomed down at them. "It is the power of Christ that compels you, who brought you low by His cross…it is God Himself who commands you; the majestic Christ who commands you. God the Father commands you; God the Son commands you; God the Holy Spirit commands you. The mystery of the cross commands you."

Pushing away the pain and the bitter cold, Susan pulled herself up, searching around her with her hands. *Where's the gun? Where the hell is the gun?*

"You are guilty before the whole human race," Raymond was shouting now, "to whom you proffered by your enticements the poisoned cup of death. Your place is in solitude; your abode is in the nest of serpents; get down and crawl with them!"

Her hand touched metal.

The man spoke again in his own voice. "Just so you know, this part…the pipe bombs…this was my idea. You think *they* need guns? You think *they* need pipe bombs? Hell, no…they've got us. They've got me! All they have to give…is permission. Inspiration. We kill each other. It's what we do. It's what we've always done."

He lunged for the detonator.

She raised the gun, fired.

The bullet slammed into his shoulder and threw him against the wall. He slumped to one side as he fell, never taking his eyes off her.

"The spirit is willing," he whispered. "But the flesh is weak."

Then the other voice came again. "*Flesh is always weak.*"

Slowly, impossibly, he stood.

No, not stood, she corrected herself distantly. He arose at a sharp angle, legs straight at the knees, *like a stick suddenly being levered upward from somewhere far below.*

And the eyes that met hers were not the ones she had seen there a moment earlier. They were the eyes of a predator.

Not human, she thought, feeling the world turn gray at the edges all around her as hysteria tightened her throat. *Not human…*

Then the room seemed to shake with Raymond's words.

"You might delude man, but God you cannot mock. It is He who casts you out, from whose sight nothing is hidden! It is He who repels you, to whose might all things are subject! It is He who expels you! He who has prepared everlasting hellfire for you and your angels, from whose mouth shall come a sharp sword, who is coming to judge both the living and the dead and the world by fire!

"*Amen!*"

The emergency lights flickered.

The figure cried out and jerked erect in torment, arms outstretched, shaking violently. He screamed as he was jerked up off the floor, and rose into the middle of the room, his face twisting with pain.

Suddenly his face snapped toward her, and for a moment she saw not one man, but two images layered over each other like a photo negative, his own and something else, something *other*. A face that was part smoke, part rage, part teeth, part blood; a face that could never be glimpsed in whole because it did not belong here, did not belong anywhere this side of hell.

Then a scream rose from somewhere deep inside him, a howl of rage and frustration and pain and fury that shook the walls. She covered her ears, trying without success to block out the scream as it went on and on and on.

Then: silence.

She looked up.

The man lay motionless on the floor, eyes open in death, his face now his own. There was no trace of the Other.

As Susan pulled herself up into a sitting position, Raymond lowered himself into the room from above. He jumped the last few feet to the floor and ran across to her. "Are you all right? Did he do anything to you?"

"No…hurts like hell though…"

"We must get you to a doctor," he said.

"I shot him," she said, looking at Mike's gun on the floor. "God…I shot him…"

"You did what you had to. I'm sorry I couldn't stop the ceremony to help you, but I knew that I'd wounded him…knew that the Other inside him had to be forcibly cast out *before* the host body died, or it would go into the nearest available body…which would be you. I couldn't allow that to happen again."

Again? she thought distantly, but filed it away as she nodded to the rows of pipe bombs. "Careful," she said, "there may be others."

From somewhere far below she could hear doors banging open, could hear the rapid approach of what were almost certainly SWAT teams racing up the stairs.

"We've got company," he said. "I better follow the wiring before they get here, make sure there aren't any more of these planted where someone could get hurt."

"Raymond—"

"It's all right," he said, "there's nothing here that can hurt you now."

He hurried out, tracing the line of wires that extended from the detonator and out the door.

She glanced at the body, whose lifeless eyes were staring in her direction, then she looked away again, remembering what she had seen.

I don't know what to think anymore, she thought numbly. *I don't know anything anymore.*

Then bright lights broke the darkness, glaring into the room alongside shotguns and men in SWAT vests and helmets.

"Civilians down!" somebody yelled. "Get a medic up here stat!"

Then, and only then, did she allow herself to close her eyes and let the world slip away from her.

Serial Killer Dead In Shootout
By Susan Randall
Exclusive to the Los Angeles News–Tribune

(LOS ANGELES) Richard Deacon Carlyle, age 32, was not the sort of man you'd notice on the street. He stood 5'9", average weight, with sandy hair and a pleasant but unremarkable face. He drove a taxi, which made him even more invisible to attention. He could drive anywhere, any time of the day or night, and no one would think twice or ask what he was doing there.

He was also the man responsible for the serial murders that had held Los Angeles a captive to terror for nearly six months. That campaign ended last night when he was killed during an attack on an interfaith convention at the Staples Center. Prior to his death, he confessed his responsibility to this reporter, a guilt that has been confirmed by forensics tests on the weapon used in the Staples attack, which matched bullets taken from his weapon with those that struck the seven gunshot victims in the arena. Additional forensics evidence linking Carlyle to the serial murders—the knife used in the attack, and other fiber and blood evidence—has been found in his apartment in Burbank.

Along with the evidence, police also found a small cache of weapons, a diary whose contents have not yet been released to the media, and a substantial amount of reading material one source characterized as "showing an unhealthy interest in satanic or cult groups."

"He was always a very quiet sort of man," said Margaret Sims, a thirty year old Sears cashier who lived next door to Carlyle since moving into the same apartment complex two years ago. "Very intense, but quiet. He mainly kept to himself."

Co–workers and friends who asked not to be identified shared their shock and disbelief on learning the identity of the man police had once characterized as the most cold–blooded killer in the history of Los Angeles.

Of the seven shooting victims, four died of their wounds at the scene, with three others still in critical condition at various area hospitals. Two dozen more were hurt, some critically, in a rush to escape the arena. A police officer was also injured in an exchange of gunfire with Raymond Weil, age 51, a civilian who ultimately shot Carlyle in self–defense, critically wounding him. The injured officer, Sergeant Mike Devereaux, received a hip wound and is listed in stable condition in Cedars Sinai Hospital. Sources at the hospital indicate he may be released as early as tomorrow morning.

"Obviously the LAPD takes it very seriously when one of our officers is shot, even when the circumstances are such that it appears to have been a mistake by both parties," Chief of Police William Darrow said in a press conference last night. "And to that effect, Mr. Weil, currently in custody on an out of state warrant, will have to answer some serious questions and face the possibility of aggravated assault charges.

"Certainly, however, the Police Department and the District Attorney's office have both indicated their willingness to factor in Weil's role in stopping the killer from taking any additional lives. There's no question that he put his life at risk to save others. The issue is whether or not he interfered in the ability of a police officer to pursue this same individual. Somewhere in this equation something approximating justice will be done."

In a press release issued today by Dr. Philip Lacroix, a consulting psychiatrist for Citizens United Against Gun Violence, Dr. Lacroix suggested that Carlyle was a disturbed personality fixated on media images of violence and pushed further into fantasies of violence by reading material based on demonology, cults and role playing games that use these same images. "It's only a small jump from a role playing game or video game where you're a demonic force slaying innocent people to acting out that sort of behavior in the real world," Lacroix said.

In his final statement, made to this reporter, Carlyle did not mention role playing games, video games or television. He stated only that he was sorry for what had happened, and that he felt he was not responsible for his actions.

Susan stared at the screen. It told the facts, but it didn't tell the *story*. She didn't know how to tell that story in a way that anyone would understand, herself included. She was still processing what she had seen and heard.

Especially what she had heard.

In the well–lit newsroom of the *Trib*, it was hard to put herself back in that room, to believe that she had heard the things she had heard, seen what she had seen. She was sure she could cobble together at least half a dozen explanations for what she had experienced that would allow her to dismiss it out of hand.

But it wouldn't be the truth.

And that was what was troubling her about the article. It relayed facts. It provided closure. It would mean people could sleep nights knowing the killer was dead. But it didn't tell the whole and complete truth.

And if she wasn't in the business of telling the truth, then what was she doing here? How could she explain to others what she could barely accept herself?

She started to glance up at the clock, then flinched in pain. The discomfort was as much from the strained ligaments and bruised muscles in her back and sides as the stitches in the back of her neck. As they were sewing up the damage from the ricochet, the doctors had found a good–sized piece of brick deep in the fleshy part of her neck, right beneath the skull. If it had penetrated just another inch or so, it would've cut right into the spinal column, leaving her paralyzed from the shoulders down.

"Looks like God was watching out after you," the nurse had said.

And that was another topic Susan wasn't prepared to deal with right now.

Two fifty–seven, she thought, staring at the article on her screen. *Three minutes to deadline.*

It wasn't the whole truth.

But she didn't think she was going to find a way to express that truth in the next three minutes. Especially when she had no real idea what that truth might be.

Resignedly, she sat back in her chair and hit SEND.

The article was done. The killer was dead. Life went on.

So why do I feel so empty?

Maybe it's residual shock, she decided. *Maybe it's the pain killers.*

And maybe it's because suddenly none of this means as much as it used to. Is that it?

I don't know. I honest to God don't know.
And I'm not going to find out sitting here, that's for sure.

Cedars–Sinai Hospital is a squat gray series of buildings next to Jerry's Deli, which provided regular deliveries of chicken soup and other delicacies to patients unable to handle one more tray of the formless, colorless meat that passed for hospital food. Most days the deli worked in coordination with physicians who had to carefully monitor a patient's eating habits.

And sometimes they did not.

But that was what rear doors were for.

That was the only explanation Susan could come up with for the tray in front of Mike Devereaux containing a Reuben sandwich, a side of chili, a hot dog with mustard, macaroni salad, two small bottles of Dr. Brown's Cream Soda, and a slice of chocolate cake.

"I got shot, I didn't have a heart attack," Mike said at her look.

"Not yet. Give it time."

He shrugged and unscrewed a bottle of Dr. Brown's. "You doing okay?" he asked.

"Yeah, I think so," she said.

"Only reason I ask is you look like somebody just died. You got that *Why* look on your face."

"Why what?"

"Not why what. Why *anything*?"

She smiled thinly. Sometimes Mike had a way of seeing things he wasn't supposed to.

"No, really, I'm fine. I just wanted to see how you were doing."

"Doctors say the bullet nicked my hip bone, but that I probably won't notice anything." He took a long drink from the bottle. "Thing that bothers me is that if he hadn't been faster than me, I would've killed the wrong guy. All these years of being a cop, I've never had to shoot anybody. Threaten, sure, but I find I don't even have to do that a lot."

At your size I can believe it, she thought.

"If I ended up making a mistake my first time out, if I would've nailed the wrong guy and had to go through life with that…" He shook his head. "I don't like being shot, believe me, I'd rather be anywhere other than here right now. But on the whole, I think it'll stop hurting a hell of a lot sooner than my conscience would have, you know what I'm saying?"

"Yeah, I think I do," Susan said. "You know—and this is something I haven't said as often as I probably should have—for a cop, especially for LAPD, you're a pretty decent guy."

"Thanks."

"I mean it. When the security gates came down at the arena you could've just called for backup and waited, but you went up there on your own because you wanted to open those doors, get the people out of there before any more of them got hurt."

"Yeah, and that did a whole hell of a lot of good. Look at me."

Susan shook her head. "Don't give me that," she said. "I talked to your boss. He said that a few minutes after Raymond and I left, you came to and crawled, bleeding, to the control panel and found the manual on/off switch to unlock the doors. He said you couldn't raise them from the control room, but once the crowd figured out the doors were unlocked, they got them open fast. If they hadn't, who knows how many more people would've gotten hurt or killed in the crush?"

Mike shrugged, looked away. Susan found it hard to imagine Mike being modest, but here it was, right in front of her. "It's a job, you know?" But he smiled at her.

"Anyway, I should go," she said. "I just wanted to come by and see if you were okay. If there's anything you need, just let me know."

"I'll do that," he said. "Thanks."

She smiled, started to turn.

"One thing?" he called after her.

"What's that?"

He pinned her with a look. Whatever may have happened to his hip, he was no less intimidating when he wanted to be, even sitting down in a hospital gown that showed more of Mike Devereaux than Susan had ever wanted to see.

"What happened up there with you three? *Really?*"

She hesitated for a moment, then said, "I'll tell you what. You get better, and when you're up on your feet, we'll go out and you'll buy me a drink. Buy me enough drinks, and maybe I'll tell you what happened, and then you can tell me what it all means. Deal?"

"Deal," he said.

Susan continued out of the hospital room and down the hallway to the elevators. She pushed the Down button and waited as a voice came from behind her.

"I thought I'd run into you here."

She turned at the familiar Russian accent to find Karl standing behind her. "I didn't know you worked at Cedars," she said.

"Three days a week. I share an office here with another doctor. Is it all right if I speak to you for a minute?"

"Sure."

They walked to a sitting area beside a window that overlooked the nearby Beverly Center. "You are well, I hope?"

"Fine," she said. "How's Raymond? I was about to go see him at County Jail."

"He's not there anymore. I posted bail for him a little while ago. Until they can finish reviewing the current situation, he is only being held on the out of state warrant from Seattle, and there is sufficient good will in his direction that I did not have to fight very hard to get him released on bail. Yes, the bail is a bit large, but I make a good living. It's nothing I can't afford to lose."

"Lose? But why would you lose it? The only way you'd lose the bail money would be—"

She didn't finish the sentence. *If he didn't show up for trial.*

"He should not go to jail, not for this," Karl said, then added, "Did Raymond ever tell you what happened in Seattle?"

She shook her head. "No."

"Then you should know. Do you remember what I told you, about his wife and daughter, and pier 39? Well, there was supposed to be a police officer on patrol the afternoon that man opened fire. But it was a warm day, and he had been out late the night before, and with no one looking, he went into his car and took a nap. If he had not been asleep at the time of the attack, perhaps fewer people would have died. Perhaps even none of them.

"The officer transferred to the Seattle police department soon afterward, perhaps out of guilt, perhaps hoping to avoid responsibility for his actions. But Raymond found out, and Raymond found *him*." Karl shrugged. "He...what is the phrase? Oh yes, he belted him. Knocked him out. I suppose it was the minimum given the situation. Certainly if it were my wife, I would have done far worse. And Raymond is capable of doing far worse even than me. He just wanted this man to know that *he* knew. And to pay back a small portion of that debt."

"I gather that's supposed to make me feel better about all this," she said. "Does it?"

She looked away. "A little."

"Good," he said. "I'm glad."

"Why? Why should it matter to you what I feel?"

"I'm Russian. We are a very empathic people, you know. I feel for others, very deeply sometimes. I feel for you. I feel for Raymond's wife as well. I will see to her needs until the day when I may be able to move her someplace...else.

"And I feel for Raymond. You see, he is alone right now. Soon he will be gone, and along with him a rather large amount of my money, but such is life. He will be free of certain obligations, and certain explanations that no one would ever believe anyway. But he will lose his home, and much of what he has come to love in that place. And he will still be alone.

"It is a terrible thing to be alone, is it not, Ms. Randall?"

She looked up, and studied his face for a very long time before answering.

Rob Klein prided himself on being the first to arrive at work in the morning, and with a few exceptions was almost always the last to leave in the evening. Susan was one of those exceptions. But by seven o'clock she had still not returned from her visit to see Sergeant Devereaux.

Maybe she went home to get some rest, he thought. *She could certainly use it after what she's been through.* He didn't know all the details, only enough to suspect she had held back some of the facts in her article, but he knew enough to feel she was hiding the full story of what had happened from him, and possibly even from herself.

It was one of the things he decided they would talk about the next morning.

With the rest of the newsroom empty, he was about to switch off the computer on his desk when the EMAIL WAITING message flashed on his screen.

He called up the email.

> TO: ROB KLEIN, HEAD MOJO
> FROM: SUSAN RANDALL, BAD MOJO
> Dear Rob,
> When I first dreamed of being a journalist, I wanted to be a war correspondent. I thought it would mean going to Europe, Iraq, exotic places all over the world. And it's true what they say, you go where the war is, but that particular truth only goes so far.
> Every day, all around us, there is a war being fought on battlefields we cannot see or choose not to see. It's a war that, until a few days ago, I didn't think existed. And though part of me is still a little unsure, I've realized that one way or another, someone has to chronicle that war. I figure it may as well be me.
> Take care of yourself, Rob. I don't know when, or where, but I'll be in touch.
> Susan.

He reached for the phone, which had her home phone number on speed dial.

He let it ring twenty five times before giving up.

Good luck, he thought before finally hanging up.

Godspeed, and I hope you find what you're looking for.

Susan stood in the parking lot at the precise time she had been instructed. The sun was starting to drop down below the horizon. She wondered what the next morning would bring, and where it would find her.

She looked up as a white Ford pulled into the empty lot and stopped next to her. Raymond climbed out and came to stand next to her, watching the sunset for a long time before speaking.

"Are you sure you want to do this?" he asked.

"I think so." She looked away from him. "I'm sorry about what I said...when you came by my apartment the last time. When I read the doctor's report—"

"No apologies necessary," he said. "I was seeing things I could not describe and they could not accept. They could not explain me any other way. I do not blame them. I could not explain me either."

"I know the feeling."

"Then perhaps we shall figure it out together, yes?"

"Maybe so." She turned back to him, searching his eyes. "The other day, at the arena, you said that it had to be forcibly expelled before the host body died, or it would jump into the next available body…and that you would not let that happen again. That's what happened in Bolivia, isn't it? That's what came into the camp? And that's why the autopsy showed that many of your team died at each others' hands; the body would be killed, then it would just jump into another one and the killing would go on."

He glanced down. "Yes. I was terrified. I was wounded, and scared, and I ran…I left them behind."

"There was nothing you could have done. If you'd stayed, you'd be dead yourself."

"I know that now. But for a long time afterward, I blamed myself, sought to somehow atone for their deaths. I don't know if I can ever atone that much, but I also know that I can't stop trying."

She nodded, understanding. Without really meaning to, she put her hand on his.

He looked over at her, and managed a smile. "We should go. We don't want to attract attention."

"You're right."

"So, tell me," he said as they walked back to his car, "have you ever wanted to see Venzuela?"

"Why Venezuela?" she asked.

He looked to the darkening sky. "I have some unfinished work there, on behalf of a friend."

He opened the car door for her, and closed it again as she climbed inside.

End

Welcome to the DarkTales...

Thank you for reading *Tribulations* by J. Michael Straczynski. Already craving more? Collectors and fans, be sure to watch for DarkTales' upcoming JMS Script Book series featuring screenplay collections from *Babylon 5* and *Crusade*—including *Crusade* episodes never broadcast. Also available for free reading at www.bookface.com. Don't miss out!

Check out the DarkTales website at www.darktales.com. We are the web's haven for writers of horror and dark fiction, as well as artists and fans. Join our horror discussion list hosted by Egroups.com, put your website into our webring or submit it to us for award consideration, visit our bookstore to purchase your favorite horror titles, and submit your works to our editors for the various upcoming anthology titles and to our inhouse electronic zine-*Sinister Element*...

Sinister Element is the quarterly online publication of the DarkTales community. Insightful commentary on current events, the best in dark fiction, interviews with prominent figures in horror, and information you just can't get anywhere else...it's all here.

DarkTales provides opportunities no author or fiction fan should miss.

Visit *Sinister Element* at:
www.sinisterelement.com

or visit the special Sawtooth Creek website at:
http://sawtooth.home.dhs.org.

Join us...

We're Bringing Horror To The World!
www.darktales.com

DarkTales Novels

DeadTimes by Yvonne Navarro $24.99
Demonesque by Steven Lee Climer $18.99
Clickers by J.F. Gonzalez & Mark Williams $24.99

Collections & Anthologies

The Asylum Vol.1 Doug Clegg and others, edited by Victor Heck $15.00
Scary Rednecks by David Whitman & Weston Ochse $18.99
Moon On The Water by Mort Castle $19.99

DarkTales Novels

Eternal Sunset by Sephera Giron $19.99
Secret Life of Colors by Steve Savile $19.99
Tribulations by J. Michael Straczynski $24.99

Deluxe Chapbooks—$8.99

Coming Soon!
Deadfellas
by David Whitman

Coming Soon!
Holy Rollers
by James Newman

In Memoriam by Mort Castle $8.99
Lifetimes of Blood by Adam Johnson $8.99
Filthy Death by James Moore & Brett A. Savory $8.99

Order by mail or via the web at:
www.darktales.com

DarkTales Publications
P.O. Box 675
Grandview, MO 64030

Shipping Charges:
$4.95 U.S.; $6.90 Canada; $10.00 overseas
(plus $1.00 per each additional book)

Tribulations was initially printed by DarkTales Publications in August, 2000, using Garamond type on 60# offset white. Cover design by Natalie Niebur. Typesetting by Keith Herber. Editorial, Butch Miller. Proofing by David Nordhaus.